THE
DARKEST
STARS

KRISTY GARDNER

THE DARKEST STARS

KRISTY GARDNER

CITY OWL
PRESS

THE DARKEST STARS
The Broken Stars, Book 2

CITY OWL PRESS
www.cityowlpress.com

Cover Design by MiblArt. All stock photos licensed appropriately.

Edited by Danielle DeVor.

For information on subsidiary rights, please contact the publisher at info@cityowlpress.com.

Print Edition ISBN: 978-1-64898-402-0

Digital Edition ISBN: 978-1-64898-401-3

Printed in the United States of America

PRAISE FOR KRISTY GARDNER

"*The Stars in Their Eyes* is chilling, thrilling, and full of emotional depth that will leave you on the edge of your seat and questioning your own reality." — *Madison Lawson, author of The Registration*

"Visceral, creepy, and disturbing. Dark horror fans will love this startling debut." — *Chana Porter, author of The Seep*

"High passion, high stakes, and otherworldly romance! Kristy Gardner delivers sultry sci-fi and a journey of self-acceptance with *The Darkest Stars*." — *J. Dianne Dotson, author of The Shadow Galaxy*

"*The Stars in Their Eyes* is a juicily twisted path through what it means to be human, what it means to be alien, and, above all, when our world is lost, what it means to find home in each other." — *Ann Fraistat, author of What We Harvest*

"At once exhilarating and philosophical, this debut dark sci-fi is a tour de force of twists and turns." — *Sarina Dahlan, author of Reset*

"*The Darkest Stars* is that rare smooth sequel that gives you just enough resolution to leave you even more desperate for the next installment. Readers will be on the edge of their seat as they run along after Calay's struggles through danger, deception, and darkness." — *Ciel Pierlot, author of Bluebird*

"A gripping tale of survival. *The Stars in their Eyes* shows us the dark, violent side of humanity, but also the promise—however out of reach it may seem—of something brighter." — *N.C. Scrimgeour, author of The Waystations Series*

"A pacy, visceral and action-packed romp through a vividly depicted broken future. *Resident Evil* meets *War of the Worlds* in this compelling debut." — *Kate Murray, author of We Who Hunt The Hollow*

"Heartbreaking and heartwarming, this book has great chaos and all the feels. It's sci-fi and adventure and romance and a must-read!" — *K.C. Harper, author of Marked For Grace*

"A harrowing journey of self-reliance and acceptance–while kicking some serious ass. *The Darkest Stars* proves even the most damaged people can heal and do incredible things." — *Heather Chambers, author of Earth Sucks*

For her.

AUTHOR'S NOTE

At the gentle request of some readers, I have included content warnings for this book, and others, on my website. If you are someone who prefers to know what they're getting themselves into (protect your mental health), please scan the QR code below or visit KristyGardner.com/Books.

CHAPTER ONE

CALAY BARELY TURNED as the pod hovered only four feet above. It clicked and whirred. She kept her gaze forward. Almost down. She didn't know why it didn't zap her into a haze of red mist. Wasn't sure she cared, either. According to Jacob, it was because she was one of Them, whether she liked it or not. After she'd found out the truth about herself—that her mother was alien and thus, so was she—she'd made it clear to him, and Them, she wouldn't be returning to their home planet. She needed to remain on Earth. For Tess. Not that Tess had much to say about it of course, but it was penance. She deserved as much, probably more.

Calay ignored the light growing stronger as it rose up her calves, traced over her knees, climbed her thighs. It rested on her belly. The warmth of it crept through the thin layers of her jacket and warmed her, despite the cold. She shook it off, veered around the unwavering light.

It wasn't so much the pain of losing Tess that gutted Calay, it was the way she'd lost her. It'd been three months since she'd felt Tess's breath against her lips, as she gasped her last lungful of air. Calay could still feel the soft flesh of Tess's neck pulsating beneath her fingers. She could still hear Tess's breathing become labored, then quiet. Quieter. Until it stopped completely. It was all Calay could do to stuff the nausea down as she trudged farther down the snow-covered street.

She'd just come from what had once been a thriving community market and pharmacy. She swung her backpack onto both shoulders and crouched low through the mangled doorway. The crushed contents of what had once been a box of cereal, snapped, crackled, and popped under her faded leather boots. The floor was littered with trash and layers of fissured mud. Or blood. It was hard to tell in the failing light. She gnawed on her bottom lip and squinted; her dark eyes peered between the shelves. It was the kind of place where someone's grandmother would have picked up her weekly prescriptions, or a person might have stopped by after work on the last Friday of the year to grab a dozen eggs for New Year's brunch, a Valentine's Day card, or a box of firecrackers. Calay could almost picture herself plucking a fifth of whiskey from the shelves, asking the clerk if they had fresh oranges. Before the Change, she'd never imagined in her wildest nightmares she'd rummage through broken racks for unmarked and expired cans of mystery meat products. The shelves dangled at odd angles, some hung by only a bolt or were propped up by whatever was deemed too worthless to carry away. Forgotten. Alone.

Like Calay.

The gray light crept through what was left of the iron cage sprawled across the doorway. It did little to reveal what was between them. She didn't dare turn on her flashlight. Not with the sun nestled so close to the horizon already. It was getting darker earlier these days. The window to scavenge for supplies or something remotely edible growing ever shorter.

The metal rattled on its hinges. Calay's heart banged against her chest. She crouched lower. Inched further into the darkness of the desolate store. She'd been around the neighborhood long enough to know she had nowhere to run. Not back here. Not now. Her best chance at survival was to go unseen. If humans were dangerous while she was a part of a pair before, they were a death sentence now. *Maybe* that's *what I deserve.*

She waited.

Listened.

She was alone.

Just the wind.

If she wanted to eat tonight, she needed to focus. She ignored the impulse in her legs to race the hell out of there. Instead, she released a shaky exhale and extended her arm. Without better light, she was going to have to risk getting her hands dirty. As she reached between the shelves, her fingers traced their cold surface and disappeared into the shadows. She swallowed, closed her eyes. There was nothing on the first one but dust bunnies and empty plastic wrappers. Same with the second. On the third, her hand grazed something soft, and she shuddered. *Something furry.* Calay gasped. She jerked her arm back, banged her elbow on the jagged metal ledge. A sharp pain shot through her forearm and into her shoulder.

"Fuck!" She gripped her arm, waiting for the throbbing to subside. When it didn't, she angled herself toward the long, dusty windows that stained the walls along the far side of the store. A sharp hiss crept past her lips. No wonder the pain wasn't going away. She'd not only caught the shelf, but somehow managed to hit it just right to slice two inches across her skin. She squinted and watched as the blood seeped from the laceration, dripped down her forearm, pooled in the cracks of the shattered tile floor. Calay ground her teeth together, pressed her lips into a thin line. She didn't have time for this. She also didn't have much of a choice.

She made her way to the back, toward the pharmacy. Dusty rays of light fought to survive the last hours of the day, illuminating each tentative, and necessary, step. She swung her legs over the counter and pushed herself to the other side. Her arm ached with the effort as she left a smear of red on the counter behind her. There was a time she would have beelined it back here to check these particular shelves before anything else. But useful medical supplies had long run out. Besides, she now knew she healed differently than other people. Faster. Because she was one of Them. For her, there was less need to have a constant supply of Ace bandages and Amoxicillin. Still, she couldn't risk trailing blood all the way back to the Loft. She scanned the nearly bare shelves. Flicked the empty bottles of herbal supplements aside. The rubber bands and condoms too. What she needed was something to clean the wound. There were about eight hundred different kinds of bacterium that could have been crawling along that shelf, and the last thing she needed was an infection. *Who'd risk their life for stale crackers or expired mystery meat then?* Calay sneered, shoved a bunch of discarded Band-Aid boxes to the floor, and found a small bottle of hydrogen peroxide. It wasn't antibiotics or rubbing alcohol, but it would do.

She shuffled her way back up front. She swung the backpack off and popped a squat as close to the gate as she dared. She needed light to patch this up and the better she could see, the faster she'd get it done. She pulled a wad of gauze out of the sack and a wheel of duct tape with one hand and gripped the peroxide with the other. A wave of pain rolled up her arm when she lifted the bottle to her teeth and twisted. The cap popped off in her mouth. She spit it to the ground before angling the protective plastic seal under her front tooth. It tore away as she bit down. The bitter flavour cloaked the back of her throat. She hastily doused the wound, allowed the fizzing of tiny bubbles and searing pain flow through her in undulating waves. She waited until it stopped and the thoughts once again roused from the coagulated corners of her mind.

Calay wouldn't be here right now if things had gone according to plan. If she and Tess were still together. If her mother and father hadn't forced her out. She frowned. This wasn't the first time she wished she hadn't been born. And neither of them was even alive to blame. Because of her. It seemed to Calay she was somehow cursed. As if it were written in the stars. Destined, even. *Everyone around me dies.* She swallowed a lump in her throat and secured a wrapping of gauze with tape. It wasn't pretty, but at least she wouldn't leave a trail of breadcrumbs behind her.

Breadcrumbs.

She still didn't have dinner.

She had to eat. She'd survive a day and a half on a couple of apples she'd gleaned from someone's yard, but it wasn't enough. It was never enough. She eyed up the shelves once again and groaned, forcing herself to her feet. The light grew dimmer. The shadows longer. She opened closets and dug underneath the register. She leaned against the counter and sighed. There wasn't much. A few cans of vegetables nearing their expiration dates and one of corned beef. A bag of dehydrated potatoes. What she wouldn't give for some peanut butter or honey. Something hot and fresh like BBQ chicken or a cheese pizza. Ice cold milk. Her stomach grumbled, reminding her it was time to go.

Calay slid the items inside her pack, shouldered it. She pried the gate open a few more inches, ignored the pulsating in her elbow, and squeezed through.

That was before the pod had found her. She'd heard it before she saw it. A distant mechanical whirring. The sound of metal on metal. A gentle hum. A click. A shiver ran up her spine. Then, the blue light appeared. It had snaked along the snow from behind. Inched across her path. It reflected off the ever-darkening sky, illuminating the street in a bright blue glow.

She didn't run.

Didn't even try.

She just kept putting one foot in front of the other.

A few months ago, Calay never would have let that blue light fall on her. She'd seen what it could do to the human body. The way people evaporated into sprays of blood and plasma. Human beings were an endangered species because of it. After the Change, she and Tess had spent four years evading the aliens. Surviving, together. Turns out, a lot can happen in blocks of four. Four months passed between the time Tess discovered the truth about Calay and when she'd left her for dead in that warehouse. When Calay came to, it took four weeks for her to uncover the truth about herself and find and confront Tess. And much to Calay's horror, four minutes with her hands wrapped around Tess's throat were enough to squeeze the tepid breath out of the love of her life. *For better or for worse.* Calay hated the number four. Almost as much as she hated the aliens for doing this to her.

To them.

With each step, the snow crunched, the fresh air caught in her lungs. It was just a light dusting when she'd first set out for the day. Now, it clumped around her ankles. *So much for not leaving breadcrumbs.* She scanned the snow for footprints other than her own. She saw none. Just an endless winter wonderland. Or nightmare. A brisk wind wound itself around the strip mall and through her long dark hair. She gathered it in her hands and tucked the ends inside the oversized green scarf she'd tied around her neck. She wrapped her arms around her waist, bracing herself. The leather jacket that would only half zip-up did little to blunt the cold. Winter was coming. Or rather, had already arrived. Early. Much too early for the west coast. Trees were still clinging to the last of their leaves, most had fallen to the ground in the frost. But instead of freezing, they deteriorated into a layer of rotting organic matter Calay had to slosh through each time she left the Loft. It reeked of decay. A constant reminder of what she'd lost. What they all had. It wasn't normal, the way the weather was behaving. The way the cold wrapped around her bones and refused to let go. Then again, none of this was normal. Thanks to the Change, it never would be again.

She crossed the road and large powdery flakes clung to her eyelashes. She blinked, kept her gaze ahead as she followed the low-rise buildings down the long narrow street. They trailed behind her like ghosts. Storefronts vacant, houses boarded up, memories long since forgotten. Dreams too. She approached a T-intersection.

To the right, the road led out of town toward the mountains. The last place she saw Tess. Kissed her. Watched the light dim from her eyes. There was nothing out there for Calay anymore. Nothing but the memory of a life she'd once lived. One that was now deader than her girlfriend. Calay shuddered. She fought to keep the memory of their time together alive in her mind. The mornings they'd made love. The nights too. The little life they'd both cherished. Even if it was all a lie in the end. The truth was, Tess had been behind Calay's attempted murder. Twice. She'd lied to Calay, betrayed her to bring about a revolution. *Genocide, more like it.* Tess had gotten it all wrong. Calay didn't have much, but that fact was something she clung to like it was oxygen. It was also the thing that was slowly choking the life out of her. There was no escape. No reprieve. No end. That fact was cloyingly bleak. It scraped against her mind as if trying to burrow through the center of her brain. Sometimes the truth of what her life had become and what she'd done was so sharp it was all she could do to keep from putting the Bowie knife that hung from her belt through her skull.

To the left, was the only future she could conceive of. And that wasn't much of a future at all.

She paused only long enough to force the tears back where they belonged—deep inside. She turned left, began making her way back to the Loft. The sun was non-existent now. The sky an endless dark gray curtain. It was silent as she plodded forward. She pretended to ignore the footprints she left in her wake, as if she couldn't care less if someone found them. *Come*, she'd say, *come quick; put an end to this endless pain for me*. Even as these thoughts circled her brain, much to her chagrin, hope prodded the back of her mind that the snow would fall fast enough to cover her tracks before someone else came upon them.

A new cycle of whirring and clicking caught her attention.

"Go away!" She called over her shoulder like the floating pod was a stray dog.

It didn't go away. It followed her. Traced her steps. Taunted her. It even had the gall to fill the dents she left in the snow behind her. *Rude*. She may not have wanted to live, but she wasn't quite sure she wanted to die, either. That was her real problem. Her existence was an unrelenting purgatory of reliving her own mistakes. Her lack of conviction. Her cowardice.

She turned the final corner to the Loft and tossed a glower over her shoulder, trying not to shiver. The pod halted, hovered behind her. It continued to flash blue light as Calay moved away. A thrum of deep vibrations bloated the air. Like a beacon. She waved the small ship off, refused to give it the satisfaction of looking back.

"Good riddance," she muttered as she approached a towering fifteen-story building.

It had been the start of development. A burgeoning metropolis, a revitalized neighborhood. Before the Change. Local boutiques would have lined the ground floors. New families and single professionals would have made the upper ones their homes. The construction never got that far. It rose from the frozen ground, a wall of unfinished concrete. It was out of place among the low-rise sprawl. But then again, so was she. The first six floors were framework. Concrete pillars. That, and if one looked closely enough, a broad scaffolding staircase hidden by painted plywood and shrubbery. The upper floors were boarded up, what windows they managed to install before everything went to shit, shattered. Calay risked a glance to make sure no one was following. Though she already knew they wouldn't be. Not with an alien pod nearby. Anyone with a decent sense to survive would have put as much distance between themselves and the pod as possible. She was alone.

She was always alone.

Calay drew the curtain of greenery back, bent down, and slipped her fingers beneath the first board. Bending deep into a squat, she shimmied the board up high enough to slip underneath. She hissed through her teeth as pain radiated up her arm with the effort. Once through, she dropped the sheet of plywood. It landed against the pavement with a loud crack. Her feet felt like lead as she made her way up a set of unfinished, concrete stairs. She'd found this place shortly after she and Jacob left the mountain—and left Tess buried in the field of wildflowers at the summit. In terms of architecture, this was the furthest thing she could find from the natural beauty and memories of that place. So far, the building seemed impenetrable.

It was her fortress. The Loft.

It also had the unfortunate history of being a temporary storage facility for the realty company. As Calay rounded the top stairs and slid a makeshift wooden door open, and a vast ocean of featureless white faces greeted her. Mannequins. She shuddered. While she knew what was waiting for her, the initial dread she felt every time that door peeled back never failed to give her the creeps. She shook it off and stepped inside, closing the door and securing it with a wooden plank. She wound her way through the maze they'd constructed of the hard, plastic bodies. Row after row, each branch a possible dead end. Having constructed the route, Calay knew how to avoid the traps they'd rigged out of fishing line and various sharp and blunt objects hidden in the ceiling. If someone were to sneak in and try to attack, they'd almost certainly be impaled with something. Calay paused before sliding open the next door. This was how they survived now. Among the faceless.

Calay shook her head, stepped through the next door, and slid it closed. She was greeted by a deep bark. The black Pitbull trotted over, its tongue lolling out its mouth, its golden eyes trained on hers.

"Hi Max." Calay smiled as she bent down. She kissed the warm spot on the back of his soft ears and he returned the affection with a few kisses of his own. Calay couldn't help but laugh, her cheek covered in slobber. His long tail whipped the air in delight. She may have rescued the dog in her old camp while she was looking for Tess, but the truth was, this dog had rescued her in more ways than she could count. "Hi boy. I missed you."

"We missed you too." The deep voice came from beyond the next room.

Calay swallowed, patted the dog on its fat head, and dragged herself into the light.

In the center, far from the windows, Jacob was splayed across a vintage couch they'd found in what had probably been the construction crew's break room. He was reading a tattered novel by the light of a kerosine lantern. *Of course.* He was always doing things like that. Reading books. Making jokes. As if everything was normal. As if everyone wasn't dead. He rested the book on his broad chest and looked up as Calay made her way across the expansive space, Max trailing at her heels. He was always doing this too. Giving her his full attention. Like she deserved it. Her gaze darted to the floor; his bore into her. She kicked off her wet boots and dumped her backpack at his feet.

"I was talking to Max," she said.

"I still missed you." The smile in his voice made Calay cringe. She exhaled and brought herself to look at him. His full lips were turned upward, the light of the lamp reflected in his clear blue eyes. "I was starting to think we might have to send a search party out after you."

"We don't have a search party." Calay's brows knitted together. "We don't have anything."

"Then it's a good thing I didn't have to send them."

"I don't know how you can be in such a good mood right now."

"Why not?" Jacob ran a hand through his dark hair, several curls falling over his forehead as he pulled himself to sit.

"We're holed up in here like two fugitives. Because we are two fugitives! The Resistance is hunting us. There's nowhere else to go. We barely have enough food to eat to keep us alive. We don't have anything, Jacob. We have no one."

"We have each other." Jacob leaned forward, setting the book aside to scratch Max under the chin. "Didn't go well out there, huh?"

"About as good as it usually does." Calay rubbed a hand across her forehead, exhaled. She knelt next to the couch, unable to bring herself to sit next to him. To feel the fabric of his shirt or the warmth of his skin. She unzipped the backpack and pulled out the food, one item at a time, taking inventory.

"Meat. Potatoes. Vegetables. Looks like a feast to me," Jacob said, thumbing each can as Calay set them down.

"This has to last us until…" Calay paused, glancing at the limited rations in front of them. "Until we can find more. It's bad out there, Jacob."

"I know it is. We'll get through it. We just have to make it through the winter. Then I'll be able to go outside more."

"That's another thing. This weather. This isn't normal Oregon weather. Not in early October. Something strange is happening."

"Either way, we knew we'd have to deal with this sooner or later, right? If not the snow, then the rain." Jacob's eyes narrowed.

"What do you mean?"

"I know the coast was your home, Calay. But if you're set on staying on planet, maybe we should start thinking about moving East. Or further South. Away from all this precipitation."

"Absolutely not."

"I'd be of more use then. I could help you more."

"I can handle it."

"I know you can, of course. You always have." Jacob peeked at her between long, dark lashes. He looked sweet. Sincere. Delicious. A shiver peeled its way up Calay's thighs as she remembered what it felt like to have those lashes graze her cheeks. Those lips on hers. Those arms around her. It had only happened twice. That was as far as she'd let things go. "I'm just saying, you aren't alone."

She wanted so badly to reach out to him. To feel the warmth of his heart against hers. From here, she could smell the fabric of his T-shirt. She longed to bury her face in it. Even with Tess gone, or maybe because she was gone, Calay couldn't bring herself to fall into him again. Couldn't reach out. Not now. She understood that, why couldn't he? Calay cleared her throat, changed her soaking wet socks before she slipped her cold wet boots back on her feet. She made a mental note to pick another pair up next time she made the trek to what used to be the shopping center. She'd only been once since they arrived here when the weather turned colder and they needed supplies. It was too dangerous to risk going more than absolutely necessary. Too many places for people to hide. To corner her. But if the skies were going to keep up like this, she'd need more than one pair of shoes if she didn't want to catch hypothermia.

"I'll be on the roof if you need me." She said, palming one of the cans and a weighted blanket from off the couch. It was gray and scratchy, but warm. That's all that mattered. She began making her way toward the door.

"Calay." Jacob stood after her. "Stay."

She stilled. Didn't dare look back at the face she knew was waiting for her. The kindness in his eyes. The adoration. She shook her head.

"C'mon," Jacob coaxed. "We'll heat some of this up. Get a little cozy. Stay dry."

"You know where I'll be if anything happens," Calay mumbled.

"I do." Jacob agreed. "I just don't know why you'll be there when there's a perfectly good, warm, dry place to spend the night right here."

Calay finally turned, the pain in her eyes on fire in the flickering light.

"Yes, you do."

Jacob pressed his mouth into a thin line and glowered. She felt him watching her as she turned her back to him again, her breath short. A sob swelled below it. She couldn't let him see her crack. If she did, his arms would be around her faster than she'd be able to say no. And then, it'd be all over. She'd fall apart and never be able to put herself back together again.

Struggling against the now foot-deep snow, Calay pushed the rooftop door open. It creaked on its hinges, echoing through the black night sky. It swallowed her whole. She made a break for the edge, dropping the can she'd brought up with her to her feet. Ignored the grumbling in her stomach. She gripped the concrete ledge. It dug into her palms, the snow stung her fingertips. She gasped for air, drank it in as the tears poured down her cheeks.

Calay was drowning in the darkness and not even the stars in their eyes could light the way home.

CHAPTER TWO

CALAY WOKE AT FIRST LIGHT. She was propped up on the ledge, under the blanket and a dusting of snow. In the harsh coldness of day, she shivered, conscious of a growing truth she couldn't escape—she couldn't keep hiding on the roof, sequestering herself away from Jacob. From everything. Despite her best efforts to freeze herself out of existence, she was alive. Tess was dead. Nothing was going to change that. It was only a matter of time before she had to accept it. Move on. Whatever the hell that meant.

At least it'd stopped snowing. The sun glowed gold behind a thin layer of cloud smeared across the early morning sky. It cast a strange pink glow over the white ground, reflected in the few windows that remained in the low-rise buildings across the industrial park. Down the street, a school bus was planted on its back end, the nose rising high in the air. She stared, imagining how it got there.

She pictured a blue beam of light shooting down from one of the Mother Ships, the driver swerving to save the children inside. The beam would have caught the back fender or maybe the gas tank, igniting an explosion that upended the bus, flipping it. As the children crawled out, the driver would have cried in horror as one by one, they were zapped into red mist.

Calay wrapped her frozen, tingling fingers in the blanket and pulled it tighter as she burritoed her body inside. She wasn't sure if that was how vehicle crashes actually worked, or if it was just something she'd seen on TV once. When there still was TV. She shuddered. She didn't want to think about it. Instead, she turned her attention to the newly fallen snow, looking for footprints. A trail of smoke. Any sign of human life across the frozen landscape. After humanity turned on the aliens, they turned on each other. So it was usually best to see them before they saw you. From up here she could get a bird's-eye view of anyone coming. Though, there were so few humans left anymore, Calay wondered if that was actually a concern, or just the residual trauma of avoiding them for so long.

What she told Jacob the night before was true—the Resistance was hunting them. After escaping the confines of their compound and killing their leader, it didn't take long for Calay to figure out she was being followed. Tracked. On several occasions, she'd been forced to hide in an abandoned building or crawl against the hard pavement, under a vehicle, to avoid capture. She'd spied the uniforms. The army-style boots. The big fucking guns. If there was any doubt in her mind (and there often was thanks to Tess's betrayal—she'd likely spend years deconstructing that mind fuck), the few people she'd come into contact with confirmed her suspicions.

They'd answered her questions in exchange for favors—a thieving here, a supply run there. They didn't trust her, and she certainly didn't trust them, but she'd been desperate. So had they. She'd tried to restrict her dealings to only other women. Their requests were less seedy, more born out of necessity than want. In the end, she'd learned the Resistance was looking for someone they wished dead. They'd promised a big payout for information about her whereabouts, including sanctuary within the Resistance itself. Calay knew that someone was her. So as soon as she finished the job she was on, she'd disappear as if she hadn't existed at all. It was for the best, really. She couldn't risk strangers finding out who she was. Where she was. *What* she was. There was no telling who might betray her, turn her in. Kill her.

Her stomach growled. Calay was going to have to go back inside if she wanted breakfast. Or at least, what passed for breakfast these days.

She tried to adjust her legs farther underneath her when one slipped on the thin layer of ice that had formed between her ass and the concrete. Her foot kicked an empty can, it tumbled away, the sound muffled by the snow. Last night's dinner. A snapshot flashed through her mind. She'd pried the thing open after the tears had subsided. Green beans. *Always with the green beans.* She was never one to be ungrateful, so she'd forced the contents down. Though if she was being honest, if she never saw another can of the damn things it would be too soon. She pushed the thought away, looked toward the horizon. The sun was getting higher. The snow sparkled as the rays cut through the trees, down the cracks of the buildings. It was beautiful. It was horrible. It wasn't right.

There was something very wrong with the weather.

Something had shifted in Earth's atmosphere, something important. Normally she could have gleaned fruit, pumpkins, all varieties of squash, potatoes, and even lettuce and peas, if they were lucky, well through November. They should have had fresh vegetables for another two months. Instead, they were barely surviving on what she could scrounge in barren supermarkets. To make matters worse, houses had been picked over one, two, three hundred times. Garbage bins and dumpsters were turning up empty. So were their stomachs. She peered down at the can again, considered licking the rim. *Like a dog.* Speaking of which, Max was probably wondering where she was. From the first moment that mutt wandered into her camp, the two of them had been a pack. Her heart ached as she realized she'd abandoned him for the better part of twenty-four hours. More than that, actually. She was going out longer and staying up here later more and more frequently. This self-imposed exile wasn't fair to him. As her eyes traced the line between herself and the door, a shiver twisted itself up her spine, and this time, not from the cold.

Footprints.

Calay's breath caught in her throat. She recounted her lack of steps that morning. She hadn't moved from the ledge where she'd crawled up late last night. Any tracks from her coming on the roof would have been long covered. These were new. She glanced around, bracing herself for movement. But there was none. The footprints also only led one way. Inside. She shook her head. *That's impossible.* For the prints to be leading between her and the door, whoever had come up there had to have started from the opposite direction. Except, there was no tread. No markings. Just one set of prints, leading directly from her spot on the ledge to the door of the building.

She popped down onto the rooftop, her legs aching and stiff. Her knees creaked as she squatted to get a closer look. Yes, these were definitely new. The snow was clearly compacted into the shape of shoe treads that were far too small to be Jacob's.

"Shit." Calay whispered under her breath. She stood, tossed the blanket to the ground, and followed them inside.

Leading down the steps, one flight after another, were small puddles of dark water, pooling like blood. *Melted snow.* Calay tip-toed her way down the stairs, floor by floor, losing the light as she went. It was too early for the sun to reach into the corners. The stairwell was set too far back from the cracks of light that found their way through the boarded-up windows. Long shadows blanketed her path, making each footfall a game of chance. Calay had to count every set to know when the floor would drop away and when she'd have a landing to catch her, should she fall. She gripped the jagged railing, the metal clawed at her palms, and her whole body vibrated with adrenaline. She was following someone down a dimly lit stairwell, and she didn't know who. Or even why. She knew what she should have been doing was racing down to find Jacob and they could tag team the search, but she'd gotten so used to being on her own.

Even in life-or-death situations such as this. Especially in situations such as this.

So instead, she inched slowly downs the stairs, her hand poised on the hilt of her knife. The puddles were smaller now. There were fewer of them. The only sound was her short, ragged breathing and the scuff of her boots as she shuffled ever deeper into the building.

She'd just started down toward the sixth floor, two still well above where Jacob should have been, when something behind her scraped against the concrete. Her hand closed around the knife, and she lifted it from her belt before it was knocked clean out of her fingers and skidded down the stairs ahead of her. A scream burst from her lips but was cut short when something wrapped around her throat and pulled her backward, through the open door to the seventh floor.

Calay clawed at the grip around her neck, her eyes wide, darting side to side. Now she remembered why they hadn't used this floor as their base. There wasn't much up here. Just an abundance of broken mannequins. Many were missing limbs or turned on their sides, laying in mounds of white and brown paint flecks. Someone had colored several of their eyes in all black. They gaped at Calay, watched her gasp for breath, as she was dragged further among them. She struggled, pushing against the weight on her throat. Pulling. Prying. The vice didn't let go. She scratched harder, her fingernails left red claw marks behind on the skin of whoever—whatever—was holding her. The Resistance, likely. She couldn't let them get her. Not like this. Not here. Like before.

The thought occurred to Calay maybe her destiny really was to die alone in a warehouse somewhere. She could just give in. Let it be over. Finally, once and for all. Then, there was breath on her ear. Calay's stomach dropped. She let her body fall still.

She waited.

The assailant pulled her closer, the warmth of their chest pressed against the chill of hers. The breath grew softer. It smelled of peppermint. Calay almost drank it in. When was the last time she'd had candy? Or toothpaste? Or a fresh Mint Julep? That was another thing she should have been able to harvest. Herbs. But they'd frozen and died in the blizzard three weeks ago. *That would make the green beans a little more palatable, a little less disgusting.* If she ever got to indulge in the displeasure of eating green beans again. If she ever got to eat anything again.

"I'm going to let go," the yummy warm breath whispered. "And you're going to remain calm."

"The fuck I am," Calay muttered between short gasps.

"You are, or I cannot be held responsible for what happens to you. Understand?"

Calay didn't know what that meant. She didn't even know if she actually wanted to live. But she did know she wanted a say in how she died, and it wasn't deep inside a room full of creepy-ass mannequins. She nodded. The grip eased off her throat, the warmth left her back. Calay was free. She spun around, her fists raised, ready to fight the Resistance. Again.

Who she saw was not at all who she envisioned.

First of all, it was a woman. The Resistance was by-and-large, a male population. Calay still hadn't figured out why there weren't any women, and at this point, she didn't care. She just wanted to keep as much distance between herself and them as possible.

Second, she'd expected to face army fatigues and standard issue combat boots. What this woman wore took her breath away almost more than the chokehold. The woman with the strawberry blonde pixie cut towered over Calay by almost a foot. Her arms hung loosely beside a black leather corset, a strap wrapped its way across one shoulder and down her back. Loose, flowing pants hung off her round hips, stemmed at the knee. Her calves were covered in black tattoos, disappearing beneath ankle height lace-up boots. Calay let her gaze trail back up the length of the woman's body as she tried to regain her footing.

"Who are you?" Calay blinked, keeping her fists raised.

"You can put those down, you won't be needing them."

"You assaulted me and dragged me in here against my will. I think I'll make that judgement for myself." Calay raised them higher.

"Suit yourself." The woman stepped back, gave Calay some space. "I'm Ash."

"Is that supposed to mean something to me?"

"Does it?"

"No."

"Are you sure?"

Calay tilted her head, searched her memories. She scoured the most recent ones—the strangers she'd mostly avoided since leaving the cave, the few she hadn't. The months before everything happened, with Tess.

The years before that. There were a lot of names, a lot of beautiful women. Ash was new.

"I'm sure."

"Hmmm. I'd hoped Jacob would have told you more about me. About yourself. Your future."

"Wait." Calay's blood ran cold. It thrashed in her veins. "You're...one of Them?"

"A Térasian, yes. Do you like what you see?" Ash grinned with her full pink lips, winked a sparkling green eye lined rimmed in black liner. A ring glinted in her button nose as the sun crested the sky and sparkled through a broken board.

Calay did. Very much. But she wasn't about to tell Ash that.

"I th...I thought..." Calay searched for the words to ask her question. She struggled. "I thought the aliens were a consciousness. That you didn't have bodies."

"Ah, so he's told you some things. Maybe he just forgot to mention me." Ash thrust her hip to one side, rested a very well-manicured hand on it. Nails, Calay noticed. The woman had painted nails. She wondered where Ash found the polish—and the interest—to do that. They were in the middle of the apocalypse, after all. "I don't blame him. Wanting to keep you for himself. What, with the way he feels about you and all. He's always been a little...secretive."

Calay blanched. She couldn't argue with what Ash was saying; Jacob was guarded with his knowledge. Still, it took everything she had not to run from the room. She didn't want to hear about Jacob's feelings for her. If she did, it would mean she'd have to confront her feelings for him too. And she couldn't do that now. Not when she'd already lost so much. It was better she kept a tight lid on them, along with the rest of her emotions.

"You didn't answer my question."

"We can assume physical form, Calay. Do you really think Jacob is the only one of us to do that?"

"Of course not. I just...I thought he was the only one who did."

"Why should he be the only one to have all the fun?" Ash flashed a smile of perfect white teeth. "Our ships are excellent protection against

Earth's elements. Your planet being mostly water and all. But they're not exactly...intimate."

Calay nodded. What Ash was saying made sense. She'd learned water was toxic to aliens. They could withstand small amounts, but an Oregon rainfall—or an abnormality like a blizzard in October—would certainly kill them. She'd taken precautions, of course. Found Jacob a proper duster that covered him head to toe. Chosen this place because it wasn't only inaccessible to most, but also well insulated from the elements, unlike structures made of wood. Living in a rainforest for an extended amount of time was dangerous, if not impossible, for the Others. That was why Calay was the one risking her life day after day, foraging for food, while he laid around and read romance novels. Last night hadn't been the first time Jacob suggested they relocate somewhere dryer. Warmer. Calay understood. She was free to come and go as she pleased. So if she felt trapped, he must have felt like he was in a prison. It wasn't that he was lazy or in denial. He could actually die.

"Why are you here?" Calay blinked, stepping forward.

"I tried to make contact with you yesterday, and you walked away. I was hoping my human form might be more effective in getting your attention." Ash closed the distance between them.

"Grabbing somebody by the throat will do that." This woman—Ash —was right on the money. Calay cleared her throat. "Yesterday, that was you? In the pod. What do you want?"

"Jacob's had his chance to tell you the truth. To get you to come home. He's failed. I've gone over his head."

"I'm not going anywhere." Calay exhaled, turned. Sidestepping her way through the graveyard of mannequins, she was almost at the door.

"We can't wait any longer, Calay. Time is running out for us. For you. For Earth."

This had her attention.

"You mean the weather." Calay turned back around to face Ash. The sun's rays were pouring in through the window behind her now. She looked radiant, aglow. Calay swallowed, grateful someone was commiserating her concerns as well as for the distance between them.

She needed to keep her head clear. "This isn't natural. I've been telling Jacob that for weeks."

"We need this planet as much as you do, and it's dying." Ash strutted forward with conviction, placing her hand on the round of Calay's shoulder. Her pulse fluttered. *So much for keeping a clear head.* "There isn't enough symbiosis between humans and the environment anymore. It's becoming inhospitable."

"That doesn't sound right," Calay scoffed. She ran a hand over the back of her neck, swiped at beads of sweat that had pooled there. The proximity to Ash, and the weight of her hand, was making Calay warm. For all the reasons. "For generations, humans have been responsible for the demise of Earth. It should flourish in our absence."

"It did. For a while. But something's unbalanced, and we need your help to fix it."

"Mine? Why mine?"

"You're a hybrid. Half human, half us. You're the bridge, Calay."

"I don't understand."

"We're building a coalition force. A connection between our civilizations. We need people like you—those who can coexist—to make it work. To save us all."

"I can't do that." Calay recoiled from Ash's touch. The idea Ash was proposing made Calay want to curl into a ball and throw herself off the roof. She couldn't bridge the gap between her and Tess, and now she was barely managing to survive herself. Never mind saving an entire fucking civilization. No, two civilizations. It was ludicrous. Worse than that, it was impossible. Calay's head hung between her shoulders, a tightness swelled in her gut. "You've got the wrong woman."

"I don't think I do." Ash pulled her shoulders back, grinned. It was the same upturn in her lips that drove Calay crazy about Jacob. For Jacob.

"Why's that?" She couldn't help herself. She had to ask.

"Because of who you are."

"And who's that?"

"Are you sure you want to know?"

"Nevermi—" Calay started to back away, her hands in the air in front of her.

"You're your mother's daughter, Calay."

This stopped her mid-stride. She pulled her shoulders back and fought the urge to turn and punch Ash right in her beautiful mouth. She had no right bringing her mother into this.

"What does that have to do with anything?" The hardness in Calay's voice was like steel.

"Oh, c'mon Calay. Aren't you even a little curious?"

"My mother's dead. She died during the Change."

"Are you sure?"

"Of course I'm sure. My father told me so right before..." A darkness fell over Calay's gaze. "Before he died too. She was murdered by the very community she'd grown to love."

"I'm afraid that's not true." Ash dropped her gaze before bringing it to meet Calay's. "Your mother is alive, Calay. And she's sent me to bring you home."

CHAPTER THREE

CALAY'S BLOOD seized in her veins, her stomach dropped. She shuffled from one foot to the other, shook her head as if trying to clear the words from her ears. She couldn't have heard Ash correctly, could she? Calay stilled, swallowed a lump that was trying to lodge itself in her throat.

"What did you say?"

Ash grinned, took a step even closer. Yes, she definitely smelled like peppermint. It reminded Calay of something, but she couldn't quite place her finger on it. It hovered in the back of her mind, almost within grasp. But unreachable. Unfathomable. Just like the words she was sure she'd heard come out of Ash's mouth.

This was impossible.

"I said your mother is alive, Calay, and she wants to see you."

"You're lying."

"You're right." Ash nodded. "*Want* isn't desperate enough, given our current situation. It's more accurate to say she *needs* you."

"I don't believe you."

Ash closed the distance between them. Their faces were inches apart. Barely. Calay's pulse quickened. She resisted the urge to back away. She was determined to hold her ground. As long as she did that, she was in control. At least, that's what she kept telling herself.

"I know it's a lot to hear, especially after all you've been through. But I need you to believe me when I tell you it's the truth. Your mother is alive."

"Bullshit." Calay's voice bordered on hostile. Her lips pressed tight into a thin line, her hands balled into fists. She didn't know what this woman—this alien—was up to, but Calay wasn't going to entertain it. She'd been through enough. Lost enough. *Just, enough.* She'd been shocked by more surprises over the last four months than most people experienced in a lifetime. Between the secrets she'd uncovered about the aliens, almost losing Max, killing her father in cold blood, Tess's betrayal and attempt to murder her—twice—and finding out she herself was half alien, Calay didn't think she could survive any more. She didn't want to. "My mother is dead."

"Did you see a body? A grave?"

"From what I was told, there wasn't much to bury." Calay choked on the words, forced them out anyway. She couldn't believe her father had lied to her about her mother's fate. Not now. Not when she couldn't ask him for the truth. She'd made sure of that. "My Dad... He told me she tried to pull us together. To close the gap between our species. But when she came out to them as Other, they tore her apart. Limb by limb. Until there was nothing left."

"That did happen, yes. But he didn't understand the biology of our species. That we regenerate."

"That's impossible. Jacob said you die if you sustain too much damage. You can't regenerate."

"That's half right. Just because we can't collect ourselves in human form doesn't mean we can't in our natural state. On our home planet. Your mother survived, Calay. Just not as you knew her. After everything that happened between the two of you, she had to let you believe she'd died so you could be truly free. Unfortunately, the time has come where we can't afford your freedom anymore. We need you."

Ash reached for Calay's hand, but she backed toward the doorway, out of reach. She stumbled into something else. Someone else. A wave of panic rose inside Calay, her heart thrashed against her chest. She gasped, turned. Caught her breath as she realized it was Jacob. As he wrapped his strong arms around her, his blue eyes brimmed with affection. Calay buried her face in his chest before she could stop herself. Before she could even think about stopping herself. Jacob squeezed her tighter against him, his breath warm on the top of her head.

"She isn't ready for this, Ash." Jacob's deep voice reverberated against Calay's cheek.

"Ready or not, here I come." Ash whispered.

"That's not funny."

"Earth has really dried your sense of humor, darling." Ash sighed. "The truth is we didn't have a choice."

"I need more time." Jacob squeezed Calay tighter.

"We're out of time, Jacob."

"You should have come to me first. Let me handle it."

"You were supposed to handle it weeks ago."

"Not everything works the way you plan for it to work. Things get complicated."

"The only complication is that you've developed a crush on the target and now you're hiding away here, trying to play house. But I'll huff, and I'll puff..."

"Ash, I'm warning you."

"Elora's had enough of your games, Jacob. Your...complications, as you call it. It's time for action."

Calay's mind spun trying to make sense of their conversation. Jacob had never referred to her as the Target before. As he'd explained it to her, the Others had heat signatures that could be tracked. He'd been searching for her mother's when he came across hers. A tingle ran up Calay's arms and into her chest. If what he was saying now was true, that he needed more time to handle it—whatever it was—then it was possible he'd never been looking for her mother in the first place. Calay held her breath; on top of the revelation that her mother was alive, there was also the awareness forming in Calay's mind that Jacob must have known that truth all along.

Calay fought back the urge to cry and instead released a guttural scream against his shirt. She pulled away from his embrace, her eyes shining with tears.

"You knew. You knew all along and you let me believe she was dead."

"Calay, please. I intended to tell you. But then everything happened. Your father. Tess. I was giving you time to grieve and heal."

"I guess you didn't think that grief might be alleviated if I knew my mother was still alive? That I wasn't completely alone? That, oh I don't know, maybe I still had someone in this world who loved me?"

"You have me." Jacob's voice cracked as the words tumbled out of his mouth. He frowned, his arms hung at his sides. "You'll always have me."

"You lied to me."

"I'm sorry. I was protecting you. I was only doing what I thought was right."

"I don't need your protection. I need..." Calay almost let "my mommy" spill past her lips, but she sucked in her breath and held it.

"Speaking of needs," Ash said, turning, "we need you Calay. I can explain more later once we get to Téras. But first—"

"Téras." Calay side-eyed Ash, wrapped her arms around herself. "What's Téras?"

"You haven't even told her where she's from, Jacob?" Ash shook her head and frowned. "It's a good thing we stepped in when we did."

"You don't have to do this." Jacob's voice dropped an octave, and his crystal blue eyes grew dark. Ash ignored him, waved her hand above her head, as if his words were an insect, hovering in the air.

"Téras is the name of our home planet. It's where we'll be going. Where your mother is leading the coalition force. Jacob was supposed to fill you in, get you home so you can help save our civilizations."

"I'm not going anywhere." Calay pulled her shoulders back, stood taller.

"You don't have to." Jacob puffed his chest.

"She does if she wants Earth to survive. If she ever wants to see her mother again."

"Falling stars, that's not fair, Ash."

"You're right. Fair would have been telling her the truth from the very beginning. Fair would have been giving her the chance to choose her own fate. Fair would be a long, long way away from here."

"Please, give me a fucking break." Jacob scoffed, his jaw hard. "You don't care about Calay, or about this planet. The only thing you care about is yourself and getting exactly what you want. Like usual."

"What's so wrong with that?" Ash's green eyes turned dark as they slid across the length of Calay's shaking legs. Her gaze crawled over her stomach, her chest, and then her face. It took every ounce of strength Calay had to not melt into a puddle, right then and there. "I always get what I want."

"Watch it." Jacob charged forward, snaring Ash's shoulder with his own.

"Oh, I am." Ash hissed, shoving him back.

"Stop!" Calay's heart smashed against her ribs, her cheeks flushed.

"I'm stopping, I'm stopping." Ash threw her hands in the air. "So what do you want, Calay? To stay here and continue playing broken house with this one?" Ash jabbed her thumb toward Jacob, rolled her eyes. "Or to come home? Finally."

The only thing Calay wanted in that moment was to get the hell away from both of them. From the truth. The lies. The gray area where she couldn't tell them apart. She shuddered under the feeling something heavy and dark was hanging over her, clinging inside her, refusing to let go. Waiting to envelop her.

A hot blackness grew beneath her feet, oozing over the concrete on which she stood. It spread like it was alive, growing, one jagged arm, then another. Calay blinked, brought her fists to her eyes, rubbed them. It was still there. Pulsating. Breathing. She tried to take a step, to move out of its reach. It crawled up her legs, weighing her down, trapping her there. It wound its way over her stomach, cloying over her ribs. She swiped at it, pulled. It was no use; it was stronger than she'd ever be.

Her gaze darted between Jacob and Ash, who were entrenched in a discussion about what to do next with Calay. Why couldn't they see what was happening? Why didn't they help her? She thought she called to them. They continued their argument. The blackness inched up over

Calay's chest, around her neck, strangling a scream. It scraped over her jaw and across her cheeks before leaking inside her mouth. It tasted bitter and like decay. As if it was rotting her from the inside. It plunged deeper, forcing the bile that was rising in her throat back down into her stomach. It wrapped around the breath in her lungs, dripped into her bloodstream. It was drowning her. One inch at a time.

The room tilted. Her vision swam. She struggled against the urge to lay down and give in. To give up.

The next thing she knew, she was outside. Her feet slipping in the snow, charging away from the blackness. Away from Jacob. From Ash. From herself. The flakes had stopped crashing down from the sky, but the ground was slick and ill-defined. Calay stumbled through potholes and over debris hidden by drifts and snowbanks. Tears flowed out of her eyes, their trails freezing against her cheeks as she plowed forward. She sobbed between heavy, labored breaths. She wasn't being careful. Or quiet. She wasn't even trying. She just needed to get away as fast as possible.

Max's barking chased her all the way to the end of the street before she stopped. Something had finally cracked inside her and she dropped to her knees. The overturned school bus behind her, she buried her hands in the snow and let her fingers grow numb. She squinted in the morning light, its reflection on the snow-capped buildings. It held little warmth, and the wind cut through to the bone. She didn't even try to zip up her jacket. Just let the cold creep inside her. Anything to stop the pain radiating from her heart, the blackness from swallowing her whole. As she clawed at the frozen ground, she realized she'd had a panic attack. Brisk, fresh air flowed down her raw and aching throat while she inhaled it in heaving gulps.

She was desperate to put as much distance between herself and the Others as possible. They had, after all, been responsible for every major trauma in her life.

The first of which was when her parents disowned her for coming out as bisexual, for being different. Yet, they knew better than most the challenges that came with that. Her mother was an alien, for fuck's sake. And they'd hidden it from her. Until her mother had died at the hands of her neighbors, and her father by Calay's own when he'd tried to kill Jacob.

The second was when the Others took the life she'd planned with Tess when they literally turned their building inside out. Calay's chest ached at the thought of Tess. The betrayal. All Calay had wanted was a life with the woman she loved. But the woman she loved turned on her when she found out she was half-alien. Half Other. Tried to murder her. So Calay had killed her too.

It was as if Calay was cursed. Destined to be alone because of the very essence of who she was. Shivering, she thought she may have been responsible for the deaths of everyone she'd ever loved, but They were responsible for breaking her heart. Over and over again.

And now, Jacob.

After everything, she'd wanted to trust him. To love him. Somewhere deep down, maybe she did. But now she'd never know. It was true she'd been hard on him. Hell, she'd been hard on herself. He wasn't wrong— she needed space to process and heal after everything that had happened. She'd hoped, once she made it through that pain, if she ever did, he'd be there when she came out the other side. Disappointment rolled over her with the knowledge that he'd lied to her the whole time. He knew from that first night he squatted by her campfire, that she was the intended target.

Her mother was alive. She'd sent for her. Jacob had kept them apart. And for what?

He claimed it was to protect her, and maybe that was true. But how could she trust anything he said ever again?

Everything—every moment, every confessional, every embrace, kiss, laugh, and fuck—had been built on a lie.

"Now what?" Calay whimpered.

Something creaked.

Calay froze. She wasn't more than two feet away from the school bus. She held her breath, stifled a sob. She listened. A gust of wind howled, rushing up the street and back the way she came. As if saying *go back. Run now.* Calay didn't move.

Another creak. Then, a third.

Something banged against the wall of the bus closest to her. She lurched to her feet. Someone was definitely inside. She backed away, into the street. She knew better than this. To put herself out in the open. To leave herself vulnerable. She wished she'd learned the same lesson emotionally. Then, a loud scratching like someone was frantically crawling over the seats. Calay spied a pair of hands crest the door of the bus way up in the air. It was all she needed to move. Whoever was in there had heard her. She was certain of it. How could they not? She'd be damned if they caught her. She briefly considered running back the way she came, to the Loft. But she couldn't bring herself to face Jacob and Ash. The Others. Instead, she surged the opposite way into town. Behind her, someone shouted. She chanced a glance to see a man in army fatigues waving a red flag from the top of the bus. Calay's heart dropped.

It was the Resistance. They'd spotted her.

Calay didn't think she could trust anyone anymore, even herself. Yet, she had to trust her knowledge of the town, turning down one side street, then another. It wasn't long ago the Resistance had captured her. Imprisoned her. Assaulted her. She'd seen how they treated the enemy. They couldn't know for sure it had been Calay who killed Tess, but they would suspect it. Of course they would. Tess had died, and Calay had vanished. She was a wanted woman, and they would do what they wanted with her. If they got their chance.

She wasn't about to give it to them without a fight.

Shouts chased her down the abandoned streets. They weren't far behind. She crashed through long, twisting shadows as she plunged down an alley. Now that she'd been responsible for finding all their food and supplies, her legs were the strongest they'd ever been. Still, they screamed for her to stop. Take a breather. Rest.

She denied their pleas and instead, reached for a metal handle and dashed through the side door of the old play theatre. The latch clicked behind her. She didn't pause to make sure it had locked. She probably should have. She just kept running.

Her footfalls pounded against the wooden floor of the stage.

She slowed. Stopped. Listened.

The only sound was her ragged breathing echoing across the theatre. The burning in her thighs subsided. Her shoulders relaxed a little. She squinted through the darkness.

The sconce lights hanging on the wall were long since smashed, the floor strewn with broken glass. While most of the seats were still in place, whole sections had been ripped out and burned, their remains scattered across the stage. In their wake, an immense hole through the floor. The red velvet drapes were singed, stained. She followed them, craning her neck.

In the rafters, she could make out the silhouette of several bodies hanging by their necks. Calay gasped, her eyes grew wide. She couldn't tell if they were men or women, adults or children. They were too high up and the room far too dark. They were still. *Likely been there a while.*

She cringed at what passed for hope these days.

She clenched her eyes shut and turned her attention back to the room in front of her. The theater used to be a place of joy. Performance. Art. Now, the whole place was marred by the collapse of humanity. It was more of a tomb than a playhouse. Calay sighed, having finally caught her breath. Then, it was stolen just as quickly.

Against the padded, tufted doors at the back, stood a man. His army uniform was smeared with something dark, his eyes like black caverns in his face. He was almost as still as the bodies above. Except for the occasional tilt of his head. He stood there. Watching her. For who knew how long? Waiting. But for what?

Calay backed toward the center of the stage. The man didn't move, but something else did.

Calay's gaze darted left. She didn't see anything at first. Maybe a trick of the light. Then a shadow stepped forward. She couldn't make out the entire shape, but there was definitely a head. Shoulders. Another person. Calay's pulse raced, her blood surged through her ears. The wooden floor behind her groaned. She spun to find a handful of silhouettes creeping up the back stairs.

She twisted to run, but tripped over her feet. More silhouettes appeared. More than she could count. The theater was bursting with them. The group converged on every available side. Dread overwhelmed Calay as she realized she was being corralled.

"Who are you?" she cried.

No one answered.

"Are you with the Resistance?" Calay's voice cracked.

They crept closer.

"My group will be here any minute. You better get out of here. While you still can." She lied. She knew it. They probably did too.

She tried to make out some details of who they were. What they were. To find some humanity in the wave of faceless creatures slowly descending. But there were no distinguishable characteristics. None of them seemed to have mouths. Or noses. Or even ears. It was just a dark horde of bodies.

This time, unlike the blackness that tried to swallow her earlier, there was no escape. This was no panic attack. It was real. Calay pressed herself against what remained of the pyre, careful to avoid the giant fucking hole in the middle of it all.

Then they swarmed her.

CHAPTER FOUR

A LEGION of bodies rushed the stage from every direction.

They surged forward like a tsunami, thundering toward Calay.

She had nowhere to go.

The closest, the man from the door, was nearly on top of her when she fell backward through the hole. She narrowly missed the splintered floorboards as she crashed through the air, plummeting into the unknown. She felt almost weightless, as if she was falling through space.

The moment lasted a lifetime. It didn't last nearly long enough.

Calay's teeth chattered, her bones shook, her neck ached as she came to an abrupt stop. She gaped, dazed if not confused. She squinted, trying to make sense of her surroundings. It seemed she'd landed in some kind of laundry chute. What were once white towels and sheets folded beneath her head and up over her arms. Now, they were marred with gray ash and black soil. Fragments of wood and melted-turned-hard-again pieces of plastic jabbed at her ribs and back. Remnants of the blaze that had caused the hole in the first place. They smelled musty and dank as if they'd never made it to the laundry machine. Just sat here, stewing in their own filth. Her arms splayed at her sides and her legs twisted, she blinked, tried to clear her vision.

Stars seemed to pendulate in the darkness. No, dust. Particles of the stuff drifted down from where she'd lost her footing. A whisper of a memory flashed across her mind. The morning she'd woke up after the Resistance left her for dead in that warehouse. No, not the Resistance. *Tess*. Calay's heart ached so hard she clutched her chest. She'd trusted Tess. She'd trusted herself. And she'd been wrong. So horribly, horribly wrong. About everything.

Calay shook the cobwebs from her mind—and her hair—and froze. She became painfully aware the only light was that which bled from above. It poured down on her, as if by spotlight. It was unnatural, she thought, there were no lights; no windows. They'd been smashed or boarded up long ago. One of the people above her must have a flashlight. If they could see her, maybe she could see them.

She peered up through the dust and the never-ending empty space. Three floors up, the opening she'd fallen through. Rimming that, a legion of shifting silhouettes. Their chests heaved, their arms stretched out overhead. She could see some reaching through the hole, as if they could claw all the way through this blackness and grab Calay. She stifled a scream, her body recoiled into the soiled linens. She shuddered, wrenching her neck from side to side, desperate to see in the darkness. There was no way they were coming down there after her, were they? She strained to listen. No stampeding footfalls overcame her. No monsters jumped from the shadows that stretched the length of the laundry room. It was silent. Too silent for so many bodies. She turned her gaze back to them.

They writhed above, hungry.

No one had—as of yet—dared to jump after her. She gaped at them, trying to distinguish one from the other. To find a clue as to who they were and what they wanted. The Resistance may have chased her from the bus and through the streets, but whoever this was, staring back down at her in the cold darkness, was not them. It was someone else. *Something* else. She was determined to put a face to...any of them. Calay squinted past the light, her eyes finally adjusted.

This time, the scream made it passed her chapped lips. It flew out her mouth and echoed through the rafters of the theater.

The reason she couldn't make out their faces before was that they had none.

Where their eyes and mouths should be were wide black holes. They lacked noses. Ears. Dimples, wrinkles, and cheekbones. In their place, a yellow-tinted canvas, adorned with bulging black veins that seemed to writhe with each violent breath. Those veins crept across their ugly taut faces and around the back of their bald, bulbous heads. Where she could make out bare skin on their arms or legs, their skin was white. Whiter than white. It was almost translucent.

Calay's stomach dropped, and she clawed at the heap of laundry. She shivered, her legs ached to move. To run. To do something. Anything. But as she counted down from three, two, one—trying to spur herself into motion—she remained. As if pinned down under the weight of their stares.

She laid there, paralyzed with fear.

There was something about the way they moved that wasn't right. Maybe it was the animalistic ferocity in their run. The way they twitched. It was deeply unsettling. They reminded her of the zombie shows she and Tess used to watch on Sunday nights. After they'd ate all the food and drank all the wine, the two women would curl up on the faded green velvet couch they'd procured at the flea market, wrap themselves in a blanket (and each other), and catch up on the latest undead series.

"Zombies aren't real," Calay whispered into the dark. Though she wasn't entirely sure she believed the words as they came out of her mouth. It wasn't that long ago aliens were considered mere creatures of science fiction.

Now, she knew they not only existed, but she was one of them. She couldn't help the chilling question from burying itself in her mind: *what if the same is true of zombies?*

Before she could shake herself clear of the waking nightmare, one of the beings coughed. Or grunted. She couldn't be sure. Then it screeched. It was a horrible hacking noise that bellowed through the theater, coming to rest firmly on her chest.

Its shape rose above the others. It grew and grew, seeming to take up the entirety of the expansive opening. Then it turned and ran. Then a second. *Oh no.* Calay had seen enough films over the years to know what was coming next. She had to move. She struggled to gain her footing, her legs slipping on the mountain of fabric beneath her. She rolled over onto her stomach, scratching her way forward.

She'd made little progress when a deafening boom thundered through the room.

She chanced a glance over her shoulder just in time to see the remaining heads rise and disappear the same way the others had.

Their footfalls fell away, replaced by several thuds. Grunts. Several loud cracks that sounded like wood splintering.

"What the fuck is going on up there?" Calay breathed in the moments that lingered between the cacophony of destruction. She tried to slow each breath, to make herself smaller. Quieter. Whatever was going on, she wanted no part.

If it was the Resistance, she hoped they were unaware of her presence. Maybe they were just doing a sweep, searching. If she was lucky, they'd pass right by her. Maybe they'd chase those things away.

Whatever they were.

She dared to hope maybe the beings that had chased her down weren't zombies after all—they were just people. After all, no person in their right might would have jumped through that hole. *Or they were clever zombies.* Calay shook her head. *That's worse. That's so much worse.*

She fought to see beyond the beam of light that was somehow still shining down on her. She wanted to run but was terrified what she might find beyond the light. In the darkness.

If she was still upstairs, she could have slipped back out the rear door. Made a break for it. Instead, she was trapped down here. Like a mouse in a lion's den.

She should have stayed where it was safe, if not comfortable. At the Loft. With Jacob and Ash. He may have lied to her, but at least he wasn't trying to kill her. Calay shook her head, ran a hand over the beads of sweat that had pooled on the back of her neck. She thought she was beyond this. That she'd finally got her impulsivity under control. Evidently, she was wrong. Again.

The racket above stopped. Calay sucked in her breath. Waited.

A shadow grew over the light. It crawled across the laundry, over her toes, obscuring her face. The silhouette was broad. Clearly out of breath. Human.

"Who's there?" Calay asked, her voice barely above a whisper.

The light shifted as the figure picked up what turned to be a heavy-duty, utility work light, like the kind her dad used to have on the farm. They hoisted it up to their chest. Shined it down. She grimaced as the beam hit her square in the eyes. It was a very Resistance thing to do. Calay's heartbeat increased, her pulse raced. She needed to know who was up there. Watching her.

"Who are you?" Calay tried again, raising her hand to try to shield the glow.

"You alright?" The figure called back.

Calay exhaled. Her shoulders relaxed. Of course.

Jacob.

He was always dashing to her rescue. Showing up when she needed him most. When she wanted him least. After the way she stormed out of the Loft, the last thing she needed right now was for him to come in and save her. Except, she very much did need him.

She ground her teeth together, licked her dry lips.

It wasn't that she was so foolish enough to think she could do everything on her own. After all, up until four months ago, she'd done it all with Tess by her side. *Look how that turned out.* But every time Jacob came waltzing in with his alien super-strength, he reminded her how weak she was. For once, just once, she'd like to save herself.

"How'd you find me?" Calay repositioned herself on the towels. Used one to wipe the tears from her cheeks. Failed. Instead, a dusting of soot followed in their place. Against her better judgement, Calay tried to make eye contact with Jacob. She knew his mannerisms well now. Almost better than her own. The subtle shifts in his body. The openness of his shoulders. She could tell he was grinning down at her. Her muscles tensed. She glared up at him. "What?"

"Do you really need to ask at this point?" He shifted his weight. The light too. "You know I can track your heat signature, right?"

"Fucking heat signature." Calay hung her head, nodded.

"You can run, but you can't hide, Calay." Jacob laughed. He actually laughed.

"That's not funny."

"It's a little funny."

"Nope. Not even a little bit." Calay crawled off the mountain of linens, stumbling as several caught around her ankles.

"Are you okay?"

"Don't I look okay?"

"You looked like you needed help." Jacob exhaled. "Badly."

"Well, I don't now." Calay exhaled in return. If not out of spite, frustration. "You can go."

"Can I though? Do you know how to get out of there?"

Calay glanced around. The blackness seemed even darker now with the light pointed so strongly on her. The last thing she wanted to do was push through it. Alone. She shook her head. Out of the corner of her eye, she watched his head bob.

"Stay there. I'll come get you."

"I'm still mad at you," she said.

"I know."

The light dimmed as Jacob retreated out of sight.

Calay found herself in pitch blackness. She couldn't see a thing. It was a vast emptiness that weighed on her chest. Her heart. Her fear. She slowed her breathing, taking long inhalations and doubly long exhalations. She tried not to panic again. Jacob would make his way down there soon, and then she'd be free.

Whatever that meant anymore.

As the intense instinct to fight or flee receded, she almost wished he'd just let her die. Isn't that what she deserved? After everything she'd done? She was responsible for so much pain. So much death. She just couldn't claim it for herself. She pulled on the edge of the scarf still wrapped around her neck. Stretched it. Brought it to her mouth and bit down on the fabric. It tasted like dust. She clenched her eyes and stifled a sob.

The shudder of a heavy metal door opening pulled Calay back into her body.

She watched the light dance across what turned out to be an enormous concrete room, sparsely decorated save for a tweed armchair that had seen better days and a handful of washers and dryers. Cracked wooden shelves lined the walls, musty books coated in grime seemed to shrink away from the light. She didn't need to pull them down to know between the covers were plays that would never be performed. Stories that would never again be read. Fictional lives, unlived.

Unloved.

"Place is a goddamned maze back there." Jacob marched straight up to Calay, angling the light down. A swooshing sound filled the space as his head-to-toe leather duster dragged on the floor behind him.

Calay rolled her eyes at the drama of it. He sure knew how to make an entrance. But for an alien who couldn't be touched by water lest they die, the jacket worked perfectly to keep the snow off him.

"See anyone?" Calay shuffled sideways. She didn't trust her feelings if she got too close to Jacob, but also didn't trust what might still be lurking in the shadows that surrounded them.

"No one on the way down, though there were probably five or so of those things when I arrived."

"Is that all?" Calay blinked, her gaze met his. She could have sworn there were more. Hundreds, even.

"Oh yeah." Jacob grinned. "Taking down five creepy-ass motherfuckers is a walk in the park for me. No big deal."

"That's not..." Calay frowned, straightened her scarf. "That's not what I was saying. I guess I just thought there were more. What were those things?"

"People." Jacob shrugged.

"They didn't look like people."

"And aliens don't look like aliens, but here we are."

"None of us are quite what we seem anymore."

"Is that what you think?"

"Maybe we never were." Calay shrugged.

"Calay, about earlier. I... I'm sorry I didn't tell you the whole truth."

"Right."

"I mean it. I wasn't trying to keep you and your mother apart. I hate to say it, but Ash was right. I should have said something sooner."

"What's up with her anyhow?"

"What do you mean?"

"You seemed..." Calay frowned, searching for the right word. "Weird, I guess. Around her."

Jacob angled himself toward the darkness. Calay watched his shoulders rise and fall with each breath. Finally, he faced her and said, "That's a story for another day."

Calay ignored him and his pouty lips, took a step forward toward the door. *Fine, if he wants to be that way.* She'd had enough of this place. Only she wasn't sure if she meant Jacob's company, the theatre, or life.

"Calay..." Jacob charged after her. "Calay, stop. Please."

"Let me go, Jacob." Calay shook him off, continued up and out through the theater. She navigated the arteries of hallways as if she'd been there before. Several times. She pushed through the back door and stepped into the alley. A fresh blanket of snow crunched under her feet. Any trace of her footsteps from earlier were gone. Erased. Like they'd never existed. *I wish.* Jacob was on her heels.

"No." Jacob planted himself in front of Calay, blocking her path. His crystal blue eyes drilled a hole into her, his voice cut through. She tried to bore one back but wasn't sure she succeeded. She worried she was edging on smoldering. "You have to let *her* go."

"Excuse me?" Calay's voice crossed from pithy to shrill. Her eyes grew wide, a fire ripped through her veins.

"I'm not trying to be insensitive..." Jacob started.

"Well, congratulations, you've overshot the landing and somehow managed on cruel." Calay stepped forward, her finger jabbed his chest. "How many times do I have to tell you? You don't get to tell me what to do. I am not yours. I will never be yours. Do you get that?"

"No, actually. I don't." Jacob's eyes grew dark. His mouth turned down in the corners, his dimples too. Calay blanched. This was not the response she'd come to expect from him. "I'm sorry for what happened. I truly am, Calay. I'm sorry the love of your life betrayed you and died. I'm sorry your dad is dead. I'm sorry you were forced to play a hand in both. You have to know though, that it's not your fault. It's never been your fault. You need to realize and accept that. Moping around here won't bring her back."

"Don't you think I know that?" Calay screamed. She usually tried to keep a lid on her feelings. Hide them. Bury them, deep down where not even she could reach them. It was how she survived. But Jacob's words hit too close to home. To the truth. To her. They exploded like shrapnel, lodging themselves in the cracks of her heart that were starting to show regular wear and tear. Evidently, they dug deep enough to not just cause a leak in the wall holding back her emotions, they shattered the damn thing. "I killed her, Jacob. Me. I. Killed. Her."

"She put you in an impossible position. It was you or her." Jacob stepped forward, placed a gentle, heavy hand on her shaking shoulder. "You were fighting for your life."

"Maybe so, but you know what?" A waterfall of tears poured across Calay's cheeks, over her chin, melting the snow at her feet. "I sat there on top of her, my hands around her neck. Her eyes on mine. And I watched the life drain out of her like air out of an air mattress. It didn't happen fast. It was slow. Painful. Do you know that when it's quiet, I can still feel her pulse between my fingers?"

"Calay…"

"And you know what the worst fucking thing about it is? I liked it."

Jacob frowned.

"I did. I liked watching her squirm and fight and fucking lose! After all she did to me, I wanted to hurt her."

"I'm so sorry." Jacob brought his hand to her other shoulder, turning her to face him. As if he could shelter her from what she'd done.

"I live with this, Jacob. This pain. I carry it around from sun up to sun down. All day, every day. I dream about it when I sleep. It's there when I eat, when I hunt, when I…if we…It's nestled inside me, and I'm afraid if we get close, it'll nestle inside you too."

"I wish that it would." Jacob's eyes were glassy now. Calay knew the Others couldn't cry. Tears were water, and water was their kryptonite, but it didn't mean their bodies didn't emulate human physiological reactions. This was as close to balling as Jacob could get. His voice cracked. "I wish I could take this pain away from you."

Jacob tugged Calay close, one inch at a time. He wrapped her in his arms. She let him. Just like she'd let him hold her at the Loft earlier that morning. And the way she let him comfort her in the barn at her childhood farm. In the kitchen of the abandoned cabin. Even before she realized what they meant to each other, she'd found a comfort in his arms. His company. Their kind.

Jacob was right. It had been the two of them, surviving.

He'd tried to reach her, to help her. To bring her back from the dead. She was the one who refused to crawl out of the grave she'd dug for herself. She flinched with the realization she was pulling him down below the surface with her. Strangling the oxygen out of them both. The same way she'd choked the life from Tess. *No, not the same way.* Because Tess was dead. Nothing was going to bring her back. Calay and Jacob had to live with that fact. Together. The truth was, despite her promise to protect him from her damage, Calay needed Jacob.

In more ways than she could count.

Her shoulders shook with the violence of her sobs. Her fists clenched at his back. He held her tighter. He brushed the rat nest of knots out of her long dark hair one handful at a time, showered the top of her head with kisses. He even wiped what was left of the ash and dirt from her face, each gesture eliciting a wince of pain from him as her tears came into contact with his skin. He did everything she needed him to do.

Everything except tell the truth.

Ash had though. Calay's mother was alive. That counted for something.

"Maybe you can." Calay mumbled against Jacob's chest, cleared her throat.

"What do you mean?"

"You're right. Wallowing in this pain isn't doing either of us any favors. There's nothing left here for me here. Not anymore. Maybe there'll be something in Galaxy 3C303."

Jacob's body became rigid. His breath shallowed against her cheek. He held her at arm's length.

"Are you serious?"

"I don't know what else to do." Calay sniffed.

"Believe me, Calay. This is the right decision."

"I don't believe in anything anymore. Least of all the words coming out of your mouth." Calay paused, watching a shimmer of pain flash over Jacob's face. To his credit, he tried to hide it. She could tell he was hopeful about this change. She didn't want to take that away from him. Maybe his hope would be enough to buoy both of them. "But maybe in time I will. On Téras."

"I accept that." Jacob tucked his hands in the pockets of his duster and nodded.

Calay shifted her gaze down the alley, glanced up at the murky white sky. The sun was almost overhead. If they were going to get going, now was the time. Her eyes met his.

"What should I pack?"

CHAPTER FIVE

THE SHADOWS on the fourth floor were already starting to transform by the time Calay and Jacob made their way back to the Loft.

The clouds grew darker, the snow deeper.

Jacob gingerly pulled the hood of his duster down and shook it from his shoulders, letting it fall to the concrete floor. He skirted around the growing puddle and made for the window facing the road. He shimmied the plywood barrier they'd constructed to block the light of their lantern and their movement. He leaned against the barrier. Calay watched him squint into the falling afternoon light, searching for signs they'd been followed.

He was so cautious with her. So thoughtful. Always looking out for her. The slightest smile crept across her mouth before she snuffed it out.

She trailed behind him, but first, picked up his coat. Shook it off. Hung it on a piece of exposed, vertical rebar off to the side of the room to dry. They both knew the risk to Jacob's life was more dangerous than ever. Earth was already over seventy percent water, so the odds of his survival low. Throw in the abominable weather conditions, and they dropped almost to zero. They had to be careful.

Really careful.

He'd taken a huge risk coming after her like that. Through the snow and ice. She shook her head, then her jacket and scarf. Hung it next to his. Jacob had saved Calay's life on more than one occasion, and now it was her turn to protect him. She had to be more vigilant over her emotions and reactions. A shiver rippled through her. *It's bloody freezing in here*. The sound of dripping water followed her footsteps when she crossed the room.

She approached Jacob, felt the heat rising from his body. She leaned closer, her forearm grazed his. She let the warmth of him seep into her. The hairs on both their arms stood up. Jacob glanced down at her, raised an eyebrow. Just the one. Grinned. His dimples deepened. Calay's stomach did backflips.

"I thought you were still mad at me," Jacob said.

She shrugged at him, furrowed her brows in reply.

"So, we're good?"

"I'd like us to be."

"Okay then. You let me know."

A moment of silence passed between them. It hovered, thick with electricity. Calay swallowed, tried to get a read on Jacob. On herself. She really did want everything between them to be alright. To make it work. But how could she do that when he wasn't being honest with her? He said he was only trying to protect her, to keep her safe. But that wasn't what she needed. *Not most of the time*, she admitted. She needed him to trust her to take care of herself.

Even if she couldn't do the same.

"I just want to make sure you're doing your job properly." Her voice was curt, but a twinge of sarcasm underlaid it. The corners of her mouth turned up. It wasn't quite a smile. But it wasn't not a smile, either. She felt Jacob's gaze on her when she turned and peered out the window. The snow was falling again. Like someone was shaking a sieve of flour over the whole town.

"It's a winter wonderland out there," Jacob said, his voice gentle.

"That, or Hell finally froze over."

"Did you just make a joke, Ms. Calay?"

"It's all fun and games until someone loses their life."

"You're on a roll." Jacob laughed.

Calay braved a glance at him, allowed the tension in her body to defrost a little. The blue in his eyes looked clearer than it had in weeks. They almost twinkled, like icicles in the crisp morning light. She watched his face grow somber and turned to follow his gaze.

The snow fell harder, obscuring the view from their perch. They could barely see two feet in front of them, never mind the long stretch of street below.

"I don't think anyone followed us," Calay murmured.

She peered at him out of the corner of her eye. They'd done this exact thing dozens—hundreds—of times since they'd arrived here. Stood on the safety of the platform, surveyed the landscape. It had shifted so quickly. The leaves turned from deep green to brilliant shades of orange and yellow. As the sun cut between them, they glowed as if on fire. Then they fell in giant heaping clumps. The snow arrived.

Calay counted and recounted the ticks they'd made on the wall. An ever-present reminder of both the changing seasons and the never-changing reality that Tess was dead. Each notch marked another day that fact was still true.

So, while the weather grew colder and the days shorter, Calay remained. Stuck inside her awful memories. But not this place. Not anymore. She'd finally agreed to return with the Others to Galaxy 3C303. Their planet, Téras. This shell of a building wasn't home, but it was the closest thing Calay had to one. And now it was possible this would be the very last time she and Jacob would stand here, like this, together.

"Where'd Ash go?" Calay wrapped her arms around herself. She wasn't sure if it was to stave off the chill or the shiver Ash's name sent through her body. There was something strange about that woman. *That alien.* Something irrevocably beautiful. And although Calay had no true reason to think it, something dangerous, too.

"Back where she came from, I suppose. She has authority. Influence. She wants more. But she's not the type to do legwork. Recon missions fall to those with lower seniority or lower-class status." Jacob shoved his hands in his pockets. "Like me."

"Why her then? Why now?"

Jacob cleared his throat and turned back to the room before leaning against the barrier. The veins in his arms rippled, the apple in his throat bobbed. Calay blinked, surprised to find herself yearning to press her lips to it. *I must really be out of it.* She slid her hands over her stomach and pressed them between her legs, squeezed her thighs. Both to keep the cold out, and her hands off him.

"Elora," Jacob hesitated, "your mother. For her to send Ash, she must really need us."

"Yeah, well, Ash said you've been gone a while."

"That's not what I meant. I meant you. She must really need *you.*"

"Right." Calay struggled to keep the strain out of her voice. The desperate desire to be loved by the one woman who was supposed to love her most. She failed.

"You'll have to ask her." Jacob pressed his lips together.

"Why did she wait this long to send for me then? If she needs me so much?"

Calay met his gaze, watched the icicles in his eyes melt as they grew darker. Almost black. Calay straightened her spine, watched him closer. His eyes had never clouded with shadows that way before, and she'd spent more time looking into them than she wanted to admit. It could have been a trick of the light, the sun setting. The moment passed and they turned bluer than ever. And drilling straight into her.

Calay exhaled, rolled her eyes, and nodded. "I guess we should get our shit together then." She turned from the window and made her way back across the room to the couch, where her stuff lay scattered across the tattered rug.

She didn't have much aside from the brown leather backpack she'd lifted from the back of someone's closet. Likely abandoned as they'd fled their house. Or never got the chance to. The house in which she'd found it stunk to high hell. Several rooms had been locked shut, and neither she nor Jacob had the urge to explore what was inside them. The smell never really wore out of the fabric of the bag. Jacob had suggested she find another, but in a way, she kind of liked it. It was a sick reminder that things were never as bad as they seemed; they could always get worse.

Calay gathered the small mound of medical supplies she'd gleaned the day before. She squatted and flipped the lid on the dented cooler they kept beside the couch. There were still two apples, most of the cans of vegetables. Jacob had sprung the lid on the corned beef, but the bag of potatoes was sealed.

She dumped all but the beef into her pack and divided up the meat onto two chipped plates.

"Dinner is served!" She announced, holding one in each hand. The sound of Max's nails on the hard floor happily responded as he trotted over. She scanned the space, which was quite dark now. The sun dipped below the horizon. The shadows grew long.

Jacob had disappeared.

They survived together by being together. It was a truth that had kept her and Tess alive. It was the opposite truth that had killed Tess.

No, that was me.

Calay pushed the thought from her mind. She'd already had one meltdown today, she didn't intend to have another.

It wasn't like Jacob to leave without saying anything, but then again, none of today was normal. She shrugged. He had to be around there somewhere. Not wasting any time, he was probably getting ready to go. After all, Téras was his home. He'd been gone from it a long time. It was hard to be away from those you loved. The places that made you feel like you belonged. The spaces that made you feel safe. Despite the fact she'd fallen apart earlier, or maybe because of it, she couldn't help but hope Téras might be that for her one day too.

But only if she got her ass in gear.

She set the plates aside, tossed half her portion to Max, and twisted the fuse on the lantern. The flame sprung to life. A gentle glow flickered over him as he gobbled the meager portion of food. It took him only a few moments to finish it. The light glowed in his golden eyes, and he wagged his tail. *Grateful mutt.* What she wouldn't give to feel the same.

She glanced at what remained of her things and gathered what little layers of clothing she had, rolled them up, and stuffed them inside her pack. She spied Jacob's book on the floor, peeking from behind the couch. She stepped forward to grab it too and placed her foot directly in the puddle of melted snow from their coats.

"Ugh."

Her sock was soaked.

She plopped down on the couch, reached into her bag, and retrieved the third and final pair of socks she owned. With them came something shiny. It glinted in the lantern's light. The muscles in Calay's back tensed, the breath shallowed in her lungs.

She held the item at arm's length. As if it might reach out and strangle her.

Caught between the creases of her folded socks was the one thing she hadn't been able to let go of. The one thing that was still theirs.

Their pendants. Two crescent moons hanging from delicate gold chains. It was the first gift Tess had ever given Calay. It was the last thing she had to remember her by. Through everything, Calay had managed to hang onto it. She'd worn hers the entire time she'd searched for Tess. Until she couldn't hang onto Tess a moment longer, and Calay watched her body float away in that cave. Lifeless.

Like their love.

She unravelled the socks and let the necklaces fall to the floor. There was a time she'd have scrambled to pick them up. Protected them at all costs. Now, she stared at them. Frozen. Stuck in a time and place that was no longer hers.

"Calay?"

"Huh?" She blinked, gazed down.

She'd managed to get the new socks half on, the wet ones discarded. Her pack lay on its side, the contents half spilled out on the carpet. Max nestled beside her, staring at the remaining plates of food. Calay wasn't sure how much time had passed or how long Jacob had been standing there. Shadows licked underneath his eyes, across his strong jaw, disappearing into the darkness of the room. His form seemed broader. More bullish. He towered over her. Calay recoiled, her heart lurched in her chest. He bent down, his thick hand seeming to hover over her face. Her mouth. She couldn't breathe.

Then, he scooped up her bag, gently tucking the items back in that had fallen out.

"Sometimes I think you make a mess because you like pushing my buttons, or maybe you just like me on my knees." He smiled, pulling his gaze to hers.

This was Jacob, she reminded herself. She had no reason to be afraid of him. When she didn't snark something in reply, he leaned forward, resting one of those broad hands on her knee. "You okay?"

Calay took a beat. Then another. She nodded.

"You sure?" The concern in his voice was palpable.

"Yeah, um..." She snagged her pack, forced a smile, and nodded to the plates. "I made dinner."

"Do you think we should just give it all to him? Since...you know?" Jacob's gaze shifted between the food and Max.

"Since what?"

Jacob pressed his lips together, refusing to make eye contact with Calay.

"Wait, what?" Her heart felt as though it might thunder through her chest. Jacob couldn't be saying what she thought he was, could he? "He's coming, right? Max is coming."

"We can't bring him with us, Calay."

"We have to!"

"We can't."

"Why not?"

"I don't know about you, but I don't think dogs fare too well in long-distance space travel. He'll do better here."

"No. We'll put him under or something. We'll figure it out. He's coming with us."

"I'm sorry, it won't work."

"We can't just leave him here, Jacob! We're a pack. He needs us. He'll die without us."

"I know this is hard. I love him too. He made it on his own before, he'll do it again."

Calay fell to her knees, wrapped her arms around Max. His floppy black ears smelled like popcorn. He raised a thick paw, rested it on Calay's arm. Tears wallpapered her eyes.

"What if he doesn't?"

"He will."

"He'll miss us too much."

"You and I both know he'll be living it up out there instead of waiting for you to come home every day. It'll be hard on him at first, but he'll adjust. He'll be free."

The coldness of the floor seeped through Calay's jeans and crawled to her heart. She didn't want Max to be free. She wanted him with her.

She hadn't been good enough to him lately. Hadn't loved him enough.

She showered him with kisses and pets. She couldn't bear to leave her best friend behind, but what other choice did she have? Jacob was right. They couldn't fly a dog into space, to an alien planet. She knew that. But it didn't make leaving him behind any easier.

Teared flowed out of Calay's eyes, down her cheeks, and into the scruff of Max's fur.

This animal had been everything to her. He'd saved her more times and, in more ways, than she could count. The least she could do was return the favor and give him the best chance at survival. The Loft had been safe for the three of them thus far, it stood to reason it would be okay for just Max. As long as he could find enough to eat.

Calay wiped her nose with the edge of her scarf and reached for the remaining food. She set the two plates in front of Max who wasted no time faceplanting into them. A hollow shell of a laugh trickled between Calay's lips.

"Good dog." Calay whispered, pressed her forehead to Max's.

"He's a good dog." Jacob kneeled, gave the dog a scratch under the chin.

He rose, gathered the blankets, and tucked them into the corner of the couch. Fluffed the starchy, flat pillows. He sat down beside it, patted the cozy spot next to him. With ease, Max bounded into the mess, turned a couple circles, and nestled down for a long winter's nap. Calay pressed her lips together, forced another sob back down where it belonged—deep inside. She pulled a sweater out of her bag, crawled closer to Max, and tucked it under his big head.

"So he remembers me."

"He'll always remember you." Jacob nodded.

"I'm just about finished here." Calay rubbed the remaining tears out of her eyes, unable to manage another second saying goodbye. If they didn't get this over soon, she might change her mind.

"Well, don't let me stop you." His full lips spread across his face and the freckles under his eyes turned up as he smiled. He ran his fingers through several locks of dark curls that fell over his forehead. The muscles in his forearm flexed under his golden skin.

It was the middle of winter, and he still had a tan. Calay yearned to trace the length of it, see where it ended. Jacob protected her. Probably loved her, even. Gods, she wanted to love him back. To trust him. To move on from Tess. To believe Max would be okay on his own. She gnawed on her bottom lip as the wishes piled one on top of the other. She wanted it all so much she could barely stand it.

Jacob pushed himself to stand but stopped mid-rise. He reached forward, picking up the pendants from where they'd landed. Just beyond Calay's reach. In that moment, she kind of wished they'd remained that way.

"Don't forget these," he said, unaware.

"Thank you." Calay took the chains from him and tucked them in the outside pouch of the bag. She pressed the snap closed as if that could contain the power they held over her. The prison they kept her in.

Jacob smiled, pulled himself up on the edge of the sofa, and then pulled Calay up too.

"Ready?"

"As I'll ever be." Which, meant not at all. Calay didn't bother to tell him that though. Instead, she hiked the pack up on her shoulder, a move she had become intensely familiar with, and nodded.

"To the roof!" Jacob turned, grabbed his duster off the make-shift hanger, and led the way to the staircase.

Calay extinguished the flame in the lantern. She glanced back at

Max, whispered a final goodbye, and tried to ignore the butterflies trying to burrow their way out of her stomach.

"SO, HOW DOES THIS ALL WORK?" CALAY SECURED HER SCARF up and over her long dark hair. Jacob sunk deeper into the duster's wide hood. The snow was falling lighter now, but the wind howled. They stood in the darkness, shivering. "I mean, how do they know to come for us?"

"While you were getting ready to go, I connected with the hive mind. Like you and I have been practicing. If one of us knows, all of us knows. Then, all they have to do is track my heat signature. They'll find us."

"Practicing?" Calay scoffed. "That's generous."

Jacob had been teaching her to harness her alien super-powers almost every day since moving into the Loft. One of which was a telepathic connection to their species. The ability to connect and communicate with other beings like them without using words.

The hive mind, Jacob called it.

When he'd first told her of their potential, she'd braved a trip to the downtown public library to research the concept. Between the water-logged spines of an expired edition of encyclopedias, she'd learned certain species seemed to exhibit a similar trait. Like ants, bees, and of all things, certain kinds of mushrooms. These animals sent complex chemicals or signalling movements humans didn't quite understand. Now, they'd never get the chance.

Science was gone. Humanity, gone. If this risk they were taking didn't pay off, Earth would be too. Calay wanted to trust. She shifted her weight from one foot to the other.

She'd been reluctant to believe anything could communicate psychically at first. While no species on Earth had an innate collective consciousness like the one Jacob talked about, the Others were not of this planet. Was it really so hard to believe now that people knew they were in fact not alone in the universe, perhaps aliens had evolved a different method to communicate? A better one?

"It takes time, especially when you haven't been integrated into the society. Reaching into the hive mind is a skill."

"One I don't have."

"Wanna try now?"

"It seems pointless. You've already signaled them anyway."

"It's not like we don't have time to kill while we wait." Jacob encouraged her. She squinted at him, dubious. "We have everything we need inside us, Calay. You can do it. Slow wide turns, remember?"

"I remember." Calay nodded.

"One step at a time."

Calay took this literally and stepped forward. She inhaled a sharp breath, her warm exhale pooling in the cold air in front of her. She did as Jacob had instructed her to do. She tried to silence the noise in her mind, raise her vibration. She still wasn't sure what that meant or how it was supposed to feel. She opened her mind, visualized a highway of energy linking herself to the hive. Or what she imagined the hive to be. Based on Jacob's descriptions, it didn't seem real. It was difficult to envision something that couldn't be described. Then again, her experience in the pod right before she'd found Tess wasn't entirely tangible either. So, she pictured that. Gray swirling matter. Warm air. Everything and nothingness, all at once. She tried to follow it up and out of her head. Into the stars. But her feet never left the snow-covered roof. Her mind didn't either.

Frustrated, she huffed and heaved her bag at her feet. Jacob's grin faded from hopeful to sympathetic. That was the last emotion she wanted to evoke from him. Or anyone.

"It's useless." Calay groaned. "I'm too..."

"Too what?"

Calay fought for the right words. For the truth.

"Too human."

"There's no such thing." Jacob said. He hoisted her bag and thrust it back at her. She took it, but only because it had everything she had left in the world inside. "In fact, that's my favorite thing about you."

"My humanity is your favorite thing about me? I'm terribly sorry to tell you this, Jacob, but people are a terrible disaster, and you have terrible judgement."

"That's a lot of terribles."

"You haven't even heard the half of them."

"Keep trying." Jacob pulled Calay by the elbow, turning her to stand beside him. "Especially once we're on Téras. You'll get it."

"Maybe." Calay sighed, allowing herself to be guided. "Do you think it'll be much longer? I mean, if they can sense you, can't you sense them? See how far away they are? I'm freezing out here."

Jacob nodded as he looked up into the night sky. Calay followed his gaze.

"Oh my god!" Calay gasped.

Not more than ten feet beyond the ledge she'd slept on the night before were dozens of silent, round white pods.

They hovered, weightless.

She tried to count them. Couldn't. There were too many. More than she'd ever seen. If she was shocked after the two pods had chased her and Jacob behind the waterfall all those months ago, she was downright stunned now.

An ocean of blue light pooled at Calay's feet and spread like a wave across the entirely of the roof. The building. For blocks farther than Calay could see.

If anyone else was seeing this, they'd be shitting their pants and running in the opposite direction. She could have used this kind of backup at the theater. Why hadn't they come for her, then? To protect her *then*? It was another question for which she'd have to wait to receive an answer.

One of the pods glided forward.

Calay swallowed. Despite knowing she was one of them, some primal fear plucked inside her. It was the sheer number of pods. Of blue lights. At the awareness of how many people had died because of them. No, not died. Exploded. Into red mist. Nothing left, nothing to be mourned. As if they had never existed in the first place. Still, she stepped toward the pod.

One foot. Then the other.

She resisted the urge to turn and run and raised her palm to its smooth white surface.

"What will it be like? Traveling in one of these?" Her voice brimmed with wonder. It cracked with unease.

"You won't feel a thing." Jacob stepped up beside her. He took her other hand. When she peeled her gaze from the pod, she saw he was grinning. Again. Didn't he understand how scary this was for her? What she wouldn't do to smother that smile off his face. Or kiss it off. She didn't have time to consider her options for long. The pod clicked. It whirred. A horrible grinding sound echoed through the air.

Calay nearly jumped out of her skin. She ripped her hand from the surface and stared.

"Actually, though." She said, trying to keep her voice steady.

"It'll be quick. Probably a little painful. You won't be fully aware of what's happening because the limits of your human mind won't be able to process it. It'll be similar to when you were in the pod before, on the mountain. But more abstract. Less…conscious." Jacob explained.

"Oh boy." Calay wrinkled her nose at him, took a shallow breath.

"You're about to travel some one hundred and fifty thousand light-years through space, Calay. Do you remember how I told you it should have taken your mother thirty thousand times the amount of time the universe has been in existence to get from where she was to Earth?"

"Yes. But she did it in a matter of days."

"Right. The alignment of electromagnetic waves made it possible. When the charge generated a super-massive black hole, that power within it atomized her particles there, reassembled them here."

"Yes, I remember. That's not a bedtime story a girl tends to forget. What's your point?" Calay didn't mean to be so short with Jacob. Not after all he had done for her that day. She just couldn't stop herself; she was terrified.

"You're about to take that same trip."

"You're saying…I'm about to be atomized?"

"And reassembled."

"I don't know about this, Jacob. How do you know I'll be

reassembled? How do you even understand the power of something so huge?"

"We've harnessed it."

"You've what now?" This was news to Calay. Yet another thing he'd elected to not share with her before now. She wondered how many more secrets he was keeping from her.

"That's what the blue light from the pods does to people. Atomizes them." Jacob sighed, rubbed his hands together. "Only, it doesn't put them back together again. We formulated it to..."

"You mean you weaponized it." Calay blanched.

"We...We didn't..." Jacob stumbled. "Yes. Okay, yes. We weaponized it. But we also manipulated it for space travel. We can cross vast distances in a very short amount of time. We can make a difference because of it. For both our planets. Our people. Which means as soon as you're ready, we can begin the journey. We can go home."

Calay turned to the night and trudged across the roof to the farthest ledge.

She pressed herself against the frozen concrete. The jagged wall dug through the holes in her jeans and into her hips. It was cold. Wet. Hard.

She clung to the two chains, held them close to her chest. They burned hot in her palm. As if they were on fire. Screaming at her. She shook her head, squeezed the pendants tighter. They were inanimate objects, it was her mind that was so loud. Her memories ablaze. The darkness she'd wallowed in for so long, a raging inferno. She knew if she curled up in there much longer, she'd burn right up along with it. This was Hell. And despite the horrible things she'd done, she wanted out.

Calay pressed her lips together, gnawed on the bottom one. She closed her eyes against the wall of tears stacking behind them.

"It's time to let go," she whispered.

She held her arm up, extended it. Then, she opened her fingers.

The two half-moons clinked together before they disappeared into the blackness.

Calay swallowed, knowing in another moment, so too would she.

CHAPTER SIX

THE SHADES of gray cloud finally dissipated.

When she and Jacob first took off, they'd plunged past her lips, down her throat, stealing the breath from her lungs. It wasn't so much an effect of the wind they threatened to carry with them, swirling like a tornado, that made her gasp for breath. In fact, the air felt calm and pleasant. It was the similarity to when she'd been transported into the pod on the mountain. It was just like this.

The Others had come for her, implored for her to return to their galaxy with them. But Calay couldn't leave Earth then. She couldn't leave Tess. It had been her home. But it wasn't anymore.

She shuddered at the simple truth: she was no longer on Earth.

She faded in and out of consciousness for only a moment. For a lifetime. Maybe several. There was no way to know. The twisting vacuum was all that ever was. All that ever would be.

When she'd come to, she knew, this time, the shadows lingering just outside her vision would be gone the moment she turned her head. So, she didn't. They existed, just beyond her understanding. Her skin. She knew there was no sense in trying to catch them. They weren't really there, in the flesh. In this place. She wasn't either.

When she'd been beamed into the pod in the forest, that floating in nothingness feeling had frightened her, but she'd also felt free. Every emotion she'd ever had flowed through her body. It was the closest thing she'd come to God in her life. If there even was such a thing and Calay doubted it very much. It was the closest thing she'd come to know what it meant to be Other. That part of herself she had never accessed before. Up until recently, hadn't even known existed.

This time, she let the feeling overtake her. Wash over her. Consume her. If nothing else, it was a brief escape from the pain she'd been carrying until now.

She'd give just about anything not to feel that.

As her breath returned and the euphoria left her body, Calay blinked. A palmful of tiny gold lights blinked down at her. Flashed once. Twice. Then they were gone. So were the clouds.

Save for the air flowing in and out of her lungs, it was silent.

The view above, a hexagonal panelled white ceiling. She sniffed, rubbed her eyes.

She became vaguely aware she was lying down. The surface was stiff, but as her hands dropped to her sides, she found it not too hard, either. It was lined with an impossibly bright white sheet. Her head was propped on a too-flat white pillow.

Her body, naked.

She pushed herself to sit and her stomach lurched. Her hands flew to cover her mouth, swallowing the bile rising in her throat. She waited. The nausea passed. But her head throbbed with the thunder of Thor's hammer. Her vision swam. Goosebumps rose across her skin. She slid her hands from her lips to her forehead. She draped them across her bare chest and over her churning stomach.

It hurt. Everywhere.

She decided Jacob categorically undersold the level of pain associated with quantum leaping two billion light-years into space. That, and the tiny insignificant detail that she'd be naked. *The hell?* Where were her clothes? She'd bring both points up with him later. First, she had to actually find him. And get dressed.

She positioned herself to stand, dropped her hands to the mattress and discovered her clothes folded beside her. *Thank the gods.* She grasped at them, wrenched them onto her body like they might disappear at any moment. Or someone might suddenly appear. She pulled her T-shirt over her head, wiggled into her jeans. Dust and chips of dried blood flaked onto the pristine floor. She scuffed her toe at them as she reached for her boots, which were lined neatly at the foot of the bed. She frowned, tried to recall taking them off. Coming into this room. Laying down here. Her mind came up blank. There had to be an explanation for it.

She gazed around while her mind rummaged for answers it couldn't find. The space was small, not much bigger than the structure she was perched on. It was aglow in a soft, delicate white light; she couldn't find the source. She blinked, trying to make sense of her surroundings. She realized it wasn't just the ceiling in the strange white pattern, it was the walls too. The floor. The whole space. Everywhere she looked were white panels. Just her and her padded cell.

She was trapped.

Before her thoughts could run away from her, another handful of gold lights winked from a door she hadn't noticed before. There was no break in the patterned walls. No hinges. No windows. But now the glowing lights raised up forming what looked to be a knob of some kind.

She stood, took five short steps to reach it, and extended her hand. Her fingers against the lights and a warm energy tingled up her arm. Like electricity, but softer. Less of a jolt and more of a wave flowing through her veins. She gasped, took a step back.

A deep sound pulsed through the air before the door popped outward and evaporated into thin air.

Calay shivered, stared.

The way it dissipated was too much like the people she'd watched die in the blue lights of the pods. She glanced behind her. This room. Something about it felt too...sterile. Too inhuman.

This place. These feelings. They were too real.

It was all too much.

She had to get out of there.

The hallway wasn't much better.

At least at the end of the long, white, padded corridor there was an actual door. With a real handle. Sunlight—or what passed for sunlight—gushed through the square window onto the floor. She searched the space for other exits. Other sets of flashing lights. She pushed against the panels, peered between them.

Nothing revealed itself. Jacob was nowhere to be found. It seemed she was alone. In an alien spaceship. On what was supposed to be an alien planet.

"Hello?" She called.

No one called back.

Her legs were woozy as she took a step forward, her boots squeaking against the floor. She took another step. Then another. Her stomach belly flopped, her head pounded.

"Jacob?" Calay tried again, propping herself up on the wall. She waited. "Ash?"

Silence.

Fuck.

Sunlight crept over her toes, then her shins.

She was almost at the door.

She tried to peer out the window but couldn't see a thing other than the glare of what felt like a million suns. She took a deep breath, reached for the handle, and hesitated. Should she go outside? Jacob hadn't said anything about where they were landing or the ecosystem of Téras. Calay didn't even know if she could survive beyond these unnaturally white walls. For all she knew, she'd open the door and spontaneously combust.

She braved a glance behind her. Considered going back to her room. Any evidence it existed was gone. The wall had scaled back up. It was one long, interminable hallway with no turns. No end in sight. Other than this one. *Do not pass go.* Calay turned back to the window. There were no shadows here. No night. It was all bright, blinding light. She raised a hand to shield her eyes. It was almost worse than the darkness she'd been clawing her way through on Earth. The panic started in her toes. It rose in her chest. She didn't know what she'd gotten herself into, but she had to do something.

This time, she didn't breathe at all. She reached for the handle, it turned easily, and the door swung open into the unknown.

She squinted, the glare was almost too much beyond the safety of what she now realized was a very tinted window. Her skin bubbled in the searing light, her feet melted to the floor. One dripped through the metal grates, onto the gray rocky planet below. The ankle bone of the other wedged itself between them, propping her up like a puppet. Her eyes boiled in her head. She tried to scream, and her voice caught fire, searing her throat. She swatted at her lips, trying to put out the flames, but they caught fire too. Until they popped like fireworks. They exploded, lodging shrapnel of bone and flesh between her teeth. She waited for the pain to come. To die. But somehow, she was still alive. Still there. Still breathing.

If she'd remember to take a damn breath.

Her chest roared for oxygen, and she drank it in eagerly. Then the world righted itself. Her vision cleared. She traced the curves of her body.

She was fine. Perfectly fine.

Her mind spun. Tried to make sense of what she'd just seen. She didn't know what the fuck that was. Whatever happened, hadn't happened at all. She pushed the tears back and gazed out from the platform on which she stood.

Her heart slowed. Her breathing, too.

The light shining in was from a domed glass sunroof at the top of what seemed to be some kind of loading bay.

It was longer than long and wider than wide. The perimeter was lined with big white barrels, each marked with a small black flame. *Fuel?* Calay's suspicions seemed to be confirmed as she gazed out at the expansive space, punctuated by more white pods than she could count. Just like the one she'd just been in.

She looked back through the door. The hallway was long too. Longer than was possible. It seemed to stretch on forever, but she could see quite clearly from the outside the pod was barely bigger than the room she'd just been in. Maybe this was part of the quantum technology the Others had harnessed. The term *weaponized* floated through Calay's mind, but she pushed it away. There wasn't time for brooding over the ethics of intergalactic warfare.

Right now she had to get—and keep—her wits about her.

"I wondered how late you'd sleep in." Ash's voice floated above Calay's thoughts.

Calay's gaze fell to the bottom of the staircase she was now gripping with both hands.

Ash smiled up at her, her full lips smirking wide and her green eyes grinning at Calay like they shared some kind of secret. She stood, her weight on one round hip, her well-manicured hand above that. Calay traced the miles of skin between where Ash's pants rested and her corset began. She tried not to stare at the tattoos underneath that played peek-a-boo every time she adjusted her stance. Calay struggled to find her breath, but this time, not because she was burning alive or suffocating in a hexagonal prison.

She shook off the urge to peel that corset off Ash, and instead, pried her own fingers from the railing and descended the stairs. She was only three from the bottom when her shaky legs betrayed her.

She pitched forward, catching her toe on the lip of one of the steps. Ash dove and in one graceful swoop, catching Calay just before she plunged face first onto the smooth floor. *Of course.* Calay sighed, embarrassed.

Ash's toned arms held Calay tight against her soft chest, her breathing was calm and Calay could feel Ash's heartbeat against her cheek. Calay's face turned pink as she did her best not to swoon.

"My hero." Calay managed, swallowing.

"It can take some time for the effects of the jump to wear off. Especially for humans." Ash said just above a whisper. Why was she whispering? Before Calay could ask, Ash continued, "take your time."

Calay wanted to. Breathing in the sweet smell of Ash, she wanted to spend all the time in the universe right here. With her. Under her. Over her. Inside her.

Calay wanted her. She didn't think she'd ever desire anybody in that way ever again.

All it took was leaving Earth and everything she'd ever known. She shook her head. *For once in your life, can you please get it together?* Ash seemed to take the action as Calay wanting to get up. She released her hold on her and turned her onto her feet. It wasn't until that moment Calay realized they weren't alone.

Jacob strode forward, his newly polished boots echoing through the port. His clear blue eyes glinted at her, and he winked from behind the curtain of dark tousled hair. His shaggy beard was neatly trimmed, his teeth sparkling white. Gone were the bags under his eyes and the faded T-shirt and over-sized duster. Instead, he wore a buttoned-up vest with a buttoned-down shirt that stretched across the width of his chest. Calay's gaze traced his dark brown leather suspenders from the tops of his shoulders to the waist of his dark pants. which were tight in all the right places.

He looked rested. Refreshed. Almost happy. *Of course he's happy. He's home. Finally.*

Calay tried to smooth the fly-aways and knots in her hair, press some of the wrinkles out of her crop top and the dust off her ripped jeans. The two of them—Jacob in his vest and suspenders and Ash in her strappy corset and tattoos—made quite the pair.

Ash stepped to the side to let Jacob through, but not without a certain grace.

He moved to fill the space between them. Watching them, Calay thought it looked almost like a dance. As if they'd done this many times before. There had to be a history between them, and she had to admit it was one she didn't want to know about. Or did she?

Watching the two of them looking at her, Calay felt feral. In more ways than one.

"How are you doing? Jacob asked, stepping between the two women and blocking Calay's view of Ash.

She thought about confiding in him about the vision she'd had as she exited the pod. The experience? She didn't know what to call it. She also didn't want to relive that waking nightmare, whatever it was. Until she figured it out, she was going to keep it to herself.

"I'm a little wobbly, I think," Calay admitted.

"That's understandable. It'll take some time to find your footing here. You'll get it."

"Let's hope my so-called natural ability to acclimate to an alien planet is better than trying to summon one." Calay pressed her lips together. She may not have been as confident as Jacob was about her belonging in this place, but she was buoyed by his hope. For now. "Speaking of acclimating, why the hell did I arrive without my clothes on?"

"Yeah, sorry about that." Jacob grinned. "It's part of the transition when we make the jump from your galaxy to ours. A cleansing, in a sense."

"I don't feel very cleansed." Calay tugged on the hem of her worn shirt.

"Not in the literal sense, but it gives you the opportunity to arrive as you are. Without the imprints of where you've come from. A symbolic new start."

A swell of emotion bubbled up the back of Calay's throat. She coughed it down. The idea one could leave their past behind and start fresh was as old as humanity itself. She couldn't help but think maybe it belonged with the rest of human civilization—buried in the ephemera of a past she'd never truly escape.

"You better not have looked," she said through clenched teeth.

"Nothing I haven't seen before," Jacob said.

"Jacob—"

"I'm teasing, Calay. I know this is a lot to take in and I'm just trying to lighten the mood. I brought you to your husk after you lost consciousness—which is perfectly normal, by the way. We all do. You just passed out faster because you're part human. But the system—the shuttle—did the rest."

"Wait, the shuttle—the pod—can do that? How?"

"We'll get to all that, but first, let's get you settled." Ash said. Her hand wrapped around Jacob's arm as she side-stepped him. He practically bowed to let her through. The fluidity to their movements wrung a pang of jealousy through Calay, squeezed. She couldn't quite name why. Wasn't sure if she wanted to. "Can I show you to your room, then?"

"Um, su—"

"That's enough, Ash." Jacob bristled.

Calay's eyebrows shot up as she watched him peel Ash's hand off his biceps and wrap his other one around Calay's shoulders. There was definitely more to these two than either of them was letting on. Calay thought to ask but then she inhaled deeply and found herself leaning into Jacob instead. Despite the makeover, he still smelled like himself. The way he had when they'd wrestled by her fire. When they'd made love. When she'd saved his life after Tess shot him. It stirred welcome feelings after what had been an intense and uncomfortable—to say the least—last few days. Only now, there was something else underneath it all. He smelled clean and new. Like leather and cinnamon. "I can handle it from here."

"You might be able to handle the task, Jacob. But something tells me you don't have what it takes to handle her." Ash's deep voice snuggled deep in Calay's mind as she and Jacob turned away from Ash and made their way down the long hanger.

"I THOUGHT THE OTHERS DIDN'T HAVE BODIES." CALAY gaped, unable to shake the memory of Ash's chest against her cheek.

The door swung open to her suite. They'd made their way through the building down several long, crowded corridors. The hallways were not unlike the one in the pod. White panelled walls. White panelled ceilings. Smooth, white floors. So much white, it was overwhelming. The difference being there were more people than Calay had ever imagined. She wasn't sure what she'd been expecting, if she was being honest with herself. But it certainly wasn't a building full of human beings.

"Everyone here looks human to me."

"It's a projection. We've evolved to have a shared-consciousness. We don't need bodies to survive, we exist beyond the physical realm. Our technology allows us to take on biological shapes when needed, though. Kind of like blank slates. Your mind is filling in physical attributes with something you'd recognize. Something human."

"Wait, are you saying you don't really look how I imagine you look?" The color drained from Calay's face. She turned to Jacob, almost reached for him. As if she had to make sure he was really standing in front of her.

"Interesting choice of words." Jacob held the door open for Calay. His other hand slid along her lower back, guiding her forward. She stepped into the room. "I really do look how you see me. To exist on Earth with its corporeal reality, I had to have a physical body of some kind. That's not something you're filling in."

"Oh, thank God." Calay released a breath. The idea she'd made up Jacob's attributes to fit a certain fantasy almost broke her. She'd always worried he was too good looking. Too sweet. Too perfect. The last thing she needed was to find out she'd made him up.

"I mean, if you like what you see..." Jacob said, as if reading her thoughts. He let the words hang in the air as he closed the door.

They were alone.

In what was apparently her bedroom.

He stepped closer to her, brought his palm to her face. For the first time since they'd left Tess buried on the top of that mountain, Calay didn't pull away.

"So how I see one of you isn't how someone, another person, would see that...Other?"

"Térasian." Jacob's voice became breathy. "And yes, exactly."

"What about gravity?

"That's artificially produced. For you."

"You made gravity for me?"

"I'd do anything for you."

"Jacob—"

"We didn't make it, okay? We simulated something like it so you'd be more comfortable. Again, because we don't have bodies, we don't need gravity."

"My head hurts."

"Would you like me to take your mind off it?" Jacob leaned down, tilted Calay's head to the side, and brought his full lips to the crease between her neck and shoulder.

Tingles spidered across her arms and down her back. They pooled between her thighs. A gentle moan escaped her lips. They'd put so much distance between what had happened on Earth and where they were now, Calay could give in.

Right now. Be with him. Again. Couldn't she?

This was supposed to be a new beginning. A future. At least, that was the hope that gnawed from somewhere deep inside her. But there would be no future if they didn't rally to save their two planets. Their species.

Calay brought her hands to Jacob's chest, wrapped her fists around his leather suspenders, feeling the gold accent rings on the harness cold against her palms.

She pulled him closer. Then pushed him back.

The spot where his mouth had been felt cold in his lips' absence.

Calay took a breath, waited for him to take one too.

"I'd like to meet Elora," she said. "My mother."

"I'll see to it that happens." Jacob nodded, retreating even further from Calay, toward the door they'd just come through.

"I just..." Calay fought to find the words. She wanted to be with Jacob. She really did. It wasn't the right time, though. It never was. "We came all this way. This is something that I need to do. As soon as possible."

"No, I get it." Jacob cleared his throat, raked the hand that had been on her lower back through his hair. "She's unavailable right now, but she'll send for you as soon as she can."

"She'll send for me? I flew billions of light-years into space, and she doesn't have time to meet with me?"

"She does. And she will."

"When?" Calay tried to keep the tremor out of her voice. "To be honest, I kind of expected her to meet us in the hanger when we landed."

"She's the leader of the coalition, Calay. She's...busy."

Calay stared at Jacob in disbelief. What exactly had she gotten herself into?

"Maybe this was a mistake," Calay said.

"It wasn't, Calay. I promise, it wasn't." Jacob opened the door, took a step backward. Calay couldn't help but feel like he was running away from her. From her questions. "Elora has some things she needs to attend to right now. She'll be available later this evening."

"What am I supposed to do until then?"

"Get situated. Recover from the trip. Relax."

Calay rolled her eyes, exhaled. It seemed she was always waiting for something. Usually the other shoe to drop.

"Okay." She plopped down on the bed. It was firm, gift wrapped in white linen. The pillow was far too flat. Almost hard. Just like the platform in the pod. "I want more of these, though," Calay said, patting the pillow.

"I'll make sure you get them." Jacob grinned. A shadow crossed his face. It lurked there. "I wish you'd let me take care of you."

"Maybe I will." Calay could tell he didn't believe that any more than she did.

"I have to go," he said. "I have a debrief to take care of."

"Can I come?" Calay rose, stepped toward him.

"No off-planet visitors allowed."

"Oh."

"Besides, you'd just be bored."

"Reporting details about a quantum mission billions of light-years to an alien planet, only to unveil closely guarded secrets, escape death twice, have the best sex or your life, and return home with one of the last remaining, long-lost prodigies of your kind? Hardly." Calay frowned.

"Is that how you remember our time together?"

"It's not a bad story." Calay shrugged.

"It's only the beginning." Jacob dipped his head, winked at her with that infuriating grin, and turned the corner out of her cabin.

The door reappeared in his place.

Calay almost laughed. Almost. Instead, she shuffled to the window that spanned the width of the room.

She stared out of the curved glass that stretched from floor to ceiling. She hadn't felt this untethered to anything—or anyone—in her life. Maybe that was for the best. Beyond the panelled walls, Calay drank in her first glimpse of the outside world. The planet, Téras.

Silver and glass towers twisted into the sky, kissing the horizon as far as Calay could see. Small mountains climbed between them, speckled with moving dots. People—physical projections of the Others' consciousness—scampered from building to building in small groups. Talking. Laughing. Hugging. In the sky, the light of a massive sun reflected in their exteriors, setting the whole place aglow in golden light. Beyond that, another planet hovered, pink and green, with several ombre colored rings around it. She could almost see them moving. If they were even real.

How much of what she was seeing was a projection? How much was reality?

Calay's head spun, her legs wobbled. She wasn't sure if it was the side effects of jumping through space that were keeping her unbalanced or the strange truths she'd already uncovered in the short time she'd been planet-side. She gazed out the window, her arms hanging at her sides.

It was all so very, very different from Earth.

If the Others were to be believed, it wasn't just humanity in danger anymore, it was the entire fucking planet. Téras didn't look as if it was suffering, though Ash had claimed as much. Calay found it hard to believe as she stared out the window at the glittering city. Then again, how much could she really ascertain from this pristine cubicle in the sky?

Not enough, she decided.

Calay turned and charged for the door. If Elora wasn't available to answer her questions, Calay would take it upon herself to learn what she could. After all, she'd come all this way. She didn't intend to let one moment go to waste.

It was time to stretch her legs.

CHAPTER SEVEN

THE SECOND TOUR of the building wasn't any more illuminating than the first. Hallway after long, winding white panelled hallway, Calay found herself walking in circles. At least, it felt that way.

She shuffled along, her boots skidding on the freshly polished floor. The squeaks of their tread chased her around every corner. The constant rush of air in the ventilation system above rattled, sputtered, then continued. Everything felt so foreign. So strange. So discomforting. This, despite the fact that everyone she made eye contact with nodded and smiled. She assumed their gestures were kind and meant to welcome her to their home, but it only served to make Calay more uneasy. She wrapped her arms over her chest. She couldn't quite put her finger on what it was, but something about the place reminded her of the time she'd spent locked up at the Resistance compound.

This was so unlike that place. The polar opposite, actually. It was more open. Bright. Friendly. From what she could see, there were no barbed wire fences. No cameras. No hordes of men, leering. This place was different. *So what's wrong with me?*

There was the possibility that her experiences on Earth, one after the other, taught her not to trust a new face. Smiling or otherwise. You never knew what was hiding beneath the surface of their shiny exteriors.

Or behind their backs. If nearly five years of fighting for her life had taught Calay anything, it was that people were the enemy. Not that these were people, per se. But they were Others.

And wasn't that worse?

Either way, she tried to return their broad smiles with several of her own, but she worried she just looked pained. Like the grimace she'd worn over the last few months was permanently etched in her face.

The other option—the more frightening one—was perhaps she'd spent so much time alone, she'd simply forgotten how to relate to anyone other than Jacob; even that was a stretch most days. As she gazed at their faces, watching them hustle past her in every direction, she warmed to the idea that they were her kind, and they'd invited her into their home. Her heart fluttered at the possibility it could be her home too.

Like Jacob said, maybe it would just take some time.

Calay rounded a corner and found herself alone. The hallway she'd just come from was bursting with activity, and this one seemed almost abandoned in comparison. She paused, trying to orient herself. She'd been walking for the better part of an hour and still hadn't found her way outside. She knew from the shuttle she'd arrived in, doors were not always obvious. Their alien tech was far more advanced than she could have imagined, but still—she should have come across at least one. A window even. Some kind of hatch or fire door.

It was just one white wall after another.

The ventilation system continued to whisper sweet nothings as she continued through the building. It was almost as if it was guiding her forward. Or urging her to turn back. She traced them along the ceiling with her gaze. This particular arrangement of vents looked oddly familiar. As did the Y-intersection ahead.

She would have sworn she'd been here before. Already zigged right. Then left. Only to end up at the same place.

Then again, every corridor looked the same.

A whisper floated past. It sounded like Jacob. The hairs on the back of her neck stood up. Calay froze. She listened. Yes, there was the muffled sound of voices. It seemed to be coming from everywhere and nowhere, all at once. She strained to make out individual words, but it was more the suggestion of words than anything specific. The harder she tried to grasp what they were saying, the more slippery their voices became.

Then, all was silent. Whoever it was had stopped talking. That, or they were never talking in the first place. The memory of the vision she'd experienced earlier flashed through Calay's mind. The fire. The burning. The smell of her flesh liquifying. She shook her head. It wasn't real. This place was.

She reached out, touched one of the walls. It was hard, cool, and smooth under her calloused fingers. The fingers that were still attached to her hand. Not exploding like Pop Rocks. *You're okay.* She glanced back the way she came. Retracing her steps wouldn't tell her anything new. She didn't know much, but she knew that for sure. Looking forward to the split hallway ahead, the only question was left or right? It was not so long ago she'd been offered the same choice before she found Tess. At the mouth of the cave. Before everything went horribly and irretrievably wrong. She'd chosen to go right back then.

Calay picked up the pace and veered left.

She almost immediately regretted her decision. She didn't have to walk far before the voices finally started to make sense. Huddled together in an alcove ahead were Jacob and Ash.

Jacob's shoulders were turned in toward Ash, their faces only a few inches apart. Calay stifled a gasp, backed out of sight. She wasn't sure why she didn't want them to see her, but something about their body language begged for privacy. She peered around the corner, kept herself tight against the wall.

Jacob's brows were furrowed, his mouth carved into hard lines as he spoke. Ash raised her hand, rested it on Jacob's chest. Near his heart. Calay shifted at the intimate gesture. This confirmed there was a history between the two of them. Something more than just colleagues. Ash stood almost toe to toe with him, nose to nose. They were close. Too close for Calay's comfort. She didn't have dibs on Jacob, and she'd been clear about her emotional unavailability. Still, there was something unsettling about the way Ash seemed to possess him. She said something too low for Calay to hear, her gestures and expression as unyielding as Jacob's. Calay wished she could hear what they were saying. Jacob tried to shake Ash's hand off him when it shot up and grabbed him by the throat. Ash forced him backward, pinned him against the wall. Calay's heart raced, and her eyes grew wide as she watched Ash's face creep from angry to lethal. The muscles in Ash's biceps tensed, the veins in Jacob's neck bulged. Calay could see even from a distance they were both vibrating with raw energy.

The idea occurred to her that maybe she should step in, save Jacob from whatever the hell this was. She inched a toe forward as she harnessed her courage but pulled it right back again when Ash brought her mouth over his, whispered something down the throat she still had her fingers wrapped around. Then, released her vice grip and stalked off, the lace ties in her corset waving goodbye behind her.

Calay shrunk against the wall. She didn't know what she'd just witnessed, but she didn't want Jacob to know she had. He brought his hand to the red scratch marks Ash's nails clawed into his neck before he charged away in the opposite direction.

"The fuck was that?" Calay muttered under her breath.

She braved a few steps in the direction Jacob had gone, unsure how to proceed. She'd never seen him at another's mercy like that. She wanted to make sure he was okay. To offer him some of the comfort he'd been so good at giving her. But she didn't trust herself not to ask him about the interaction.

Instead, she turned and stomped after Ash.

The hallway almost seemed to shrink before it opened up to a bustling dining room. She more than a little relieved to have once again finally found herself in a central hub. An escape from the sound of air vents and whispers.

She scanned the rushing bodies in every direction, Ash was nowhere to be found.

The Others continued to smile at her from a distance. She had to remind herself these weren't actually people. They were aliens. The Others. Their physical selves were only projections from her mind. Every time she began to approach one, it gave her a wide berth. She wasn't sure if they couldn't communicate with someone who was part human, or simply chose not to. She made a mental note to ask Jacob when he came back. Eventually.

The sound of cutlery and plates clinking together made her stomach rumble. She couldn't remember the last time she ate. Her jaw dropped. There didn't seem to be any food to speak of, but the sounds nonetheless, of people eating, filled the air. She swallowed, the idea all these people—these Others—were mere projections was overwhelming. She came here to find the truth but how could she trust the truth when she didn't even know what was real?

She steadied herself on a nearby table that looked like it had never been dined at. The chairs even still had the plastic on them. Like they hadn't ever been unwrapped. *That can't be right.* But Calay was so disoriented, she didn't tug on that thread further. It was just another question on top of the pile of questions that had yet to be answered.

She needed to get some air.

Farther, beyond the shrink-wrapped tables and chairs, there was another hallway. One no one seemed to be entering or exiting. It was darker, too. *One of these things is not like the other.* That had to be the way out.

Calay pushed herself upright and made a break for the corridor.

She was right—the lighting was dimmer. Almost as if the bright light of the main hallways had been turned down. The walkway glowed amber, the walls ensconced in long shadows. It was alright though; Calay only needed to see the floor. Where she placed each footstep. She made her way deeper down the long, dark hallway. The sounds of the cafeteria faded. The ventilation too.

With every few steps, Calay became more and more aware she may have made a mistake. This corridor didn't seem like it would bring her outside after all. It seemed like it led to the basement. She shivered, despite the pleasant warm air. She'd never been much of a fan of basements. Their long, creaking stairs. Cold, unfinished concrete floors. The monsters that lived inside them.

Calay thought she might turn back when the outline of a doorway became clear. It was not unlike the exterior door to the shuttle. *One of these things just doesn't belong.* Rectangular. No panels. A window at the center. Only unlike the impossible brightness of the pod window, this one was deathly black.

She slowed her steps. Inched the final few feet to the door. Brought her face near the glass. Then against it. It was like the only thing that existed beyond that window was nothingness. She wasn't sure which was worse—basement bogeymen or the darkness of oblivion.

Maybe it was a Clean Chamber; a small room between the inside of the building and the outside. It was possible the lights were on motion sensors. But why would they need a Clean Chamber if the atmosphere was safe to breathe? Calay tried to make out shapes beyond the window. Space suits. Oxygen masks. Anything that would give some indication she shouldn't go outside without adult supervision. But she couldn't see a damn thing.

The familiar feeling of panic rose in Calay's chest. She tried to tamper it down with a few deep breaths. She counted back from twenty. When that didn't work, she tried to solve her problem by finding a switch on the wall or another handful of gold winking lights. Nothing worked. She struggled to get enough air in her lungs. Beads of sweat pooled on her neck. If she didn't get out of this building sooner than later, she was going to have a meltdown. Here. At the end of a very long, very dark hallway. Alone. On an alien planet. Calay doubled over, tried to catch her breath.

"Fuck it."

She reached for the handle and was about to pull the door open when a set of green eyes rushed the door through the darkness.

Calay screamed, stumbled back. She tripped over her own feet. Again. Then, fell flat on her ass.

Ash pushed the door wide open and charged toward her.

Calay, while relieved it wasn't some deep-space monster coming to eat her insides, couldn't shake the image of Ash's hand around Jacob's throat. She scuttled backward, eyes wide, legs flying in all directions. Ash's hands wrapped around Calay's ankles. She straddled the space between Calay's legs, hovering over her. Calay was pinned to the floor.

"Shhhhh," Ash said. "Hey, hey now. You're okay."

Calay was decidedly not okay. Ash seemed to be around every turn, just out of Calay's reach. Yet always ready to reach for her. In the stairwell at the Loft. In the loading bay after they'd landed. Now, here. Calay didn't trust it. Didn't trust her. But then she remembered Ash hadn't seen her watching them in the hallway. She didn't know Calay knew about the fight between her and Jacob. The way Ash had whispered down his throat like she owned him.

She could use this.

"I'm sorry, I...I was just looking to get outside. I shouldn't have been down here," Calay said between breaths.

"No, it's my fault. I didn't realize someone else was on the other side of the door," Ash said, not removing her iron grip on Calay's ankles. "I'm glad it was you."

"Me too." Calay cleared her throat. "I mean, I'm glad it was you too."

"What were you doing all the way down here?" Ash's gaze fell to where her hands rested on Calay. Her grip loosened, her touch soft.

"I thought maybe it was the way out."

"Looking to leave us already?" Ash batted her eyelashes, feigning disappointment.

"No, of course not. Just looking to explore."

"I like exploring too." Ash's fingers caressed Calay's ankles. They crept behind her calves, the backs of her knees. They came to rest on her thighs. Calay's breath shallowed. The moment hung between them, thick and heavy with want. Almost as heavy as the warmth of the weight of Ash's palms on her legs. Calay reached for Ash's hands, intertwining their fingers, and grinned.

"Pull me up?"

"If I must." Ash sighed. She pushed herself to her feet before pulling Calay to hers.

"Thank you." Calay smiled, dusting herself off. There really was no need. Like the rest of the building, the corridor was immaculate. Calay couldn't help but wonder how they kept it so clean. She hadn't seen janitors or Roombas or anything. Surely there had to be dust on this planet. Dirt of some kind, right? Calay released Ash's hands from her own and rubbed them over her clothes. The only thing that came off on her pants was what she'd brought with her from Earth. It had worked its way into her bones.

"You're welcome, though I think I liked it better when you were on your back." Ash flashed an eyebrow.

Calay's mouth went dry, her pulse quickened. She felt that same tingle between her legs as she did when Jacob had kissed her neck earlier. She took a wide step around Ash to distract herself from the fantasies snowballing through her head.

This time, Ash raised both eyebrows. "But this is good too."

"Is this the way out?" Calay reached for the door.

Ash shimmied herself between Calay and the handle. She leaned against it. Caught Calay's gaze with her own.

"You really should rest."

"I've rested enough."

"Maybe you'd like to use up some of that energy."

"Exactly what I was thinking." Calay grinned. "Which is why I'd like to get some air."

"I could give you a lot of things, you know." Ash closed the distance between them. Their chests met at the top of short breaths. Calay would have sworn she could feel Ash's heart through their clothes. Maybe it was just her own, beating so hard it might crack a rib. Ash brushed several strands of hair from Calay's face before she gathered them in one hand, pulled them over Calay's opposite shoulder. Tugged on the ends.

"Oh yeah?" Calay could have stepped back. Probably should have, but she didn't want to admit Ash intimidated her. Or that the proximity to her had such an intoxicating effect on her, either. Given everything Calay had been through and how far she'd come to get to the truth, she was an expert at lying not just to others, but to herself too.

"But most of them would involve taking your breath away, not giving you more."

"Mission accomplished." Calay exhaled. She'd intended to use Ash's advances to her advantage, but somewhere along their flirtation, Calay found herself advancing back. As Ash gazed into her eyes, Calay struggled to maintain her grip on what was strategy and what wasn't.

Calay knew Ash was dangerous. Seeing how she'd treated Jacob confirmed that. She knew it was wrong, but it only made Calay want her more. She traced a line along the hem of Ash's corset where the fabric met her bare skin. Her tattoos. "How many of these do you have?"

"Would you like to find out?"

Calay found herself nodding.

Ash's fingers met Calay's, she pulled them to her mouth. She slid one between her teeth, wrapped her pouty pink lips around it. Calay sucked her bottom lip between her teeth, swallowed a moan. She stepped forward, erasing the small amount of space left between them. Ash released Calay's hand, pressed her own into the fleshy pads of Calay's hips.

"Still need to get that air?" Ash nuzzled Calay's hair, her voice melted behind her ear.

Oh, right. Air. Calay had been on a mission to get outside. A mission for answers. She knew better. This was getting out of control. She fought to maintain her perspective. What her objectives really were. The whole damned reason why she came to Téras in the first place.

It wasn't this.

"I'm sorry, I do." Calay peeled herself out of Ash's embrace and put a good, safe, three-foot distance between them.

She tucked her hair behind her ears and exhaled.

"You're a better woman than me, Calay." Ash's shoulders slumped, but her eyes grinned as she spoke. "I promised I could take your breath away, and I'm about to. Come with me."

Ash treaded past Calay back down the long hallway, toward the kitchen. It didn't take long before her form became a silhouette. Had it grown darker down here since Ash had come through that door? Calay risked a glance back at it. The black window. The expanse of darkness beyond. Calay couldn't imagine what was back there, if not access to the outside. The question was, did she even want to?

The echoes of Ash's footfalls began to fade. Calay turned and ran after her, catching up to her just as she reached the cafeteria.

"What are you talking about?" Calay grinned.

"You must be hungry, yes?"

"Starving." Calay admitted. Even the mere mention of food made her stomach roar.

"What are you in the mood for?"

"Are you taking the piss?" Calay glanced across the room, confused.

The strange echo of diners dining continued to float through the air, but no one was eating. It was as if a banquet of ghosts surrounded them. Her brows knitted together. She squinted sideways at Ash. "There's no food."

"As a shared-consciousness, we don't need to eat. No bodies, remember? But you do."

"Wait. Wait wait wait wait wait..." Calay struggled to keep up. Yet again. "Are the sounds in here also projections?"

"No, those are speakers. Forks, knives, spoons, plates, cups. All those things are inanimate. We can't assume their forms any more than you can project them. They exist as material objects. So do speakers, I might add. You can't have a projection without a biological foundation. There has to be a spark there. Life. As you know it. Without it, all there is, is death."

Calay bristled. She'd heard those words before. On Earth. In the pod. When they'd warned her that was all she'd find on the mountain. And she had. The death of Tess. Of the life she once knew. Of herself, in a way.

She wasn't ready for the sudden wash of emotions Ash's words ignited. She couldn't let the tears come now, though. Not here. In front of Ash. Instead, she reached for impudence.

"Well, that's dark."

"Not dark." Ash's hand found Calay's. It was tender and warm. Ash's grip tightened when she led her across the room. "Death is where no life can be. Where one exists, so does its opposite. Self and Other. Did Jacob really not tell you any of this?"

They stopped in front of a standalone block of reflective glass in the middle of the cafeteria.

Calay gazed at herself in its smooth surface. Her long brown hair was frizzy and frazzled. The bags under her eyes dark, and her skin pale. Like she'd been on a week-long bender of substances with the beautiful people she inhaled them off of. It had been a very long time since she'd engaged in a night like that. Well before she met Tess, even. That was a lifetime ago. Probably several. But she remembered the look well. She squinted, peered closer. She looked tired. And frail. Maybe Ash and Jacob were right. She needed rest.

"He told me some of it. He told me a lot of it, actually. You know, I wasn't exactly the easiest to deal with." Calay couldn't explain it, but she felt the need to rush to Jacob's defence almost as strongly as the need to keep an arm's-length between them. Maybe it was the amount of times he'd come to her rescue and protected her, or simply the way Ash had throttled him earlier.

"Oh, I'm counting on it." Ash winked, squeezed Calay's hand. She reached for Calay's other one and placed her fingers on several gold blinking lights Calay hadn't noticed before. *Just like in the pod.* Ash continued, "you can have anything you want. Think of it. Imagine it. Picture it in your mind."

Calay did. She imagined the one thing she'd wished for with all her heart since the Change happened and food caches had started to dry up. A deep tone throbbed from within the machine. When it stopped, Ash reached through a wide slot in the bottom of the box, pulled out a white tray.

It was empty save for the center. There, a peanut butter and honey sandwich on white bread with a tall glass of cold milk.

"Huh." Ash laughed, handing the try to Calay.

Calay blinked, disbelieving. The sound of Ash laughing was almost as shocking—and delicious—as what Ash handed to her.

"I would have gone for something a little more exotic, but you do you, boo."

"Is this...Is this real?" Calay's mouth hung open, her eyes wide. She gripped the tray with both hands, terrified it might slip out of her grasp and disappear at any moment.

"As real as your finger between my lips." Ash leaned in and kissed Calay on the same spot—the exact same spot—as Jacob had earlier. A tingle crept around the base of Calay's spine, but her attention remained locked on the sandwich.

"Can…Can I? I can eat this?"

"Eat it. Look at it. Fist the damn thing. It's yours." Ash called over her shoulder as she waltzed out of the kitchen, leaving Calay to enjoy the fruits of her imagination. Calay prayed it wasn't her nightmares. "Eat. Sleep. In a few hours, you'll feel good as new."

Calay didn't even make it to a nearby table. She sank to the floor right where she stood. The swarms of Others, cloaked in human form, flowed around her like a fast-moving river. She was the rock. Strong. Steady. Sure. Her hands wrapped around the soft, moist bread. It dented underneath her fingertips as she gripped it and brought it to her mouth. It smelled sweet and faintly of wildflowers. As she stuffed the first bite in her mouth, the honey melted on her tongue. The peanut butter clung to her teeth. The bread disintegrated with each chew.

It was everything she'd hoped for and more.

She took another bite. Then another. It was all she could do not to stuff the whole thing in her mouth in one bite. Calay shook her head. She could tell herself lies all she wanted, but underneath the layers of savory sandwiches and sexy aliens, she knew she wasn't a rock. She wasn't strong. She wasn't solid. And she sure as hell wasn't sure about anything at all.

She was the salmon. Swimming upstream and against the current. It was dangerous territory, leaving the safe waters of the Pacific Northwest, into the unknown.

A part of her yearned for the comfort of that place. It wasn't perfect, but it had been home. At one time. She didn't know what that was anymore. She'd hoped she'd find it here, on Téras. With the Others. Still, Calay couldn't shake the feeling that something was off. It was far too perfect here. Too beautiful. Too much like a strange dream come true.

Calay knew what they said about things that seemed too good to be true.

They were.

CHAPTER EIGHT

IT WAS LATE that night when Elora finally sent for her daughter.

Calay, unable to sleep, hadn't been able to shut her mind off. She stared at the ceiling; a gentle warm orange light emanated from somewhere she couldn't see. It ran the perimeter of the room. The soft gray sweatpants and sweater she'd found on her bed when she returned from the cafeteria with a belly full of peanut butter and honey twisted with each toss and turn. The firm mattress seemed to only grow harder with each rotation until finally, she flung off the covers, padded over to the room-length window, and stared at the emerald glowing city below.

She still hadn't figured out a way outside, and as the hours ticked by, she'd become more and more restless. A clump of bread lodged itself between her teeth. She tongued it furiously as she paced back and forth. She wasn't sure how the Others measured time, but the cracked watch at the bottom of her bag told her she'd arrived close to eighteen Earth hours ago. Assuming it was still working as it should. Between the simulated gravity, artificial oxygen, and thousands of entities masquerading as human, Calay was finding it harder and harder to tell what was real and what wasn't. She huffed, her breath pooled on the curved glass. She brought her thumb to it and traced circles. It felt like she'd been running through a maze all day. Trying to find a way out. To get some answers. To maintain her grip on reality. She tapped the tip of a jagged fingernail on the glass. Patience had never been her strong suit.

The knock came not long after.

Now, as an unnamed Other in a white suit led her down a labyrinth of twisting corridors, Calay couldn't help but worry the moment had come too fast.

"Are we almost there?" She asked.

The Other waved their hand forward and nodded, their shaved head reflecting the white domed lights above.

Calay was eager to see her mother again, but as the distance closed between the two of them, she became more nervous. A dampness pooled on the small of her back. Her palms itched. Her throat became dry. How many times over the years had she wished to reunite with her mother? Yearned for it. Ached, even.

They'd left their relationship on unsteady terms at best. After she came out as bisexual, her father and mother had grown cold and eventually, when she'd brought Tess around to meet them, they'd kicked the two of them out of her childhood home. Sure, they'd given her a choice, but it was an impossible one: be a good girl and marry a good man or leave. They explained they were worried her being different would cause the family pain; it would make life too difficult. Through her tears, she'd pleaded with them to love her. To accept her. She'd told them they were asking her to do something she couldn't. She could no sooner live their lie any more than she could leave her home. But it wasn't her home anymore. It was theirs. And they'd made it very clear as long as she was living under their roof, she'd live by their rules. So she'd left. With Tess's hand in hers. And until she returned with Jacob four months ago, she hadn't looked back.

She couldn't.

It hurt too much.

"Is Jacob meeting us?"

No answer.

Calay sighed. She hadn't seen him in hours. With the exception of when they were imprisoned by the Resistance, this was probably the longest she'd been without him since they met. No one was forcing them apart now, like they were then, were they? Before they'd left Earth, she'd been so sure she couldn't get close to him again. Now that she had some distance, she wasn't feeling confident she wanted that, either. The last Calay had seen of Jacob was him stomping away from Ash in the hallway pretty much identical to this one. And the one before it. And the one before that. Calay shivered. No wonder she couldn't find her way out of the building.

It really was a maze.

She had no plans to escape, no reason to. Yet. But the idea she couldn't escape if she wanted to sent a wave of anxiety through her veins. She closed her eyes, took a deep breath. Téras was going to be her new home. There was nothing left for her on Earth. At least she had friends here. Jacob. And Ash. Okay, perhaps *friends* was too strong a word. She didn't know what to call them. Their relationships were... complicated. There was also the possibility she even had her mother here. Maybe. If Calay was being honest with herself, she wasn't sure how they'd ever recover from what was. Really, how could she forgive Elora after everything that had happened and the judgement she cast on Calay?

The cherry on top of her pain sundae was finding out Elora was different too. She was Other. All along.

Calay's stomach lurched. She swallowed, forced the nausea down. She'd be damned if she was going to lose the first peanut butter and honey sandwich she'd had in years to the glossy white floor. Instead, she focused on putting one foot in front of the other.

They walked for what felt like hours. It wasn't nearly long enough. When they finally arrived at a panelled door, the Other who'd led her there stepped away and retreated down the hall without a word.

"Thanks for the escort!" Calay called, stared after them. Her breathing became shallow. Her arms felt like lead, her legs too. A darkness rolled in the pit of her stomach, tried to climb its way across her chest. Usually, she could blame the Others for the trauma and pain she felt. This though was all family.

Part of her wanted to turn and run back to her room. To Earth. But she'd come so far. This was what she came to do.

She raised her hand, looking for the gold lights, but saw none. There was no handle. No knob. Just a dark cut out in the shape of a door through the familiar hexagonal pattern. She stepped backward, trying to get a better look when a loud swoosh echoed through the hallway and the fabric of the door evaporated before her eyes.

Beyond it, a blue glow illuminated a wall well armored in dials and knobs. Dozens of gray and white screens depicted the many hallways of the building and the immediate outside surroundings. Intrigued, Calay swallowed her trepidation and stepped through. Inside, the walls were almost black. The floor too. A static hum hung heavy in the air. It was so very different from the rest of the building.

She approached the wall of screens, entranced by the Other's movements. They flickered in and out of focus on the screens like ghosts, their features or limbs hovering separate from them, then reforming. As if the technology couldn't quite register their human form. Her projection of it. It was disconcerting, watching them appear and disappear before her eyes. A reminder this place was not what it appeared at first glance. Or second.

The sound of someone clearing their throat pulled Calay from the digital ghost world.

She didn't have to look to know who it was. Her mother used to make that sound any time she missed curfew or borrowed her father's truck without asking.

Calay straightened and turned.

Elora loomed before her. All six feet of her. Her cropped silver hair twinkled in the blue light, her brown eyes—almost black, against her pale skin—softened as they took in Calay. She stepped forward, thigh-high slits in her olive green hooded tunic revealed dark fitted tights underneath. A leather harness stretched across her chest. Jacob's suspenders were similar, Ash's strap across her shoulder, too. Come to think of it, almost everyone Calay had seen was wearing a variation of the strap. Calay wondered if it had something to do with rank and made a note to ask Elora about it later.

If they got that far.

Elora's beaded earrings swung as she moved, chunky-heeled boots echoed around them. Calay knew her mother was pretty, but she'd forgotten how blinding her grace could be. Not for the first time, Calay wished she'd inherited some of that magic. But then again, all the Others had an ethereal beauty to them she couldn't put into words. A magnetism she couldn't resist.

"How did you...?"

"I didn't. You did." Elora tilted her head toward the door. "Motion sensor."

"Ah." Calay replied. A tsunami of emotion bubbled inside her. She had so much she wanted to say to her mother, but no words came to mind. She desperately wanted to run to her, to be held in her arms. She also wanted to scream.

After a bloated pause, she decided the best way forward, if she really wanted to repair the damage that had been done, would be to start gentle.

"Calay."

"Elora."

"What happened to Mom?"

"You lost that title when you disowned me." Calay's lips drew into a thin line. *So much for gentle.* This was not going to be easy.

"I didn't..." Elora started but stopped herself. She pulled her broad shoulders back. "Your arrival coincided with one of the busiest and most successful tests we've accomplished in recent memory. I'm sorry it took me so long to send for you."

"Well, that's one apology down."

"I deserve that." Elora winced, nodded.

"You deserve a lot more."

"I'm not disagreeing with you, Calay. I'm..."

"You're what?"

"I understand you're mad. You have every right to be angry with your father and me."

"Don't talk about Dad." Calay sneered, reaching for the nearest console to steady herself. The memory of him falling under the sharp prong of a pitchfork flashed through her mind. The blood. The pain of losing him after she'd only just found him again. Calay pushed aside the urge to fall apart right then and there. Had she bitten off more than she could chew by coming here? Was it too soon?

No, she could do this.

Elora was tough, but she wasn't callous; even when she'd kicked Calay out of the house, she had her reasons. If Elora knew Calay had murdered her father in cold blood only a few short months ago, she'd never have brought him up. Jacob had his debriefing earlier; maybe he didn't tell them everything. He could have kept some of her secrets for just them. The idea warmed something inside her for the briefest of moments before Calay forced herself to meet her mother's gaze.

"I only want to talk about you," she said.

"All right, let's talk about me."

"You hurt me."

"I did." Elora folded her hands in front of her.

"And?"

"What do you want me to say, Calay? I screwed up. A lot of times." Elora sighed. "I'm sorry. I'm so sorry. For all of it."

"What exactly is all of it?"

"You want me to itemize my failures as a mother?"

"I've met you halfway. Hell, I've met you more than halfway. I've flown to another fucking galaxy. Now it's your turn to take a leap of faith." Calay crossed her arms over her chest. She held her breath, nodded, not giving another inch.

"Okay, fine. If that's what it takes to get you on my side." Elora stood taller, if that was possible. She closed her eyes and when she opened them again, they shone with tears. "I'm sorry I trusted Jacob to look after you while you struggled without me. I'm sorry I lied to you about who and what I was when you were younger. And more than anything, I'm so, so sorry I didn't stand up for you when your father insisted you couldn't stay with us."

"Funny, that's not how I remember it."

"You're right. I told you to go. Your father and I, we agreed, before you were born, to be an allied front. I tried to talk him into letting you stay. But he thought it was too dangerous. Too risky in the community."

"Yet he married you. An alien. But a queer daughter was too much to handle? I find that hard to believe. That doesn't make any sense, *Mom*."

"Your father had his reasons. I'm not saying they were good ones. I can't speak for him. I can only speak for myself. I need you to hear me when I say I'm sorry. I didn't protect and love you like I should have. And I've regretted it every single day since you walked out that door. I should have fought harder for you. I will fight for you. You are the reason I'm here now. You are…everything. To me."

"If that's true, why didn't you come for me before? Why did you let me struggle on Earth, alone?" Calay pouted, grinding her teeth.

"I did come for you, my daughter. I was the one in the ship that transported you in the woods. It was me you were speaking to all along."

"Why didn't you tell me at the time?"

"Would you have believed me?"

"No," Calay admitted. What Elora was saying was everything Calay wished she'd one day hear from her mother. She'd dreamed of it. Prayed, even. And she didn't even believe in God. But she'd put it out there, into the universe. The question itching the back of her mind was whether it was too late or not?

As if able to hear Calay's thoughts, Elora continued. "I know it's taken me a long time to get here. Longer than it ever should have. But if you give me the chance, I won't let you down again."

Calay nodded, her gaze fell to the floor. She wanted to believe Elora. But she was so angry. So disappointed.

"Please, Calay. I love you. Give me the chance to prove myself. If not as your mother, then at least as your leader. We have an opportunity to save both our civilizations, and I cannot do it without you." Elora dropped to her knees. The slits in her pants fell open, her beaded earrings clacked. Calay gaped as Elora folded Calay's hands in hers.

Right. Beyond their happy little family reunion, there was the issue of saving the planet too. *When did life get so complicated?* Things were so much easier when Calay only had to worry about feeding herself and Jacob. Now, she had to figure out how to keep Earth and all its species alive. Including an invasive alien one. *This is going to be impossible.* Calay offered Elora a reluctant nod. Elora pounced on the opportunity.

"Let me show you." She rose from Calay's feet and crossed the room in what seemed like one giant stride. Calay padded after her.

"Is this the security room or something?" Calay asked, trying to take it all in.

"Close. It's our Strategic Operations Room. We call it the SOR."

"Sounds painful."

"You always did have a clever sense of humor." Elora grinned as she reached up and activated an invisible digital screen.

A spectrum of colors exploded. An array of detailed schematics and maps appeared in the air in front of them. Several were depicted in languages Calay didn't understand. There were probably thousands of them, layer upon layer.

"What is all this?"

"It's how we're going to save Earth."

Calay let the effect of those words sink in. The flutter of hope they inspired somewhere deep inside her. Like it could actually be a thing. Doubt followed close on its heels.

"Okay." She cleared her throat. "How?"

"Are you sure you want to know?"

Calay reached up to touch a map written in what looked like ancient code. It swirled under her fingertips. A blossom of warmth threaded through her veins. Her breath caught short as the hieroglyphic-like symbols slowly gained meaning. She tried to form full sentences from them, but they were more general ideas. Something about truth. Loss. And acceptance. She scanned the document, bringing both hands to the transparent surface. There was no English. No images she could understand. Yet, it made sense. Somewhere deep down inside her. It all connected.

"What language is this?"

"Yours." Elora replied, stepping beside her.

"What?" Calay's eyebrows shot up. "I don't recognize this."

"You call us the Others. We call ourselves Térasians. You are one of us. If not yet in spirit, in biology. I know it may take some time for you to accept that, but that doesn't make it any less true. What exists here, exists in you. You are what is. That's why you understand the symbols."

"I don't, entirely. Just fragments."

"That's a start. You'll get more the longer you're here. Once you fully integrate, you'll pick up more of our language. Like I told you in the pod, where one exists, so does its opposite. You may be part human, Calay, but you are also Other. You are also Térasian. You're home."

An overwhelming sense of gratitude filled Calay, as well as trepidation. For the first time, she wondered if there wasn't a real reason for that sense of foreboding she kept feeling; maybe it was simply the opposite of the other feelings she was experiencing.

The greater the emotion, the stronger its reaction.

"It doesn't feel like home." Calay retreated from the display, a chill settling in her bones. She once again crossed her arms over her chest, hung her head.

"It will. And when it does, we will live side by side forever."

"I still don't understand how. There are mountains of information here, and I'm only getting pieces of it."

"We'll go through it together, my daughter. You, and I, and other hybrids like yourself. They're making their way here as we speak."

"Wait, what? They are?" Calay blanched. Her heart fluttered. The possibility of meeting others like her was almost too much. She'd be able to actually talk to them. They'd understand how she was feeling. What she was going through. Jacob was a confidante, but he'd never really get her experience. Not in the same way she needed him to. These Others, like her, would. Finally.

"It's only a matter of time before they get here. Then our coalition will be complete. I see a bright future for us, Calay. A very bright future."

"After everything..." Calay turned to face Elora and found her mother's arms wrapping around her. Calay's body went rigid. Her heart raced.

Elora pulled her close and Calay almost fell apart right then. She smelled just as she remembered—like warm sunshine and dirt. Calay wasn't ready for this. For any of it. Still, they had to start somewhere.

Slowly, one inch at a time, and as the tears poured out of Calay's eyes, she brought her arms up and around Elora's waist.

Through muffled sobs, she mumbled, "if you think so."

"I know so." Elora pulled away and held Calay at arm's length. Her palms rested on Calay's shaking shoulders.

Calay sniffed, trying to stand taller under the gaze of the mother she thought she'd never see again, never mind hold. A tight smile wrapped itself across Elora's mouth.

"It will all work out as I've planned. And it's all because of you. We can fix this."

Calay didn't know whether Elora was talking about their relationship or their civilizations. Maybe it was both.

Their eyes met and for the first time in a long time. Despite her best efforts, Calay couldn't squelch the hope that blossomed inside her for what could be. Elora seemed so confident. So powerful. Gazing through the strange blue light, Calay thought Elora's eyes looked inhuman.

Calay realized they were.

This alien intervention could be exactly what Earth needed to recover and right the failing ecosystem.

It could be exactly what Calay needed to heal.

CHAPTER NINE

THE SAME TÉRASIAN arrived shortly after to escort Calay back to her room. Racked with emotion, that was the last place she wanted to be. She'd spent enough time stuffed in there, waiting for the next phase of her life to begin. Holding out for answers that never seemed to come.

Now that she'd finally met with Elora, Calay was confident she'd done the right thing by coming to Téras. She didn't quite know what the plan was to save their civilizations, but her mother promised all would be revealed the next day once they'd both gotten some much needed rest.

After the other hybrids arrived.

Calay's heart skipped a beat and her steps felt lighter just thinking about it. Others. Like her. She'd never met anyone like herself before. Or if she had, she wasn't aware of it. She couldn't help but wonder what they'd be like or if she'd know they were the same when she saw them. Did they too go their whole lives not knowing who—or what—they were until recently, like her? Had they known they were special? Suspected it? The questions rolled around her mind faster than she could keep track of them. She exhaled, grateful that after all this time, it seemed she would indeed uncover the answers she was seeking.

But first, what she wanted more than anything, was to talk to Jacob.

Before they arrived, Calay didn't have a mother. She had no home. And she certainly wasn't optimistic about the future. It had been only one day since they'd arrived here and everything had changed. Now, she even felt different. Stronger. Brighter. Almost happy. Twenty-four hours ago, that would have been impossible. Everything Jacob had promised back on Earth was coming true. They could build a real home here. Save the planet and what was left of humanity. And even—just maybe —the two of them could create a life together. As Calay followed the Térasian down the long white hallways, she swiped the remaining tears from her eyes with the cuff of her sweatshirt. She knew what she had to do. If they were going to move on, as Jacob had pleaded with her on so many dark, cold nights, she needed to stop hiding in the shadows or disappearing onto rooftops by herself. She had to unlock the doors she'd sealed shut and air out the rooms of her heart.

She'd tell him everything.

Her knuckles came down hard on the door to Jacob's cabin. The Térasian bowed and retreated as silently as they'd arrived. Calay watched them go, growing smaller and smaller the further they walked down what seemed like a never-ending hallway. Had she come all that way? Calay hadn't even noticed. She'd been deep in thought about what she should say and how she should say it. Jacob knew what had happened on Earth. The things she'd gone through. He'd held her while she cried. But he had no idea how terrified she was of getting close to him—or anyone—ever again. She shivered, pulled the sleeves of her sweater over her shaking hands. She shifted her weight from one foot to the other. Waited. Where was he? She needed to talk to him before she lost her nerve. She raised a fist again, ready to knock a second time, when the door swished and evaporated.

Jacob was standing on the other side, in a matching sweatsuit, but his was black. His dark curls spilled into his eyes. He squinted into the light of the hallway, a grin etching its way across his full lips.

"Isn't a text common courtesy."

"I'm sorry?"

"Before a booty-call. You should have texted to let me know you were coming over."

"That's not why I'm here." Calay grinned back, despite her nerves. "Besides, I couldn't text you if I wanted to. Nobody's had phones for over four years."

"Oh, right." Jacob ran a hand through his hair. "Tin cans and string then?"

"If that's what it takes for you to let me in your room, we'll arrange something."

"Where are my manners? Come in." Jacob stepped aside, waving Calay forward with a broad sweep of his arm. Calay strode into the dimly lit space. The same orange light that was in her room glowed here too. It was gentle enough as to not keep anyone awake. Assuming they could fall asleep in the first place. She hadn't. But judging by the pile of sheets on the bed and the way Jacob rubbed his eyes, he'd had no problem doing so. Her eyes adjusted and she could make out the edges of the side table, the curve of the mattress, the shape of Jacob's full lips.

"You were sleeping," she said.

"Only a little."

"I'm sorry."

"I'm not."

Calay's gaze darted between the bed and the floor. She wanted to meet Jacob's stare and launch into a full explanation of why she was there, but she didn't know how. She'd spent so long bottling her feelings up, she was afraid if she took the lid off, they might never stop pouring out of her. She bit her lower lip, chewed. Instead, she opted for logistics.

"I haven't seen much of you the last twenty-four hours," she started. "Where have you been?"

"I know, I'm sorry. I had the debrief, like I said. I've been off-planet for a while."

"That's weird." Calay scuffed her toe on the floor.

"What's weird?"

"When you say 'off-planet' I think Earth, but you mean this place. Téras."

"This is my home. For me, Earth was the alien planet." Jacob shrugged, his cheeks grew red. "I guess this is all pretty disorienting for you."

"It's not normal."

"I'm sorry I haven't been around more. We have protocols. There's been a lot of catching up to do. I was pretty tired after everything so I came back here."

Calay nodded, noting he made no mention of the heated conversation with Ash.

"I thought they might have put us together," she replied. Now it was her turn to blush. She was grateful for the lack of lighting. "In the same cabin."

"Is that what you would have wanted?"

Calay shrugged.

"I guess not."

"I didn't think so. You…" Jacob sighed, as if trying to find the right words. "I don't know if you've noticed but you've been kind of stand-offish recently. I figured you'd want your space."

Of course, Jacob was right. He was always putting her needs above his own. Trying to guess what she wanted. She didn't know how he could always figure it out when she couldn't.

"That's not what I want now." Calay stepped forward.

"Oh no? And what do you want now?" Jacob raised his eyebrows.

She wanted to press her lips against his. To feel the weight of him on her again. She wanted to be with him. But more than anything, she wanted to tell him the truth.

"Your jammies aren't gray." Calay tugged on the sleeve of his sweatshirt.

"Black is for ops. Gray is for guests." Jacob tugged the sleeve of hers in return.

Calay's brows furrowed. She dropped her head, trying to hide the disappointment spreading across her face. They saw her as a guest, she realized. *I'm not one of them.* So maybe it wasn't to be her home after all.

"Hey, they're just temporary, okay?" His fingers brushed past the wall of her hair as it fell forward, hiding her face. He cupped her chin, tilted her head up, forced her eyes to meet his. "You'll get black ones once you complete training."

"Are you sure?"

"Are you?" Jacob closed the distance between them. His breath was soft and warm against her skin as he spoke. "Calay, I know this is a lot to absorb. The possible end of the worlds and all that. Is this really what you want?"

"I..." Calay gazed up at him. Her stomach did back flips. She searched his face for a reason not to say the thing she was about to say. He didn't give her one. Like usual, his expression was open. Vulnerable. Hers. "I don't often know what I want. But after everything that's happened here in this short amount of time, I know now. And I want to tell you something, Jacob."

"I'm all ears."

Calay cleared her throat and made her way to the bed. She sat down and tapped the spot next to her. Jacob crossed the room and sunk down beside her. Their legs fell against each other and neither bothered to move them. Calay forced herself to ignore the warmth of him against her. She met his gaze. His crystal blue eyes were trained on her. As if he could see inside her.

This was it. Now or never.

"The way I've been since...Since it happened. It hasn't been because of you. It's been all me." Calay paused. Jacob nodded, just a little. *Fuck, why is this so hard?* She continued, pushing the clumsy words over her teeth and her lips. "I died that day. Not literally, obviously. But maybe spiritually? Emotionally? I don't even know. I think I felt my soul leave my body the moment I squeezed the life out of her, Jacob. I died with her and these last four months I've been trying to come back. To you. To life. But it's been dark. So fucking dark. And I didn't want to pull you into the darkness with me."

"Calay, you could never—"

"No, please. Let me get this out."

Jacob zipped his lips with his fingers and grinned. *Damn, that grin.* Calay took a deep breath. Exhaled. Tried to steady the tremor in her voice.

"You saw me at my very worst. I...I killed someone. I killed my girlfriend. In cold blood. You watched me. I know you've told me it was self-defence, and it was. But that doesn't make the fact that everything I knew about her was a lie. Or that I murdered her any easier. It killed me inside. And I didn't want it to kill you too. So, I thought it was best if I kept my distance. I've been terrified of getting close to you again. I pushed you away. But I think by doing that, I made everything a lot worse. For both of us. Jacob, I've never felt tethered to anyone the way I tethered myself to Tess. And when I lost her, I thought I'd lost the last thing I had in this fucked up world. I'd already lost both my parents. My home. Society. And then her. It all fell apart. I had nothing. But I see now that I had you. *Have* you. You've been beside me through everything and shown me nothing but…"

"But what?"

"You've shown me nothing but love."

"Are you saying you love me too?"

"That's the thing. I'm not sure I can love you the way you want me to." The realization struck Calay like a bolt of lightning. A sharp pang of heat flushed her cheeks. Darkness edged her vision. She ignored the urge to jump to her feet and run right out the door. "I don't know if I can love anybody like that ever again. But, I want to try."

"Does this make us a couple?" A smile grew across Jacob's face, lighting his blue eyes even brighter.

"I can barely make sense out of myself right now, I'm not ready to make sense out of us." Calay's mouth turned down at the edges. It was the first time she'd said those words out loud. Possibly the first time she even acknowledged them. It felt good to give her truth a voice and at the same time, an unease wound its way through her guts. She knew this wasn't what Jacob wanted to hear. He'd made it clear how he felt about her while they were still at the farm. She didn't want to lead him on but she also refused to promise him anything she couldn't deliver. This was the best she could do right now. The best she had inside her. She watched his smile fade. "It doesn't mean I don't care. It just means I need time."

"I'll give you anything you need. You know that Calay. Take all the time in the universe. I'm not going anywhere."

"It'll be pretty hard to, given we're on an alien planet." Calay smirked.

"It's not alien to me. And soon, it won't be alien to you either."

"I should have listened to you before. We should have come here much sooner." Calay reached for Jacob's hand. He embraced hers with both of his. "I don't always agree with your methods and I'm going to need you to be completely honest with me from now on. Tess's lies messed me up. Every time you're dishonest with me, even if you're looking out for me, makes the pain way, way worse. I don't want you to protect me. From anything. If I'm going to be here, I can take care of myself. You tell me the truth, no matter what. No lies. No omissions. No secrets. Got it?"

"Understood." Jacob's voice dropped an octave.

Calay allowed her shoulder to lean against him. She could tell he meant it. She smiled. "Good. Thank you for listening. And for giving me the space to say what I needed to say. I've been holding all this in for so long. I wanted to tell you sooner. I just…didn't see the point."

"Why not?" Jacob brushed Calay's hair behind her ear.

"I didn't see what good it would have done. I was…unreachable. And there was no reason to think things would get better." Calay swallowed. "But coming here has changed all that. I think there's a real way out of this mess. For all of us."

"You know what?" Jacob whispered into Calay's ear. "I think you're right."

A shiver crawled across Calay's skin. From the first moment she found Jacob in her camp all those months ago, she couldn't stop her body from reacting to his. They were drawn to each other like two magnets. It was as if they were destined to be together. One way or another. She peered up at him from behind her lashes and the fire blossoming in her eyes set a match in his.

His hand tightened around hers, the other slid around her waist as he pulled her closer. She could feel the rhythm of their hearts through their shirts. His mouth hovered over hers, less than an inch apart. The space between their lips was alive with energy. Calay would have sworn she could almost see it moving. She could certainly feel it.

She let that moment hang just long enough to feel the electricity plunge through her veins before she pressed their mouths together.

His soft, full lips tasted like caramel and woodsmoke. Calay devoured it.

Before Jacob could get both his arms around her, she swung her leg over his and straddled him. She pressed her tongue past his teeth and kissed him deeper. She'd wanted this for so long. How long had it been? It felt like millennia ago they'd laid together. And yet, it could have been yesterday. Their bodies moved in sync, even with their clothes bunched between them. When her hips rose, so did his. When hers fell, his were right behind. Her fingers traced the hem of his sweatshirt, the tips grazed his chiseled stomach. Gods, it had been *too* long.

She inched the shirt over his waist, his hard chest, and up over his head. Their faces pulled apart. Their eyes met. Slowly, she pulled hers off, too. Jacob drank in the sight of her, his eyes blazing, clear, and wide. She brought his hands to her breasts. Then his mouth. Her back arched under the warmth of his tongue. The nip of his teeth.

Then, Calay went in for more.

She kissed him with a hunger she couldn't satiate. She needed more of him in her mouth. Now. She reached for the waistband of his pants. Her hair tumbled forward, cloaking their faces. Jacob released her ass, gathered her hair in his hands. He wound it around his fist, pulling it tight at the base of her neck. He tugged just enough to make Calay groan. It was enough to push both of them over the edge.

Jacob wound his free arm around her and flipped her onto her back. A giggle escaped Calay's lips but it was cut short by a moan when Jacob's mouth found her collarbone. His arm outstretched above both their heads, he held her hands there.

She was pinned beneath his hips.

The tips of his fingers followed her mouth, tracing a line from her chin, to her neck, all the way across her stomach before his hand reached inside the band of her pants and cupped the warmth of her. Calay nearly came right then.

She ached for more.

Moments later, her cozy joggers were off. His too. She wanted to beg him to enter her, but the words wouldn't come. The blood her brain needed to form them was pulsing between her legs. She ached to feel him inside her. She let her body speak for her. But for probably the first time ever, he refused to give her what she wanted. Instead, he took what *he* wanted.

He kissed her belly button, the crease of her hips, her wetness. A desperate heat pooled between her legs and spread through her limbs. Jacob released her arms and gripped her thighs. He kissed her deeper. Longer. With quick, gentle strokes of his tongue, Calay's chest fluttered. Her body melted. And then it tensed.

She tried to breathe into the feeling but her air was stolen in exquisite rapture.

Her fingers wound through the loose curls in Jacob's hair as waves of pleasure rolled over, under, and through her body.

When she relaxed, so did her grip on Jacob's tresses. His hand found her mound and he cupped her again.

Calay shuddered with warmth. She didn't know why his palm over her felt as reassuring as it did, but she welcomed it.

He slowly kissed her soft stomach, pausing to put each of her nipples in his mouth, sucking gently. He released her and kissed her cheeks. Her eyelids. Her forehead. And her mouth.

He took his time, showering her in affection. Tenderness. Safety.

Then, he slid inside her, filling her with the thickness of his cock. Calay came again. When they were finished, she was on top and collapsed on his chest with him inside her. Her whole body shook with feeling. Physical and emotional.

"That was…" She exhaled against his skin.

"You're welcome," he replied, trying to regain his breath. She didn't have to look at him to know he was smiling.

"You're fucking welcome." Calay laughed and pressed herself up to look at him. Yes, he was smiling. His eyes twinkled in the delicate orange light. She slid to the side and Jacob wrapped his arms around her, holding her close.

"Thank you." Jacob kissed the top of her head.

"It was good before," Calay started, "but it's never been like that, right? Tell me I'm not crazy."

"You're not crazy."

"But actually."

"Do you remember I told you the sex was better here?"

Calay's cheeks flushed, despite what they'd just done together.

"Yes."

"Well..."

"But you don't even normally have bodies."

"So?"

"So, what's the point?"

"What do you mean?"

"I just don't understand what the point of sex is if, as a species, you don't have bodies. You obviously don't need it to procreate. It seems redundant."

"Was I the only one who experienced what just happened?" Jacob smirked, raised an eyebrow.

"Of course not." Calay ran her finger down his chest. "This whole world is new to me. If I'm going to make it my home, I need understand."

"I'm trying to explain it to you. Why do you do it?"

"Why do I have sex?" A whisper of a laugh floated through Calay's voice.

"Yes, you. Or humans in general."

"Because it feels good." Calay paused, chewed on her bottom lip. "And because it makes us feel something different."

"Different from what?"

"Anything. Everything."

"So it's escapism for you?"

"Sometimes, yes."

"With Tess?"

"No." Calay halted at his mention of her name. Wrapped in the arms of someone else, it felt wrong, somehow. Even if she was dead. She swallowed and chose her next words carefully. "With Tess sex was something else. It was us. Our essences. Together. It was special."

"And with me?" Calay felt him tense beneath her.

"Of course not." She bristled.

"Calay—"

"Okay, yes. The first time we did it, in the cabin, I used you. Just a little. You just looked so good, and you were kind to me, and I couldn't take my eyes off that stupid, pouty grin of yours." Calay brought her eyes to his and found them smiling. "But after that I started to fall for you. Feel things for you. Jacob, every time since then has always been about us. It's meant something. We mean something. To me."

"It's meant something to me too."

"But I've used people in the past. To feel better about myself. To feel connected to others. Sometimes the pain of being alone is too much and all I want is someone to hold onto. It makes the hurt more bearable."

"Is it so hard to believe the same could be true for me?"

"I guess The Térasians seem like such an expansive, limitless species. Why bind yourself into a corporeal form if you don't have to?"

"Limits can actually inspire connection. Creativity. Passion." Jacob's eyes darkened, he lowered his gaze to her mouth. "Some things are worth binding ourselves to."

"Stop." She pushed back against his chest. "I'm being serious, Jacob."

"So am I. Meeting you has changed everything about my existence, Calay. The closer we become, the more whole I feel. Getting to make you scream is just a bonus."

"But…"

"Do you really want to get into explanations right now?" There was that grin in his voice again. The one that made her feel like they had all the space and time in the world.

"Not even a little bit." Calay smiled.

"Good." Jacob squeezed her tighter.

For the first time in more sleeps than she could count, Calay didn't sneak off to spend the night alone. There was no other place she wanted to be than right here. With him.

Her eyes grew heavy and her limbs still. It seemed today was a day for firsts. She didn't know what that meant entirely, and she didn't need to. Like she'd told Jacob, she was only just figuring out this whole living without Tess thing. With a little patience and compassion, maybe she— along with both their civilizations—might just make it through the end of the world. Jacob's heart slowed, his breathing deepened. With each gentle breath, Calay's head rose and fell. Each motion strong. Steady. Sure.

That night Calay drifted off to sleep listening to the rhythmic sound of Jacob's heartbeat with the understanding that she may have been the salmon, but maybe Jacob was her rock all along.

CHAPTER TEN

A GENTLE SWISH and a tingle up Calay's spine woke her with a start the next morning. Standing over them was the same Térasian who'd dropped her off the previous night. Now, they gazed down at her and Jacob's naked forms wrapped around each other under the thin veil of a sheet. The intent focus of their green eyes unsettled Calay as they cocked their head. She gasped, gripped Jacob's hand with one of her own, the sheet with her other. She pulled it up to her chin and sank lower.

Jacob stirred, nuzzled the top of Calay's head with his lips.

"Ready to go again?" He purred against her hair.

"Jacob." Calay hissed. "Jacob, wake up."

"Oh, I am."

"There's someone here." Calay tugged again on his hand, not daring to let him—or the sheet—out of her grasp.

"Hmm?" Jacob opened his eyes. Calay used her own to guide his gaze toward the end of the bed. His shoulders tensed beneath her head. A grunt escaped from somewhere deep within his throat, vibrated against Calay's forehead. He pulled has arm from around her and propped himself up onto his elbows.

"Haven't you heard of knocking, Thana?" Jacob said through gritted teeth. Then, out the side of his mouth, "There's a lady present."

"I can see that," Thana replied in an even voice.

Calay's mouth fell open. It was the first time they had bothered to answer a question and Calay had asked a lot of them on their long walks through the building. She couldn't place the inflection. It ticked up at the edges and muddled the harder consonants. Their thin, dry lips barely moved as they said the words. It wasn't an accent she recognized. She wondered if this was the closest she'd heard to their original dialect. The one that existed beyond their corporeal, human-like forms.

Thana blinked, unmoving. "The lady is wanted in the SOR."

Calay's brows furrowed. *Already?* Elora promised they'd get started the next day, but Calay didn't realize it would be this early. If she had, she might have spent the night in her room after all. The last thing she wanted after the tenuous ending with her family was to be seen as irresponsible. Frivolous. Irrational. She came here to do a job, and she meant to do it. She didn't need to embarrass herself, or her family, the way she used to. Before she'd met Tess. It felt like a lifetime ago she'd lived that life. Made those mistakes. Not that her unhealthy coping mechanisms didn't have a purpose. She'd found comfort in the bottom of a bottle and the arms of strangers with good reason.

At least this time it was in the arms of a familiar one. For once, she'd owned her feelings. Gave them a voice. Intentionally sought Jacob rather than just falling into him because he was the closest, most beautiful thing she could reach. This had been her choice. She had to give herself props for that. Besides, it was none of Elora's business what Calay did in her free time.

Still, despite everything that had happened between them and the pain her parents caused her, a small part of Calay couldn't help but yearn for her mother's approval. Her acceptance. Her love.

"I think the SOR can wait," Jacob said.

"No, it's okay." Calay rested her hand on his bare chest. "I'll go."

"You don't have to, Calay. After all you've been through, you get a bit of time to process it. You deserve to rest."

"I hardly think what we did last night could be called rest."

"It's what I'd intended we'd do this morning too." Jacob peeked at Calay from behind his long lashes, licked his full lips.

Want rippled through Calay. She glared at Thana. Their expression remained unchanged. Neutral. Inhuman. Calay sighed.

"I should go. Maybe my mo…Elora, has a reason to get started now."

"But *we* just got started now."

"You brought me here for a reason, Jacob, and it wasn't this." Calay allowed her hand to run through the soft curls of his dark hair.

"Fine." Jacob groaned. "Do what you must."

"You know I always do." Calay turned her attention to Thana. "A moment?"

Thana continued to examine her and Jacob with their wide stare. Calay's knuckles turned white as she clung to the edge of the sheet.

"Please?"

Thana pivoted and left the room as silently as they'd entered. Calay watched the door reappear and when she was confident they were alone, peeled herself from Jacob's embrace and threw back the covers.

The air of the cabin was pleasantly warm, though she cringed as her bare feet hit the cold hard floor. Still, after the excruciating winter they'd left behind only a few days ago, she could hardly complain.

She sifted through their discarded clothing, searching for her own. As she pawed her way through the dark room, she felt Jacob's eyes following her every move.

"If you don't stop watching me, I'll have to ask you to leave too." Calay giggled. Her hand flew to her mouth, she gasped. The sound almost stopped her dead in her tracks. She didn't giggle. Not anymore. She didn't think she ever would again. But she just did. This alien planet was having its way with her in more ways than one.

Her fingers grazed the soft, fleecy fabric of her gray jumper. Jacob's gaze persisted. She met it with her own, then watched him watching her. She slid her pants on first. Then her sweatshirt. She pulled her long dark hair back and over one shoulder, stood with her hands on her hips.

"Enjoy the show?"

"I never thought I'd see you like this again." Jacob sighed as he reached for her.

Calay let him pull her to the edge of the bed. She pushed against it with her knees, refusing to be brought back into the folds of the messy sheets. She had important work to do, and she was afraid if Jacob managed to get her underneath him again she might never leave.

"Neither did I." Calay admitted, gnawing on her bottom lip.

"I'm glad I did."

"So am I."

"So stay."

"You fought for months to get me to this planet to do the things that needed to be done, and I'm damn well going to do them." Calay returned his smile, shook her hand from his. "I'll see you later, okay?"

Jacob nodded and rolled onto his back, his hands behind his head. The sheet barely covered his...everything. She swooned. *No wonder Thana had stared.* She turned to go before she lost her nerve.

"Calay?" Jacob called over the swooshing sound of the door evaporating.

"Yeah?" She turned back.

"Be careful."

Calay smirked and walked out the door. *Careful.* Only a few days ago, Calay would have told him she couldn't afford to be careful. Now, with so much balanced on winning whatever fight was ahead of them, it was the only way forward. She didn't know what Elora had planned, but Calay couldn't imagine a scenario where they succeeded if they weren't minutely careful.

In the cold light of day, Calay wasn't sure she was up to the task of saving two civilizations in one fell swoop. It seemed too big. Too hard. Too bloody impossible. But Elora had a plan. Or so she'd led Calay to believe, anyhow. And now she was being summoned to find out what that plan entailed.

The least she could do was try.

The door swished shut behind her, and Calay found Thana standing at attention against the white panelled wall.

"Ready?" Calay said.

They nodded, mute once again. Evidently, Calay wasn't important enough to warrant a reply.

As if in response to Calay's thoughts, Thana's green eyes honed on hers and held them just long enough to make Calay's skin crawl. Then they turned, silent as the grave, leading the way back down the long corridor to Elora's strategic operations room.

THE NEXT TWELVE HOURS WERE A TORRENT OF information.

Calay swiped through endless charts and diagrams projecting The Térasian's data. The number of pods they'd lost. The casualties they'd suffered. Their success rate. She reviewed evidence that without her help, that rate, over time, would drop to zero. She analyzed disturbingly detailed maps of Earth, outlining where the Térasians thought clusters of humans continued to resist, as well as how many were likely to be saved, and how many they might lose in the process. Elora offered generously detailed schematics outlining the Térasian population, the total number of ships they still had docked, and why it wouldn't be enough. Not on their own.

As Jacob had told Calay months before, there were far fewer Térasians than humans, even after so many people had been killed. The last four years hadn't improved the numbers on either side. That was why they needed Calay's help—and that of other hybrids—so badly.

Numbers, theories, and symbols formed a maze in Calay's brain. It climbed higher, more complex. A labyrinth of information. Her mind spun at the sheer velocity at which it was presented. She fought to keep up, to keep her wits about her and make sense of the intelligence being hurled in her general direction.

As she tried to digest it, she couldn't help one nagging question that seemed to have burrowed its way deep inside her mind. Even as Elora presented more facts and figures, more evidence, there was one piece of the puzzle that just wasn't fitting for Calay. Before she could ever agree to anything Elora was asking, she needed an answer.

"Wait," Calay finally said. She swallowed, leaned against the wall and rubbed her eyes, exhaled.

"I realize this is a lot to absorb. Should we take a break?" Elora replied.

"No. It's a lot, but it's okay. I think." Calay shook her head.

"Good, then let's continue. We're short on time and long on details. We have no time to waste. Let's get to the meat of it, shall we?" Elora strode across the room and pulled up a whole new library labelled Co-Exist Strategy. "As I was saying, the only reasonable way for us to live together is to work together. This is how we'll do it."

"Hang on just a second." Calay stepped forward, rustling the courage she needed to address her newfound mother. "I get that you want the Others, err, I mean Térasians and Humans to work together, and that somehow hybrids are in the middle of all that. I'm guessing that's what we're about to get to."

"You've always been smart, Calay. You guessed right." Elora nodded.

"But there's something I don't understand."

"What don't you understand?"

"Why are we doing all this?"

"What do you mean? I've told you—if we don't, neither of our species will survive."

"Sure, right. I get that. But why even ask for the help of humans? Of hybrids? When Térasians invaded Earth, they didn't come peacefully. People died. Most of us, actually. They shot first, asked questions never. It was War of The Fucking Worlds. So why are you helping them now? Why should they help you?"

"We never wanted to hurt anybody." Elora clenched her hands in front of her legs.

"But you did. You hurt a lot of people."

"We're deeply regretful about that."

"Regretful? That's all you have to say for wiping out an entire species? My species."

"It was the way it had to be."

"Was it? Please, explain it to me. I don't understand why so many people—everyone I loved—had to die!"

"Our preliminary research told us our arrival wouldn't be met with peace. From that, we deducted humans would be hostile." Elora's mouth tightened. "So we came prepared. We weren't wrong."

"Wait, what research did you do?"

"As you know, I arrived on Earth long before the Others, as you've called them, arrived. Thanks to the radiated electrical storm I was transported through, I met your father and made Earth my home. That doesn't mean I wasn't in communication with Téras authorities while I was there. Or that there weren't more of us already on planet."

A coldness crawled through Calay's veins.

"While I was growing up..."

"Yes, yes. I was sending transmissions back here. Others followed. Like Jacob. They came on a mission to rescue us. And you, I might add. But as we came to know more about people, we learned we could never arrive peacefully. Humans are a fearful species, violent by nature. They proved that when they tore me apart once they found out what I was. That I was Other."

"Kind of like how you threw me out of your house when I came out to you as bisexual?"

"Point—and jab—taken. Yes, like that."

"So you came in with guns blazing."

"We entered Earth's galaxy with the knowledge that to get our kind —and their offspring—back home safely, we may have to sacrifice a few human lives."

"My god, Elora. You sacrificed more than a few. The Others turned almost seven billion people into red mist!" Calay gripped the fabric of her pants. She pushed down a wall of tears threatening to spill out of her eyes as memories of that first, fateful day flashed through her mind.

Her apartment building falling apart around her and Tess. Their lives literally upended, brick by bloody brick. The terror on her neighbor's faces as their loved ones disappeared in front of them. Then, everything that came afterward. She'd lost count of the horrors that haunted her day by day. Night by night. The worst of it was the constant fear she'd be murdered, or worse. Bodies rotting where they fell. The relentless hunger. The need to kill or be killed.

Tess.

A wave of nausea rolled through her. She lunged for the nearest receptacle—a waste basket that looked as clean as the day it was placed there—and threw up the waffles with strawberries with whipped cream she'd manifested and messily eaten with her fingers on her way to meet Elora.

Her mother kneeled beside her, pulled her hair out of the splash zone. Her hand was warm and strong as she rubbed small circles on Calay's back.

Calay wiped her mouth on the edge of her sleeve and sat back on her heels, cleared her throat.

'Do you even know what you've done?" Her eyes brimmed with tears.

"I'm sorry you suffered." Elora offered Calay a dark swatch of lace-rimmed fabric she pulled from the pocket of her flowing pants.

Calay's heart lurched. It was such a familiar movement. How many times did her mom do that same exact thing when Calay was a child? She shuddered as she acknowledged this woman would never just be her leader. She was her mother, too. No amount of galaxies or pain could change that. She didn't want it to.

"Believe me, I know what we did," Elora added. "It's why I'm trying to make amends now. Far too many lives have been lost, Calay. Please, help us to ensure we save as many as possible."

Calay accepted the handkerchief, sniffed, and wiped her nose.

"Can I show you something?"

Calay wasn't sure she had much of a choice. Still, she wanted to believe what Elora was telling her. She needed to. She nodded.

Elora pulled Calay to her feet. Tucked in the shadows of the dark glow of the room, between the far wall and a long panel of knobs and switches, was a cylindrical glass tower Calay hadn't noticed before. It was barely the height of her, coming up only to Elora's shoulders.

"This is going to change everything," Elora said. She twisted a few dials and reached for a lever. Inside the container, delicate white shapes appeared. They hovered before swirling up and around in circles. Slow at first, then faster. They formed a funnel, narrow at the top, wide at the bottom. "Do you know what this is?"

Calay had an idea, but it seemed impossible. This far away from Earth. On an alien planet. At their command. Still, the shape of the fluttering formations was unmistakable.

"Snow?" Calay asked.

"See? Smart."

"But, how? And isn't this thing dangerous? Snow—water —is toxic for Térasians."

"That's why it's here. Under lock and key and my eye. We've been experimenting with it, doing tests. Earth is over seventy percent water, it's the lifeblood of your planet. It only makes sense we understand it. Control it. Our research shows Earth is undergoing a massive environmental shift right now. The delicate equilibrium that has allowed generations of people to survive is on an axis. You might have noticed the strange weather shifts where you were."

"Portland shouldn't have had snow this time of year. Even if it did by some fluke of the weather, it shouldn't have had as much." Calay nodded.

"Exactly. The patterns are all wrong. We intend to right them." Elora reached for one of the dials, began to turn it counterclockwise.

The funnel of flakes grew wider in the center, then evened out to make a long tube.

"How?"

"Restoring the human population."

"What could that possibly do?" Calay blinked.

"There's an imbalance. If we can revive the number of humans on Earth, balance will be restored."

"That doesn't sound right." Calay scoffed. "Humans were literally destroying the planet before the Others arrived. I'm not saying what the Others, ugh Térasians, did was right by any conceivable approximation. But if there's one good thing that could possibly be pulled from all this, maybe they saved Earth. From us."

"People weren't bad for the planet, Calay." Elora smiled, turning the dial down to zero. The snow melted and clung to the glass in thick drops. "Their way of life was. The systems they protected. Neoliberalism. Hyper-capitalism. Over-consumption. If one good thing could possibly be pulled from all this, it's that humans get a second chance. A reset. If we repopulate Earth with people who believe in our coexistence, we can build anew. From the ground up. And fix everything."

Calay had to admit, it sounded good. Imagine what they could do for humanity by creating systems that put people's needs ahead of corporations. By choosing community over consumerism. That prioritized being instead of doing.

Still, she wasn't quite buying it.

"There's no way humans can have that much of an effect on the planet. It's too big. We're too small."

"This is something humans never understood. It's one of the many reasons their planet was in the state it was. Every single species has that much of an effect on the planet. You're all part of something bigger and more interconnected than you can imagine. But humans are the only ones with hubris big enough to abdicate their role in it."

"And brains evolved enough to question it."

"Exactly."

"Okay, so pretend I accept everything you're saying is true, and I go along with your big plan. If people are inherently violent and fearful, what's to stop them from just doing what they did all over again? To the environment and each other? To you?"

"We will give them a better option."

"What kind of better option?" Calay strained to keep her tone even, she was getting impatient. It felt like she was doing mental gymnastics just trying to get a full answer out of Elora.

"We won't be starting at ground zero. There are still thousands of humans alive who remember the old ways. And we don't want to take that from them. Humans are a fascinating species, after all. Highly intelligent. Often curious. We understand there will be those who wish to return to what was. Who will depend on or desire superfluous creature comforts, regardless of how it might affect the greater good. We merely aim to give them a better way to enjoy those comforts."

"Okay..." Calay squinted, concentrating.

"We will give them the one thing humans couldn't gain for

themselves. Something that will allow them to enjoy their lives and the amenities they've come to depend on, without bringing harm to their environment. And, it'll make us indispensable to their way of life, thus ensuring both our survivals on Earth." Elora flipped another switch on the panel.

Calay wrapped her arms across her chest, waited.

"An alternate fuel source."

An immense fire roared to life inside the tube.

Calay gasped, jumped backward. She stared at the flames, enraptured by the remaining water steaming and evaporating against the glass. In its place, a familiar blue light glowed from below. Calay shivered, despite the heat. It was identical to the lights in the pods. The ones that turned people into plasma.

Orange flames licked up the sides of the cylinder, kissing the roof. Sparks flung themselves back into the raging inferno. *Wait, what is that?* Calay looked closer. Inside, amongst the growing flames, dark eyes seemed to peer back at her. A mouth curved into a large oval. If she didn't know better, she could almost make out the outline of a face. Melting flesh as the cheeks peeled off in chunks. She could hear the haunting echo of a high-pitched scream.

Elora's hand came down on her shoulder. Calay jumped again, made eye contact with her mother. When she looked back at the fire, the mirage was gone.

"What's the fuel?" Calay retreated, increasing the space between herself and the flames. The face that only moments ago seemed to be staring back through the glass walls. She shrugged and cleared her throat. It must have been her lack of sleep and perhaps a trick of the light. That would teach her to stay up all night with Jacob. Rest. She just needed rest.

"It's not of the Earth. A new compound we created here." Elora once again twisted the dial the other way, and the fire disappeared.

Calay released a breath. The room seemed darker now. Colder. More ominous.

Elora turned and marched back to the strategy hologram, glowing green. "With this technology, we can co-exist. We won't only survive,

Calay. We will thrive. It'll be hard, but now, with your help and others like you, we are in the position to change things. For the better."

"I'm still not clear on what it is I'd do exactly. What would my role be?" Calay asked, following Elora.

"I've shown you our data and our science. Our strategy—what your role will be, my daughter—is exactly what I want to talk about now. You exist in this very special sphere that we, as Others, cannot. You have experience we will never understand. You can use that expertise to influence humans to accept our proposition. You'll be the bridge between our two civilizations."

"You want me to talk people into going along with this?" Calay balked, grinning. "I don't know if you've met me, but I'm not exactly the most charismatic person on the planet."

"You and others like you, yes. Charisma has nothing to do with our success, Calay, as I'm about to show you."

"Others like me." Calay's heart skipped a beat. "Yesterday, you said other hybrids would be arriving soon. Are they here now? Can I meet them?"

"They are here, yes. Some of the Térasians are arranging a meet and greet as we speak. Before that though, Calay, please. I need your word on this. Will you lead our hybrid division?"

"Wait a minute. Who said anything about leading?"

"You are my daughter. The love of my life. My shining light, Calay. Last night, I promised you we would get through this together. Side by side. I can't think of anyone who would be a better fit to lead our coalition to success."

Truthfully, neither could Calay. But that was because everyone she knew was dead.

"What about someone from Téras? Jacob maybe? Or Ash? Surely, there has to be somebody more qualified."

"It has to be a hybrid." Elora cupped Calay's face. Calay swallowed as best she could and held her breath. "It has to be you."

"What if it doesn't work?" Calay's voice was smaller than she'd intended.

"It will." Elora nodded, her gaze trained on Calay's. Her hands slid down Calay's arms, and she took her hands. "Let's repair our worlds. Together."

Something nibbled at the back of Calay's mind. Everything Elora said made a strange, twisted kind of sense while also being wholly out of a science fiction novel. Calay was overwhelmed with information. With feelings. She wasn't sure which way was up or down right now, and it wasn't even lunchtime.

Still, they had the data. The facts. The truth, if what Elora was saying was to be believed. If their plan worked, they could do something she and Tess never would have been able to do on their own—get her life back.

"I don't know if I have what it takes."

"I know it, my girl. You trust me, don't you?"

The color left Calay's cheeks. She could do a lot of things, but trusting someone was one of the few she wasn't sure she was capable of anymore. Her trust had been broken so many times. In so many irretrievable ways. The openness in Elora's expression tugged at Calay's heart. She wanted to trust. Dear gods, she wanted to trust. Maybe it was like Jacob had told her—at some point, she had to move on. *Spearheading a team to defend the planet and save our civilizations from extinction is definitely moving on.* Calay scrunched her face and blew the breath she was holding through her teeth.

"Fuck, okay." Calay nodded, crossing her arms over her chest. "I'll do it."

CHAPTER ELEVEN

CALAY'S PROMISE haunted her the rest of the day. It echoed through her mind, clutched at her breath. Whenever she thought she'd found a moment's peace, the memory would come crashing back like a rush of wind, sending shivers up her spine.

"I'll do it."

Despite running through the details with Elora, Calay still wasn't convinced she was up to the challenge of leading the coalition. Hell, she wasn't even sure she was prepared to attend the meet and greet with the other hybrids. Those who would be her team.

Wherever they were.

Elora said they'd arrived, but Calay had yet to run into a single one.

After their conversation yesterday, she'd decided a break was indeed what she needed. That, and a good long nap. She'd made her way to the cafeteria only to find she wasn't hungry. She stood in front of the reflective magic food machine thing, her image reflected back to her on its smooth surface. Dazed and overwhelmed, she didn't see herself. She didn't see anything.

She just kept replaying Elora's words in her head. Sorting through the facts and figures. Trying to understand how the Others—the

Térasians—knew so much about humans. They knew more about people than people knew about themselves. And Calay was being asked to trust them while she herself knew almost nothing about the aliens.

A memory flashed through her mind. One of Jacob sitting by her fire. It was from the first time she'd met him. He'd known who and what she was all along. Always one—or several—steps ahead of her. Calay felt like she was constantly trying to catch up to him. Aside from the benefit of saving both their species from total annihilation, maybe the benefit to leading the coalition was the opportunity to finally understand the truth. To be part of something bigger. To belong. But if that was actually the case, why did it feel so wrong?

A loud "thunk" pulled Calay from her thoughts.

A Térasian with short red hair and almost gray colored skin bowed before her, their amber cloak billowing onto the floor. Calay's brow furrowed, confused by the reverent display. That is, until they pulled upright after having retrieved a tray from the machine with a nondescript bowl of mash.

Calay cringed, shuffled backward, and mumbled an incoherent apology.

The Térasian didn't bother to make eye contact. Instead, they huffed and shuffled away on what looked like spike heels, the tips of which clacked on the shiny surface of the floor.

She squinted after them, shooting barbed thoughts at their back. *Excuuuuse, me.* She couldn't help but wonder what aspect of her mind came up with those shoes. Wasn't that what Jacob had said? Everything she saw in the Térasian physical bodies was a projection. What did the manifestations Calay saw say about her? She wasn't sure she was ready to pry the top off that can of worms. Instead, she sighed, rubbed her eyes. It wasn't their fault she was hovering in front of the food. *Right, food.* She tried to imagine something delicious. To picture it in her mind, as Ash had instructed.

All Calay could think about was war.

Images of humans and aliens fighting. Dying. Earth in some kind of permanent winter. That was the trouble with promising to save the world. Your word was not only your bond, it was also a death sentence if things didn't go according to plan. Calay shuddered. Afraid of what might pop out of the slot in the bottom of the machine, she settled for what appeared to be a glass of grapefruit juice.

After returning to her room, it sat untouched, dripping condensation on the bedside table. Calay collapsed on her bed. She closed her eyes. But she couldn't shake that panicked little voice in the back of her mind telling her this place wasn't what it seemed. As she breathed in and out, methodically slowing her breath and trying to calm her thoughts, the feeling creeped around the corners of her mind. Tugged at them. It wound its way behind her eyelids before plunging down her spine and settling in her chest. Calay's eyes snapped open, she held a hand to her racing heart.

Something wasn't right.

Flustered, she pushed herself to sit and tried to gather her thoughts. But there were too many of them talking over one another. Her legs grew twitchy. The thumping in her chest wouldn't slow. She needed to clear her head somehow.

To do *something*.

She slipped off the standard-issue sweatsuit and reached for the crop top she'd arrived in. It'd been somehow cleaned, along with the rest of her clothes, and stacked neatly on the small chair beside her bed. It was a gentle comfort being in her own clothes. She pulled her scruffy boots over her dark ripped jeans and secured her hair at the base of her neck with a stretched-out hair band she habitually wore around her wrist. She shrugged on the scarf that had seen better days and the leather jacket that fit like a second skin. She exhaled.

She was going for a walk.

Calay's knuckles rapped on Jacob's door.

She waited. She knocked again.

No answer.

Calay pulled on the ends of her ponytail to keep her hands from shaking, then she clenched her teeth. The anxiety rolling through her body was threatening to crush her. She didn't know many people in this place, and she was still wasn't used to Jacob not being at her beck and call. Regardless of her emotional unavailability over the last several months, the two of them had been a pair. A team. Together with Max, a pack. Her heart ached at the memory of leaving her dog behind. Maybe that was part of the unease she was feeling. She'd grown accustomed to having both of them around. She liked it, even if she wasn't willing to admit it until this moment. She missed the wag of Max's tail. Jacob and his stupid grin. The ease between them.

She banged a third time and was met with silence.

"What'd that door ever do to you?"

A tingle of warmth curled through Calay. She turned to see Ash's black-rimmed green eyes honed on her, her full pink mouth turned up at the corners. An abstract tattoo peeked out the collar of the corset that swayed in all the right ways as she closed the distance between them.

"I was looking for Jacob." Calay's pulse quickened. Only this time it wasn't because of the panic that had now firmly settled in her stomach. It was the intensity with which Ash was peering at her. As if she was the only other thing in the universe. She cleared her throat. "Have you seen him?"

"I've seen too much of him, if you ask me." Ash paused to angle her shoulder against the wall. Calay turned her eyes up, following Ash's movements. They were elegant. Confident. Sensual. Calay found herself wanting to trace them with her fingertips. Ash's eyes sparkled, as if she were reading Calay's thoughts. They traveled down the length of Calay's body, then back up. "I haven't seen nearly enough of you."

Calay's eyes widened, her cheeks flushed.

"I, uhh." Calay pressed her lips together and swallowed the butterflies trying to make their way up her throat. "I'm right here."

"I see that." Ash leaned closer. She was nearly a head taller than Calay. Her hand hovered beside Calay's face before tucking a stray strand of hair behind her ear. "And what, exactly, are you doing here?"

"I was going for a walk. I thought maybe Jacob would want to join me." It took everything Calay had not to shift her weight forward and kiss Ash right that moment.

"Ah." Ash nodded. "And does he?"

"He's not answering. I mean, I don't think he's here."

"Well, that's unfortunate."

"Yeah, I really need to move a little. Get outside and stretch my legs. I can't seem to figure out a way out of this place though." Calay closed her eyes, swallowed. "Do you want to come with me?"

The moment hung between them. Then another. Calay dropped her eyes, worried she'd misread the conversation. Ash's intentions. If she had, she'd be mortified. A warmness began to spread its way through Calay's cheeks again.

"I'd love to come. *With* you."

Calay's breath caught in her throat. It was all she could do not to throw herself on Ash that moment. Ash beamed at Calay a billion-watt smile, winked.

"Great." Calay peeled her gaze off Ash, refocused it down the hall. "Which way?"

Ash took Calay's hand in hers and without a word, pulled her in the opposite direction.

They walked for what seemed like miles. But that was impossible. Calay knew that. Still, they never seemed to pass the same place twice. Though, as she'd discovered, every hallway looked just like the last, so she couldn't be sure.

"How much farther?" Calay finally summoned the words to ask.

"You said you wanted to walk. We're walking." Ash smiled, squeezed Calay's hand.

"Yeah, but I meant outside. The view from my cabin is amazing. I feel like I've been cooped up in this place since we got here."

"One step at a time. Are you saying you've seen all there is to see here?"

"Hardly. This place is enormous." Calay side-eyed Ash, whose attention was still focused ahead of them. She steeled herself and decided to try her luck and press Ash for more information. "I still don't know what was in that room you came out of yesterday."

"Not much down there, really. Storage. I'm afraid it's not terribly exciting."

"Oh." Calay sighed. Tried another tactic. She brought her fingers to the inside of Ash's wrist, teased her soft skin with the tips. "I was hoping for a little more excitement today."

"Have you seen the loading bay?" Ash turned to level her gaze at Calay.

"Only when we first landed."

"Want to see it again?"

"Really?"

Ash shrugged.

"I don't have access."

"You have me." Ash winked again, ran her hand up Calay's arm.

Calay's stomach flipped. She'd learned a lot from Elora about the Térasian plans and procedures, but the possibility of getting up close and personal with alien tech, without the threat of imminent death, was more than she could resist. Especially if she was going to be leading the troops into some kind of peacekeeping mission. Finally, she might be able to understand more of what really happened the day the aliens invaded Earth. What their technology was really designed for. What they were capable of.

"Absolutely." Calay winked in return. "Let's go."

THE GLASS ROOF OF THE LOADING BAY CURVED ABOVE THEM. A pinkish gold hue radiated across the room. The massive sun's rays were blindingly bright when they arrived on planet, but now, black shadows crept the impossible length of the space as the sun arched beyond the horizon. Calay halted on the landing and watched Ash descend the steep metal stairs until she disappeared from view.

There was a coldness to the space. A hollowness. Despite the fact that the bay was packed with white pods. Hundreds of them, maybe thousands, punctuated the darkness. They were lined in rows, stacked one on top of the other in columns. She couldn't tell what was holding them in place. There didn't seem to be hoists or lifts, there wasn't even shelving or ladders. They just sat there, in mid-air, motionless and silent. Calay pushed a swell of panic down, reminded herself she was one of Them. An Other. The pods wouldn't hurt her, even if they all came to life that moment. Even if she was fully human, here, the blue light was not what she once thought it was. Térasians were a peaceful species. They didn't want to do harm. If Elora could be believed. Calay scanned the ocean of pods in awe. She couldn't help but wonder if there were so few Térasians left, who flew them? Maybe that was why they were on-planet, instead of in space, among the stars. Or perhaps they were meant for an army. A coalition. Her coalition.

The crumbs of an idea entered Calay's mind.

"Ash?" Calay called out.

There was no answer.

She pressed her lips together and carefully made her way down the steep staircase.

She hadn't noticed it before, but when she reached the bottom, she realized the panelled floor was pearlescent and reflective of the stars shimmering in the growing night sky above, blue lines glowed beneath the surface. They wound their way across each square like ribbons.

She followed one. It wound deep within the loading bay until it stopped abruptly beneath one of the pods. The way the colors twisted back on each other and disappeared from view deep below the surface, Calay guessed they had to be fuel lines or charging cables. She would have asked, but Ash was nowhere to be seen.

"Ash? You here?" She tried again.

Nothing.

Calay couldn't figure her out. She was slippery. There, and then not. Appearing and then disappearing. It had become a recurring theme since Calay arrived and she wasn't sure what to make of it, or even if she should. Ash stirred something inside her. Something dangerous. Despite Calay's best efforts to resist, she wanted more of it.

But first, she wanted to know more about the ships that had ruined her life and the lives of everyone she knew and loved.

Remembering the way the pod transported her back on Earth to that swirling, liminal space, Calay raised a tentative hand to the shining, white surface. As her palm connected with it, it was cold. Hard. Irritatingly unresponsive.

Calay frowned, grumbled under her breath, and tried again.

Nothing happened.

She scanned the outside for a button or latch but found none. She already knew she wouldn't. There was no obvious way in or out. Not for the human eye, anyhow. *Not the human eye.* A wave of excitement crested through her body.

The pods likely worked the same way their telekinetic powers did. The same way the machine manifested food in the cafeteria. It was a hive mind, after all. And that meant their technology was connected. She just had to harness it. If she could harness it. She and Jacob had practiced and while she'd yielded no success as of yet, Calay wondered if being here, among the Others—among the stars—might inspire a stronger pull.

Calay stomped her feet. She shook her arms loose. Then cleared her mind. She focused her energy on the pod in front of her. In her mind, she pictured being inside the pod. She didn't know what that looked like, but she drew from her experience back on Earth, on the mountain. She pictured gray swirling clouds, a warm and pleasant air, completeness in its entirety.

Breathe in, breathe out.

The hair rose on the back of her neck first. Then her arms.

Calay gasped, opened her eyes. Her focus faltered and the energetic charge dissipated almost as quickly as it appeared.

"Oh my god." Calay stifled a squeal. Was this what it felt like? To connect to the hive?

"Again." Ash commanded, her voice low. She appeared from behind one of the towers of pods, following the same blue ribbon pattern, which was now aglow below their feet.

"Where'd you go?" Calay's hand flew to her chest, feeling the pounding of her heart.

"I was just checking a few things. Seems the show is right here, though."

"I did a thing. I think I did *the* thing."

"You did. Do it again."

"I don't know if I can."

"Of course you can." Ash narrowed her eyes.

"But…" Calay glanced down at the floor, breathless. Embarrassment flooded her cheeks. She was just getting her footing; she wasn't sure her connection was stable enough to continue with Ash's gaze on her. If she was. "You're watching me now."

"Do you want me to look away?" Ash stepped closer.

Calay bit her lip, raised her gaze to meet Ash's.

"No."

"Good." Ash nodded. "You have everything you need inside you, Calay."

A pang of guilt riddled its way through her. They were Ash's words, but Calay had first heard them from Jacob. Maybe it was a Térasian turn of phrase. Still, being here, alone with Ash, felt wrong. Though perhaps even more damning were Calay's thoughts of what she wanted to do with her. Like she was betraying Jacob somehow.

"Again." Ash commanded, her voice deep and gaze fierce.

Something melted in Calay. She wanted to succeed, to prove to herself she belonged here. Yet at the same time, she had an unexplainable urge to please Ash. She cleared her throat. Ignored the warmth between her legs. She visualized the pod again. Focused.

This time, the energy swept over her at once. Her hair stood up, a thrum of vibration echoed through the room. Something shifted inside her, huge and foundational. She was no longer alone. She wasn't even herself. And yet, she'd never felt surer of anything in her life.

The lingering emptiness she'd carried around most of her life seemed to evaporate. In its place, a wealth of impassioned confidence. Something full and satisfying. Something satiating. It poured into every one of her cells. Her thoughts. Any doubts she had were erased. She knew them and they knew her. Intimately. Her attention spanned eternity, and then it routed in on the pod as it clicked and whirred.

When Calay opened her eyes, the white orb bounced to life. It hovered. Blue light poured out of the bottom, waiting. But it wasn't just the one in front of her. It was all of them. Calay turned in a slow circle gaping as the way they hovered, as if waiting her command. Tears filled her eyes. She'd done it. Connected with the hive mind.

Finally.

Calay was about to gush as much when the ground seemed to shift beneath her. Her knees buckled. Her vision grew dark. She had the foreboding sense the ground was rising to meet her.

CHAPTER TWELVE

When she came to, the air was cold as ice in Calay's lungs. The back of her head was warm. The hard floor nestled against what she assumed must be countless bruises against her back.

It hurt. Everywhere.

Her eyelids fluttered. Through the haze of what was quite likely a concussion, an all-encompassing whiteness filled her vision. No, it had edges. An orb. *A pod.* A pod was hovering directly above her.

Its blue light trained on her toes. Calay's breath caught in her throat. She fought to sit upright, but the soft warmth cradling the crown of her head traveled to her shoulders and over her chest. It rested there, holding her where she lay.

She struggled harder, fear rising in her chest. She had to get out of there. Had to escape. She couldn't die. Not now. *I have to save Tess.* Tears sprung from the corners of her eyes as she clawed at the smooth floor. She gasped for air. Screamed.

"Hey, you're alright." Someone said in a soothing voice. Calay wasn't sure if it was coming from within her mind or the alien craft hovering above her. "You're okay."

"Help! Somebody help." Calay's voice rasped. Her fingernails dug into the weight still pressing down on her collarbone. It found flesh.

"Ouch, stop Calay!" The voice hissed. "You're okay. You're safe."

A vision appeared before her. A woman. She gazed down at Calay, her soft, chunky, strawberry-blonde hair aglow in stars. Her green eyes were wrought with concern, her brow furrowed. She wore a cute little ring in her button nose that glinted in the blue light. She was beautiful. An angel. There, perhaps, to take Calay home. But she couldn't leave, not without Tess.

The woman raised her hands and clutched Calay by the shoulders. She was shaking her. Then, the angel slapped her. *Not an angel.* A warm sting wound its way across Calay's cheek and behind her eyes. The fog in her brain cleared, the white swirling shadows vanished.

Reality rushed in like a tidal wave.

The vision peering down at her wasn't an angel. Far from it. An Other. Like her. Ash.

Calay was on Téras. Two billion lightyears away from Earth.

And she didn't have to save Tess; Tess was dead.

A chill ran through Calay. She shuddered, shook off the memory of Tess's lifeless face. She focused her gaze on Ash.

"What happened?" Calay whispered.

"I thought I lost you there for a second." Ash's hands slid over Calay's arms and down her back. Ash pulled her to a seat.

"I...I felt the connection to the hive. And then, I don't know. Something happened. Everything got really quiet. And dark. And then I was back on Earth, before...Before."

"You passed out."

"Did I? How long was I out?"

"Long enough to give me a scare. I've never seen someone couple with the hive so quickly. Or so powerfully. You fired up every ship in the loading bay. I'm not even sure I could do that."

"I what now?"

"It was impressive, but you overexerted yourself. It happens."

"It does? Why didn't you warn me?"

"It's not uncommon for young Térasians to have similar experiences. They're not as severe as the one you had, but harnessing that much energy takes a toll the first time or two." Ash rose to her feet and pulled

Calay along with her. "You're half-human, I wanted to see what you could do."

"You wanted to see what I could do." Calay scowled.

"I want to see a lot more than that."

Calay ignored the way Ash's words raised her pulse.

"I could have been seriously injured. I likely have a concussion. I could have died!"

"Hey now." Ash laughed, tightening her arm around Calay. "We've got you. I've got you. As I recall, you were feeling a little wobbly the first time you were in here too."

"Last time I was in here, we'd just flown several billion lightyears across the universe. You'll have to excuse me if it's taking my body a bit to catch up."

The floor pitched when Ash let go of Calay, and she immediately regretted her sarcasm. She steadied herself against the closest pod. She almost stumbled after Ash but didn't trust her legs to do what she told them. Or any other part of her. Ash lit something on fire inside of Calay. Something she thought died along with Tess.

She wanted more.

"I'm sorry for my tone. I didn't mean that." Calay said.

"Yes, you did." Ash narrowed her eyes.

"Yes, I did." Calay pulled her shoulders back, nodded.

"I like that you say what's on your mind." Ash raised an eyebrow. "That you tell the truth."

Guilt wrenched in Calay's stomach. Since Tess died, Calay *hadn't* told the truth. She'd buried it deep inside. Until now. She'd hid from it. From Jacob. From herself. She'd laid down in the darkness, waiting for it to swallow her piece by broken piece.

It wasn't until coming here, to Téras, that she started to let some of the light back in. For the last four months, Calay had turned the volume down on her life to zero. She couldn't bear to face it. To hear the irrefutable verity of what she'd done. What they'd all become. And what might lay ahead in a future that had yet to be.

Now, it was as if someone had cranked that volume up to ten.

Suddenly there were emotions. Truth. Information. Family. Reality. Gods, it was overwhelming; it was life.

Calay didn't think she'd ever live again after she squeezed Tess's last breath from her throat. Yet, here she was. On an alien planet. In a galaxy far, far away. Surrounded by the very pods that had ended life on Earth as humanity knew it. She couldn't decide if that was a fucking revolution or just plain fucked up. Either way, a rush of adrenaline curled around her spine.

She was here.

With Ash. Wanting Ash.

"I like that about you too," Calay said.

"What else do you like?"

"The other day, did you mean it when you said you could take my breath away?"

A devilish smile crept into Ash's vivid green eyes.

"Come with me."

Ash took Calay's hand and pulled her into the blue light of the pod. Calay steeled her stance, hesitated. But only for a second. She couldn't stop herself. Didn't want to.

The blue light crept across her toes, over her ankles. Then it was everywhere. It was all Calay could see. Ash wrapped Calay's hands in hers and closed her eyes.

For a moment, everything stilled, then she felt the floor of the loading bay disintegrate beneath her feet. The air around them. Until they were surrounded by a circle of long white curved columns, thick with bumpy ridges, like tree trunks. At the top, they branched out in winding, gnarled patterns. They stretched the entirety of the walls and overhead, disappearing beneath the smooth surface of the gleaming white floor. Similar to their cabins, effervescent, soft orange light emanated from some unknown source. There was a single panel of dials and switches embedded in one of the columns. Other than that, the space was empty. There were no apparent doors or furnishings. But why would there be? The Others didn't have physical bodies. Not when Calay wasn't around to project them.

"Are we...?" Calay's mouth dropped open, her eyes grew wide.

"Inside one of our shuttles?"

"A pod?"

"Yes."

"How does it fly?"

"I'm not sure you're ready for that quite yet."

Calay turned her attention away from Ash. She wanted to argue. To protest. To get a straight answer for once. But this was cool. In fact, if Calay was being honest with herself, Ash had more than delivered on her promise to show her around.

Now, she wanted to get up close and personal with the tech that had destroyed Earth. The tech she'd soon enough be in charge of as leader of their coalition. She was walking a fine line between being a bridge and a traitor. She wasn't sure which side she'd land on in the eyes of history, but she hoped it was the former.

It had to be.

She reached out and ran her hand along one of the columns. It was surprisingly soft, given the uneven, ridged looking structure. It dimpled beneath her fingertips, sprang back slowly. It made her think of the memory foam mattress she and Tess had bought shortly before the Change. They'd saved for months to afford something so luxurious, but they'd intended to spend a lot of time in bed. Together. A wave of sadness rippled through Calay. Tess was gone. That life was over. She pushed the memory aside, focused on what was in front of her.

"Why is it like this? Is it a conduit for the hive somehow?"

Ash grinned, her gaze trained on Calay's every movement. For once, Calay didn't mind. The self-consciousness she'd felt earlier in her company was tamed by her curiosity.

"How do you see out of them? How do you know where you're going? There are no windows or controls."

Calay shuffled across the pod. It wasn't much wider than she was tall. The sound of Ash's boots on the floor followed behind her. Slowly, Calay became aware of the proximity between them getting smaller. The air between them becoming warmer. When she turned around, they were separated by only a few inches.

"What's the purpose of these rafters? Where do they go?"

Ash gazed down at Calay, her mouth upturned at the corners. Calay's heart thumped against her chest, butterflies. She leaned into it. It was as if being inside one of the pods somehow made the stirring inside her more acceptable. Less illicit. Or maybe the thick alien walls simply gave Calay the privacy she needed to distance herself from what had been. She allowed herself to be in the moment. To be watched.

"There's a better use for your mouth right now than asking questions," Ash purred.

Calay swallowed, a failed attempt to stifle a moan. Ash raised a finger to Calay's parted lips, traced the bottom one. Calay grazed it with her tongue before taking Ash's long, delicate finger in her mouth. She wrapped her lips around the tip and nibbled.

"Better." Ash nodded, levelling her gaze. Her finger slipped from Calay's mouth, followed the line of her jaw before coming to rest on the soft spot between Calay's neck and collarbone.

Calay breathed in short, shallow gasps as Ash backed her one step at a time, slowly, against the wall.

Calay forced her arms still by her sides, let the intensity of Ash's gaze melt into her. It was all she could do to not pull her against her body and devour her. Want flowed between Calay's legs while she sifted through the mud of her thoughts. Guilt twitched in her mind. But why shouldn't she give in to her desires?

Tess was gone, she was never coming back. Calay had to accept that and move on. She also hadn't promised herself to Jacob. In fact, she'd done the exact opposite. It was true they were a team, but that's all they were. He needed to accept that and respect her boundaries for once. She'd told him she needed space to figure out who she was. To process everything that was happening. And she wanted this—right now—to happen. Calay nodded, ever so slightly, under the weight of Ash's palm against her throat.

Ash's hot, pink lips were over hers. She released a gravelly moan inside Calay's mouth. She could have melted. Her tongue lapped Ash up, eager for more.

Calay wrapped her arms around her waist, pulled her closer. Their bodies crashed together as Calay collapsed against the wall, gripping the leather strap of Ash's corset between her fingers. She undid the clasp, loosened the satin straps on the back. She let her own jacket fall from her shoulders.

Ash's hands found Calay's lower back, slid up the inside of her T-shirt before she pulled it over her head, discarding it on the floor. Her hands were warm, and her long nails clawed at Calay's skin. They climbed, one vertebra at a time, finding the soft indent where her head met the top of her spine. Ash wound them around Calay's ponytail, and she tugged, exposing Calay's neck. Ash's teeth carved a line from her jaw to her chest, her breath hot and moist. With the flick of her wrist, Ash unclasped Calay's bra and pulled away.

Breathless, Calay gazed at Ash. The freckles on her nose wrinkled as they grinned at each other. Calay shifted, let the bra slip over her shoulders and down her arms.

Ash grabbed it with one hand and spun Calay to face the wall with the other. She raised her arms above her head. Ash held Calay there with her round hips, her full breasts pressed into Calay's back. Calay quivered, her hips arched. Ash's tongue foraged for shivers behind her ear, she nibbled on the lobe. Her nails grazed the inside of Calay's wrist and gently pulled it up to meet the other, bringing her palms together. She flung the bra over a branch-like rafter and wound it around Calay's wrists.

"Do you want this?" Ash whispered. Calay's skin tingled under her warm breath.

Calay didn't know what was happening, but she knew she wanted it. More than she'd wanted anything in a long time. She nodded, fervently.

Ash secured Calay's hands and then guided her own through Calay's hair, around the front of her body, cupping her breasts, pinching her nipples. Then they grazed her soft stomach, over the button on her jeans. Ash unlatched it, slowly, painfully, undid the zipper. One tooth at a time. Calay's hips bucked as the tips of Ash's fingers found the front of Calay's legs. Ash pulled Calay tight against her body. She reached her long arms between Calay's thighs and parted them, tracing the seam of her jeans. Calay sighed, she ached to reach for Ash. She couldn't get close enough. She craved her underneath her skin. Inside her.

"Please," Calay moaned.

"Please what?" Ash growled.

"Please, Ash?"

"Nope."

Calay blinked. She had an idea about what Ash wanted her to say, she'd experimented with this kind of play in the past. Enjoyed it. Very much. Was this actually happening? A thrill rolled down her spine.

"Please." Calay took a breath, exhaled. "Mistress?"

"Good girl." Ash growled in Calay's ear.

Ash's fingers dipped inside the top of Calay's jeans. She explored the warm places between Calay's legs, cupped her wetness. They moved in slow circles between her flesh and the fabric, exploring every crevice. Ash palmed the soft curls at the top of Calay's mound before releasing her. She tenderly slipped off Calay's boots. Slid her jeans over her hips and down her legs. Calay had never felt so exposed. And so turned on. Ash turned her to face her, her arms still extended above. Calay drank in the sight of her. Her layered, messy hair. The wildness in her black-rimmed green eyes that somehow seemed to see deep inside of Calay, all the way down to her bones. The hunger in her smile. Ash kicked off her boots. Pulled the strap of her corset over her shoulder and let it fall to the floor. Loosened the band on her flowing pants and let them fall too. Ash stood before Calay, naked. Fuck, she was beautiful.

Ash stepped forward, took Calay's face in her hands, and kissed her deeply.

Then she dropped to her knees.

She kissed the tops of Calay's thighs, the roundness of her belly. She inhaled loudly. Then her mouth was on Calay. Between her legs. Wildly. Calay shook in her binds as she straddled Ash's face. Ash's hands grasped Calay's ass, held her where she wanted her. Ash kissed her deeper. Harder. Wetter.

Calay panted, ached, moaned.

A flutter of heat ruptured between Calay's legs. It vibrated through her body, into her chest, all the way through to the tips of her toes and her fingers. Coming one after the other, she held on to each crashing wave as if her life depended on it. It was a rush of pleasure and pain, a moment suspended in time. Until it slowed, and her body convulsed with aftershocks.

Ash smirked, pushed herself to stand, her mouth tracing Calay's skin the entire way.

She reached above and released Calay's hands. Calay spun to face her.

She pulled her back to her mouth, hungry for more.

The two women slid to the floor, their soft breasts pressed together, their warm bellies dotted with sweat.

Calay straddled Ash, her mouth wet against her soft skin. She may have come, but she wasn't nearly done yet. Calay kissed Ash's neck, her belly. Her tongue plunged between Ash's legs. Her hands did too. It didn't take long for Calay to make her come, savoring Ash's pleasure. The grinding of her hips. The arch of her back. The taste of her.

Afterward, they took a moment to catch their breath.

Calay was reeling, trying to make sense of the emotions and feelings still rattling her body. Her mind. She flung her arm to the side, searching for her clothes. This wasn't anything like how it was with Jacob. There wouldn't be cuddling or sweet jokes. The promise of something bigger. There wasn't a future here. And maybe Calay liked it that way after all. Maybe this, whatever this was, was exactly what she needed to put distance between herself and everything that had happened. Maybe this was hers, and hers alone.

Ash propped herself up on her elbows, Calay felt her gaze on her.

"I told you I could take your breath away."

Calay bit her lip. The mere mention of Ash's promise threatened to steal it away again.

"Like I said." Calay smiled from behind the curtain of her lashes. "I like that you tell the truth too."

Calay turned, now dressed. She watched Ash stand and lace herself back into her corset. As they pulled on their boots, the hair raised on Calay's arms. The air vibrated with a gentle hum. The energy seemed to shift.

"What's happening?"

"We're getting out of here before Elora has a chance to catch us." Ash grinned.

"No, the hair on my arms. It feels electric. Like it did when I connected to the hive."

Ash's eyes narrowed, she sighed.

"What is it?" Calay asked.

"It would appear we're too late."

"What do you mean?"

"Someone's already found us."

Ash took Calay's hand once again, and closed her eyes. Calay gripped Ash's fingers tighter as the floor fell away, the walls evaporated. Calay waited for the drop in her stomach and clenched her eyes shut. When she opened them, she and Ash were back outside the pod, standing hand in hand in the loading bay.

The sound of somebody clearing their throat caught her attention.

She turned to see Jacob staring at them, his mouth pressed into a firm line, eyes wide, arms crossed across his chest.

Calay knew this look.

It was the same one he wore when Tess provoked him by kissing Calay in the cave. Before everything went so horribly, irretrievably wrong. The moment simmered between them. Calay's mind spun. The guilt she'd felt earlier firmly rooted itself in her chest as a lump, thick and heavy. She tried to meet his gaze, but he wouldn't look at her.

He was focused on Ash.

"Jacob." Ash's voice spun his name like a spider spinning a delicate, dangerous web. One Calay worried she was already caught in.

"Jacob," Calay echoed, her voice not nearly so self-assured.

"I thought I told you to stay away from her." Jacob said. His blue eyes were glazed over with...what? Rage, if Calay were to guess.

"She's a big girl, Jacob. Calay can make her own decisions."

"She doesn't know what decisions she's made. Or what she's getting herself into. What you are."

"Oh, I think she has a pretty good idea about what she got herself into. Give her a kiss. You can probably still taste me."

Calay flinched, her brow furrowed as she watched Jacob's

shoulders sag and fold inward. He practically winced. She implored him to look at her, but he wouldn't meet her eyes. Would barely acknowledge her.

"You have no right."

"I have as much right as you, dear lover."

Calay's eyes widened at the pet name. She gaped at Ash and then Jacob. Was it possible she'd inadvertently inserted herself into an alien love triangle? She recalled the fight she'd witnessed between them in the hallway before. She hadn't asked either one of them what it was about. She wasn't sure she wanted to. Maybe it was reckless; maybe it was none of her business. As she watched the anger boil between the two of them, she couldn't help but wonder if their quarrel had been about her.

Either way, she'd made a mess. She was going to have to clean it up.

"I'm right here, you two." Calay fumed. She stepped forward, blocking Ash and Jacob's line of sight so they both had to look at her. "Don't talk about me as if I'm not."

"You shouldn't have come here," Jacob said, finally meeting her gaze. His eyes were cold, unyielding.

"Do you mean to this planet? Or the loading bay?" Calay bristled. It was the first time she'd questioned whether Jacob really wanted her around. He'd never looked at her like this before. Not even after she'd tied him to a log and left him for dead. She knew in a way it was her fault, coming here. With Ash. But she could have lessened the blow to them both if she hadn't gone to Jacob the night before.

"And what exactly is it that you're doing here, Jacob? Hmm?" Ash slid beside Calay, patted her ass on the way by. Her boots echoed through the cavernous space as she made her way toward the metal stairs. Calay waited, watched the way Ash sashayed away from them, like she was pleased with the damage she was leaving behind. As she reached the door, she called back over her shoulder, "Don't stay down here too long lovers, I wouldn't want to get jealous." The door slammed shut with a click behind her. Calay peeled her gaze from the platform and trained it on Jacob.

"Are you two…? I mean, have you two…?"

"No, well, yes." Jacob stumbled over his words, wrung his hands at his sides. "Not anymore. Not for a very, very long time."

"Didn't end well?"

"You could say something like that."

"I didn't know, Jacob. If I had, I wouldn't have..." Calay swallowed the rest of her sentence. Took a small step toward him. Started to reach for him but pulled her hand back as he opened his mouth to speak.

"You don't know what you've done." Jacob shook his head, dropped his gaze to the floor.

"What I've done is none of your business, Jacob. Look, we talked about this. I'm sorry, okay? I'm sorry this hurts. I never wanted to hurt you. Ever."

"It's not about that."

"Then why won't you look at me? You keep looking away, like you can't stand me. Do you hate me?" Calay's eyes swelled with tears.

She'd opened the door to her heart and with it came the very thing Calay had avoided for so long: vulnerability. It was so much easier to wall up and hide. At least that way, Calay didn't have to worry about what Jacob really thought about her. As she peered at him, she watched a chasm open between them.

He was judging her. Like her parents. Like Tess. Like she often judged herself.

She'd made a horrible mistake and the worst part was, she liked it. A pit sunk in her stomach at the realization. She owned her decision. Her choice. Her truth. As she peered at the vast distance blooming between her and Jacob, Calay winced with the pain of being punished for it.

"I don't hate you. I could never hate you, Calay."

"What is it then?"

"Ash is...complicated. She's only going to hurt you."

"Has it ever occurred to you that I might want her to hurt me?"

"What?" Jacob frowned.

"You're so kind to me, Jacob. You're sweet. And gentle. And good." Calay huffed, looking for the words. Or rather, looking for the words that would lessen the blow. She searched her mind, trying to figure out how to say what she wanted to say without sounding like a complete psychopath. Jacob's mouth hung open, waiting. *Fuck it.* "I don't want to be good."

"Calay—"

"No, let me finish. I want what she does, Jacob. I want it so badly."

"Calay, for fuck's sake, she's going to break you!" Jacob shouted, his voice booming across the loading bay.

"I want her to break me!" Calay yelled back. She tugged on the ends of her hair, stomped her foot.

"What are you talking about?"

A deep sigh escaped Calay's lips. She couldn't make Jacob understand. He was good. She wasn't. She wanted to believe in the future Elora promised. To trust that she and Jacob could find their way back to each other in time, whatever that meant. To live up to the hopes and dreams and expectations he had for her. Sweet Gods, there was so much pressure. But before any of that could happen, Calay needed something only Ash could give her.

"She and I are the same."

"What does that mean?"

"Darkness."

"Calay, you're not darkness. You are light. You are the essence of light."

"I don't feel light."

"But you are. You might not see it, but you are. You're the sun, and the moon, and every single star in that sky." Jacob pointed at the glass dome, awash in twinkling stars. He rushed forward, took her face in his hands. "You're everything. You're my everything. You are my light."

Calay shook her head, tears forced their way out the corners of her eyes. She tried to pull away, to keep them off his skin. He flinched, letting her tears roll over his forearms, but didn't let go.

Jacob pressed his lips to hers, then pulled her into his arms. She breathed in the smell of his shirt, the warmth of his embrace. She nuzzled her face into his chest, leaned into him, let herself be cradled in familiarity. She worried it might be the last time. Her shoulders shook as he held her. He showered the top of her head with kisses that were so different from Ash's. They were unhurried. Tender. Sweet. Even after all

Calay had done to Jacob, there was love in every single one. Ash's were more...malevolent. Which, underneath it all, was exactly what Calay deserved.

"Please, listen to me." Jacob mumbled into her hair. "Ash is dangerous. She's hungry for power."

If only Jacob realized how well Calay knew that. She brought a hand to her wrist, could still feel the edges where the straps of her own bra had dug into her flesh. She shivered.

"I don't know what that means."

"It means Ash isn't what you think she is."

"I'm not what you think I am."

"Yes, you are. I know who you are, Calay." He squeezed her tighter. "I wish you knew it too."

CHAPTER THIRTEEN

THE DOOR to her cabin fizzled open, and Calay plodded through. She glanced around. It was as she left it. Her single bed made with the corners tucked in tight. The glass of grapefruit juice on the small white table, stale and still. Nothing had changed, yet everything was different.

She peered through the window, yearning to somehow get out there among the Others, and yet, wanting nothing more than to make the pain from today disappear. She was finally going to take that nap. First though, she was going to get into her jammie-jams.

She'd been looking forward to slipping into something more comfortable. Something less...lived in. Something that didn't smell so much like Ash. She'd left the gray sweatsuit half-folded on the end of her bed, beside her bag. She checked under the bed, inside her pack. It was gone. As she turned, surveying the small room for any dark corners she might have missed, Calay's hand flew to her mouth, and she gasped.

Hanging on the back of the door that had reformed once she passed through it was a dark blue pantsuit. A black leather harness wrapped around the waist, adorned with gold clasps. A matching ribbon of gold fabric lined the cuffs. She ran her fingers over the starchy material. It was simple, elegant, and looked like it was cut to fit. She huffed, released a shaky breath. Calay was unsure if she was pleased to have graduated from the standard-issue sweats or disappointed.

This made her decision to join the coalition—the Others—real. Once she slipped this on, there would be no going back. She'd ached to belong —to have a place she could call home—longer than she could remember. Her fingers traced the leather, her mind fluttered to the straps on Elora's outfit. Ash's. Even Jacob had worn a similar one when they first arrived. This was it. The symbol that she was now officially one of Them. Calay grinned despite the lagging ache in her heart.

In the white and blue light shining from the glass towers outside, Calay peeled off her Earth clothes. As she starred down at them, a rumpled pile on the sparkling clean floor, she made a mental note to ask Jacob about showers—though she wasn't sure that'd even be an option. Water was poison, after all. She shrugged and slipped into her new uniform. She gazed at her reflection in the window, gaped.

She was right—every cut, every angle, designed just for her.

Beyond her visage, the outside world she still hadn't managed to explore buzzed with activity. It was the middle of the night; didn't Téras ever sleep? She plopped down on the firm mattress. She sighed, threw herself back on the bed, and wrapped her arms around herself.

How did she get here?

She'd flown, of course. In an alien pod. With the Others. She'd spent the better part of over four years running from them and now she was not only on their home planet—by her choice, no less—she was fucking two of them. Oh, and she couldn't forget the fact she'd agreed to partner with them. Align her cause with theirs. Everything about the Others gave her life meaning now.

It was who she was. What she was.

She shook her head, ran her palms over the fabric of the new uniform. Less than a week ago, she'd been living in a derelict building, fighting for everything. Expired cans of food. Dirty water. A decent night's rest. Well, she was still struggling to get her claws into that last one. The point was, while she was still on Earth, she couldn't let her guard down for a moment or she'd be risking her life. Jacob's. Now, she had a warm bed to sleep in. Clean clothes. A family. And waffles, even if she couldn't keep them down. The memory of each sweet, fluffy bite made her stomach growl. She realized she hadn't eaten since this morning. How could she? She'd been tasked to save the world. What would Tess think of what she was doing? Who she'd become?

A sad girl. A mad girl. A traitorous girl.

Not only was she now a murderer, she was collaborating with the enemy. The Térasians, as she'd learned they were called. Her mother. Calay thought she'd never see Elora again. Yet here she was. Asking her to join her. To stand beside her. To love her. How many nights had she wished for that very thing? It was everything Calay ever wanted to hear.

A whimper escaped past her lips; along with the other horrible things she'd done, she'd also broken Jacob's heart. The wound in his eyes when he'd found her in the hangar with Ash gutted Calay. If looks could kill, she should have been dead. She wanted so desperately to allow herself to depend on him, but how could she lean on him when she couldn't even lean on herself?

Calay rolled onto her side, starred out the window. A hollowness filled her chest. Tears blurred her vision. She pushed them down. She watched the human-shaped Térasians shuffling from building to building. They balanced on the same strange shoes as the red-haired one in the cafeteria, and their clothes billowed and flowed around them. Yes, everything was different from what it'd been a few days ago.

She had a place. A people, so to speak. And a purpose.

So why did she still feel lost?

A neon sign flashed in the distance, advertising some kind of charging station. It seemed so far away. So unworldly. So numb. Something bristled inside of Calay. A question. As if she needed to add another one to the ever-growing mountain of unknowns in her mind.

Why would a Térasian sign be in English?

It occurred to her it could be a projection, like The Other's physical forms. Something her mind couldn't understand in its original shape or language, and so the hive molded it into something she could. She still didn't get how it all worked.

Her shoulders slumped as she realized she might never understand.

She sat up, rubbed her eyes. Her stomach growled again. There were an infinite number of problems running through her mind, but there was one she could solve. And it started with more waffles.

THE CAFETERIA WAS QUIET FOR ONCE. CALAY WAS GRATEFUL for the reprieve. She had enough noise running through her head, a bit of peace and quiet would probably do her good.

She made her way across the room, past the chairs still lined with plastic and bubble wrap. She'd carried visions of thick whipped cream and liquid honey in her mind the whole way here. She approached the shiny silver machine at the center when the lights flickered off.

She halted. A few moments passed. Her stomach growled. Again. Did she brave the darkness only to risk a fractured toe or bruised knee walking into a table she couldn't see?

She was just so hungry. And tired. And tired of being hungry.

She was about to inch her way toward where she knew the box would be when the lights came back on, without event. *That was weird.* She stepped forward, but a sputtering of light caught her attention. It was coming from down the hall at the far end of the cafeteria.

Calay's pulse quickened. Ash had told her there was storage down there. "Nothing terribly exciting," were her exact words, if Calay remembered right. Nothing about this trip had been boring, and Ash's words felt hollow. Like she was evading Calay's questions. Hiding something. Jacob had warned her Ash wasn't what she thought, that she was hungry for power. Calay still didn't know what that meant, but maybe the answers lay in whatever was beyond the door at the end of that hallway.

A rush of curiosity fuelled Calay's legs, propelling her forward. She bypassed the shiny box with the food and made straight for the corridor. She moved quickly. If she was caught now, she didn't know what they'd do to her. Sure, they'd given her a sparkly new uniform, but she wasn't really one of them. Not yet. She still had no clearance to access secure areas of the building. She hadn't even met the hybrids who'd supposedly just arrived. She was among the Others but was still Other to them.

The lights flicked above, Calay's breath caught in her throat. Something echoed back the way from which she'd come. She kept moving, chanced a glance behind her, bracing herself for what might jump through the shadows that disappeared and reappeared with every flicker of light. But she was alone.

She reached the door. It was as she remembered it—unlike the rest of the ship, this one had no white panels. It was rectangular, a large, black window at the center. She peered through the glass and couldn't see a thing. For all she knew, there was nothing beyond this gateway but oblivion. *Or things that go bump in the night.* Calay shivered, her heart thumped against her chest. She wrapped her hand around the cold, metal handle. Which was another thing none of the other doors seemed to have. They operated with motion sensors, movement. This one was secured with a good old fashioned steel bolt. As if the Others wanted to keep people out. Or lock them in. Calay shook off the creeping anxiety oozing down her back. This could be her last chance to find out what, exactly, was down there.

She squeezed the handle and slipped through; the door latched firmly behind her.

The blackness was impenetrable. Complete. The most terrifying thing Calay could have imagined. While she knew it was going to be dark, she'd expected some of the light would have fought its way through the window behind her. It didn't.

With breath short in her lungs, she shuffled forward, her hands tracing the wall for a light switch. The toe of her boot caught on the lip of what she was sure was a sharp, metal grate. She stumbled on it, the metallic sound echoed through the dark space. One, two, three flailing steps and a long metal bar caught her by the hips. She grasped at it. A railing. Where there was a railing, there were stairs.

Her arms extended along the bar, she took baby steps, hoping she wouldn't pitch forward to her death. She was right. The railing was long, cold, and straight, until it curved sharply downward.

She lowered a foot to find a narrow foothold. Her other one followed. Taking each stair one at a time, she climbed down further into the darkness. One minute passed. Another. It seemed the staircase would never end. The blackness, too. It was as if what she was feeling inside had finally bubbled up and out of her, swallowing her whole.

After what felt like a lifetime, the feeling of grates beneath her feet ended, giving way to a smoother, more slippery surface. Calay imagined in her mind's eye she was likely standing in a room not unlike the loading bay. If that was true, she'd reached the bottom.

Still, she clung to the railing. Her breathing shallow and ragged. It was the only sound and it was deafening. She thought about calling out, just to cut through the silence, but the risk of getting caught somewhere she didn't belong sent a chill down her spine, which was already coated in cold sweat. Besides, it was highly unlikely anyone would hear her. Down here. In the dark. Alone. There was nobody down here with her.

Was there?

Calay clenched her eyes shut, tried to slow her thoughts. She swallowed the lump forming in her throat. Of course she was alone. But then, as much as she tried, she couldn't stop the question from circling in the corners of her mind: what *was* down here?

She pried her cramped fingers off the railing. She tried to recall the layout of the loading bay. It had been a ridiculously large room. Brimming with pods. Through the glass dome, she'd seen stars. When Calay looked up here, none of their twinkling light made it down to her. It was just more darkness.

She didn't know how that was possible, but then again, nothing from the last week seemed real. Yet, it existed. Calay focused on that fact. That, and physics. *The room must have four walls, for fuck's sake. There has to be a switch somewhere.* With the railing as her starting point and her arms stretched ahead, Calay made her way to what she guessed was the closest wall.

She bumped into it a few thousand moments later. It was ridged, formed by several curved columns, like the inside of the pods. *That's new.* The loading bay's walls had been smooth, like the floor. So why was this one different? She traced the surface, inching forward, desperate for something, anything, that would shed some light on her current situation.

She found what felt like a button. Small, flat, recessed against the wall. This had to be it. Her mind spun as she realized it could be a button for anything. It could open a wall in the side of the building, like a garage door. She still wasn't sure if the human-part of her could survive in the alien atmosphere. That could be bad. *Really bad.* It could be an alarm. If it was, it might alert the Others of her location, she could get in serious trouble. As if she wasn't already in serious trouble. For all she knew, the button could be a destruct switch, and she'd incinerate herself and anything else that was in that room.

She took a deep breath. Exhaled.

She pushed the button.

A loud buzz filled the air. A mechanical whir. Then there was light.

Calay covered her eyes, winced. It was bright. Brighter than bright. It made her yearn for the darkness she'd wanted so desperately to escape. She covered her face with her hands, peeked through the pink gaps in her fingers.

Calay shrieked.

She stumbled back against the wall. It lacked the softness of the pod interior and the ridged edges cut into her back. Her thighs. She stuffed her hands in front of her mouth, trying to silence the echo of her voice cresting across the space. Her eyes grew wide, unable to look away as she scanned the never-ending nightmare before her. A wave of nausea churned in her stomach, threating to turn her insides out.

She waited, paralyzed by the fear radiating through her body.

When nothing moved, she released a breath.

She ran her hands along her legs. Slid down against the wall. Recounted what she knew. She and Jacob had flown across the universe to his—her—home planet, Téras. She'd just entered through the door at the top of the very long, very steep metal staircase and made her way here somehow, without knocking into any of *them*. She was in a room, like the loading bay—wide, cavernous, big enough to swallow an army of alien pods. Shuttles, Ash had called them. Only now they weren't shuttles.

They were her mother.

Calay breathed between her knees, tried to make sense of what was before her. *This isn't right. This can't be right.* But she didn't know what was right anymore.

She peered at the rows and rows of mother figures from her crouched position. They stood, still as the grave, one row after another for as far as Calay could see.

There were so many. Thousands. And they looked just like Elora.

It took everything Calay had not to turn screaming for the door. She could run, but if she did, would they come after her? The thought made her blood run cold. She fought against the urge to lie down and wait for her heart to finally give out and instead, resolved to get a closer look. She'd wanted to find out what was beyond the door at the end of the hallway. She'd gotten her answer. *Be careful what you wish for.* She bit her lower lip, inhaled a sharp breath, and pressed herself to stand.

As quietly as she dared, she made her way through the rows of Elora look-alikes.

The resemblance to her mother was uncanny. They were the same towering height, the same voluptuous proportions. They even wore her cropped silver hair the same way. Elora's deep brown, almost black, eyes starred back at Calay, lifeless. Cold. Dead.

A surge of anger rippled through her. Her mother was Other, but she belonged to Calay. She'd just gotten her back. After all these years. Calay pursed her lips and balled her fists against her sides. These monstrosities had no business wearing Elora's strong cheekbones or delicate nose. Her thin, soft lips and pronounced jaw. That face was for laughing and smiling when Calay and her dad surprised her with breakfast on Mother's Day. Her long fingers were for gardening and pruning flowers. Her arms were for hugging. The little girl inside Calay raged at the replica's existence. These were not her mother. Even though they donned the same olive-green hooded tunics with slits in the thighs that Elora wore. The same black tights underneath, the leather harnesses strapped against their chests. The big, beaded earrings and clunky heeled boots.

As Calay gazed into one of the clone's faces, a wall of tears sprung behind her eyes. The stony expression on its face reminded her of the day she'd come out to her parents. The moment her mother had stared at her, dead eyed, from the front window of the house, watching her daughter drive away from their family farm for the last time. After they'd forced her to go.

Calay had nowhere to go now.

She dropped to the floor and screamed again. She screamed for the time she and Elora lost because her parents wouldn't accept her as queer. For the life she'd been forced to take from Tess. For the pain she couldn't escape, no matter where she was in the universe. It haunted her and everyone she loved. Calay's voice gave out and her screams subsided. She grovelled at the feet of the mother-figures, and she cried. Tears streamed down her face and onto the smooth, blue ribboned floor.

She wanted to help her mother, to save their planets. But how could she do that when she couldn't even save herself? Or Jacob? She regretted what she'd done to him, and what she would likely still do to him as long as he clung to her. He didn't deserve that. He deserved better. But better wasn't an option. This was who she was. What life was now. And Calay wasn't entirely convinced that life was worth saving.

Nothing was worth this torture.

Calay sniffed, stood, and reached up, her hand shaking both from fear and outrage. Her fingers grazed the face of one of the mother-figures. The skin was surprisingly supple, pulled tight across its high forehead and crest of its brow. She traced a line to its cheek. Poked it. Again. Harder this time. She wanted to claw its face off. To destroy them all. For being here when they—her mother—should have been with Calay all those years. Instead, she'd been here, on Téras. Alive.

Unless Elora wasn't alive to begin with.

Dread crept through Calay, one inch at a time, as an understanding dawned on her.

Her mother was Other. They could survive a lot, but not everything. Jacob had been clear before—if they sustained enough damage, they couldn't regenerate and repair themselves. They were as capable of dying as a human being. He'd told her as much after Calay found out she was half-alien herself. So if Elora really had been torn to pieces and scattered across the community in which she'd raised Calay, she wouldn't have survived. Corporeally, or otherwise. She would have died, as bodies do. As her father did when Calay buried that pitchfork in his brain. He said himself there was nothing left after the mob attacked Elora. Calay needed more answers about that day, but she'd never be able to ask him.

The realization itched at Calay's mind.

Her legs begged for her to run from this place. From the truth. But as she stood at the centre of that room, surrounded by mother-lookalikes, she couldn't. Not anymore. She was done with running. Maybe Jacob was right. She wasn't entirely darkness. Not yet. It was time to shine a light on the truth about who—and what—she *really* was. About where she came from.

Calay had seen what the Others could do through the hive mind. She'd harnessed a glimmer of it in the loading bay. Imagine what she could do with it in time. As a species, they could communicate across galaxies. Transport themselves and others like them to distant places. It was how they piloted the pods and if they could animate ships with their minds, what did they intend to do with these? An army of Eloras. A revelation rolled through Calay's body. Her mother was dead. So for her to exist here, row after terrifying row in this place, that meant...her mother was never really her mother.

She was one of these. Whatever *these* were. Always had been. Her memories and personality were likely transferred telekinetically, from one to the next. Through the hive.

If that was true, everything Elora told Calay since her arrival had been a lie.

Elora wasn't her mother on Earth.

She wasn't her mother now.

She was something else.

CHAPTER FOURTEEN

THIS MACHINE. This alien. Whatever it was, was not human. It wasn't even Térasian, was it?

Blood rushed through Calay's ears. Her heart thundered in her chest. She tried to wrap her thoughts around the lifeless face in front of her. What the implications might be. If what Jacob told her was true, the Others didn't have physical forms, so theoretically, they might have a warehouse full of human bodies to inhabit should the need call for it. Like when they—when he—appeared in her camp that first night. But she knew, deep down, they didn't.

She shook her head, fought through the mental fog threatening to drown her. The Others, in a way, shape-shifted, depending on the species they were trying to pass for. According to Jacob, and even Elora herself, every "person" Calay saw was a mental projection. A physical manifestation her tiny human brain could comprehend. So why the fuck were the bodies in this room all the same shape? A human shape? The shape of her mother?

Calay resisted every instinct she had and squinted, peered closer.

The face certainly looked like her mother. She grazed its cheek with the palm of her hand. It felt like her mother. Calay, bracing herself, leaned in and inhaled. It even smelled like her mother.

"The fuck?" She whispered as she pulled back and found its near-black eyes, wide open, and trained on her.

Calay's hands flew to her mouth. She stumbled backward into the next row of Eloras. She tripped on the long flowing fabric of their pants and landed hard on the smooth floor.

"Ouch!" Calay's teeth chattered together upon impact. A metallic taste filled her mouth. The inside of her cheek pulsed. She'd bitten it. She took a moment, plying the sharp ache with the tip of her tongue. Something inside her implored her to move. *You're wasting time!* But she knew, all the way into her bones, it was already too late. Her skin tightened into a mountain range of goosebumps.

She took a deep breath, pushed her hair out of her eyes, and forced herself to look up.

She was surrounded.

Dark silhouettes, lit from above, peered down at Calay. A memory floated through her mind of the day Ash had shown up at the Loft. When Calay had run away from them. From the truth. To the theater. She'd fallen through the floor, landed in the soft pile of soiled linens. When she'd gazed up, all those shadows were looking down at her, daring her to move. She'd reminded herself then that zombies weren't real. But monsters were.

Calay pressed herself against the cold, hard floor. She'd survived then. Would she survive now?

She shut her eyes, hoping it was just another hallucination. She opened them, stared. *Nope, still there.* Their eyes leered back. They were like black holes threatening to swallow her. Still as the dead. As if someone had frozen them in place. Yet, she knew that wasn't the case at all.

They were alive.

Calay's gaze darted from one to another. An endless sea of mother-shaped bodies. As they statued around her, something wasn't quite right about them. Their heads seemed too small atop their wide shoulders. Their backs too round, as if bulging out of the seams that held their tunics together. Their arms and legs too long. They'd looked normal only a few moments ago. Well, as normal as a sea of Elora replicas could look, anyhow.

Calay almost laughed at the absurdity of it. The panic that had dug its way into her gut, firmly planted itself inside her. She felt it growing, like a child. A horrible, horrible child. It gnawed at her insides, clawed to get out. She felt it climbing its way through her stomach and up past her chest. It scraped at her throat. A scream formed in Calay's mouth, but no sound passed her lips.

The shapes began to move.

Their chests heaved, their arms stretched. Some reached further than others, their fingers grazing the top of her head, tangling in Calay's hair. She scrambled backward. Bumped into a pair of legs. Another set of arms. They curled around her wrist, moulding to the curves of her body like putty. Another wrapped around her neck. Hands grasped around her waist. They pulled violently, as if trying to reach inside to yank her insides out. Cold breath pooled on her cheeks.

They were coming for her.

They were here.

The scream that was waiting, so impatiently, to make itself heard erupted from somewhere deep inside Calay. It poured from her throat as the bodies pressed her against the floor, which seemed to melt beneath their weight. Her flesh sizzled where their skin met hers, as if on fire. The smell of burning hair filled her nostrils. She spun, clawed at the grip they had on her, desperate. She resisted their pulls, struggled against their restraints.

If she didn't do something soon, she was going to die.

Alone.

In the hangar.

In the universe.

In her pain.

It was all that ever was. All that ever would be.

No.

The instinctual need to survive, despite her best efforts to sabotage herself up until this point, drove Calay forward.

Half crouched, half standing, she leapt through the heaving wall of black. The soft fabric of their clothes felt like sandpaper, scratching. As if it too could grab hold. Swallow her. Slough off the outer layer, expose the raw flesh beneath. She came out the other side, her shoulder collided with the floor. She left a layer of skin on the smooth surface as she pushed herself to stand. She barely noticed the searing pain it left in its place.

Thousands of mother-figures were standing, facing her. She hadn't seen them turn. Hadn't heard them. Even now, they made no noise. It was silent save for her raging breath. Their dark eyes clung to her like oil.

She forced herself away from them, toward the door at the top of the staircase. Would she make it? They moved so fast. So silent. So inhuman.

Calay turned and ran. Her feet pounded against the metal stairs, the echo reverberating through her teeth and across the vast room. The door was so impossibly far away. But she'd done the impossible before, hadn't she? She'd traveled across an alien-ravaged country. Found the love of her life. Then killed her. She'd survived then, she'd survive now.

She had to.

She took each step like it might be her last. Thrusting one heavy boot-laden foot after the other, she climbed. Higher, faster. The door was closer now. Her thighs burned, her lungs screamed for oxygen. She didn't dare a glance back, couldn't afford the risk of falling or slowing down. She focused on nothing but landing each footfall. Heard nothing but the sound of rushing blood in her ears. The door grew nearer yet. Her arms flailed at her sides, lashing forward for momentum. Her legs begged to give up. To rest. But the door was right there. She could almost reach out and touch it. If she could only make it a few more feet.

She pictured being back on Earth, in Jacob's arms. Thought about how if they made it out of this alive, she'd get her shit together. Make things right. For him. Finally.

Her fingers clasped around the cold metal. To die now, when she was so close. She couldn't. Light from the hallway on the other side glowed beyond. Her fingers clumsy and swollen, she wrangled the latch. *Push the handle down. Push the handle down. Push the fucking handle down.* Calay pushed the fucking handle down.

She flung the door open wide, it banged against the outer wall. She was in the hallway. But she wasn't safe. Not yet. She whipped around, her hair caught in her mouth, whipped her eyes. She dove forward, reaching for the door as it slowly hissed on its hinges.

"C'mon." Calay pulled against the hydraulic resistance.

With a satisfying click, the latch locked. Calay gasped for air, slumped against the cold white exterior surface. It was bright. Almost blindingly so. She exhaled. The door was closed.

She was on one side of it. Those *things* were on the other.

She knew that still didn't mean she was safe.

She bristled, brought her face to the window. Leaned closer. She prayed to the stars she wasn't about to come face to face with one of them. She didn't. She pressed her hands against the cold glass. Peered into the darkness. She couldn't see them down there. Not a single one. Though she could feel them. They were staring at her. With those black eyes. And the faces that looked so familiar, so foreign.

She'd almost died.

A shudder whirled through Calay. If they'd wanted to kill her, they would have. She was well within their grasp, as evidenced by the tears in the arm of her new uniform. The friction burn on her shoulder. The rat's nest that was her hair. So why hadn't they charged after her?

She wasn't going to wait around to find out whether or not they were going to change their minds. Instead, she turned and ran as far away from that room of nightmares as possible.

SHE HURLED HERSELF DOWN THE HALLWAY BACK TO HER room and her pulse didn't slow until the cabin door swooshed shut.

She grabbed her bag, stuffed what little she'd pulled from it back inside. The uneaten cans of vegetables. A few balled-up articles of clothing. She found herself lamenting the loss of the sweatshirt again. Small comforts went a long way when she was so far from home.

After she was forced out of her parent's house, she'd found solace in her new apartment, cozying up with a cushy blanket and a good book. Hot mugs of Sleepytime tea. The warmth of Tess's embrace.

The sweatshirt had felt like that. If only a little. Calay sighed, scanned the room.

The apples sat untouched on the window ledge. She wasn't confident wherever she and Jacob were going to end up would have the same food technology as this place, so she reached for one. It squished like Jell-O between her fingers.

"Ew!" She dropped what she could to the floor.

It splattered at her feet. A ripe, rotten scent hovered in the air. A sticky fruit sludge coated her hand. In the rising sunlight, it glistened.

Calay gagged, reached for the blanket on her bed. She cleaned her hand off the best she could, discarded the apple into the trash. The fruit was gone, but the smell wasn't; it lingered. *What would cause a perfectly good fruit to go rancid so fast?* Calay cringed, pulled her gaze from the garbage can to the view outside.

Beyond the wall-length window, the sky was aglow in purples and pinks. The moons were curving beyond one side of the horizon as the enormous sun crested the other. Long shafts of silver and glass caught the warm rays, deflecting them in every direction.

She searched her mind, tried to make sense of the apple. The Eloras. All of it. She stood there long enough to watch the shadows retreat from the mountains, their white and gold peaks sparkling under the rising sun. With the ever-growing light of the day, Calay almost allowed herself to imagine what she'd experienced in the basement was just a very bad dream. That she was on Téras, reunited with her long-lost mother and together, they were going to save Earth. That the Térasians were a peaceful, highly advanced species, and they were going to usher the human population back into their humanity.

If she closed her eyes and tried hard enough, she could almost believe it.

Almost.

The moment she reopened them, the fantasy gave way to truth. The mother-figure's cold, dead eyes that were far too wide, too monstrous, peering down at Calay. The feeling of their long, bony fingers scraping at her skin. The fact that her mother died on Earth and yet, somehow, against all logic and imagination, she existed. Here. By the thousands.

No, this wasn't right.

This was very, very wrong.

Calay needed to get the hell out of there, and Jacob was coming with her. She didn't know where they'd go, but there was a whole planet of places she'd rather be than this one. If only they could figure out how to get the hell out of the building. There had to be a way. She was sure of it.

She leaned her forehead against the curved glass. Slowed her breathing. She rationed that if the stars in her eyes were a roadmap home to Téras, then maybe there was a building map or something stored somewhere in the hive mind too. It made sense, didn't it? The hive had granted her access to power the pods. Jacob used it to communicate with the Others in other galaxies. Someone, somewhere, must have a layout of the building. She just needed to connect with it.

Calay inhaled a sharp breath, her warm exhale pooled on the glass in front of her.

She cleared her thoughts. Closed her eyes. Imagined the energy she'd felt earlier when she'd summoned the power of the pods, pulsating through her limbs. The hair raising on her arms. She opened her mind, visualized an interconnected freeway of information. She pictured the gray swirling matter enveloping her. The warmness of it. The feeling of everything and nothingness, all at once.

She could feel the hive.

It was close.

A thrum of buzzing swarmed the room. As if it were alive.

Then, silence.

Nothing happened.

Calay blinked open her eyes, looked around. She felt no great pull to the All-Being she'd experienced before. She was still in her cabin. Shaking and alone. Nothing had changed.

"Damn it." Calay hissed. Why was this so hard? She'd done it earlier with Ash. Then Ash's words came back to Calay. "Again," she'd said.

"Right." Calay nodded and readjusted her stance.

She softened her gaze, took a big breath in. Exhaled. Focused. She pulled on that intangible, hollow pit that had always lived deep inside her. The one that never felt full, no matter where she was. What she did. Who she fucked. It was the ache to belong. To breathe. To be loved. It was constant and it had, over the years, nestled in Calay's soul. She tugged on that string. Of never being good enough. Never being strong enough. Just simply never being enough. All of it was the Otherness inside her. It was something she'd resisted. Something she had yet to claim. An ache vibrated through her body with the knowledge of what she now knew, and she didn't want to. The secrets the Others carried. The truths she'd discovered. Yet, she needed to own that connection, now more than ever.

The hive lived there. Her truth did, too.

An inky feeling strummed in her stomach. It raced across her limbs. It almost seemed to explode out the top of her head, her body trembled with the force.

The buzzing filled the air again.

A haze of silver lines exploded across her vision.

The landscape outside the window faltered.

Calay gasped.

"What the fuck was that?" she whispered, allowing the powerful energy to drain from her body.

She searched the view through the glass. Everything was as it had been a few moments ago. She watched the small dots of Térasians moving outside from structure to structure. The sun continued to rise. A bright blue, long-necked bird soared above it all, as if keeping watch. It was peaceful. Serene. Perfect. She swallowed, bit her lip. *Too perfect?* She didn't know what she'd done, but she was compelled to find out.

She did it again.

As the energy of the hive flowed through Calay's blood, the peaceful scene outside split in two.

Then three.

Fissures cracked across the terrain, as far as she could see. Calay frowned, brought her hand to the window. No, it wasn't the glass. The fractures were beyond, outside.

The room seemed to shake with her effort. Her limbs too. She needed to hang onto the connection. She remembered Jacob's gentle encouragement, "you have everything you need inside you, Calay." She tried to clear the questions pinballing inside her head, to allow the buzzing to fully consume her.

To be here, now.

Then, her mind caught hold of a ragged edge, and a rift cut across the landscape and tore it apart like an old sheet of paper.

Téras disappeared, and in its place, a nightmare.

Calay didn't think it could get worse than the cloned mothers in the basement. But it did.

The room tilted when she saw they weren't on a planet at all. What she was standing in wasn't a building. She was aboard a very large starship, hurtling through deep space. So deep, the stars didn't even shine.

For as far as she could see out into the distance, there was nothing. Only a jet-dark blackness, dotted with what looked like big fucking rocks.

Tears filled Calay's eyes. She swiped at them, pressed herself harder against the arch of the window. *This can't be real?* She coaxed herself into the shape of the glass.

The buzzing ceased, replaced by the sound of rushing blood in her ears. In the ship's wake, rocks were pulled along, colliding violently with other debris. Her gaze followed the trail, one dark round shape at a time, finally coming to rest on what appeared to be, if she didn't know any better, a planet. The wide, round curvature was unmistakable, visible in the darkness only for the red fire raging from deep within its fractured, crumbling surface.

They weren't pulling just any regular space-rocks behind them, she realized, it was pieces of that planet.

From the moment she arrived at this place, nothing had been what it seemed. Elora had manipulated her. What she'd believed to be true—

everything—had been a lie. Calay trembled, her vision darkened. She clawed at the glass, trying to maintain a hold on her reality. Any reality.

She dry heaved as she sunk against the window, her legs collapsed beneath her. She gasped for breath but found none. Panic coursed through her body.

She was trapped.

She tried to look away from the destruction.

From the fiery, dying planet.

From the truth.

But even as she lay there, weeping on the smooth white floor, Calay already knew.

What she was looking at was Téras.

What else could it be?

The Others had destroyed their home planet, and now, they were coming for hers.

CHAPTER FIFTEEN

CALAY DIDN'T WANT to die.

She'd thought so at one time. Several, actually. Over the last four months, it had occurred to her how easy it would be. How meaningless. Humanity was gone. Tess was gone. And if the Others had their way, Earth would be too, soon.

So where did that leave her?

Without any real connection to a place, or to people, what value did life have? She'd wanted to belong somewhere so badly, to find a home she could call her own. She'd followed Tess across the country to make a place for herself. Then across the Pacific Northwest. She'd given up her family in the process. Herself, she realized, as she boxed herself smaller and smaller to fit into Tess's world. It wasn't until she was free of Tess that she realized how big the outside world had truly become. How dangerous.

She snivelled and her shoulders shook with sobs. She curled into a ball on the floor and wrapped her arms around her knees.

Of course, she'd understood the dangers of the Others on Earth. Watched them level her apartment block. Then their city. Finally, their world. An entire civilization was brought to its knees, grovelling.

Begging. The aliens were relentless. As was Calay when she'd grappled with Tess in that cave. Wrapped her hands around her throat. Squeezed. Calay shuddered. *We always hurt the ones we love the most.* But that wasn't entirely true, was it? She'd fought for their love. Done everything she could to nurture it. Maintain it. She'd risked her life after Tess went missing. She'd risked Jacob's. Even now, billions of lightyears away from Earth, she'd done what little she could to shelter what remained of Tess. Calay had locked herself in loneliness. Somewhere Jacob couldn't reach her. Where no one could. Except the ghosts of past lives. They haunted her. Taunted her. Attached themselves to her memories. To her heart. She couldn't escape them. Every time someone reached down into the depths and grazed Calay's outstretched arm, she'd pull it back. Afraid to ask for the help she desperately needed. To risk losing anyone else. To love. She'd given up everything for Tess. In life and in death. Maybe that was the problem.

Calay had nothing left.

It was all so empty. *She* was empty.

Or at least, she was, until now.

Now, she had a purpose.

Dragging her legs underneath her, Calay inched her way to sit. She propped herself on her knees, took a deep breath.

She stared out at the debris rippling in round waves behind the ship, the remnants of a planet, and a hollowness filled her chest. What species had died there, in the explosion? What lives were forsaken? New tears formed in the corners of her eyes. She blinked them away.

In the vast darkness of deep space, the destroyed planet looked almost unreal. As if she was watching it on a movie screen, or it was happening to somebody else. That's the way she'd experienced most of life now. Everything she'd ever loved felt so far away. So impossible. So...not hers.

She'd had about enough of that. There wasn't much she could do about the past. But there was plenty she could do about the future. *Her* future.

She clawed at the window, pushed herself to stand. Her legs

wobbled, she took a moment to steady herself. To focus. There was no denying the truth: she was half Other. An ache rippled through her heart. She didn't want it to be so, but it was. Facts were facts. She didn't know if she belonged on Earth anymore, if she even had a right to be there in the first place. She knew she definitely didn't belong here, either. Among Them. They'd asked for her help, implored her to take on their cause. And she'd reluctantly agreed. That was before Calay knew what the cause really was.

Something wrenched loose in her chest, as if the ghosts clinging to her were ripped from her body. Her soul. It didn't feel exactly free, but it was lighter. She steeled her resolve. Earth may or may not have been Calay's true home, but she'd be damned if she was going to let the Others destroy it.

The strap of her pack dug into her fingers as she snatched it up from the floor and headed out the door of her suite in search of Jacob. He might have been Other too, but he was her friend. He was in love with her, for fuck's sake. He'd know what to do.

She tore down the corridor, one foot falling in front of the other as she raced through the hallways.

It made sense now why they all looked the same. Why she could walk for what seemed like hours and never find a way outside. Some corridors looped back on themselves, others fed into offshoots which inevitably shepherded her back the way she'd come. Some were just dead ends. They sprouted like tentacles, creating the illusion of a vast building. Different pathways. Options. But they were all the same. Like the ship was endlessly eating itself, swallowing her whole. There were no real choices. No doors. Why hadn't she seen it before? *Buildings have doors, idiot.* Of course, ships had doors too. But if Calay had learned anything about the Others in the last several hours, it was that they were less than forthcoming. They hid things in plain sight, behind obscurities, and lies. She must have walked every inch of this place since she'd arrived. Felt every wall. She'd found nothing. Except for the loading bay. There had to be a hatch of some kind there, right? The pods had to get in somehow. *They have to get out too.* She made a mental note to pull on that thread later. There wasn't time right now to explore what that might look like. First, she had to get Jacob, and then they had to get the hell out of there.

Pushing her legs faster until she reached Jacob's room, Calay slid to a stop. She rapped on the door harder than she needed to. It slid open almost instantaneously.

Jacob stood on the other side, his smile widened as he scanned her uniform.

"I have to talk to you," Calay said.

"So now you're ready to talk?"

"Jacob."

"I see you already got your first halter. It's official, you've achieved rank."

Calay frowned. So the leather harnesses did mean something. She knew it. It didn't matter though. Nothing did. Except getting Jacob back on her side.

"Jacob, please…"

He looked at her, his eyes narrowed before they gave way to a mischievous grin. He motioned to step back, Calay's shoulder collided with his chest as she pushed her way past. "Please, after you."

"I found out something terrible."

"I should have warned you about the food. It looks fancy, but most of it comes from a box." Jacob's gaze followed Calay inside, the door swooshed shut. He leaned against it, crossed his arms over his chest.

She blinked. "What?"

"Can you imagine how gutted I was when I found out the mac and cheese was made from freeze-dried noodles and powdered sauce? Garbage."

"No, Jacob I'm serious."

"So am I. That processed food will kill 'ya."

"Jacob!" Calay screamed. She balled her fists at her side, slowed her breathing. "Stop!"

"Aye aye, Captain." Jacob nodded, his face solemn.

Calay stared at him in the cabin's golden light. Her legs trembled. Her lower lip, too.

"Okay, I'm sorry. I'm stopping, okay?" Jacob's brow raised; he stepped forward.

Calay nodded, she surprised herself by reaching for his hand. He took it in his own, his elegant fingers clasped her short, stubby ones. She starred at them, wound together, before pulling her gaze up over the veins in his forearm, the bulge in his biceps. She gazed at his pouty mouth, the chisel in his cheekbones. Finally, she met his eyes.

"Whatever it is, we'll handle it." He nodded. "Like we always have."

"I don't know how we'll handle this." She shook her head.

"Slow wide turns, right?"

"Right."

"Okay, so tell me. What terrible thing did you find out? Aside from the pre-packaged food."

Calay took a deep inhale. Exhaled. Steadied her breath.

"The Others. They aren't what they seem."

"What do you mean?" Jacob squeezed her hand.

"They…" Calay searched for the right words. For any words. "They aren't what they've said. They—Elora—told me they were trying to save Earth. To save humans. But I don't think that's true. I saw something. Outside my window."

"What do you think you saw?" Jacob's lips pulled tighter at the edges for just a moment before he relaxed them. Calay almost missed it. Almost.

"I saw…death." Calay's voice cracked on the last syllable.

"You saw death?"

"I broke through the hologram on my window, and I saw rocks. Big ones. There was a long line of them, Jacob. I didn't think it was real. It couldn't have been. But it was. It was!"

"Hang on a second. What do you mean you broke through the hologram?"

"The city. It was just a picture. A video. A simulation. It wasn't real." Calay gasped for breath as the words finally started to tumble out of her mouth. They were awkward and felt too big for her lips. The truth often was. It was part of the reason she hid so much. Why she resisted letting others in. She swallowed, pressed on. "I tried to use the power of the hive to connect with a larger information circuit. To find a way outside. A door. I needed some fresh air. I felt stuck, and it didn't make sense. Something felt wrong. So I pushed. And then the outside wasn't outside anymore. It shattered and I could see everything. We aren't on a planet at all."

"I see," Jacob said. Slowly. Too slowly. "And instead of the city, you say you saw rocks?"

"Yes, I saw rocks! I followed them all the way behind the ship and there was a planet. On fire. Téras. It's been destroyed. They blew it up."

"I don't believe it."

"It's true, Jacob. I saw it."

"Okay. Hang on." Jacob shook his head, released Calay's grasp. He paced across the room before flopping onto the bed. He ran his hands over his face. "If Téras has been destroyed, and we're not on planet, then where are we exactly?"

"We're on a ship. The Others' ship. You must know this."

Jacob nodded, cast his eyes down at the floor, said nothing.

"They destroyed Téras. They're going to destroy Earth too," Calay continued.

"What?"

"I don't know how to explain it. But I feel it. I know I'm right. Maybe it's a subconscious part of me that's connected to the hive mind? Maybe it's intuition. I don't know where it comes from. But something's felt off since we got here. It's been worse since I found that horror house of Eloras they keep in the basement."

"I'm sorry, what now? You didn't…"

"Thousands of them. Elora clones. They attacked me. That's why my uniform looks like this." A chill crawled around the base of Calay's spine, pulled taught. She shivered. "Jacob, the woman running this ship isn't my mother. She's…something else. She's one of them."

"One of them?"

"She told me humans attacked the Others first. That killing humans was just self-defense. That we could save both our civilizations. But she lied. It wasn't true. None of it was fucking true. Everything she told me is a lie. I think aliens attacked Earth. Just like they attacked Téras. There's nothing left of that planet or the life there. And...I think we're next."

"How can you be sure you're right?"

"Because..." Calay faltered. Her words caught in her throat. Jacob's question stung. He'd never second guessed her before. But he was right to ask. She was often wrong. She'd made a lot of mistakes in her life. More than she could count. It was a big part of the reason she'd kept her distance from Jacob before this. Why she'd locked herself away. Why she resisted his kindness. How could she be sure about something as important as the fate of the planet when she couldn't even trust herself to make good decisions? Calay shook her head, closed her eyes. "Come see what I saw. Come to my room and see it for yourself."

"I don't know if that's such a good idea, Calay."

"You'll see I'm right."

"This is insane."

"I know what I fucking saw, alright? I know what I'm saying is true. I'm not crazy!"

"I'm not saying you're crazy, Calay. I would never—"

Calay squinted, waited for him to finish his sentence. The moment hung between them, thick and oozing with unspoken words. Her jaw fell open, she closed it. Air passed between her lips, but barely reached her lungs as her breathing shallowed. Suddenly, Jacob's absence since their arrival took on a new meaning. The fight between him and Ash in the hallway. His warning her about Ash's intentions. A swell of disgust surged through Calay.

"You knew."

"I knew what?" He leaned forward on his knees and clasped his hands in front of him.

"All of it."

"Calay..."

"I mean, I knew you had to know we weren't on planet. You had to know we were aboard an alien ship. But I thought...I hoped you were kept in the dark about the rest of it, like I was."

"It isn't as simple as that."

"Isn't it, though? You intend to destroy a planet—my planet—and you say that isn't simple? The Others are going to kill an intelligent species. Ecosystems. Life as we know it, for god's sakes!"

"I got you off. You're safe here."

"I'm the farthest from safe I've ever been."

Jacob reached for her, tried to pull her to him. She wrenched her arm away, backed against the far wall. The coldness of it took away what little breath she had left. She forced what she had to say next through clenched teeth.

"Did. You. Know?"

Jacob's head fell between his arms. "I knew."

Calay's vision swam.

"How could you?" She spat. "Was anything you said to me ever true?"

"Everything I said to you was true, with a few liberties. I was tasked to go to Earth to look for others like us. To look for you, Calay. Elora personally told me not to return until I had you."

"What? Why me? That thing in there isn't even my mother!"

"We need people like you, Calay."

"Like me?"

"Hybrids."

"For what, exactly? If not to make peace, what for?"

"Calay..." Jacob pleaded.

"What the fuck for?"

"As bait. We need hybrids to act as bait. To trap the remaining humans."

"Trap them for what?" Her voice was barely above a whisper.

"For energy."

The ground seemed to shift. Calay's body shook with emotion. She imagined all the people on Earth who she would have sentenced to death if she'd gone along with the Others' plan. If she hadn't asked questions. If she hadn't connected with the hive or trusted herself. If she hadn't tried harder. She struggled for air, fought to remain standing. She pressed her back against the wall, willed herself to remain upright.

She would not fall apart. Not here. Not in front of him.

She pressed her lips together, pulled back her shoulders.

"Are the other hybrids even here? Elora said they arrived while she was...indoctrinating me."

"No, they're not here. They're still on Earth. Not everyone was as pliant as you. We're still working on them."

"You plied me? Come on, Jacob. Say it."

"Say what?"

"Say what you really mean. Why am I here and they aren't?"

"I told you. You were more...malleable."

"Oh, come on! You're saying I was desperate. Lonely and desperate, so of course I said yes when the pretty man batted his ridiculously long eyelashes at me. You used me! All this time, I was just a mission to you, wasn't I? You never cared about me. You never loved me. Every time you were there for me, all those moments, when we were together. Oh my god, Jacob. I trusted you...I...I let you inside me!"

"No, never. All of that was real." Jacob rose.

Calay stumbled backward, the rawness of her shoulder aching as she fell against the door. Jacob crossed to Calay, winced as she winced.

"Please, Calay. I never intended to fall for you, but I did, okay? Every tender moment between us was real. Those moments still are. They're the best parts of my very long, very dark life. You are my light, my love, my everything."

"And yet you'd have my entire species murdered."

"They're not your species. You're one of us."

"I'm both, Jacob! I am both! You'll never know what that feels like. To never truly belong. To never have a home. I was finally starting to feel like I could find a place. Here, with you. With the Others. But now..."

"Let me explain."

"Explain what? That you've lied to me this entire time?"

"That's what I'm saying. I've never lied to you, Calay. Not even now, through all of this. Have I denied your claims once? I promised you I would never lie to you, and I've kept that promise."

"Lies by omission are still lies."

"Yes, I was dishonest by not telling you the whole truth." Jacob sighed, his face pained.

"Not just the truth, Jacob. I don't even know how to wrap my mind around what you've done. What you're going to do." Tears trailed down Calay's face, her voice cracked with a hoarseness from yelling. "I can't even conceive of it!"

"I was trying to change it!" Jacob shouted back. "I've spent the entire time we've been here trying to convince Elora what we're doing is wrong. Don't you see? I got to know you. I got to understand your kind and for all of humanity's faults, of which you have many as a species. But you deserve a chance to rebuild. I fell in love with your planet. The natural beauty. The complex elegance. The way humanity perseveres. You embody it all. Humanity deserves to live. You deserve to live."

"Oh, do we now? How benevolent of you. As a representative of my species, I can't tell you how much that means to us." Calay clasped her hands together, feigning righteousness. "So, what then? You just move on, find another planet to crush?"

"Please, we can fix this." His voice quivered.

"There's nothing left to fix."

"We can find a better way. Together." Jacob glanced at her from behind his long lashes, a grin curled in the corner of his mouth.

"Fuck you!"

Jacob flinched, his hands fell by his sides. He almost seemed to shrink in front of her as his shoulders folded in. Calay tried not to care about the pain that settled in his face. Even with rage and shock flowing through her, she couldn't stop a pang from resounding in her heart. She might not have let him in before, but that didn't mean he didn't have a hold over her. A home inside her. Nestled, somewhere deep in the darkness. She'd caught glimmers of the possibility of opening up to Jacob, like the other night. When they'd laid in each other's arms. She'd tried to seal that off with Ash, but it persisted. Despite her best efforts, hope had bubbled back up. Even in the harsh light of the worst things she'd discovered, Calay had still hoped Jacob could be by her side. To save her. Calay was broken and even now, after everything, she cared enough about Jacob to not break him too.

If she was being honest with herself, she'd loved him just as much as he loved her. But she couldn't afford that kind of honesty.

He'd betrayed her. Over and over again. Each truth revealed an even deeper level of deceit. Cruelty, even.

She couldn't let him close to her. Not now.

Not ever.

And certainly not when her planet needed saving.

CHAPTER SIXTEEN

A SWELL of gray swirling matter bubbled in Calay's veins when she tugged on the hive and the door to Jacob's cabin evaporated. She turned and ran from his room before her heart had the chance to pull her back.

She was done with him and whatever the hell was between them. She realized she couldn't quite call it love, not really. Even though they both felt loving feelings for the other. Calay believed true love was pure. Kind. Selfless. She'd thought she'd found that with Tess. Then, with Jacob. As it turned out, she'd been wrong, yet again.

She had yet to find that kind of love in her life. Her parents weren't patient or forgiving. Tess had been self-serving. Dishonest. And Jacob… Jacob had violated every value love was supposed to protect. On a galactic scale.

No, whatever existed between them was not love. It was toxic. Not that Calay wasn't flawed too. Ever since the truth came out about what Tess had done to her, she'd lost the ability to love. At least, in the way she'd dreamed of loving. It wasn't that she didn't want to. She did. She tried. She failed. She couldn't trust herself to love someone properly. Free of fear. Free of distrust. Free.

So she hid. She walled up. She ran.

From Jacob's cabin, down the winding labyrinth of halls, unsure of where she was going or where she'd end up. She put as much distance between herself and Jacob as she possibly could within the confines of the ship. Her lungs burned, her thighs ached for rest. She finally came to a stop at the very far end of a very long corridor.

She bent over, thrust her hands on her knees, and paused to catch her breath. She waited for the echo of footfalls. Voices. Some kind of thunderous explosion to match the breaking of her heart. The only sound was that of her labored breathing. An occasional whimper. The rustle of the coarse fabric of her uniform. Calay stayed this way a long time. But the air around her was far from peaceful. The lights flickered. The air condensed. She tried to force herself still, but her body shook under the weight of finding out what she feared most was real: she was alone.

Just as she finally managed to slow her breathing, she heard it. A rustling, rhythmic and constant. Almost like swooshing air but deeper. More impenetrable.

Swish swish swish.

She listened, tried to determine which direction it was coming from. It grew louder. Seemed to fill the entire hallway.

A lump formed in Calay's throat. The sound was everywhere, all around her. In moments, it seemed to exist inside her. She shook her head, trying to free herself. It was relentless. Whatever brief peace she'd found in this place when she'd arrived was gone.

She had to do something. But what?

She took a few steps farther down the hallway.

The lights cut out. She hesitated. The lights returned, flickered some more. The noise didn't stop. Whatever was making that sound could be right around this wall. She braced herself, positive she was about to come face to face with...something.

She was stranded in deep space on an alien ship. She didn't know if the human laws of physics applied here. Or if there were even darker horrors than she'd already uncovered. The tension that hovered all around her could be anything. She gathered her courage and turned the corner. Found nothing. Just another endless corridor under quivering lights.

Calay released a breath, turned back around the way she'd come. If she was going to get off this ship alive, she couldn't go running blind. She had to be smarter. More careful. Figure out what her next move was. The idea seemed ludicrous—the challenge, impossible. She was so far away from home, entrenched in secrets. Lies. Violence. How would she ever make it back?

She rubbed her eyes, pulled her gaze up from the floor and down the long, flashing hallway. Something dark crowded at the other end. What was once a corridor was now a mass of black. No, not black. Green. And silver.

It was an unending sea of Elora lookalikes.

The lump that had lodged itself in Calay's throat bubbled up as a loud gasp. An icy chill crept through her limbs. Her eyes filled with unshed tears.

"There you are." Ash stepped forward out of the throng. They bobbed with her movement, almost pulsating with energy. Their black eyes trained on Calay.

"Ash." Calay sniffed.

"I've been looking for you," Ash purred. Her voice was silken, dripping with hedonistic desire.

"What for?" Calay bristled.

Suddenly Jacob's warnings about Ash took on a more sinister connotation. He'd warned her Ash was hungry. That she wasn't what Calay thought she was. She was dangerous. Calay had thought he'd said those things out of jealousy or because he was hurt. Now she knew better. The Others wanted to harvest humans for energy. She didn't know what that meant exactly, but she knew it wasn't good. If Ash really was vying to make a name for herself, to substantiate her power as Jacob predicted, Calay didn't want to be fodder for it.

"Just to talk."

"You haven't wanted to 'just talk' since I met you."

"You got me. I don't think much of your way of communicating as humans. Mouths can do so many more interesting things than talk." Ash crept closer, closing the distance between them. Her full pink lips curled upward, her glistening white teeth chattered together. As if chewing on the air.

Dread crept along Calay's spine.

"I don't think our mouths have any business being near each other, and I don't have anything left to say to you, Ash." Calay shuffled her feet backward, chose her words carefully. She didn't want to mince meanings, and she certainly didn't want to piss Ash off and risk sending a wave of Eloras on herself.

Calay glanced past Ash, watched their mother-like forms swarm behind her. They kept their distance, like crossing some unseen boundary might flip a switch inside them as it had in the basement. Calay could almost still feel their long fingers tangling in her hair, clawing at her limbs.

She continued to back away.

"Well, that's disappointing. I was hoping to get closer to you. Much closer."

"I'm not sure that's possible," Calay said, recalling her mouth on Ash's skin. Ash's tongue inside her. Their hot, sweaty bodies pressed together. She closed her eyes, swallowed. She pressed herself against the wall, rooted herself in the present. *Keep her talking, you'll figure this out.* When Calay opened her eyes again, Ash was close. Too close.

"Well now, that depends."

"Depends on what?"

"How much more of you I get to eat."

Calay blanched. "What?"

"Earlier was just an appetizer. I want more."

"You're sick." Calay's voice cracked.

"Come on, Calay. Superior species eat inferior ones all the time. Humans are weak. Isolated. Dying." Ash seemed to transform as the words poured past her teeth and out of her mouth.

The color of her lips tinged gray and cracked down the middle. Her green eyes sagged at the sides, hollowing into wide, dark circles. The black liner around them melted down her face. A billow of brown dust clogged the air, and in the pale shadows, she seemed to double in size. A hump raised on her back, shredding the corset which fell to her feet. Her breasts heaved before disappearing into a throbbing, gray, raw-looking bulbous body covered in pustules and spines. Her skin sunk between rows and rows of protruding ribs on either side of her hump. Patches of short, wire-thick hair jutted out in every direction. She heaved forward, her legs bending backward at the knee and her arms elongating into sharp, razor-like malformed limbs. They looked broken and poorly healed. As she balanced on their pointy tips, she walked like it too, teetering back and forth. Her voice deepened still, as if she were chewing on gravel. No, teeth. Rows and rows of serrated teeth filled her mouth, slicing into her tongue, her lips. Something tar-like oozed out of her mouth. It stunk. Like death.

Calay gagged. "Oh my god."

"We're forbidden from using hybrids as energy sources for the starship, but that doesn't mean I can't personally extract some from you if I eat your insides. Just a little. You'll still be able to perform your function."

Calay didn't know what this thing was. Not anymore. She stared wordlessly at the creature before her, her eyes wide. She cringed, remembering the strange heels the Térasians wore in the simulation outside her window, the one in the cafeteria. Horror flooded Calay. They weren't shoes, they were their actual legs. She added another item to the list of things she now knew: the Others did indeed have physical bodies. The human bodies the Others adopted weren't a projection from Calay's mind, it was from theirs. To hide their grotesque, nightmarish true forms.

"I want to see you writhe." A putrid smell filled the air, coating Calay's skin.

"Stay back!" Calay choked on the urge to throw up.

"You have a choice, Calay. Let me have a nibble, give me some of that hybrid juice. Or submit to chaos and pain."

"Not much of a choice."

"You can always choose, Calay."

Calay shivered, a heaviness burrowed in the pit of her stomach. Those were Jacob's words. How many times had he reiterated that very phrase to her? *You can always choose, Calay.* But it was always an impossible choice, offered against a rock and a hard place. He—the Others—used it to squeeze her into doing something she didn't want to do. It was just another manipulation tactic. A method of coercion. So she couldn't blame them when things inevitably went sideways.

She recounted her choices: colluding with Jacob. Renouncing the Resistance. Sacrificing her father. Murdering Tess. Leaving Earth behind to come to Téras. Aligning with the Others. All of it led to one place— here. That, and her complete and total isolation and the death of everything and everyone she loved.

Calay wept. She swiped at the tears, choked on the sobs. They used the illusion of choice to groom her. To make her second guess herself. To get her to do what they wanted. The realization hit her harder than Ash's breath. She'd never had a choice. The Others had taken that away from her. From humanity. She'd only ever done what she needed to do to survive. To make it another day. In Their world. On Their terms. Under Their control. Yes, she may have taken Tess's life, but it was because of Them that Tess was dead.

For a moment, a weight lifted off Calay. Something she'd been carrying for far too long. None of this was her fault. She'd done what she's had to do. She'd adapted. She'd survived. And now they wanted her to choose between being slowly eaten or dying painfully, torn apart by the mother-figures.

This choice wasn't only impossible, it was perverse.

Calay hit her limit.

"Over my dead body." Calay growled. *Watch your tongue, Calay.* But even as she rolled the warning through her mind, she already knew. It was too late. "Go fuck yourself."

"Chaos and pain it is."

The horde surged forward.

Calay's blood ran cold. Her skin prickled with sweat. She willed her legs to move. Her whole body screamed to run. She was paralyzed by the sight of them clamoring over each other in the narrowing hallway.

Their arms twisted the wrong way as they pushed themselves higher up the walls. Their legs bent back at the knees.

Calay's mind tried to grasp onto some sense of what she was looking at. Aliens? Robots? Projections from Ash's or Elora's mind? She hadn't had time to ask, nor had she wanted to. She didn't need to know because she already knew everything about this was wrong. They'd be on her in moments. Calay stumbled backward against the wall. She nearly choked on her tongue as she struggled to breathe. It felt too big in her mouth. Too intrusive. Like the mounting rush of inhuman screams coming from the Elora army as it piled closer.

Their faced contorted, their eyes grew darker, jaws opened wider than any human mouth should. Calay reminded herself these horrific, familiar faces were not human. They were not her mother.

Something wiggled free in Calay's mind. Her limbs too. She turned to run and butted up against the wall, tripped over her feet. Their breath bore down on her. The scraping of their nails against the floor inched closer. She could feel them. About to pounce. Rip her limb from limb. *Not today.* Calay had a planet to save.

Bent at the waist, she scampered forward on her hands and feet, a mockery of the disjointed, beastly throng behind her. She pushed herself upright. Then she ran.

She tore around the corner at the far end of the hallway. Then another. She raced down the corridors as fast as her legs would carry her. Just as she'd escaped alien pods in Seattle, when she'd been searching for Tess, Calay would escape them. But how? In the city she'd been free. Able to duck down dark alleys and under vehicles. She knew those streets. Navigated them more times than she could count. Then again, hadn't she been doing the very same thing in these hallways since she'd arrived? Even as her heart thundered against her chest and panic coursed through her veins, Calay focused.

She knew this ship. She could do this.

She came to one of the tentacle junctions. Whipped around the closest wall. Doubled back the way she came, one floor lower. She pictured the next intersection of hallways and the one after that. She anticipated each curve and hairpin twist. Leaned into them as if she'd known this ship her whole life, not just a few days. In a way, as part of the hive, maybe she had. Deep inside.

She didn't want to admit it, but these horrible creatures were a part of her. They were inextricably linked. That didn't mean she had to give in to them or the darkest parts of herself. For the first time in as long as she could remember, Calay had a real choice. She could succumb to the darkness, let them destroy her. Destroy Earth. Or she could fight. For the planet. For herself. For the light.

Jacob's words rang through Calay's mind as her feet pounded against the floor, her lungs begged for air, her shaking thighs burned. He'd told her she was his light. What if he'd been grooming her, but not as she'd originally thought? What if he'd prepared her for this moment all along? She hated him for how he'd betrayed her. And yet, it was possible if he hadn't, she wouldn't be where she was now. Calay recounted the times he'd pressed her. Lied to her. Coerced her. She forced herself to shake the idea from her mind.

He may have tricked her, but it wasn't because of him that she was fighting. Her strength was coming from within. Her love for her home planet, for humanity. For herself. She may have been Jacob's light, but she was also her own. A torch, guiding her way through the hallways of the Térasian ship in the reaches of dark space, all the way fucking home. For once, Calay trusted her intuition. Made the decision to trust herself.

The heavy sound of breathing and rhythmic swooshing of fabric echoed through the halls.

They were gaining on her. Calay pushed forward. Still, their long fingers fumbled in her hair. They scratched along the sides of her boots.

She reached her room, the door swooshed shut behind her.

She skidded, stopping only when she slammed into the floor to ceiling window on the other side. She blinked, still shocked by what she saw. Flashes of the shining city of Téras glitched in and out, cut with snapshots of the darkness of deep space. It didn't matter what was out there anymore.

She steadied herself, glanced back at the door. She willed it to remain shut through the power of the hive. She had to keep her wits about the threat from inside. She listened as one by one, the mother figures crashed against the door.

It was relentless.

Unceasing.

If they were controlled by Ash's thoughts or her connection to the hive, it might never stop. They could feed off each other's desires, Ash's commands. They could keep coming. Forever. Until they finally wore Calay down. She was still new to this whole hive thing, she didn't know how long she could hold them back. She tucked herself behind the end of the bed and pressed her hands to her ears.

She didn't bother to wipe the tears from her cheeks or the hair from her eyes.

Out of breath—and options—Calay waited.

CHAPTER SEVENTEEN

CALAY WASN'T sure how much time had passed until the banging finally stopped.

Her knees ached, her tears dried. She pulled the watch free from her pack and stared at its shattered face. It had so diligently reported Earth-time since she'd arrived. Now, the short arm stood still at two and the long one just shy of eight. 2:37. She didn't notice when it'd stopped. If it happened when she tore through the holographic image outside her room, or after. Either way, she didn't take it as a good omen.

Peeling her shaking hands off her ears, she placed them on the mattress. She eased herself out of the crouch and onto the bedspread. She stilled. Listened. Yes, the sound of Elora lookalikes charging the door had stopped, but she wasn't convinced the deafening silence was much of an improvement. She didn't want to think about what it could mean. If it meant anything at all. For all she knew, they were gathered on the other side. Hungry and waiting.

Fear rippled across Calay's skin. If she made it out of this alive, her nervous system was going to need to sleep for a month. She turned, peered out the window. Focused her connection on the hive mind to hold back the flickering, unstable projection of the city. Her shoulders relaxed, but her mind didn't. The horrors of deep space were as she'd left them. Plymouths of rock hurled in their wake, floating in negative space. Everything was dark. She exhaled. For a moment, she worried they'd somehow transported across the universe and returned to the Milky Way Galaxy. But there was no sign of Earth. For now, her planet was safe. Even if she wasn't.

She knew she couldn't stay in her room forever. There was too much at stake, and this ship wasn't her home. She was never really truly one of Them. *Thank the gods.* She had to get back to Earth ahead of the Others.

Warn people. Save them. Save herself. Somehow.

To do that, she'd have to go out there. Beyond the confines of her cabin and into the belly of the ship. She had to stop the Others. Figure out a way to get back where she belonged.

Alive.

Calay stood and paced before crossing to the door. She pressed her ear against it. Listened yet again. It was silent as the grave. She shivered. *Don't say grave.* She took a deep breath and was about to will the door open when a gentle knocking resounded from the other side.

She clutched her arms to her chest, froze.

"Who is it?" Even as the words crossed her lips, Calay cringed. It was too normal a question. Too familiar in this strange place. Too harboring of violent possibilities.

"Come out, come out..." Ash cooed in a sing-song voice.

Calay's eyes grew wide, her mind spun. *What kind of game is this?* She wasn't sure if she should answer. If it would help. She didn't know what Ash was getting at, but it seemed as long as this door was between them, Calay could hold her off. At least until Jacob found them. After she'd confronted him, it wasn't like she could storm off the ship and leave. Surely, he'd come looking for her at some point, wouldn't he? Didn't he always?

A loud crack boomed on the other side of the door.

"The fuck was..."

A long, white protrusion exploded through the door.

It pulled back.

Then again.

Harder this time. Louder.

It splintered the material of the door, sending serrated shards of it toward Calay's face. One barely missed her eye.

She screamed, staggered sideways, her hands flew to her mouth. She pressed herself against the inside wall.

The thing that had come through the door retracted a second time, leaving a gaping hole. In its place was Ash's face. More human than monster, her skin was still bulging with pustules. Her cheekbones weren't quite right. The tattoo on her neck seemed to have melted down her chest, over her collarbone, below the top of her corset, which barely hung on her body. Her shining white teeth were too large for her mouth, her lips stained with the remnants of black ooze. The cool air that drifted through the hole smelled of something foul, something decaying.

She peered at Calay, one eye wider than the other.

"Let me come in." Ash hissed.

"Noooooo!" Calay screamed. "No!" She clawed at the wall. At the brittle skin of her arms. The hem of her shirt. She had to get away. She had nowhere to go. She knew it. They both did.

"Then I'm coming in after you."

"No."

Ash's face disappeared from view. Calay stared as she tossed the thing she'd used to break through the door through the hole. It was a leg. A human leg. No, one of the Elora legs.

Calay winced at the bloody, pulpy mess at the joint. So they were biological. *Inhuman.* That was the word that had played on repeat in her mind since she found them in that room, but they were alive. Somehow. Calay retched.

Then it began again.

The herd smashed against the door. It shook under the thunder of their weight. The window on the other side of the room rattled, if that was even possible. The bed too. It seemed the whole fucking ship did. She realized they were going to bring down the door.

Calay cringed, braced herself. She watched in disbelief as their faces caught on splinters and sharp edges. It tore at their skin, it ripped off like weathered paint chips. Yet, they kept coming. Emotionless. Mother-faces. Their jaws open and their eyes like black pits.

She had a sudden vision of the mannequins in the Loft. The way so many of them had been missing limbs, or discarded, turned on their sides. Someone had colored their eyes in all black. She couldn't help but wonder who'd done it. If it was a warning, somehow. An omen of things to come. Calay's teeth chattered, her skin crawled.

She was not going to die. Not like this. She refused.

Her gaze darted across the room for something—anything—to defend herself. She scanned the bed. The side table. The impossibly clean white floor. The sparsely decorated room offered no reprieve. There was nothing.

Except the leg.

The idea of touching it made Calay want to vomit.

She sprang from her huddle against the wall and dove for the leg just as a tsunami of bodies flung themselves through the door. She pitched herself underneath them, sliding across the floor and into the pile of goo that had pooled. She grasped for it, the ache in her shoulder screeched; a nauseating reminder of just how human she really was.

Clinging to her only weapon, Calay gripped it to her chest. She sucked as much air through her clenched teeth as she could and watched a barrage of green, black, and white wash over her. They didn't stop. Probably couldn't from their momentum. Instead, they went right past her, hurled themselves into the window. They tumbled over each other. Just as one righted itself, another would crash into it. Like a train jumping its tracks, one car slamming into the next. There were hundreds of them. Perhaps thousands. She didn't exactly intend to wait and find out.

This was her chance.

She pressed herself against the floor, crab-crawled forward with her one free hand and the power of her legs. She tried not to scream. Not to draw additional attention to herself. Not to trip the Elora-figures up as they threatened to stomp her to death. Still, she felt their grasping fingers reaching for her. Saw their dark eyes searching for her. Smelled the deep stench of rot fill the room.

She chanced a glance backward.

They were still heaving themselves into each other. Behind her was a long trail of blood. *It's not human. It's not human. It's not human.* She repeated the mantra to herself over and over, clawing her was to the doorway. *More importantly it's not mine.*

A pair of Doc Marten style boots blocked her path. Calay knew who it was. Of course she did. She didn't waste time looking up to confirm her suspicions. She didn't need to. Didn't want to see that horrible, half-human, half-alien face again. Not now or ever.

Instead, she positioned her hands below the foot of the amputated leg, gripped around its cold ankle, and plunged it skyward. She heard a wet *thunk* as the blunt, bloody end collided with Ash's nose. A guttural, animal sound erupted from Ash's throat as she stumbled backward and fell. Dots of red littered the floor. The walls. The ceiling. How much of it was from Ash's nose and how much was spatter from the amputated leg, Calay didn't know. Didn't care. She just had to get out of there.

She pulled herself away from the stream of mother-bodies and clamoured to stand.

"You're one of us, you know." Ash muttered. Her hands were cupped over her face, Calay assumed to try to staunch the flow of blood.

"I'll never be one of you." Calay spat, standing over Ash. She still gripped the leg, ready to swing again if she had to, thankful Ash stayed where she was. Cowering on the floor, glaring up at Calay.

"You're part of the hive mind now. Connected to it. There's nowhere you can go where we can't find you."

"I know."

"Resistance is futile." Ash's chest heaved, she coughed.

The voice Calay had once thought sultry and alluring now sounded menacingly sick. As if she were diseased. Dying. Maybe that was the Others' problem; they had nothing left. They were doing everything in their power to survive, even if that meant others had to die. They were a species fighting for their lives.

But then again, so was she.

She forced herself to bring her face to Ash's. Levelled her gaze with hers. She pulled her shoulders back, dropped the leg. She took a long, slow breath, trying to calm the tremor in her throat. "It doesn't mean I can't try."

Calay righted herself and ran.

She didn't look back as Ash's voice bellowed behind her. Didn't concern herself with what the horde of mother-figures were doing now. She just focused on putting one foot in front of the other and creating as much distance between herself and the Others as possible.

The thrashing and pounding of their mutant bodies against the glass grew quieter. So did Ash's screams. Calay's pulse quickened when she started around each corner and she braced herself for an attack. None came. The ship seemed almost deserted. The projections, gone. She wondered how many Térasians were really left? How many of the projections had been real, alien forms in the first place? Jacob said they were a species on the brink of extinction. He'd told a lot of lies, but maybe he'd been telling the truth about that. It would make sense. The idea of a ship brimming with those grotesque monsters almost made Calay curl into a ball right then and there. But that would do her—and humanity—no good. So she kept running.

She meant what she'd said to Ash. Calay had no idea if she was going to survive or not. She didn't know if she could somehow turn off her connection to the hive mind. She had to admit it was unlikely. Or if she'd be able to return to Earth and save the planet. Or herself. But by gods, she was going to do her best. But first, she needed time to figure out what her next move was. And she wasn't going to do it with her whole body begging for rest. Despite Ash's warnings, Calay needed a place to hide.

THE HALLWAY WAS LONGER THAN SHE REMEMBERED. DARKER, too. The cafeteria behind her, abandoned. Calay turned, faced the door at the far end. She tried to ignore the lingering feeling of their long fingers in her hair. Their arms and hands clawing around her waist. The impossibly long flight of stairs out. Or in. The last place they were going to look for her would be down there. In the basement. Where Calay's nightmares aboard the ship had first begun. Which meant it would be the best place to buy herself some time.

She forced her legs forward, tampered down the urge to flee.

She reminded herself the mother-figures weren't down there. That she'd be safe. Well, as safe as she'd be anywhere else on the ship. Maybe safer. It was no different from the loading bay. It was reinforced. Protected. There was a possibility that it could work like a faraday cage on the hive mind. Calay shrugged as she piled one weak rationale onto another. The truth was, she had no idea whether this was a good idea or not. There was only one way to find out.

As the door clicked shut behind her, Calay gazed across the cavernous room. She'd left the lights on when she'd escaped earlier. They cast the space in a blinding white glow. The room seemed big before. When it was stuffed with the lookalikes. Calay bristled at the memory. Her fingers gripped the metal railing. Now, empty, it was impossibly huge. She clung to the idea they were unlikely to look for her here and forced herself down the staircase. Her boots clinked with each step as she made her way down. They echoed loudly. Too loudly. She rushed each one until she reached the smooth floor. She peered down the long, wide runway. That's what it was, wasn't it? Another loading bay. Only here the Others stashed monsters instead of pods. *Not right now they're not.* Calay dashed to the small, flat switch on the far side of the room, dropping her bag from her shoulder in her urgency, and cut the lights.

Darkness blanketed her.

Her legs trembled. Her heart too. She waited, listened. The mechanical buzzing of the lights disappeared. The uniform's fabric was rough against her skin. The feel of it under her fingers, repulsive. She couldn't wear this. Not anymore, knowing what she now knew. Panic rose in her throat. Her heartbeat quickened. She had to get this thing off.

Her backpack.

She knew it was there somewhere. On the floor. She'd packed her T-shirt and jeans. If she could just find them. She didn't dare turn on the lights in case someone passing by saw them. If she was being honest with herself, she didn't want to look at this room anymore, either. Every time she opened her eyes, she kept seeing those dark, dead, mother-like eyes staring at her.

Calay traced the wall with her fingers, her hands shaking against the columns. She made her way back to the front of the space, found the edge of the staircase. It was only a few short paces from where they'd grabbed her. She got down on her hands and knees, started patting the floor. Like the rest of the ship, it was impossibly clean. As if several thousand pairs of feet hadn't nearly trampled her to death down here only a few short hours ago.

She spread herself across the floor. She stretched her arms over her head, extended her legs straight. Rolled around, back and forth. She reached into the dark, desperate. She kept waiting for something to grab back, was grateful it never did. She made herself as long and wide as she possibly could to find the pack faster. It had to be there.

Her right foot collided with something. It was soft, pliable. Calay recoiled in the dark, fearful someone was down here with her. That it might be something else. Something new.

She didn't have time to waste. Couldn't wait for whatever it was to come and get her.

She lunged forward, grasped at whatever it was. A yelp escaped her lips at the familiar feeling of leather between her fingers.

Her backpack. She'd found it. She'd actually found it!

She unclasped the buckle, tore open the top. She reached through the opening, felt the contents, pulled out the clothing she knew was inside. She found herself almost laughing as she peeled the horrid uniform off in the darkness. A squeal escaped from her lips as she shed the top, buttons clinked as they hit the floor. She quickly replaced it with the familiar fabric of her T-shirt. The denim on her pants was soft and worn. She pulled it up over her hips and shivered. *It's clothes*, she reminded herself. *Just clothes.* There was something about being in them that made her feel like she'd returned to her skin. Her own kind. It was a small victory. She'd take it.

She barely managed to pull her boots back on when the sound of the door clicked shut.

Calay sucked in her breath. Clutching the bag between her hands, she held very still.

The echo of heavy shoes on the metal landing wrapped a coldness around the base of her spine. She shivered, the tassels on her bag rustling as she shook. She looked up, peering through the blackness, trying to get a view of who was above. She saw nothing. She inched toward the nearest wall, as if she could press herself against it and disappear. But even as she stepped gently, the sound of her tread on the floor was made ever-louder by the hollow room.

She waited. Hoped. No, she prayed whoever it was would go away.

They didn't.

The darkness grew longer. The moment too. Calay's neck ached from craning into the blackness. Then, his dark silhouette crossed in front of the window in the door.

"I know you're down here, Calay." Jacob's voice called out from above.

Calay swallowed.

"What are you doing here?" She called back.

"Where are you?"

Jacob flicked on the lights. Calay shrunk under the glare, shielded her eyes. As she waited for them to adjust, she listened to the sound of his steps as he descended the stairs and made his way across the room. After all this, she didn't trust Jacob, but she knew he wouldn't hurt her. Even now. Besides, she could run. But to where? Once again, she was out of options.

"How'd you find me?" Calay dropped her arms to her sides.

"How do I always find you?"

"Heat signature? Even down here?"

"Even down here." Jacob nodded, thrust a hand through his dark hair, then both of them into the pockets of his jeans. The veins in his arms rippled. The fabric in his shirt stretched when he shrugged. His blue eyes bore into her.

There was a time not so long ago she would have yearned to be pulled against that shirt. Into those arms. In fact, it wasn't long ago Jacob had done just that, in a room just like this. But those days were gone. While Calay blamed herself for not following the rules, in the cold light of the empty bay, in the far reaches of dark space, she finally gave herself permission to blame him too.

"Why did you find me?"

"You know Ash is coming for you, right?"

"She can try."

"I don't want you to get hurt, Calay."

"Too late." Calay's voice was laced with barbs.

"Ouch." Jacob's brow furrowed.

"Tell me about it."

"I'm sorry it's come to this. That you can't see me the way you used to."

"That's a weak fucking apology, Jacob." Calay shuffled backward. He was too close. He was always too close. "Besides, I don't need your pity. You did this to us. To me."

"I never wanted to hurt you. I never meant to cause you any more pain than you've already been through."

She raised her eyebrow, smirked. Had it always been this way? Him twisting her experience, manipulating her feelings? Her heart? He may not have wanted to hurt her, but he deliberately did things that would. She was putting a stop to that now. The Others had taken so much from her, but they wouldn't take her dignity. She knew now what mattered most to her and while she was well aware of the fact she was far from "pure," she wouldn't make herself small for anyone else ever again. She refused to crumple into the box Jacob wanted to put her in. To live in constant fear. She finally felt like she'd earned her spot in the universe, and she wasn't going to give it up without a fight. She'd stay true to herself, despite the nerves flooding her body. It was about time something felt right.

"I know what I've done can't be undone, okay? I get that." Jacob sighed. "But that doesn't mean we can't stop Ash or Elora from doing worse than they already have. I just want to protect you."

"Stop."

"Why won't you let me help you? Just this last time?"

"For the final time, and for the love of gods, hear me, Jacob. I don't need your protection. I don't need your help. Now more than ever."

Jacob cringed, opened his mouth to say something. Calay didn't give him the chance.

"I loved you. I did. And I believe you loved me. As much as you could. But not in the way I needed you to. You did everything you could to control me."

"For your own good."

"See? That's not love! Don't you get it? That's...something else. Something I don't want to be a part of. Something I *can't* be a part of. Maybe I knew it the whole time. Somewhere, deep down. Maybe it wasn't really me I was hiding from. Maybe it was you. All along."

"I'm sorry."

"So am I."

"But I'm not sorry I met you, Calay. I'll keep fighting for you. For your species."

"So will I," Calay said.

Jacob was free to do as he wished. He was a grown man. She couldn't control him. Wouldn't want to. Not the way he felt compelled to control her. As long as he stayed far the fuck away from her, Calay would be satisfied.

She nodded, hitched the backpack over her shoulder, and trudged past Jacob. Her heart ached when the smell of his T-shirt clung to her as she made her way to the stairs.

"Calay, wait."

She turned.

"What are you going to do now? There's nowhere to go."

"There's one more place I can go."

"Where?"

"If I've learned anything this trip, it's that the Others are part of me. For better or for worse. Anything you can do, I can do too. And I'm going to do it better."

"What does that mean?"

"The Others couldn't take me down before. I've survived five years, and frankly, I've had enough. I'm going to deal with them once and for all."

"How are you going to do that?"

Calay smiled. For once, he was the one with the questions. She still didn't know exactly how she was going to fix things, but she knew what her next steps were. She knew what she had to do. Finally, she had the answers.

"I'm going to the source."

"You can't."

"Like Hell I can't. I'm going to Elora."

Jacob blanched. He stepped forward. He seemed to almost reach for Calay, but his hand dropped to his side when she drew her lips into a thin, tight line.

"She'll kill you," he said.

"Not if I kill her first."

CHAPTER EIGHTEEN

THE DOOR to the Strategic Operations Room dissolved with an effortless swoosh and fizzle as Calay approached it.

She hesitated.

She'd expected it would have been more difficult. On the way here, she'd even, if only for a moment, regretted leaving the severed leg behind. She'd figured it worked to break down the door to her cabin, why not this one? Turned out, she hadn't needed it after all. A rush of warmth flooded Calay. She couldn't tell if it was relief or nerves.

On the one hand, she didn't have to crash through walls to get to Elora. After everything that had happened that day, it was a small miracle. Her body ached, her shoulder throbbed. She wasn't sure she had the fight she needed in her anymore. In its place, a dark void.

On the other hand, she was about to confront the closest thing she had to a mother now. It didn't matter Elora wasn't really the woman Calay grew up with, she looked like her. Talked like her. Smelled like her. For all intents and purposes, she was her.

Except she wasn't.

This aberration had manipulated Calay to exterminate her own species.

The fight she worried she'd lost sparked in her veins.

"Are you coming in or not?" Elora called.

Calay steeled herself. Stalked through the open door.

She squinted in the dim lighting, searching for Elora. Each step felt as if it might be her last as she made her way further inside.

Something flashed at the corner of her eye. Flickered.

She turned to find Elora flipping through holographic schematics, skulking in the shadows. *Right where she belongs.* Calay forced herself forward. Closer. If she was going to do this, she wanted to see Elora's face.

After all, this was personal.

Calay wrung her hands in front of her, gathering her courage to say what she came here to say. Elora's shoulders were pulled taut, her back straight. At a solid six feet, she'd always towered over Calay's five-foot-four frame. But now, she seemed even bigger. Almost unreachable. Her cropped silver hair glowed in the light radiating from the images, her dark eyes reflected them as if burning them into her memory. She continued to swipe through diagrams, her olive-green hooded tunic casually dangling off her wrists, as if Calay wasn't standing right there. As if none of what happened, had happened. Surely, she must know, and yet, there she was. Calmly reviewing plans Calay recognized as their strategic offence. The plans for their coalition. The plans for *her* future.

A future that would never be.

"Can I help you, Calay?" Elora finally said.

Calay couldn't tell if it was impatience in her voice or impunity. Until she knew for sure, she'd proceed with caution on the hope—albeit a distant one—that Elora was not the monster Calay believed her to be.

"I came here to talk to you. Woman to woman."

"Is that so?" Elora shifted her weight from one hip to the other, her black tights peeking through the slits in her flowing pant leg. The heels of her chunky boots clunked on the floor.

"Yes." Calay's voice was smaller than she intended.

"Well then, we have a problem, don't we?"

Calay was taken aback. She inhaled a shaky breath. She'd felt so sure coming here. So confident. But something unsettled her now. She shook her head along with the image of the Elora-figure's distorted faces charging after her. It was more than that. It was the fact that Calay—staring at her mother's face, hearing her voice—was struggling to once again maintain her grip on reality. Everything she'd known up until this point was untrue. She clenched her eyes shut, swallowed, opened them again. No, she could do this. She knew what was real. What wasn't. Mostly.

"What problem is that?" Calay said.

"We both know I'm not a woman."

Right into the deep end.

"You're right." Calay steadied her legs, slowed her breathing. "I know everything."

The leather harness across Elora's chest creaked when she reached and swiped the hologram from view. She turned to face Calay. Their gazes met. As Calay searched the dark pits of Elora's eyes, looking for the mother's warmth she'd known as a child and upon her arrival here, she ground her teeth together. Bit her lip. This Elora was not her Elora. Never had been. Her presence was both familiar and foreboding at the same time. Safe and unsafe. Life and death.

"And?"

"What do you mean 'and?'" Calay balked. "I know. I know what you are. I know what you intend to do. What you've done. I know everything you've told me about the coalition is a lie."

"I ask again." Elora huffed, exasperated. "And?"

"And what?"

"And what do you intend to do about it?"

"I'm here to stop you. To stop this from happening."

"Is that what you think?"

"With or without your cooperation." Calay didn't know if it was actually possible, but she had to believe it was.

"Calay." A slick, twisted smile crept across Elora's face. "Why can't you just, for once, do what you're told?"

"It hasn't worked out too well for me in the past."

"Nothing has worked out too well for you in the past." Elora growled.

Calay flinched. She was sure she felt her heart crack in her chest.

Focus, this is just another manipulation tactic. Don't get pulled into it. She blinked back tears and took a deep breath.

"Elora, please. Jacob changed his mind. You can too."

"Jacob is weak. He's been compromised. By you, I might add. Normally I'd feed you into the energy encapsulation incinerator and use you for fuel for what you've done to him, but I believe it just goes to show how valuable you are. If you can turn one of our own, you can certainly control the humans. Get them to do as we wish. You're an even better asset than I expected, my girl."

"I'm not your girl." Calay's voice dropped several decibels. "I found the bunker full of clones."

"My, you have been busy." Elora rested her hands on her wide hips.

"Are you one of them?"

"One of what?"

"One of those...those things!"

"If you think it'll make a difference, and it won't, I'll tell you." Elora sighed as if the biggest, most important conversation in Calay's life—in the history of humanity—was merely an inconvenience. "I was, once. My consciousness was projected inside this body. Before that, I was mindless, like them. Following orders. As you should have done."

"Jacob told me the Others didn't have bodies. That you were just a consciousness. But that wasn't true, was it?"

"No, as you discovered in the hallway with Ash. My actual form is shielded within this one. The others are in stasis in another section of the ship, sleeping. Waiting for the day we can be free again."

"Free?"

"When we wake up, we will be free to roam the Earth."

The mental image of those long legs, humped backs, and teeth-filled mouths flooded Calay with dread. In her mind's eye, she watched the blue oceans turn black, the skies gray, the lush forests die. She imagined the Others, in their organic forms, picking at the rotting carcases of dead humans. Animals succumbing to their own thirst and hunger. A planet devoid of life. A world lost.

Did the Others really have the power to do all that?

"You said there were others on the ship, in stasis, sleeping. I was told you were nearly extinct. How many of you are really left?"

"More than you'd like."

"All those projections I saw in the hallways when I arrived...The number of your look-alikes in the basement. There were hundreds of them. Maybe thousands."

"Try millions, Calay."

The color drained from Calay's face.

It made complete sense. Why hadn't she thought of it before? One small alien ship with a handful of Others couldn't end the world, but millions of them could. If they projected their sentience into the pods and their physical bodies on the ground, they effectively doubled their army. A chill crept down Calay's spine.

"The invasion, it was just the beginning."

"Phase One, yes. And it was very successful."

"And this is Phase Two?"

"Phase Two was all you, Calay. Your species. We were delighted when we saw how quickly you turned on each other. We had no way of getting to you once you saw us coming. Not without risking the lives of our own. You're a brute species, but a clever one. So, we waited for you to kill yourselves off."

"But you need us for energy..."

"Not all of you." Elora smiled. "Just a few."

"That's Phase Three. The Hybrid Coalition." Calay was surprised to find herself nodding as she pieced their plan together.

"Now you're getting it." Elora nodded back.

"Is that why you look like my mother? To convince me?"

"Calay, you convinced yourself. The Térasian elders created this shape. Their evidence on human behavior showed it might make you more...agreeable, if we adopted a form that inspired some kind of emotional connection. Then, when they realized how meaningful you would be to our plans, they duplicated it. All for you."

"Me?"

"Well, you and hybrids like you. We have rooms full of mother-figures. Father-figures. Friends and family. They all belong to the likeness of some hybrid who is going to join our cause."

"I suppose it was just dumb luck I stumbled into the one that looks the most like my mom?"

"Of course not. Your connection to the hive pulled you to them. It's only natural we seek something familiar in the foreign. You may not have been aware of it, but you were connecting to their consciousness. The same way we all connect to the hive. That's how I already know everything you've uncovered about us. And why I know you won't do a damn thing to stop us."

"Yes, I will. I'll do whatever it takes."

"You stupid girl." Elora hissed. For the briefest of moments, her eyes bulged, her jaw widened. She cleared her throat and continued. "You'll do as you're told. Or you, Jacob, and everyone on your planet will find its end."

"It's already found its end. That's what I'm trying to stop!" Calay tried to tame the shrillness in her voice. Things were escalating. Quickly. It was bubbling in the air between them. "You don't have to do this."

"Of course I do. You've seen our last planet. It's gone. We need a new one."

"What happened?" Calay pleaded. She wanted so desperately to understand. To make it make sense. To have hope. To find a way to save Earth. Maybe if she could get to the bottom of what happened to Téras, she could staunch the demise of her own planet.

"There was nothing left there for us."

"But why did you destroy it? Surely there was other life. Why not just leave peacefully, find a new place you could call home?"

"What's the saying you humans use?" Elora tapped her chin, feigning thoughtfulness. "If we can't have it, no one can."

"That's insane."

"It's a biological necessity."

"No, you're wrong. There's plenty to go around. There's enough for everybody."

"You know better as a species than anybody, that's not true. We're not so different, you and me. You sucked your planet dry, raped the natural world. And now we're going to use the only resources left. The only ones ripe with fuel."

Calay swallowed.

"Humans," Elora said.

"This is wrong."

"I warned you when I transported you into the shuttle in the forest, Calay. There is only death on Earth now."

A vision of gray swirling matter floated through Calay's mind. She could almost feel its gentle swirl against her skin. She'd thought about those words many times since she'd come down off the mountain. Wondered if she'd heeded their prophesy, would Tess still be alive? It was likely she would be. Calay would never have found out Tess was the leader of the Resistance, or that Tess had arranged to have her killed. They wouldn't have fought. Calay would have mourned the loss of their love and gone on without her, never the wiser. She may have still ended up at the Loft, with Jacob and Max. Would she still be here, on this ship? Or was the fact that she'd killed Tess herself the very thing that drove Calay to the far reaches of space? The questions rolled over in her mind, one after the other. The possibilities. The "what ifs." When she was brought aboard the pod on the mountain, Calay thought the Others had been warning her about Tess's death. But it was bigger than that. Bigger than her. Bigger than all of them.

It didn't matter what brought her to this moment. It only mattered what she did with it now.

"I won't let you do it."

"Be careful, Calay." Elora's voice grew hard, her eyes narrowed. "You might be important to our cause, but you aren't irreplaceable. Not like your girlfriend."

"What the fuck does that mean?"

"You think I don't see what you do? What *you've* done? You talk high and mighty about saving the human race as if it deserves saving. But I've seen how you use each other for your own gain."

"I...I don't know what you're talking about." Calay stammered.

One of the biggest regrets of her life was not fighting harder for humanity. She and Tess had struggled to just survive for so long, she eventually gave up the idea of taking back their planet. They talked about it at first. And of course, there were the rumours about groups taking down pods. Hell, she'd even built the camp Jacob wandered into that first night under the eye of one. But over time, ideals faded. Hope wilted. Dreams died. Together, eventually, she and Tess had even stopped responding to people's shouts for help. Started hoarding their food. Stealing from others. They did what they needed to do to survive. At the expense of everyone else. Anyone else. But that wasn't their fault. That was what the Others had done to them. Wasn't it?

"Oh, come on now, Calay. I've seen what you've done with Jacob. Several times, I might add."

"It wasn't like that." Calay's cheeks reddened, her shoulders caved inward.

Her second biggest regret was being weak. Needing Jacob. *That way.* She'd known better, before. Knew what she had done was wrong. Especially when Tess was out there, missing. Calay had tried to justify her relationship with Jacob and all the things they did together. Despite her efforts, she couldn't explain it away. Really, she didn't want to. Unless someone had gone to the darkness like she had, and survived, they wouldn't understand. She'd just been so lonely and afraid. Jacob had felt like home, then. Now…Calay didn't want to think about what he was now. Her heart ached, her stomach dropped. For Elora to call her out felt like being whipped by her own dirty laundry.

"And Ash. What the two of you did in my loading bay. Calay!"

She didn't have a retort for that one. That was pure self-indulgence. Self-sabotage, if she was being honest with herself. Ash allowed Calay to wallow in her pain. To dive into it. Swim around. It was the kind of connection that allowed her to completely disconnect from everything else. It had been unhealthy, but it was what she needed. She wasn't about to apologize for it. Not here. Not now. To Elora.

"Don't you think if you really loved your girlfriend, you would have been better to her? Didn't she deserve better?"

"My girlfriend is dead." A lump lodged itself in Calay's throat, her vision swam.

"You sure seem to have gotten over her fast." Elora smirked.

A surge of rage flowed through Calay. Elora had no idea how much she mourned Tess. How she regretted every single moment she wasn't with her. The extent to which she blamed herself—part Other or not—for Tess's death. She tried to ignore the vision of Tess's face under the shimmering blue water of the cave. The feel of her heartbeat pulsating between her fingers. She'd played and replayed what happened between her and Tess in her mind a million times. Things couldn't have gone differently. She was sure of it. She focused on what was here. What was now. She knew Elora was trying to manipulate her again. To trick her.

"That's none of your business. She betrayed me. If I didn't do what I did—"

"Then maybe you'd still be together."

"No." Calay shook her head from side to side. Like a fool, she'd almost accepted the loss of her previous life. Previous *lives*. There was the one she cautiously navigated with Jacob these last few months. The one she'd so carefully built through the years with Tess. The one where she was just a girl who wanted to be loved by her parents. With each new turn, she had reinvented herself, only to lose another piece of who she was once the dust settled.

Then she'd been brought here. Coming to this place couldn't get her closer to Tess, but there had been the hope, however fleeting, that Jacob and she could have a future together. She clung to it, twisted, wrung it of life. Still, she'd wished one day, someday, she and Jacob would find their way to each other. That she'd find her way to herself. But then she'd come face to face with the woman she'd called Mom. Or at least, this thing that looked like her mom. And then those horrible, twisted clones. And all of it shattered.

She shattered.

Or at least, she thought she had. An awareness climbed Calay's thoughts—somehow she'd survived. She'd fought, and fucked, and ran, and here she was. There was something growing inside her that hadn't been there four months ago.

A strength. A resilience. A truth. Something she believed but couldn't quite name yet.

For once, it wasn't for someone else. She hadn't found it for Tess. Or

Jacob. Or her parents. It was all her own. It had given her the courage to go to Elora, stop her from doing what the Others intended to do. Calay was prepared to kill her, if necessary. Wasn't that what she'd told Jacob in the basement? And yet, pinned under Elora's stare, trapped here, she couldn't even keep her feet beneath her, never mind end the coming apocalypse. What humans had endured for more than four years would pale in comparison to what Elora was about to do to them. They weren't prepared for what was coming.

Despite whatever it was that was growing inside her, Calay wasn't either. She swallowed, forced herself to meet Elora's bitter gaze.

"Maybe you haven't put it together yet, honey." Elora rushed forward.

Calay staggered, trying to maintain the distance between them. She tripped over her feet, halting as she half-stumbled into the console of dials and buttons. She threw her hands back, trying to hold herself up. The sharp edges dug into the backs of her thighs.

Elora only stopped when their chests were an inch apart.

This is not how this was supposed to go. It wasn't how anything was supposed to go.

Elora loomed above, her breath like ice on Calay's skin. She thrust her arms on either side of Calay like the long, white columns in the basement. The pods. There was nowhere for her to go. There was no escape.

"Put what together?" Calay whispered.

"You murdered Tess for doing the exact same thing you're trying to do now."

CHAPTER NINETEEN

THE ROOM SPUN on its axis. Or maybe it was just Calay.

Elora's words lodged themselves inside her. They nestled somewhere deep and dark. Somewhere she hadn't allowed herself to go before. She couldn't. Because if she did, she knew there would be no going back to the world as it was. To the person she'd been. After a lifetime of self-doubt, she'd finally started to trust herself. In doing so, she'd come here. To Elora. To the truth.

It was about to split her in two.

She grasped the console, it dug into her palms. She gripped harder. If she could just make the outside hurt more than the inside, maybe she'd...what? Survive? She sneered, stifled a half-laugh, half-sob. Maybe she didn't want to make it through this after all. She resisted Elora's words. Her gaze. A raw, overwhelming sensation washed through Calay. Over her. Like a tidal wave.

Gods, Elora was right.

Calay was no different from Tess.

Tess had been fighting the aliens. She'd known all along how dangerous they were, the lengths they would go to destroy humanity. She'd done everything in her power to stop them. Even at the expense of Calay's life. Tess hadn't been wrong in trying to have Calay killed. She'd been smart. All these years, Calay hadn't looked far enough ahead. For her, each moment with Tess was about survival. One day at a time. How often had she told herself—told Tess—that if they avoided detection, they'd be okay? As if that would be enough.

Calay needed it to be. If it was, then maybe she'd be enough.

If only she had been willing to look deeper, maybe she would have seen what Tess saw. Grown with her. Maybe Tess would still be alive. They'd be together, united. In the end, Tess saw the Others for what they really were. A cruel, hungry, alien species who would be satisfied with nothing short of total annihilation. The Others wanted one thing and one thing only—the death of every living human being on the planet. They'd do anything to get it. And the worst part of it—she was, at a core level—one of them.

A monster.

That was why Tess had done what she'd done. Why the Resistance was so militant in its memorandums and propaganda. There was no room for compromise. No time for delay or weakness. When Calay was held prisoner at their compound, she didn't find evidence the Resistance knew the full breadth of the Others' plans, but they saw them coming, nonetheless. Tess saw them coming. She was on one side of the fight, Calay was on the other. And she hadn't even known it.

The fate of humanity wedged between them.

Calay shivered, cold sweat covered her body. Her view of Elora became a watery, waving blob of green and black as her vision swam with tears. The dim lights of the lab and switches on the controls glistened beyond the wall of unshed tears.

Calay had mourned Tess over the past four months, but she was able to wake up each frigid morning on the top of the Loft, freezing and alone, coated in a dusting of snow, because she told herself she'd done what she had to do. That Tess deserved to die because of what she'd done to her. She had been so sure of it. She had to be. Tess's death had to have meaning. Calay told herself she'd done it to save not only herself, but the world. But all this time, all those mornings, she'd been wrong.

She'd murdered Tess.

In doing so, Calay had sentenced Earth to its death too.

The dam broke and tears poured down Calay's cheeks, dripping off her chin, onto the floor.

"How does it feel, daughter?" Elora said from somewhere off to Calay's left. "To know you killed the only woman who ever loved you?"

The aching cavern in Calay's chest grew wider. She sobbed harder. She didn't need Elora to elaborate. Could read between the spiteful lines. Understood what she was implying.

"Why did you ever bring me here?" Calay said.

"We just went over that, Calay. No sense in beating a dead horse. Or a dead girlfriend."

"Stop it, please."

"You did this, not me. I tried to help you."

"Help me?" Calay swiped at tears, cleared her throat. "You used me!"

"Hurts, doesn't it?" A consistent clicking forced Calay to turn and face Elora, who was positioned next to the cylindrical chamber, in front of a series of knobs and flashing lights. She was twisting them, each sounding-off with a flick of Elora's wrist. She tapped the glass as small white crystals formed inside. "We learn from the best, my girl. Now do you see? Human's wretched existence is a waste of life. It will be better utilized to sustain ours. I told you this was going to change everything."

"The snow?"

"Water, Calay. It's toxic to Térasians, but it's unmatched in its ability to generate power."

"You want our water…"

"Your planet is predominantly water. Unfortunately, humans have been wasting it by watering lawns and funneling it into plastic bottles your planet will never break down. Imagine our delight when we found out the second highest source of water on your planet were human bodies."

"What are you saying, Elora?"

"What do you think I'm saying? Our experiments have shown it doesn't matter whether we funnel water into the chamber as a pure form or stuff one of you in there. On its own, water burns more cleanly, and we can convert it to energy more easily, but you should see how long one of you will keep our starship running. The shuttles. We can even convert you into a sustainable food source if we get desperate."

"What kind of food source?" Calay braced herself.

"Anything your mind can dream up, the hive can manufacture." Elora's eyes darkened, her lips curved into a slick smile.

Calay blanched in the dim light of the room, making her appear more ghostly than she already felt. Nausea churned her stomach as she pictured the reflective glass tower in the cafeteria. The honey and peanut butter sandwich. The waffles. The grapefruit juice. Each mouthful. It wasn't magic after all.

It was cannibalism.

She wretched.

"How?"

"Energy never disappears, Calay. It merely transforms." Elora tapped the glass of the tower again.

"You burn people in there? Alive?"

"We can make pieces of you last for weeks."

"That's horrible."

"Depends who you ask. We find it rather ingenious." Elora strode back toward Calay, reached for her hand. "Two birds, one giant fucking spinning rock in space."

"Get away from me." Calay recoiled. The console was rubbing her thighs raw. Her palms too.

"Don't be so melodramatic. You're one of us."

"I'll never be like you."

"You already are, Calay."

"I'm not."

"You're an alien, for better or for worse. You're a part of us as much as we're a part of you."

"That doesn't make me evil. Not like you."

"You're a liar. A murderer. An adulteress. You can't be trusted. Do you really think you can return to them now? As one of them? They'll never accept you. Not like we will."

"You want to feed off human beings, Elora!" Calay shook her head, batted Elora's arm away. She pushed herself past Elora's towering frame, making her way across the room to the holographic display. She pulled up the strategy Elora had been flipping through when Calay first arrived. A silence fell over the room as she swiped through each slide. The ones they'd discussed together. "All these plans. They could have worked. What you said before, about saving our civilizations. Why not follow through with them? We could have done it."

Elora sighed, strode to meet Calay. She brushed Calay aside along with the slides. In their place, she pulled up a jarringly familiar view.

Calay hadn't seen it since they'd ran screaming that first morning of the Change. It was the first time she'd seen it from this side. The Others' side. It was their apartment building in vivid detail. She could almost hear the leaves rustling in the trees that lined their cobblestone street, smell the hot dogs in the cart at the end of the block, and feel the ridges of the brick steps of their six-story walk-up beneath her feet. She gazed at the yellow curtains she and Tess had found at the thrift store around the corner, rippling in the morning breeze. Then, blue light.

The sight made Calay's heart wrench. It was now gone. All of it.

So many of the horrible things that followed the invasion weren't about survival at all. It was about pleasure. She couldn't deny Tess had been right about everything—the aliens were dangerous and needed to be stopped at all costs. But Tess had missed an important threat. The one Calay had fought so hard to protect them from: other people. Calay had spent over four years avoiding human interactions. There was no way to tell who was good or who was bad, who would do the wrong thing for the right reasons. She couldn't even tame the monster inside herself; she'd done things too. In the end it didn't matter. What did was that she kept herself and Tess safe. That they had each other. Watching the scenes flip from one horrific scenario to another, Calay couldn't believe the two of them survived as long as they did. It certainly made her attempts to make a case for humanity more difficult. To see how they could recover after everything that had happened. But if she'd made it this long, this far, then others must have too.

"Good people still exist. That's something worth holding on to."

"The human part of you makes me sick." Elora scoffed. Calay ignored the twinge in her heart. She never really had her mother's approval on

Earth. She wouldn't have it here, either. Not that she'd ever admit it, deep down she still yearned for it. "You're a selfish, fragile, wasteful species. You just saw for yourself. After we arrived, you watched how quickly your weak civilization fell and how fast you turned on each other. Your precious world is gone, Calay. You killed it. There's nothing left to save and yet, you insist on wanting to do just that. Despite logic and evidence, you continue to hold onto hope. It's desperate and revolting."

Calay exhaled, shrugged. Elora was right that humans had acted selfishly. They were wasteful of time, energy, and resources—but they weren't inherently bad. They were products of their society, weren't they? Isn't that exactly what Elora had said last time they stood in this very spot? Calay may not have drunk the whole jug of Térasian Kool-Aid, and she hated to give her credit, but Elora had gotten a few things right. That meant people could change. For the better. For their future.

"Most people are good."

"Is that what you think? After everything! Seriously?"

She pulled her shoulders back, brought herself to face Elora. She released a shaky breath. She couldn't bring Tess back, and that was now the greatest regret of her life. Calay's duality may have caused an irreparable rift between herself and Tess, but it also granted her access to something Tess could never have achieved. Tess likely still would have been trying to take down pods, which Calay now saw was barely a ripple in an ever-growing tide. Tess's plans were like skimming a rock across the ocean; Calay had the opportunity now to pull the drain on the whole fucking thing. Maybe she should have let Tess kill her. But then again, if she had, she wouldn't be here to do what needed to be done.

"I don't know for sure, but it's what I believe," Calay said.

"Then you're useless to me."

Elora's jaw unhinged. A black cavern formed where her mouth should have been. Her lips cracked and lost their color. Her eyes sagged and her skin became waxy. Calay cowered. Elora was transforming out of her human form, back to her natural shape. Like Ash. Calay's heart raced, she struggled for breath. She couldn't go through that again. She had to do something.

Anything.

So she lunged.

She grabbed Elora around the waist and flung her across the room. She didn't let go. Instead, she gripped harder, refusing to let Elora's ugly outside match her inside. The two tumbled over each other hard against the floor, their legs flailing as each one tried to right herself and gain the upper hand.

They came to a stop against the glass of the tower at the far end of the room. It shuddered under their weight, but thankfully, didn't shatter.

A moment passed. Maybe two. Calay's mind was fuzzy, her vision darkened.

She brought her hand to the back of her head. She was already developing a bump. She must have hit it in the fall. That meant she had a concussion. She squinted against the dull ache throbbing at her temples, glanced at Elora. Any traces of the scary Térasian alien that was about to bust out of the human skin-suit was gone. She looked like Calay's mother again. *Oh, good.* Calay had succeeded in stopping the transformation, but this version of Elora was almost as scary as her natural form.

"Was that really worth it?" Elora growled, pushed herself to sit.

"I told Jacob I'd do anything to stop you." Calay growled back.

"And I told you that you might be important to our cause, but you aren't irreplaceable. If you keep fighting, I will end you. We'll find another. You aren't special."

"Maybe not." Calay coughed, cleared her throat. "But I meant what I said."

"So did I."

"I'll kill you if I have to." Calay knew pushing Elora was a risk, but it was a necessary one. Like Elora had told her when Calay had first arrived, they were playing a game of chess.

Since this all began, the Others were predicting how humans would react, what their next steps would be. Then they positioned themselves to win. They were always eight moves ahead, taking pawns—people— one by one. That was about to change. Right now, Calay expected Elora was calling her bluff. Shifting her pieces along the board to call checkmate where Calay would be captured and have no choice but to go along with their plans. Because hadn't she always? Sure, she'd struggled to reunite with Tess. To survive when the aliens attacked. But when push really came to shove and she was staring into the bleakness of the ill-fated future, Calay always gave up. Went inside herself. Made her world small. Turtled, as Jacob liked to call it. So Calay had to do the thing Elora didn't expect. She had to position her Bishop and take the Queen.

She had to fight.

Elora threw her long leg over Calay's short body, still sprawled on the ground.

Calay clawed at Elora's thick fists as they balled the neck of Calay's shirt, dragging her up against the glass. Her head rebounded off it, the pounding reverberated through her bones. Elora's hands wrapped around Calay's neck. Her black eyes bulged. Calay fought for breath against the cold grip of Elora's stare, her impossibly long, icy fingers. They were like a vise around her throat. Relentless. Calay felt the life being squeezed out of her. *Come on, Calay. Fight.* Calay's legs flailed, her lungs burned. How poetic it would be if she were to die the same way Tess died, for doing the same thing Tess had been trying to do. Maybe they really were meant to be, and this was the universe's way of bringing them home to each other. A homecoming of sorts. Once and for all.

Calay's human body weakened under Elora's alien grasp. She needed help, even if that meant turning to the one thing she wanted to get away from more than anything. Her dark side. Her Other side. She may not have been special, but it was that commonality—the utter mundaneness of being—that was her superpower.

She'd yearned so long to belong somewhere. To someone. She'd missed the opportunity right in front of her. She wasn't entirely human, but she wasn't entirely Other, either.

She was both.

The lights flickered. The hum of the hive filled the room. If connecting to the hive mind brought Ash's army down upon them, then so be it. Calay was surprised they hadn't come for her already. Elora must have been holding them at bay. *It figures.* She had to have some pair on her to think she could do all this. Fool Calay. Destroy humanity. Win. Calay focused her thoughts, her mind pulled on Elora's.

Elora's eyes flashed with surprise, then rage.

Calay had only a moment to summon her mental energy and tug on Elora's consciousness, but it was enough.

A rough, raspy roar exploded out of Elora's mouth, her breath acrid against Calay's neck. Elora's grip loosened and Calay swung. Her fist connected with Elora's jaw. Elora's back arched with the force, and Calay pushed her the rest of the way, sending her sprawling. Calay gawked, inhaled swooping, deep breaths.

There wasn't time to recover. She had to move.

Calay, fight.

She scrambled to her feet, made for the control panel. It wasn't until now she noticed the delicate white flakes swirling inside the glass chamber. They hovered, whirring in rapid circles. How did Elora get it to melt? Did it matter? Water was lethal to the Others. She just had to somehow get the stuff out of the container.

Or get Elora in.

The last thing Calay wanted to do was kill anyone else. She'd seen enough death to last her a lifetime. Several, probably. But she couldn't let the Others follow through with their plans. If she could just figure out which button to push. A way to open the column. Then she could stuff Elora inside. Close it. If Calay could do that, maybe she could just lock Elora in while she figured out how to stop an alien army from taking over the planet and killing every human on Earth. No one would have to die. *This is crazy, of course someone has to die.* That was the way of the universe now.

Calay was determined it wasn't going to be her.

She threw a quick look over her shoulder. Her not-mother was still splayed out on the floor. Unconscious.

Calay rushed to the chamber. Ran her hands over every inch, desperate to find a lock. A latch. A hidden compartment. There had to be a way to get something inside. Elora had said as much. They'd done experiments. On people. She shuddered. She didn't want to think about it. She just wanted to secure Elora, figure out how to save Earth, and get the hell out of there.

Her eyes grew wide as the swirling snow melted and pooled.

Her heart leapt in her chest. Her stomach dropped.

She spun on her heels.

Then everything went black.

CHAPTER TWENTY

THE WORST PART about being trapped in a far-off galaxy on the alien ship wasn't that Calay had lost Jacob. Though as she came to, she felt that loss.

Deep within her heart. Her mind. Her spirit.

It hurt. Everywhere.

She forced her eyes open, blinked, starred up at the dark ceiling. Small dots of light winked back. Their gentle light forced a sharp pain in the back of her head, pressing pause on each memory as they scrolled through her mind.

The night she'd met him in her camp, and he'd offered her the rabbit. The smell of the cabin the first time they'd found comfort in each other's arms. The second in the barn. The gentle look in his eyes when he revealed she was one of Them, and the friendship that followed.

She winced. It had all been a ploy. Part of some grand plan to manipulate and get her on the Others' side. He insisted those moments were real, and maybe on some level, he truly believed that. But she couldn't. Not anymore. The idea seared the edges of her heart, daring it to continue beating. As if with each pulse, a little more might be burned away. With every breath, her chest ached.

Breathe in. Breathe out. Just breathe.

It wasn't that Calay seemed to make mistake after sloppy mistake. She was willing to admit she hadn't asked enough tough questions. Hadn't fought for the answers she needed to hear but didn't want to. She'd needed to believe what the Others told her. Because if she went along with it, she'd finally have the home she'd longed for. Months had gone by. Years. Most of her god damned life, and she'd never really fit in. Not in their world. Not Tess's. Not even her own. So when they promised her a place she could belong, a place she could contribute and make a real difference, of course she'd jumped at the chance. She'd had misgivings and lingering doubts that etched at her mind, but she didn't trust herself. After Tess's betrayal and the knowledge Calay had gotten everything wrong for so long, how could she? So she'd ignored her intuition and rushed headlong into the embrace of the Others' lies because it was what she wanted to hear. Calay saw what she wanted to see. Until she saw things she couldn't ignore.

Do. Not. Panic.

It wasn't even the herd of Eloras, or the fact that Calay had finally been reunited with who she thought was her mother, only to have her ripped away once more. As Elora said, if Calay had done what she was told, kept her nose clean, everything would have worked out as the Others had planned and Calay could have gone on believing she'd come home to mom.

She should have known it was too good to be true.

Elora was dead. The mother she knew, gone. Her father had told her so, hadn't he? When Calay and Jacob first arrived on her childhood farm, Peter had seemed unwell but sane. But who knew when he actually lost his mind? In the span of a day, he went from frying bacon with Jacob in the kitchen to nearly beating him to death.

Calay's eyes shot open, her heart lurched.

Oh my god, no.

Just like Tess, her father had tried to do the right thing, and Calay had killed him for it. Buried a pitchfork in his skull. Maybe he'd known more about the Others' plans than he'd let on. Calay thought he'd gone crazy, but what if all this time he was actually trying to keep her safe as he'd claimed? And now, she could never ask him. Because he was dead.

Both of Calay's parents were gone. And for one reason or another, it was her fault. But even this realization wasn't the worst part of the whole ordeal.

It was that she couldn't control any of it. The feeling of helplessness. All this had happened and there wasn't a damn thing Calay could do about it. Nothing she could change. If she could go back to the day the Others invaded, maybe she'd do things differently. At the end of everything, she had to live with herself. With the choices she'd made. The only question now was for how long that might be.

She groaned, felt the ground list. No, it wasn't the ground. It was her. Someone—or something—was tugging on her legs. She slid along the floor, a few inches at a time. The motion gnawed at the gash in her shoulder.

She was being moved.

She had to pull herself together.

The lights dimmed, a shadow crossed over her. She peeked from behind her lashes, watched Elora lean over the console. She adjusted dials, turned the big round one counterclockwise. Her hand hovered over the gray switch, she hesitated, turned toward Calay.

Calay clamped her eyes shut, hoped against hope she might be able to buy herself some time if Elora didn't know she was awake.

The shadow passed again. She heard a swoosh, like air pressure releasing.

She focused her gaze, looked around. Confusion flooded her body. Then dread. *So much for time.* Elora had somehow released the door to the glass chamber. Calay watched her apply pressure on the glass as it popped out and slid up the side of the tower. It raised about three feet in the air, then hovered.

Waiting.

How much of Calay's life had been wasted the same way? It seemed she was always waiting. For someone to accept her. To love her. To give her the things she needed. After the Change, she'd delayed taking action against the Others, and Tess made other plans. Calay failed to own her truth, and Jacob substituted his. Before Ash showed up at the Loft, Calay might have gathered food and supplies, did what she had to to keep her and Jacob alive. But she hadn't lived. She'd merely existed. Waited to die.

She'd felt so out of control. She'd clung to anything that gave order to the chaos. Finding Tess. Avoiding Jacob. Coming here. Maybe they weren't so much mistakes as coping mechanisms. A chance to feel less fragile. Less afraid. Less alone. And yet, the harder she pushed, the more alone she was. None of the decisions she'd made had brought her closer to the things she really wanted.

Acceptance. Love. Truth.

Okay, maybe she'd achieved some truth over the last four months. But the fact was, the truth hurt. The ache in her head throbbed as if in response. For the first time, Calay thought maybe that was okay. Maybe the worst thing about this whole experience came from resisting the pain. If she just leaned into it, accepted it, maybe it would be easier to deal with. To navigate. To surrender control and let what would happen, happen. Calay starred into the empty chamber. It seemed to stare back.

Once again, and maybe for the last time, she had a choice to make. She pressed her lips together, propped herself up on her elbows. She swallowed as Elora turned, positioned herself between Calay's feet and the chamber.

"Last chance, my daughter." Elora thrust her hands on her hips. "Join us."

Calay's revelation boosted her bravado. "I've already told you where I stand."

"I wish you wouldn't make me do this." Elora sighed, grasping for Calay.

"Oh, fuck off, Elora. I'm not making you do anything. We're adults. We make our own decisions." She kicked at Elora's hands, tried to shuffle backward.

"You're right." Elora stood straight, towered over Calay. "I'm going to enjoy this."

"Go to Hell."

"You're the one who's going to burn." Elora wrapped her arm around Calay's ankles and began pulling her, inch by inch, into the chamber.

Calay screamed, she thrashed her arms wildly, reaching over her legs for Elora. She'd watched the way the flames swallowed the air inside of the glass. She didn't want them to swallow her too.

An image floated through her mind. One from when she first arrived here: as she exited the pod, her skin bubbled, dripped through the metal grates of the loading dock; her bones wedged between them, held her up like a puppet; fire raged in the back of her throat.

Fear pulsed through Calay, certain she'd foreseen her own death.

Was this really the end?

It couldn't be. Not now. Not when she'd come so far. Not when she had to stop the Others.

She flung herself one way, then the other. Elora was too strong. Calay, too weak. Too tired. She hadn't rested enough. Hadn't eaten enough. Her nervous system was shot. Still, this couldn't be it. She felt it in every part of her being. And finally, she was ready to trust that inner-knowing. That feeling. Herself.

As Elora dragged Calay's body fully into the chamber, Calay tried something she hadn't before. Instead of resisting, she surrendered. Her whole body went limp.

Just like when Calay had tugged at Elora's mind through the hive, she caught Elora by surprise. The weight of her legs nearly bowled her over. Calay watched as she stumbled sideways, propped herself against the glass.

Calay's eyes narrowed. Just because she was surrendering didn't mean she wouldn't fight. For her life. For humanity. For what was right.

The glass of the chamber shook as Calay wrenched her legs from Elora's hands and sprung to her feet. Her vision darkened at the edges, her head swam. Still, she plunged forward, driving her throbbing head into Elora's stomach.

Elora wheezed, the air knocked clean out of her.

This was Calay's moment. She turned to run but was wrenched back by her hair. Elora managed to grab two fistfuls of it.

Calay twisted, swat at Elora whose eyes had begun to sag once again. Her skin tinted gray. The olive-green tunic bulged on her back. A sharp smell bloomed around them.

Calay gasped, her eyed widened in horror. If Elora was to shift in the tube with both of them inside, Calay was finished.

She turned her back to Elora, gathered her courage, and screamed as she charged toward the door, leaving two clumps of hair behind in Elora's hands. A loud, wet, ripping sound followed Calay when she tumbled out the opening. Her scalp felt like it was on fire, her stomach heaved. But there wasn't time for that. She spun on her heel and tried to steady her shaking legs. She wanted to run from this room, but she knew she'd never escape back to Earth, limbs and life intact if she did that. She'd have to do something horrible if she wanted to survive. Something that could very well destroy her.

She'd told Jacob she'd kill Elora if she had to. But even after all this, staring through the glass at the heaving, half-mother, half-alien thing that was gripping Calay's scalp and her dark hair in her unnaturally long, jagged fingers, she hoped it wouldn't come to that.

Their gazes met. Both of them ceased to breathe. The moment froze between them, cold, hard, unyielding. Elora no longer looked human. As Calay peered closer, she realized she didn't quite look Other, either.

She leered at Calay, her neck bobbing like a bird's, and her eyes grew darker. Her tongue darted in and out of her cracked lips, like a snake. *Or a very mean, very agitated alien.*

Calay's gaze darted to the open door of the chamber. Could she get to it before Elora got to her? It was worth a shot.

A deep, dark growl emanated from behind the glass. Calay lunged. Out of the corner of her eye, she saw Elora did too, her legs bent back on their haunches. Calay jumped, slammed her palms on the top of the glass.

The door dropped down, melting at the edges and sealing the sides as if it had never opened. The tower shuddered against the weight of Elora's monstrous form hurling into it. She roared with each attempt, and streams of phlegm clung to the glass.

Terrified it would burst outward, Calay cowered, pressed herself against the console, threw her arms over her head. The glass never broke. She huddled there, staring in the darkness, watching Elora thrash against the walls of the chamber. Willed herself not to look away. She may have locked Elora inside, but that was only the first step. If she didn't finish this, it would never be over.

Elora called humans selfish and wasteful, but the Others were rapacious. Their true desires, insatiable. They wouldn't stop until Calay and everyone like her were dead. Rounded up, butchered, and used as energy. Calay had to wait Elora out. Do what needed to be done.

She covered her ears with her forearms, her eyes with her palms.

Eventually, the sounds stopped.

She peeked at the chamber to find Elora had turned back into her mother-like, human form. Any traces of the alien inside were gone. She stood, her nose practically pressed against the wall. The glass fogged under her breath.

Calay rose as well, approached. Her breath hitched in her throat when Elora made eye contact with her. *You're okay*. It seemed to Calay that Elora was trapped in there. She would remain that way until someone rescued her. No one had. Not yet, anyway. It was possible Elora had blocked Ash and her horde through the hive mind, or maybe this room was reinforced like the basement, blocking her signal for help. Calay swallowed, she had to admit there was also the possibility Ash was holding them at bay, waiting until Elora was gone, and then they'd storm the room, shred Calay to pieces, and secure her bid for power. The uncertainties piled up in her mind. She tried not to read too much into it. Instead, she focused on what was in front of her.

Elora.

"No one's come to help you," Calay said.

"Nor you." Elora cocked her well-defined eyebrow. "He would have before. But then again, he was under my command."

Another truth. Ouch.

Elora was right. Jacob had always come for her. Rescued her when she needed saving. She'd finally convinced herself she didn't need him. And yet, it still stung that he didn't need her. That maybe—likely—he'd only ever been following orders.

"I don't need help."

"No, I suppose you don't." Elora tapped the glass with her long nails. The beds were laced with black, the tips sharp like serrated knives. So she wasn't entirely back to her human-form. The beast inside her must have been aching to get out. "What exactly is your plan now, Calay? You can't leave me in here forever."

"I know that." Calay released a shaky exhale, let the tension in her shoulders drop. For the moment, she seemed to be safe. She raised a hand to the glass, dropped it, and sighed. "I wish you'd never sent for me. You know that? I wish you'd stayed dead."

"Well, I didn't. So what's your plan, girl?"

"I'm still figuring that part out," Calay admitted.

"Your impulsiveness always amazes me, Calay. You never think things through."

"You took everything from me! From us." Calay rushed the glass. "Jesus! Excuse me if I need a moment to gather myself, *mother*."

"The things we took were never yours to begin with."

"Tess and I were happy. Jacob and I could have been, I think. The world was fine as it was…"

"Your world was broken. It still is. I'm going to clean up the mess humans made. Take back the natural order of things."

"Genocide isn't natural!"

"It isn't genocide when the ones being exterminated are animals. Like I said before, the superior species always comes out on top. We feed on our prey."

"You know…" Calay pulled her shoulders back, her lips pressed tight. Elora had no idea of the power she was unleashing inside of Calay. With every syllable, she felt more confident the Others didn't know what they were getting themselves into when they attacked Earth. When they attacked her. Her body quivered. Her soul too. "Some animals on Earth disguise themselves as prey, but they're really the predator."

"Please." Elora scoffed, looked down her nose at Calay as if she were a bug.

"We are not your prey," Calay growled.

"That's what every species says, in their own way of course. Then their planet falls, like the last. It's only a matter of time."

"How much time do you need, exactly? You've gone to such lengths to destroy us. To take over our planet. It's been almost five years and you still can't kill us. What does that say about you?"

"We will succeed…"

"With our help! You can't do it without us. You have all this hate inside you. This ugliness. And it isn't enough. It'll never be enough."

"You'll never be enough." Elora hissed. "You were never enough for us to love you. You weren't enough for Tess—she'd rather see you dead. Jacob doesn't love you. Ash used you. You're nothing. Nothing!"

She'd done it. Elora had finally said the words Calay had dreaded she'd hear her whole life, from the very mouth she feared she'd hear them. Her deepest, darkest fears dragged kicking and screaming into the cold dim light in front of her. There they were. They hung heavy between the two women.

Calay slowed her breathing. She braced herself for the tears to come. To fall apart.

When one moment passed, and then another, she almost smirked. Her fears were as real as ever, they would likely be with her until the day she died. Which, Calay admitted, could be any moment. But the fact was, Elora's words carried no weight. They were hollow. And for once, Calay's heart felt full.

She may not have had her parents anymore, Ash's passion, Jacob's comforting embrace, or Tess's love, but she had herself.

"I'm enough." Calay stepped backward, increasing the distance between herself and the glass tower.

"You don't really believe that."

"I do, actually." Calay took a deep breath, let it flow through her lungs. "All my life I've been told I'm not. But hearing it now, from your hateful mouth, after everything you've done, it doesn't matter. I don't need your approval. I don't need anyone's approval. I'm getting off this ship, and I'm going the fuck home."

"There's no home to go back to, Calay. Your planet is dying."

"Not if I have anything to do with it. People may have done some pretty shitty, horrible, fucked-up things, but most of us are good. We'll come back from this. Like we've come back from everything else."

"This isn't like everything else."

"You don't think I know that? God, the things we've been through. The things you put us through!" Calay turned to the control panels. Her hand hovered over the knob. "Are you even a little sorry for what you've done to us? What you've done to other civilizations? Other planets?"

"We do what we must to survive."

That was what the Others got wrong. No one had to die for their survival. Between the Others resourcefulness and human's resilience, they could have thrived. Built a world where both their species could grow together. One free of the plights that had plagued humanity: Inequity. Injustice. Environmental collapse. One overflowing with love and abundance. But that future would never be realized. Hate would never save their species. Calay realized arguing further was futile. The Others would never be satisfied. They'd never be satiated. And they'd never stop coming for Earth.

It was all that ever was. All that ever would be.

"There wasn't any other way for this to end, was there? One of us was always going to have to die." Calay's voice shook with emotion.

"Clever girl." Elora sneered.

"And you weren't ever going to let me go, were you?"

"You were going to be useful to us. One way or another."

"I'm sorry it's come to this," Calay said and meant it. She was sorry for everything. For all that had happened in the last four years. For what would happen in the next four. She didn't know where they went from here as a species. She didn't even know how she was going to get home.

All she knew was this was it. Her moment. Humanity's.

"You still haven't answered me. What are you going to do, Calay?"

"You said it yourself, Elora—there's only death here now."

With a flick of her wrist, Calay snapped her fingers over the gray switch on the controls and lit the chamber ablaze. She squinted against the brightness of the flame. Shades of red and orange licked her eyelids.

She forced herself to watch.

Elora's skin bubbled in the searing light, her feet melted to the floor. One dripped through the metal grates. The ankle bone of the other wedged itself between them, propping her up like a puppet. Her eyes boiled in her head. Calay thought Elora tried to scream and gaped as flames erupted from her throat. Elora swatted at her lips, tried to put them out. But they caught fire too. Until they popped like fireworks. *Pop Rocks*. One at a time, lodging shrapnel of bone and flesh between her teeth. Somehow, she was still alive. Still there. Still breathing.

Calay shuddered. The vision she'd had of herself melting on the platform of the loading bay hadn't been her death. It had been Elora's. Her mind reeled. Somehow, she'd predicted—seen—her demise, but how? Had she somehow connected to something through the hive mind? Was time experienced differently here? And why her? Once again, Calay was flooded with questions she'd never get the answers to.

As if in response to Calay's thoughts, Elora collapsed onto her knees. Her flesh oozed away, revealing the horrific form stuffed inside. Gray and sickly green limbs, a bulbous body, patches of wiry hair. It remained a lump in the bottom of the cylinder.

Calay flicked the switch to off.

The fire burned itself out on the remaining chunks of human bio matter.

What if fire couldn't kill the Others? What if nothing could? The thought sent a chill through to her bones, despite the residual heat radiating off the chamber. She waited. Held her breath. Peered closer.

The alien body writhed on the floor, its limbs twisted at unnatural angles. Its face was a raw pigment of decaying flesh and bone. A scream caught in Calay's throat as she inhaled sharply. She couldn't make herself turn away from the way it sprawled across the glass. Raked the floor. Bent in ways no living thing should. Calay's hands clawed the control panel, blindly fingered the buttons, looking for the switch to light the chamber again.

Then, the alien body turned to ash, streamed like sand through the grates.

Everything grew silent.

This time, the world didn't right itself. It never would again.

Calay brought her hands to her chest, her heart slowed. Her breathing too. Her mind spun. This thing was not her mother, but it was the closest semblance she had left of one. Or at least, it was.

The ground rose to meet her, or maybe it was her legs finally giving out. It was hard to tell. They'd gone numb. They'd seen her through so much today. She knew they'd have to see her through the following days as well. However many she had. She may have ended Elora, but *this*? This was far from finished. There was still a ship full of aliens who wanted to see her—and the rest of humanity—dead.

She'd handle them.

She would.

She just needed a moment.

CHAPTER TWENTY-ONE

WHEN SHE FINALLY RAN OUT OF tears, Calay let the coldness of the floor seep through her skin. She pressed her cheek against it, grateful for the respite from the heat still rising from the chamber. Had it been minutes? Hours? She couldn't tell. It didn't matter. Time was irrelevant. All that mattered was this moment.

Here.

Now.

Move.

She pushed herself to her feet. The pain in the back of her head almost brought her to her knees. She steadied herself on the console, pulled her scarf off, wrapped it tightly around the wound with the hope she'd heal soon enough. *At least physically*. The room was quiet. Too quiet.

She glanced at the empty chamber. Raised her hand to the glass. The warmth radiated up her arm. A hollowness filled her chest. Any trace of the alien she'd called Elora—Mother—was gone. And with her, the dream of family. Calay swallowed the knowledge it hadn't been her mother she'd just burned alive. It'd been a monster. A horrible creature that wore her mother's skin like a suit. She was glad it was dead.

She scanned the grated floor. She exhaled, her arm grew heavy. She let it fall to her side. She'd been so foolish. So naïve. She'd wanted her mother's love more than anything. So much so she was willing to fly to a distant galaxy to be with her, even if it meant she'd never see Earth's surface again. The truth was, deep down, despite her bravado, she had just wanted her parents back. Her family. She should have known it was a pipe dream. An impossible one. Night after night, she'd wished upon star after star for it. But the light had long gone out.

For all of them.

The memory of Tess's almond brown eyes growing dull drifted through Calay's mind. Gods, how she'd loved her. Tess had been everything. Her truth. Her hope. Her world. The Others had taken her from Calay. Through Jacob's deceit, they'd convinced her Tess was the bad guy. But the Others were the evil ones. And now that Calay knew what she knew, she couldn't trust Jacob. She'd thought he'd been there for her, supported her. Loved her. And maybe in some sick, toxic way, he did. But it was because of him that her father was gone. Now, her mother too. His dishonesty led Calay here. To the place where she'd finally had to say goodbye, once and for all. To Tess. To him. To her mom.

If Calay was being fair to Jacob, her relationship with Elora had gone up in flames long before Calay flicked that switch. It had died when her parents kicked her out of her childhood home and disowned her because she'd been different from them.

Calay's mouth turned down at the sides, she stifled a whimper. They'd been horrible to her. The Others had been horrible to people. And People had been horrible to each other.

Still, Calay couldn't help but wonder if there was a way back from all of this. Not for her and her family. That was finished, and she'd regret how it ended for every remaining day of her life. But maybe there was still a chance for humanity. She sniffed, wiped away the remaining tears and snot from her face. As long as there was air in her lungs, Calay was sure there must be. The Others took away so much from her, she'd be damned if they got to take that too.

She wanted to help the human race and save the planet. The ideas the Others had planted in her mind had firmly taken root and were growing. There had to be a way to fix things. It was the only reason she was still standing. She couldn't see quite what it was yet, but she would. She would figure things out. Because that's what she did. Despite everything. She survived.

The lights cut out, the room plunged into darkness.

Calay stiffened, held her breath. *What now?* Of course, she knew what. The end of Elora was not the end of the Others. She was all too aware she was still trapped on an alien ship, two billion lightyears away from Earth.

The lights flashed once. Twice. Came back on.

She only began to breathe again when a penetrating beeping noise boomed through the ship. Calay clamped her hands over her ears, winced. It was deafening.

She shot forward, the door fizzled into thin air as she focused her energy to open it. Threads of it clung to her arms, her legs, her hair. Like silly string that had melted on a sidewalk in late August. She swatted at it, pulled. Sticky on her fingers, it fell to her feet in big clumps. *This is new.* Calay shook her head, stared with wide eyes as she watched the material meld with and disappear into the smooth floor. It was possible Elora's energy still somehow fused the door together, and Calay was breaking through that. Or maybe Ash was trying to lock her in. Or the ship itself was.

There was something about the way the material in the door returned to it. As if it belonged. It hadn't occurred to Calay before now that the ship might have an innate intelligence. A hive mind of its own or one that connected to the Others. If that was true, she was in even more trouble than she'd originally thought.

She glanced down the corridor.

The bright white lights flickered, creating snapshots of an empty hallway. A shadow. Movement. Then, whatever it was, was gone again. She pawed at her eyes, strained to see through the strobe-like effect. The beeping continued. It was even louder out here. Calay didn't think that was possible. None of this should have been possible. It should have been firmly contained between the beginning and end credits of a fucking science-fiction movie. Yet here she was, living it. If she was going to survive, she couldn't keep hiding in that room. It was only a matter of time before they found her. In fact, they probably already knew where she was and what she'd done.

As if in response to her thoughts, the rhythmic sound of coordinated steps echoed below the beeping.

They were coming for her.

She didn't want to believe the hive mind was real, but the persistent hum she'd felt vibrating through the air since she arrived told her otherwise. Not to mention the fact that she was learning to harness it. She'd witnessed its power firsthand. The way it transported people. Transformed places. Destroyed them. She'd used it to get inside the pod with Ash. When she'd broken the holographic barrier between the outside world and her cabin window. Then, once more against Elora. If she could just concentrate beyond the beeping and buzzing and boots, maybe she could use it against the rest of the Others too.

They wanted Calay for her ability to shift across boundaries. To use her for their purposes. They thought the human part of her made her weak. Easy to control. To manipulate.

The reality was, being human made her strong.

They couldn't have been more wrong. Calay started keeping a tally of the things the Others had messed up: their assumptions about humans, about her. It proved they were fallible. And if they were fallible, they had weaknesses. Weaknesses she could exploit. For as much as the aliens had studied people and learned to forecast their behavior, they couldn't predict what she would do. Who she was. Or even what she was. Her very existence defied expectations and labels. That was something she could use.

The hallway seemed to grow smaller as Calay's confidence grew.

Ash was right: there was nowhere to go. Not so long as the ship— and *They*—still existed. Earth would never be safe. Neither would she. An idea wallpapered Calay's mind. It unfurled slowly, one inch at a time. She swayed as the full realization rolled over her.

She had to destroy the ship. Kill them all. End this.

She braced herself on the wall, closed her eyes, let the idea sink in. She could do this, but first, she needed a plan. *Or at least, part of a plan.*

She'd made too many mistakes by acting on impulse. She was going to be smart about this. She glanced inside the SOR. At the controls. The holographic data and diagrams. The chamber. It was all here. In one place. A shiver ran up her spine.

It was only moments ago she'd watched Elora burn to ash. If fire killed her, it only made sense it could kill the rest of them. But Calay couldn't just set the ship ablaze, could she? She was in the middle of deep space. She still needed a way out. A way home, to Earth.

The pods.

If Calay remembered right, they operated on the hive mind. She could control one, focus her energy and guide herself back to her home planet. She knew enough about how the Others transported themselves the vast distance to Earth. If she pictured it in her mind, focused hard enough…Would she make it? Of course, there was the possibility that if the main ship went down, it stood to reason the pods might too, but what other options did she have? Elora had said there were thousands— millions—of them hibernating in another area of the ship. She could try to find them, kill them in their sleep, but what if she failed? Besides, she might not ever make it that far. She didn't even know where that area of the ship was. Didn't even know the first place to begin looking. She didn't think it was possible she'd find them and finish the job before Ash and her Elora army found her.

Their footfalls grew closer. By now, they were almost as loud as the beeping.

They'd be on her in moments.

Calay had no other choice.

She gathered what strength she had left, turned, and made for the loading bay.

She wasn't sure if she was running toward danger or away from it. Each slap of her boots echoed down the empty hallway. How could she have ever believed the ship would be teeming with other hybrids like her? Surely some would have been there before her, but she'd wanted to be special. The first. Her so-called mother had been the captain of the ship, after all. So why not her?

Calay shook her head, focused on not tripping again. What she wouldn't give for an army of her own now. The sound of marching mothers filled every hallway. Every room. Every cell in her mind. For all she knew, they were nowhere near where she was. Or they could be around the next corner. A place had never felt so empty and so crowded at the same time.

She plunged down the stairs into the hangar where she'd first arrived, her feet heavy against the metal stairs. Seamless white pods bounced in mid-air, blue light emanated below them. Calay wasn't sure if she'd powered them up by connecting to the hive, or if it was someone else. They'd been so still before. So eerily quiet. Now, she knew where the hum was coming from. They seemed to pulse where they hovered, as if breathing. Alive. There was no time to wait and see if the blue lights would turn on her and blast her into a plume of red.

She ran to the closest barrel along the permitter. It was marked with a flame, just as she remembered. She hesitated for just a moment. She wasn't sure why the Others needed fuel. The pods operated on the hive mind. The ship seemed to do the same: the fizzling doorways, the hallways ever-changing and shifting, and the way it re-incorporated the stretchy gum-like material after Calay was caught in it when she left the SOR. The only thing she could come up with was the energy had to come from somewhere beyond the Others. A core source at the center of it all. It was why they wanted Earth. And her. *Too bad.* Calay tried not to think about what Elora had told her about where the Others had gotten it from. Who had died for it. It could have been somebody's mother. Their lover. Their child.

A pang of rage gave Calay all the strength she needed to knock a barrel onto its side and roll it back to the front of the room. She gazed up the long staircase while she caught her breath.

She tipped the barrel up so one edge caught the lip of the first stair. Gathering as much weight behind her as she could, she let it rest against her shoulder and pushed. The barrel inched its way up as she thrust with her hip, the metal bottom shrieked against the metal grates. She winced, hoping the sound wouldn't draw Them to her. *Not much I can do about it now.* Sweat was already dripping from her hairline onto the back of her neck. She swiped at it with one hand while balancing the weight of the drum with the other. *Good. Next.* She grunted and repeated each motion until she reached the door at the top.

She shoved it out the door and began rolling it down the long hallways back to the Strategic Operations Room.

Three quarters of the way back, a chill washed over Calay when the sound of marching finally stopped. The beeping too. The lights even ceased flickering. She would have expected she'd feel relief. But sheer panic flooded her veins.

She turned. Ash stood behind her, half transformed, backed by the horde. Their clothes torn from forcing their way through the splintered door to her cabin. Their skin too. Their chests heaved with want. A distinct feeling of déjà vu washed over Calay. She was tired of this game. Tired of Ash. Tired of running.

"Oh, come on!" She yelled in Ash's direction. "Didn't we just go through this?"

"We'll keep going through this until you submit, Calay." Ash's gravelly voice moaned. Her cropped, strawberry-blonde hair was cloaked in sweat. Her brow furrowed. She leered from behind long lashes that seemed to be melting into the dark circles around her eyes. The Ash she'd known was gone, and in its place, a half-alien, half-human seething monster.

Calay had to acknowledge there were many of them, and only one of her. But they'd underestimated Calay. She'd already taken down their Queen. Surely, they must know that, given the hive mind, but she wasn't going to be the one to bring it up. Just in case. She almost grinned at the knowledge. Despite the impenetrable lines of their collective force, she felt for once, she might stand a chance. She might get out of this alive. If she could just get the barrel back to the Strategic Operations Room.

"That's not going to happen," Calay said.

"Oh, I think it is. It'll hurt less if you don't run."

"I doubt that."

"You don't have to make this about you, Calay. This can be about our future. You can contribute to that."

"You mean your future."

"Well, I mean the collective "our." But yes, the future of Térasians."

"That's not my future."

"I think you'll find that it is. One way or another."

Calay glanced forward. The hallway that led to the SOR was only a few feet ahead. She could cross the threshold in twenty, maybe thirty steps. She had no idea if the door would hold after she'd plunged through it earlier, or if it would even work at all. For all she knew, she'd be putting herself in an enclosed space from which she had no escape. She tilted her head—wasn't that what the whole ship was anyhow?

"We'll never stop coming for you."

"Tell me something, Ash." Calay herded her courage, leaned against the barrel, and pulled her shoulders back. "Did it ever occur to you that maybe I'm coming for you?"

"I told you." Ash smirked, clearly not buying Calay's bluff. "There's nowhere you can go where we can't find you."

Calay exhaled. If this was the way it had to be, she'd take her chances.

"Come and get me then."

Calay heaved the barrel forward with her hips, sending it spinning ahead of her. She ran after it. It rebounded off the wall at the end of the corridor. She lunged over it, her foot guiding it down the adjoining hallway.

Calay hit the wall, spun to see the swell of mother-figures bearing down on her. Their jaws unhinged, feet pounding against the floor. Calay sucked in a breath. This time there was no door to slow them down. No wall to hide behind. They were coming full speed toward her and if she didn't move, she wouldn't even survive the impact of their force, never mind the torture Ash had planned for her. Calay pushed off the wall and dove after the barrel, screaming as she pitched onto her sore shoulder. Something popped. Her vision darkened. Everything went numb. Her arm dangling precariously at her side, she held it in place with her other hand and forced herself to her feet. Her lungs screamed for air as she ran down the hallway.

Ten steps.

Five.

She was about to push it the rest of the way with one final kick when her head wrenched back. Someone had a hold of the mess that remained of her hair.

Her scalp screamed as Ash pulled Calay backward, spun her around to face her, and pressed her slimy, cracked lips to Calay's.

Calay gagged, shoved Ash away.

She felt herself slam into the wall across from the open door of the SOR. Her legs nearly buckled as the barrel dug into the back of her knees, pressed between them and the wall.

The mother-figures flooded the hallway, cutting off her escape. Calay was trapped. She peered across the hall, her vision wet with tears. The dim lights glowed blue and green. The chamber sat empty. It was only a dozen feet away, yet it was so far.

She raised her one good hand to the back of her head, felt a wet stickiness coat the palm of her hand. She blinked, dazed.

She fought to free herself, but with the use of only one arm, she couldn't do much but scratch and claw at the onslaught of bodies. So she did.

Calay screamed, she flailed. She couldn't let them win. *No, not now. Please, not now.* The light of the hallway dimmed as they crowded around her, pressing her against the cold, smooth white expanse of the ship. She peered between their long, translucent grasping arms, desperate for a way out. There were Elora's black eyes. A rolling sea of her silver hair. There were so many of them. In moments, their features blurred, an unwavering mass of bodies. Calay's legs grew weak. Her heart thundered in her chest. Maybe she'd been wrong all this time. She thought she could save Earth. Save herself. Finally. But the world as they knew it was gone. And soon, she would be too.

This place, for all the evil that resided here, had given her a gift. It had given her hope, and just as quickly, it'd snatched it away. Her heart ached at the thought. Sadness, regret. They washed over her not only because she was a victim of the Other's hate, but because she'd done so much damage herself. There were no innocents. Not anymore. She'd done horrible things. Made terrible mistakes. As she stared out at the ever-growing horde of aliens and the amassing darkness, the worst part of all of it all was knowing she'd wasted one wonderful chance after another to build a real life.

It was true it could never look the way it might have before the Change. The Others had seen to that. Humanity put the final nail in the coffin. But they could have built something new. Something different. Calay dared to wonder if they could have built something better.

Society was broken long before the Others showed up. Elora wasn't wrong about that. People were selfish. They consumed too much and cared too little about those living in the box beside them. Connected through screens, instead of in each other's arms, and then wondered why they felt so lonely. Isolated. Empty. Calay had made the same mistakes as everyone else. It was the way of the world then.

After the Change, things didn't get better. For any of them. She wanted to mourn that. To give herself permission to give up. She had to admit, after a lifetime of being mistreated, judged, rejected, broken, lost…in the end, she'd been cruel. All she'd ever wanted was to belong and be loved. How many nights had she fallen asleep, afraid she'd never find that?

What she didn't realize until recently was that love was inside her the whole time.

Jacob had told her as much. "You have everything you need inside you." His voice echoed through her mind. The greatest tragedy of Calay's life was that she hadn't realized this before now. She'd let the good slip right through her fingers and wallowed in what was left. She didn't give anyone a chance to love her. To be there for her. She orbited around them like a far-off planet—visible if you were patient enough to look, but impossible to reach. She'd taken her pain, much the way the Others took theirs, and weaponized it. She kept everyone at arm's length. Everyone except Tess. And look where that had gotten her. Calay was alone. The end could not be avoided. None of them could escape it. She swallowed, choked back tears. She knew in her heart if she ever had the chance to return to Earth, she'd do it all differently. But alas, death had come for her. As it comes for everyone.

Calay stiffened, she gathered her strength. That didn't mean she couldn't fight in her final moments. For what was right. For the world that could have been. One more time.

For *her*.

The snarls of the horde seemed to grow louder at her resolution. Calay didn't waver. She growled right back. A deep throaty sound that started deep in her stomach, rolled up her throat, and rumbled past her lips. She fought to get her good arm above the crowd. Threw one punch. Then another. Her fist landed, her knuckles became raw with impact. She screamed, kicked, shouldered any of those unlucky enough to come within close range. She heard their noses crack, watched their heads snap back with each blow. Her gaze darted across the bulging beast of bodies while they continued to flow into the corridor.

They moved like one entity, heaving relentlessly forward. Ash stood among them. Silent. Still. Smirking. Calay's brow furrowed as she forced herself to make eye contact. She tried to clear her mind, connect to the hive. She grasped at wisps of gray matter. A swirl of air above her head. A light buzzing entered one ear, then flew out the other. She blinked, fought harder. Tried to focus. If she could just get a grip on the edge of Ash's consciousness, maybe she could turn the mob against her. After all, Calay was one of them, wasn't she? If Ash could control the mother-figures, why not her? Like Elora said, there was nothing special about her. She was just like them. One of many. But Calay couldn't concentrate.

There were too many arms reaching for her. Too many mouths breathing on her neck. She barely had enough room to take a breath, let alone control an army.

This was it. Ash was right. Calay's attempts to drive them back were futile. She closed her eyes, sighed. Pulled her shoulders back against the wall. Dropped her head. Waited for it to all be over.

That was the way of the world now.

It was all that ever was. All that eve—

Her mantra was cut short as Calay fell backward. A firm grip clutched the back of her shirt, another wrapped itself around her waist. She thought she heard Ash's voice rise above the noise of the screaming army before a loud swoosh filled the air.

Then, everything was silent.

CHAPTER TWENTY-TWO

A BLINDING light faded as Calay peeked from behind her lashes. Before her was a white wall flecked with blue specks. She reached out, touched it. Hard, smooth, and teeming with energy. She was still on the ship. And she was alive.

The horde was gone. Ash too. Calay couldn't even hear them.

She stood, but barely. Her shoulder throbbed. The back of her head ached. Her mind begged for rest. She swayed as she turned, her legs unsteady beneath her. And could hardly believe her eyes.

She was surrounded by stars. They shimmered from beyond a wall of glass. Their lucid starlight so bright it reflected off the white floor. The ceiling. She looked behind her, as if to be certain Ash hadn't appeared as soon as she turned her back. She had a way of doing that. The blue flecks winked in reply. Calay realized the wall reflected the stars too. They were everywhere. The brightest twinkling lights she'd ever seen.

She recognized them. The constellation that glowed in front of her. She'd seen them before.

In her own eyes.

Her heart thudded in her chest, and a new awareness flooded her mind. She'd began this journey on Earth, unaware of who and what she really was. The Resistance—and by extension, Tess—had uncovered the map behind her dark brown pupils. The stars meant to guide her home. Only home wasn't where she'd ended up. This place was the farthest from it. She'd made it to Téras, or at least, what was left of it, only to realize she truly belonged on Earth. An idea carved a space at the back of her thoughts. In a long, twisting, agonizing way, she'd come full circle. If the stars led her here, maybe they could lead her home too. But first, she had to figure out exactly how she was going to get there.

She turned back to the wall of glass. Limped a couple steps but stopped short. At the center of the room, beside a raised platform showing a holographic image of a spinning dead Téras, and leaning against the upright barrel of fuel with his hands tucked in his pockets, was Jacob.

"You've got to be kidding me."

"I know you told me to stay away. But you needed help an—"

"You really have a way of showing up at the last minute, you know?" Calay said, her brows knit together.

"I like to make an entrance." Jacob shrugged, dark curls fell in his eyes.

Calay almost laughed, but the sound died in her throat. Jacob's witticisms and banter didn't have the same pull on her as they once did. They couldn't. Not anymore. So she sighed instead and pressed her lips into a firm line.

"Thank you."

"Really?" Jacob blinked from behind his long lashes.

"You're right, I did need help." Calay sniffed, nodded. "I would have died just now if not for you."

"Good, I'm glad you see it that way." A trace of a grin crept across his lips.

"Is this the bridge?" Calay took a few tentative steps forward. "This is where you control this thing?"

"It is." Jacob nodded.

"I had no idea it was right here the whole time. I guess I figured it would be more obvious. Like at the head of the ship or something."

"Elora didn't like sharing more than she needed to." Jacob trailed behind Calay while she made her way across the room. "She didn't like wasting time, either. Spent most of hers between this room and the SOR. She designed the starship, kept them close together. She was nothing if not efficient."

"You say that like she's gone." Calay turned to Jacob, her eyes wide. She still didn't know how much traveled through the hive mind. Like with Ash, she didn't want to ignite something in Jacob by volunteering she'd killed their leader. He'd done so much to protect her, Calay didn't think he'd hurt her. After all, he loved her. Despite everything. Still, she proceeded with caution.

"She is." Jacob leveled his gaze at Calay. She swallowed. There was something about his ice blue eyes that cut right through her.

"And she's definitely dead?"

He nodded, stepped closer. She could feel the heat radiating off his body. If she wanted to, she could almost reach up and press her mouth to his. If he hadn't betrayed her, that is. There was a time she would have fallen into his arms. Let him blanket her with his warmth. His kisses. His touch. Instead, she bit her lip, took a couple of steps back.

"How'd you do it?" Calay asked.

"How'd I do what?"

"How'd you save me? And I swear to God, if you say heat signatures again, I'm going to lose my fucking mind."

"Nothing that advanced, I'm afraid. I opened the door."

"I didn't see a door."

"You were pressed flat against it. I opened it, pulled you in, and closed it before they could come through."

"Won't they follow?" Calay blanched, turned her gaze to the wall, remembered the onslaught of bodies that hurled themselves through the door to her cabin. "Break it down or something?"

"The ship responds to the hive, and my connection is stronger than yours. I can reinforce the barrier for longer. It won't last forever, but it'll do for now. Besides, Ash used most of her energy to animate and coordinate the Legion."

"The Legion…" Calay settled on the word, rolled it over her tongue. It felt wrong.

"That's what we call them."

"I call them fucking terrifying."

"No doubt. You're safe for now. Ash will need to rest."

Calay nodded, chewed on this. Her suspicions about the ship were right. It did maintain some kind of intelligence, but not so much that it had its own mind. It worked in tandem with the Others. She shouldn't have been surprised. Their tech was advanced far beyond anything humans had developed.

"And then what?" Calay turned back to him.

"You tell me."

"We're on your ship. In your galaxy. I just want to go home."

Calay crossed the room, passing several docked pods embedded in the wall. Blue light glowed below them, they hummed at the ready. A long, elevated platform of controls lined the one across from them. Above the buttons and dials was a series of holographic screens. She peered closer. She didn't recognize the symbols, though she assumed they must be Térasian in origin. They had the same hieroglyphic-type symbols as the documents Elora made her review. Several of the displays charted various constellations, intergalactic pathways across the universe. She touched one. The graphic ripped outward under her fingers before returning to its original position. She leaned forward and winced as the movement sent a sharp pang through her shoulder.

"You're hurt." Jacob slid beside her.

"I'm fine."

"You're not fine. Let me look at it."

"It'll heal soon enough, won't it? That's what we do."

"It'll heal poorly if you don't put the joint back in its bloody socket. It's dislocated, Calay. I can tell from the way it's hanging off you."

"I can do it myself." Even as she said the words, she knew they weren't true. The last thing she wanted to do right now was rely on Jacob. But who else did she have? Tess was gone. Ash, gone. Elora, gone. Her friends, family, everyone she'd ever known or loved, gone. That was the thing—people didn't survive alone anymore. Did they ever? She squeezed the fleshy part of her forearm. The sharpness of her chipped, broken nails brought her back to the present. They survived together, or they died.

"Fine." Calay turned so her dislocated arm faced Jacob. She cast her eyes downward. "But this is the last time."

"You got it." He smiled.

"I mean it, Jacob."

Now it was Jacob's turn to sigh. Calay watched his shoulders sink, his smooth, wide hands hover over her arm. His chest fell with a shaky breath. A small part of her wanted to comfort him, tell him everything was going to be alright, but she couldn't stand the thought of another lie between them. There'd been too many already. She didn't know if she'd make it off the ship under the weight of any more.

"I know." He nodded, gently leading her to the platform at the center of the room. "Come over here."

Calay watched as Jacob swiped the image of Téras away, then offered her a seat.

"Aren't you sad it's gone?" She asked as she slid onto the cold metal surface. "That was your home."

"It was one home of many." He guided her to lay down. Raised her bad arm to the side and then over her head. "We've had others. We'll have more again."

"How can you be so apathetic about it? That was a whole planet, Jacob. The Others—you—used it and then threw it away like garbage." Calay gaped up at him. She'd wanted a place to call home for so long. She couldn't imagine being so flippant about having somewhere to truly belong. To feel safe. She added it to the ever-growing list of reasons why it couldn't have worked between them. Why it never would.

"Home is where this is." Jacob grinned as he tapped Calay on her chest. The gesture was too sweet. Too confusing amid the knowledge she could no longer deny about him. The Others. It was too much.

"Let's just get this over with." Calay fixed her gaze on the ceiling.

She didn't know how to speak to him anymore. Not since she found out the truth. They'd both done what they'd done, said what they'd said. There was no way to fix what was. It was over. They were over. She tried to ignore the warmth of his hands on her skin. The way it still sent shivers up her spine.

"Take a deep breath." Jacob rotated her hand and reached it across to her other shoulder.

On the exhale, he jerked her arm sharply. She yelped as a loud pop signaled the ball joint was put back in place.

"Sorry," he said. He guided her arm back across her body and pulled her to sit. "It'll be sore for a while. Try not to use it too much."

"Thanks. Again." Calay nodded.

"I know you don't want to hear it, Calay, but I'd do anything for you."

"Then take me home, Jacob."

"This is your home. With us."

"There's about a million reasons outside that door that would argue it isn't." Calay thrust her newly mobile arm toward the white wall. She cringed. He was right, it was sore.

"It could be if you'd give me one more damn minute to sort this out."

"No, it can't." Calay sighed. She gazed at the controls. The screens. The never-ending ocean of space splayed out before them. A phantasmic nebula of blue and gold bloomed in the distance. A stream of matter glowed beyond it. At the center, nothing but darkness.

"Is that it? The storm my mother, Elora, went through?"

"That's it. It's how we get to Earth. How you got here."

"You have to let me go."

"I don't think you understand, Calay. You can't escape. I can try to live without you, but Ash won't. They won't." Jacob pointed at a monitor at the far end of the console.

Calay's blood ran cold. She inched her way across the room until her nose was practically pressed against it. Row after row, column after column, white bubbles filled the screen. They looked like the pods, but instead of a solid white exterior, they were translucent. They seemed to swell with life. Inside, dark, bulging shapes. She could almost make out their long, twisted limbs. Patches of fur pressed against the sides. They shimmered in pale blue light. It was the same light that emanated from the pods. The one that had obliterated her neighbors. Civilization. Humanity. It had turned human against human. Lover against lover. And now, they wanted to use it to separate her from her home planet. Her *home*. Jacob might not have cared about his planet, but she wasn't about to let hers go so easily.

"This is what the fuel's for." Calay whispered. "You use it to power...*this*."

"They're hibernating. They can't connect to the hive when they're asleep. The fuel as you call it, keeps them alive. It keeps the whole thing running while they're in there."

"Let me get this straight." Calay peeled herself away from the display to face him. She thrust her hands on her hips, steadied herself. "You want to destroy Earth and use humans as energetic meat sacks so a bunch of aliens can get their beauty rest?"

"Come on, Calay. You're over-simplifying it. We're only doing what we have to do to survive. We need energy to power the ship. The Reservoir."

"You call that place the Reservoir?" Calay whispered. The idea of a storage facility of Others was too much. Elora had been telling the truth —there were millions of them. Waiting.

"It's the lifeblood of our species. It's how we survive between one planet to the next."

"And you'd kill us just to get there? You don't have anywhere to belong, Jacob. You kill innocent lives to survive, but there's nothing beyond that to make your lives worth living. Just more killing. More death. Don't you see how wrong that is?"

"Of course I do!" Jacob's arm shot out, his fist collided with the platform where the hologram of Téras had reappeared. He barely grimaced, but she could practically feel the reverberations that surely jostled his bones roll through the air. He rushed forward, tried to clasp her hand in his. She pulled away, folded her arms across her chest. "I need you to listen to me, alright? I told you, I've changed my mind. You, Calay, changed my mind."

"It's a little late for that now, don't you think?"

"I could have convinced them. I just needed a little more time."

If Jacob was out of time, where did that leave Earth? Or her? How much time did humans have before the dam of aliens was released?

"Elora was right." Calay shook her head. "We can't exist together."

"You and I can."

"No, we can't. Don't you see, Jacob? I might be part Térasian, but I'm part human too. And humans will always be fuel for the Others. For you. I mean, your natural physical body is the same as theirs, right? The same as Elora's? As Ash's?"

Jacob ran his hand over his mouth, dropped his gaze to the floor.

"Jacob?"

"Yes, of course it is. But I would never reveal it to you. Never hurt you. You have to know that."

"No." Calay shook her head, chewed on her lower lip as she collected the words she needed to say. She added another item to the list as to why their relationship had to come to an end. She was learning to be more vulnerable, to stand up for the truth. He, on the other hand, had to obscure it just to be with her. "I don't know that. I can't. Not after everything that's happened. The Others and I will always be enemies."

"Even me?" Jacob's voice cracked even as he stood taller, pulled his broad shoulders back. He looked every part the beautiful, strong savior he always had. Her knight in shining armor. Her protector. Her rescuer. Only he couldn't save her anymore.

"Even you."

Whatever was left of her heart shattered. She watched as his did too. She could almost hear them break in unison. Jacob's shoulders shook. Her breathing slowed. His full lips parted. She gasped for breath. One that wasn't tainted by the pain between them. She knew she'd hurt him, time and again. She'd never forgive herself for that, but he'd hurt her too. He'd never understood her. Not really. She'd always wanted something he couldn't give her. A home. Calay had found that place within herself now. Even if it was padded with fractures of a broken heart.

A broken world.

But it was her world.

A tremble crawled across her skin with the realization she not only had everything she needed inside her, but everything she needed in this room too. She'd planned to blow the damn ship up. She hadn't figured out how she might save herself, but now she not only had a container full of flammable liquid, she had a wall of pods in which to escape. Most of the Others were asleep, and if what Jacob was saying was true, they'd die if they came out of their cocoons. Which meant they'd keep on sleeping and burn along with everything else. If she was lucky, Jacob's hold on the hive would last long enough for her to get away before Ash and her army could do anything about it.

"I'm sorry," she said.

She strode past him and reached for the barrel. She felt his eyes on her as she pried open the top and dumped it on its side. Dark liquid oozed across the floor. It was thick and smelled of burnt oil. Calay choked back the urge to gag as she pushed aside the knowledge of where the liquid came from. She tried not to think of Elora's face melting in the chamber. Or the way the streets of Seattle burned after the initial invasion. So much had happened since the Change. Too much. Calay rolled the container from one end of the room to the other until it was light enough for her to muscle it into her arms.

"Calay." Jacob's voice dropped several decibels, but he didn't move to stop her. Like he said, he'd do anything for her. *Even let his own kind die?* He watched as she poured what was left over the controls. "Don't do this."

"Or you'll what?" She taunted. She caught his gaze, dared him to stop her. Hell, she'd like to see him try. He dropped his head, crossed his arms over his chest. "I'm sorry," she repeated.

"You will be if Ash catches you."

"If Ash catches me, I don't think I'll be alive long enough to feel remorse." Calay tossed the empty barrel at her feet. Kicked it away. Sparks shot into the air as circuits failed. A trail of blue smoke rose between the panels. She could already see flames licking the glass where the console met its edge.

"You know there are more out there. In the universe. On Earth. I know you don't want to hear about heat signatures, but you have one. You always will. They'll come for you."

"I'm counting on it."

This time, Calay meant it. She'd hid from the Others for far too long.

She was finished. With running. With Jacob. With all of it. She wasn't going to let them push her around anymore. She'd fight until she had nothing left to fight for. Even if it was just herself. Because she was enough.

The flames spread quickly as they ate their way across the fluid. In moments, the room was almost completely engulfed. The heat was unbearable.

She stood in front of one of the pods. It hovered before her. Ready. Waiting. To take her home. She wasn't sure if she'd be able to get back to Earth, but everything she'd experienced since being on this ship told her that she might. The stars in their eyes would be her guide.

She had to try.

She cleared her mind. The air grew cool. White and gray lines appeared in front of her vision. The air swirled around her. The hair on the back of her neck rose as electricity vibrated between her and the white orb. A loud hum filled the smoke-filled air.

"I'm not going to beg, Calay, but I have to know." Jacob's voice boomed through the roar of the fire.

She turned, trained her gaze on him. He was beautiful. He was awful. He was everything that had gone wrong in her life. It wasn't his fault, in the grand scheme of things. He was a product of his environment. She was a product of hers. They were from different worlds. Literally.

He blinked at her through the flames. His blue eyes glistened with what looked like tears. If she didn't know better, she'd say he was crying.

"That morning after we last made love, you said we meant something to you. That I meant something to you. And now you're just going to leave me here to die? After everything we've been through? Why?"

A sharp pain lanced through her heart. She swallowed, knowing this was probably the last time they'd ever see each other.

"Everything we've been through has been a lie."

With that, Calay allowed the floor of the bridge to disintegrate beneath her feet. Then the air. She transported herself inside the pod.

She found herself standing among the long, white, winding columns.

Their soft, ridged edges sprouted from floor to ceiling, spreading out in gnarled, winding patterns above. An effervescent orange light emanated from some unseen source. The air was cool, but was it safe?

Almost in response to her thoughts, the walls began to glow red. They flickered with light. *No, with flames. Shit.* Calay's pulse quickened. She had to figure out how to fly this thing, and fast.

She lunged for the single panel on the wall. She pressed buttons, turned dials. It didn't seem to do a damn thing. There had to be a way to fly the pod. The Others did it. She could too.

She tried to slow her breathing, to turn down her thoughts. She knew it operated on the hive mind. She just had to connect to it again.

Calay stomped her feet. Shook her arms loose. She focused her energy on the pod, allowing the gray swirling clouds of the hive mind to wrap around her. A warm and pleasant air pulsed through the space, completeness in its entirety.

Breathe in, breathe out.

The hair rose on the back of her neck first. Then her arms. She visualized being back on Earth. Feeling the dirt between her toes. The cool water of a stream on her skin. The warm sun on her face.

As she inhaled, the air shifted from cool to stifling.

She coughed, jarred from the meditation. The gray swirling clouds disappeared. The walls got redder. Then, they melted, flowing around her feet like lava. It rushed over her boots and singed the hem of her jeans. She would have sworn she smelled her hair burning. Calay could hardly breathe. She gasped, but no air entered her lungs. Just smoke. Lots and lots of smoke. She scanned the flames for Jacob. She called for him. Once. Twice. She screamed. He was gone.

He'd left her to die. And didn't she deserve it? She'd just done the very same thing to him.

Calay braced herself and forced her eyes open. She stared as the fire washed over her.

Then, her stomach jumped into her throat. She had the distinct feeling she was falling.

Through space.

Her hands flew to her chest as she inhaled the clean air she was sure she'd never taste again. Her eyes grew wide when she realized her lungs ballooned with each drink. She could breathe. The heat from the fire was gone. In its place, a pleasantly cool, thick atmosphere. It laid upon her like a weighted blanket. She took respite in it, tucked into the folds.

Calay had given up everything to come to a planet she knew to be Téras. To this strange place called Galaxy 3C303. She'd lost everything too. She didn't think she had anything left to lose, but she'd been wrong. Her heart ached, but her body felt lighter. Maybe it was zero gravity. Or maybe she'd finally let go of something she'd carried for far too long.

Something that wasn't hers to begin with, after all.

As she plummeted through wormholes and constellations, Calay finally let go. She didn't know where she was headed and for the first time, she was okay with that.

The stars unfolded in streams of light. Fast and then faster. Until they turned dark. She imagined herself crawling inside them, stuffing her body into their sharp corners, looking out. Her limbs conformed to their edges. Her mind too. The history of the universe stretched out before her as if looking through a fish-eye lens. Strange and disproportionate.

Nebulas blossomed.

Worlds formed.

They died.

A sense of grief flooded through Calay. Then, relief. Emotion rolled over emotion, as if one feeling was tied to its exact and equal opposite. It was the entirety of everything, together but separate.

She felt free.

The vision exploded in a firework display of white. She squinted into the bright light, saw nothing. Felt everything. Her body tingled with energy, as if every cell was falling asleep, one by one.

Her eyelids grew heavy.

Her mind slowed.

And then, she lost consciousness.

CHAPTER TWENTY-THREE

THE AIR WAS cold as ice. She took a deep breath, and it burned over her tongue, all the way down her throat, and into her lungs. Her chest ached. It wasn't just the air though. It was the ground beneath her. It dug into her back, hard as rock. *Rock.* That meant she wasn't in the pod anymore.

She was somewhere else.

She bolted upright. Gazed around. Her mouth dropped open. She crawled onto her knees, slowly turned in a circle. She couldn't believe her eyes.

There was woodland forest, as far as her eyes could see. White and black birch trees mingled with Douglas fir and Sitka. They sprung from the snowpacked ground in an eruption of green and white, their wide, billowing branches rose high into a gray sky. Her breath puffed in small clouds as a laugh escaped past her lips, the sound dampened by the snow. She fell back, allowed herself to relish the feeling of the frozen ground beneath her. She let it cool the friction burn that still radiated heat out of her shoulder, the spot on the back of her scalp where her hair had been torn out. It felt better than she ever could have imagined.

She'd done it. Like, actually done it.

She'd returned to Earth.

The pod she'd escaped in lay embedded in the ground next to her, a few feet away. The snow had melted beneath it, the ground scorched. The mystery of how they worked wasn't quite solved, but somehow, she'd harnessed the power of the hive and gotten her ass away from the Térasian starship and back on planet. She shook her head, wondering if she'd ever really understand the Others' technology, or whether she even wanted to.

Before she agreed to return to Galaxy 3C303, she'd been training for this. For her escape. Her liberation. She and Jacob had practiced connecting to the hive mind together. She'd failed every attempt. Except for when it mattered. It might have taken a two billion lightyear road trip to finally figure it out, but that was the point of adventure, wasn't it? Clear your mind. Learn something new. Come back stronger. Calay grinned.

She'd seen horrible things in that place. Things that would haunt her dreams for the rest of her life. She'd almost died. *Almost*. In the end, she'd made it. Again. She'd survived. She shuddered under the weight of the knowledge that for the first time, she didn't have anyone else to fall back on.

It was all her.

A feeling fluttered in her chest. A memory. Before she'd woken up here, she'd been dreaming. Tangled in an ocean of cozy sheets with Tess, their limbs curled around each other. Their kisses soft. The air smelled like coffee and cinnamon. Tess's almond brown eyes twinkled while she brushed a lock of hair out of Calay's eyes. The soft morning sun pooled on their skin. Outside, she could hear the bell on the hot dog cart. The laughter of the kids in the street. The clanging of pots and pans of their neighbor doing dishes near the open window below them.

"You and me?" Calay whispered.

"You and me."

"'Till the end?'"

"'Till the end." Tess peered at Calay from beneath her long dark lashes, the dimples in her cheeks turned upward.

Calay kissed them, one by one, before she brought her mouth to Tess's. Tasted herself on Tess's lips. This was their Sunday routine. As it had been for as long as they'd lived together. In the building that no longer existed. The scene fizzled away like the doors aboard the Térasian ship and was replaced by darkness. The shadows in the cave where Calay finally tracked Tess down. The muzzle of a gun. Space. The last thing Calay saw was the winking of stars. The ones behind her eyes. Her map home. Only, it wasn't home. It was the furthest thing from it. It was a place of nightmares.

Gratitude flooded Calay as she gulped in the icy air. Savored it.

This was the end.

It had come sooner than she'd anticipated. For all of them. She'd always imagined she and Tess would grow old together, collecting plants and those funny little ghost figurines Tess loved so much. They were supposed to lay on a beach somewhere, getting gray and wrinkly and saggy and beautiful. Together. Humanity was supposed to advance. Cure cancer. Feed the world. Maybe make another trip to the moon or colonize Mars. Calay shuddered, but not from the cold. If people had known what was in space, what was coming for them, would they have been more prepared? Would they have been able to prevent their own extinction?

Unlikely.

If this whole ordeal had taught her anything, it was that control was an illusion. People would do their worst. And their best. Every action had a reaction. A consequence. And the Others would have come, just the same. There was no sense lamenting the past or asking "what if?" She couldn't change it. All she could do was choose her next step. Make her next decision. Move forward.

She grabbed a handful of snow, let it melt in her palm. She never thought she'd be so glad to be half-frozen to death, surrounded by snow. Water. With the planet's ecosystem so unpredictable, so fragile, and so wet, the Others were going to need to rely on hybrids more than ever. They'd planned for a lot of things, but not this. Not the effect humans had on their environment. Or the absence of them. The Others hadn't given people enough credit.

That would be humanity's greatest weapon.

Calay rubbed her palms together, cupped them over her mouth. A breeze curled through the trees and swept across her skin. She couldn't sit here in the freezing cold like a snowman. She had to move. For better or for worse, she was human and she'd die of exposure if she didn't find somewhere warm and dry. She pressed herself to stand, unsure which way she should go. She peered through the forest. Tucked behind a wall of ferns, she spied something she hadn't seen while she was still on the ground. Her heart lurched.

Is that…? It couldn't be, could it? *No.*

She rushed forward, stumbled through the snowbanks that billowed from the base of trees. She scrambled up the hill. Climbed over a fallen log dusted with moss and snow. Dirt caught under her fingernails, and the air burned in her lungs. Still, she wouldn't stop. She couldn't. Not until she touched the damn thing. Made sure it was real. It was.

Another pod.

Her mind spun as she tried to come up with an explanation for why it was here. So close to where she'd crash landed. She chanced a glance back to where her orb still lay embedded in the dirt, motionless. Compared it to the one here. Yes, the snow was freshly melted. The dirt that should have been frozen solid was soft between the pads of her fingers. Whoever—whatever—flew this thing landed not long ago. It was too coincidental. Too unlikely. A lump swelled in her throat.

Someone had followed her.

She placed both hands on the cold, smooth exterior. Silenced her raging thoughts. Listened. Her heart thundered against her ribs. Shhhh, she thought. She pulled on every possible thread she could grab through the hive mind, searching for who it might be. Any sign of life. Of danger. She whimpered as she knelt in the snow. Waited. Nothing responded. She clenched her jaw, unsure if that was because she was back on Earth, or because the pod was empty. She broke into a cold sweat, concentrated harder. She couldn't detect a signature, let alone the unmistakable feeling of Jacob's presence. Or Ash's. Whoever had followed her here wasn't inside the pod any longer. They were outside. They could be watching her every move.

She squinted, gazed through the trees. Stood there longer than she probably should have, watching for any flicker of movement. Listening for the telltale crunch of snow or snapping of branches. Bracing for the horrible screech or moans of the horde. Any sign that she wasn't alone. The only evidence of someone nearby was her own. Her footfalls in the snow. The sound of her ragged breath. Still, she waited. Watched the shadows retreat as the gray sky grew lighter. It was a new day. And with it, new horrors with which to contend. She knew there would be Others. Jacob had told her as much. She just didn't think it would be someone she'd already met.

Or left to die.

She hadn't been prepared for anyone to make it off that ship. Against the relentless aching in her heart, she'd expected Jacob to burn among them. Calay stifled a sob. She never wanted to hurt anybody. Least of all someone she loved. Despite the odds and complicated nature of their relationship, she did love Jacob. She could admit that now. To herself. In the private silence of the forest. And yet, she'd left him behind so she could save herself.

He was right—they'd been through so much together, but they were worlds apart. It would never work between them. They wanted different things. Calay broke her own heart when she'd left him; she could live with that, at least. For the first time in her life, she'd chosen herself. She'd never forget the pained look on Jacob's face when they said their last words to each other, but she also couldn't forget what he and the Others would ultimately do to her home planet.

To her.

She just wished she knew if it was him who had tracked and followed her yet again, or if it was someone else.

Like the past, Calay had to admit there wasn't anything she could do about the pod. Whoever had come, had come. She was sure she'd have to deal with them later. She inhaled a deep breath. Peered up through the canopy. The gray clouds were beginning to part, the view above dotted with patches of clear blue sky. Despite the reprieve from the unseasonable storm, she imagined the worst was yet to come. She had to find somewhere warm and out of the elements. The cold was wrapping its way around her bones, and she wasn't sure how much longer she'd last out here.

A flash of light caught Calay's attention. She squinted in the direction it came from. To where the trees parted.

She slid down the hill and over an embankment. She tried to hide her path, stepping on moss and ferns, balancing on rocks and branches lodged in frozen mud. After all, if she could track someone through the snow, there was no reason to think they wouldn't also track her.

Even now, with winter conditions blanketing the landscape, blackberry brambles clawed at her pant legs. Ivy caught in her hair. As if pulling her back under the cover of the dense forest. Or to another time.

Calay was flooded with memories of weekends spent camping with her father. Meeting Tess under the hidden cover of nature. Running through the undergrowth for her life, with Jacob, away from the pods. Those were other versions of herself. Other lives. They no longer existed. There was only now.

Calay pushed forward.

The hill crested and the trees came to an abrupt stop.

The Resistance compound sprawled across the frozen ground, dark and foreboding. The mesh overhang did little to conceal it from this angle. Then again, they weren't concerned about hiding from people. In fact, the more humans who found them and could join their cause, the better. It was the threat of pods flying overhead. Calay imagined from the top it blended right in with the surrounding brush. She ignored the nagging feeling in her gut that told her to turn around and run. Instead, she looked closer. From here she could make out details the Others wouldn't.

Barbed wire lined the top of concrete walls, casting long, strange shadows across the ground. Her eyes settled on the very spot she'd been assaulted by Guy that morning in the yard. It was the same place she'd met Adam. The last place she ever thought she'd return. A sliver of sunlight crept across the landscape, over the guard towers, before it disappeared behind a curtain of dark clouds. Her gaze drifted to the moat snaking around the perimeter. The one that had almost claimed her life.

Why here?

When she imagined returning to Earth, this place never once entered her thoughts. Her understanding of the pods was that they were connected to the hive mind. If she could picture where she wanted to go, her atoms would reassemble there once she made her way through the jet stream. *Right?* So she'd visualized her apartment. The farm. The cave. The Loft. She'd hoped she would have ended up somewhere she'd felt at home, once, however fleeting. Somewhere comforting. Warm. Safe. Where she could gather herself and figure out what her next steps were.

Not this place.

Anywhere but here.

Calay wrapped her arms around herself, her brow furrowed. A pit settled in her stomach.

She knew why.

She'd wanted nothing more than to go home; maybe this was the closest thing she had to that now. The compound was the last place Tess had lived before she died. Before Calay wrapped her hands around Tess's throat and stole her life from her. Her mission. Humanity's chance to survive.

Individuals could take down a pod. Small groups might be able to coordinate attacks against one or two aliens on the ground, if it ever came to that. But it wouldn't be enough. Not before. Not now. Not ever.

Calay shook her head, gnawed on her chapped bottom lip. People needed to come together as a group if they were going to come back from what the Others had done to them. The aliens were organized. Strategic. They had intimate knowledge of human behavior.

Calay knew their secrets too, though.

She'd seen their plans in great detail. Learned about their species and how they survived. More importantly, how they died. Every one of them —Jacob, Elora, and Ash—had told her how instrumental she and other hybrids were to their plans. The Others were without a planet and were running out of time. If Calay was right, they wouldn't regroup. They couldn't. They needed somewhere to go, and they'd already spent so many resources claiming Earth. Not to mention the fact that she'd escaped.

They were coming for her. For Earth. And when they did, she'd be ready.

She swallowed, knowing that if she really meant what she said about stopping the Others, she wouldn't be able to do it alone. She'd need help. An army. A resistance.

She pulled her shoulders tight. The muscles in her back ached. Her head throbbed. Her mind spun circles around where she stood and what her next steps had to be. *Fuck.* She didn't want this. She'd spent over four years avoiding it, hiding in the forest. Behind her fear. In the rubble of what had been their lives. Society had crumbled and with it, so did Calay. But as the starship burned in her wake, she'd built herself back up. She'd looked death in the face and lived. Hell, she'd beat its ass. Now, louder than the thunder of her heart, was the truth of what she knew what she had to do.

She'd lead the Resistance to victory.

She'd pick up where Tess left off, continue her work. The good she was doing. She'd leave the rest where it belonged—in the past. As an organization, they weren't perfect. Their methods were in serious need of tweaking. Their cult-like mentality had to go. Women needed to be protected. Hybrids, too. Like her. If they were going to win this war, Calay knew humanity—in all its forms—had to come together. Fight together.

Survive together.

Big, chunky snowflakes landed in her hair, clung to her eyelashes. She blinked them away, brushed them off her arms. They obscured the landscape. This wasn't normal. Not at this time of year. The planet was broken, but if Calay could come back from all this, maybe the world could too. It was possible that given the right amount of time, they'd fix the climate. Stop the change. Right the wrongs that had been done to them. By them. They had to defeat the Others so they at least got the chance to try.

Calay began making her way down the steep embankment, careful not to slip on the icy patches, toward the yard.

The Resistance had been searching for her. Hunting her. The last thing they'd anticipate was that she'd come right to them. She raised her arms in the air, took a long, slow, deep breath, and readied herself for capture. *Slow wide turns.* She knew the road wasn't going to be easy.

This was going to be the most difficult thing she'd ever done.

Things were indisputably going to get worse before they got better.

But that was the thing about going to the dark place.

The darkest stars still shine.

Thank you for reading! Did you enjoy? Please add your review because nothing helps an author more and encourages readers to take a chance on a book than a review.

And don't miss more in *The Broken Stars* series with THE STARS INSIDE US available now. Turn the page for a sneak peek!

Also be sure to sign up for the City Owl Press newsletter to receive notice of all book releases!

SNEAK PEEK OF THE STARS INSIDE US

The noise in the cafeteria was almost loud enough to drown out the screaming in Calay's mind.

She gripped the aluminum tray with white knuckles, surveying the expansive room for the first time. Long rows of plastic tables formed the dining area. Resistance members hunched over their own trays, shoveling nondescript globs of leafy green vegetables and some kind of thick paste into their hungry maws. She squinted, cataloguing each bobbing head, one by one. Men. Everywhere she looked. The room was heaving with them. She shuddered. Slivers of grey light peered through rectangular windows lining the concrete walls. The scraping of spoons on metal reverberated through her mind, aggravating the headache she hadn't been able to shake since she'd arrived. Every atom in her cells vibrated, reminding her—not for the first time—she shouldn't be here. They hadn't stopped reminding her since she made the decision to take the first step down off that ledge, toward the compound.

As she'd knelt in the snow, her arms raised high above her head while they'd shoved the barrels of their guns into her ribs, she knew convincing them to fight together was going to be the hardest thing she'd ever had to do. Harder than living without her parents. Harder than existing without Tess. And definitely harder than escaping an alien starship millions of lightyears away, leaving Jacob for dead, along with everyone else she'd ever loved.

She thought she'd prepared herself for the challenges ahead.

She couldn't have been more wrong.

It'd been six weeks since she'd crash-landed back on Earth and walked through the front door of the Resistance. Well, walked was an overstatement. It was more like they'd dragged her through it by the skin of her neck.

Calay pulled her stiffening shoulders back at the memory.

Six weeks since they locked her in a four-by-four cement room with steel-grated floors. Five weeks since they strapped her to a gurney, flipped her upside down, tried to force their version of the truth out of her. Four weeks since she told them to go fuck themselves and drove her point home with an elbow to one guard's nose and another's groin. Three weeks since she resolved to fix the damage she'd done. Two weeks since they finally took the zap-straps off her wrists. One since they promised she'd be released into the general population.

And they'd made good on their word.

Here she was, free to roam as she so chose. Only now, as she chewed on the truth of what she'd gotten herself into, she wasn't so sure she was ready to swallow it.

Calay lurched forward at a sudden jolt to her left side. Her tray angled sharply. Half of the beige contents slopped on her Resistance standard-issue black boots. She threw one hand up against the cold wall, steadied herself. She didn't know how things worked here, but she knew she'd have to be tough in this place. Not let anyone push her around. Even though she was a woman. *Because* she was a woman. She turned to give her assailant a piece of her mind and gasped, her breath catching in her throat as she sized up the person who'd shoved her. He was a beast of a man. He towered over Calay's 5'4" frame. He had to be at least a foot and a half taller than she was. Probably more. Wider, too. His thick neck bulged at what looked like seams. *No, scars.* They traveled up his throat, over his right cheek and eyelid, and across his bald head before disappearing under army-green fatigues. His grey eyes—the one he still had left—tore through Calay's bravado. She shrank under his gaze. The last thing she wanted to do was get pulverized before she'd even begun her mission. In front of everyone.

More bees with honey.

She tried to apologize, to make amends for whatever slight she may have caused by simply being at the wrong place at the wrong time, but no sound made its way past her lips. A menacing growl rumbled past his. It hovered between them before he mumbled something about new recruits and plodded toward the nearest table. Several Resistance members scattered out of his way as he forced himself down between them. His attention turned to the people in front of him, Calay allowed herself to breathe again.

That was close.

She chanced a glance back. The line for food was getting longer, the number of free seats, fewer. The energy, unruly. She shuddered and forced her shaking legs forward, aiming for a spot in the exact opposite side of the room.

Calay set her tray on the table, felt a foldable plastic chair bend under her weight as she sat down, and tried to make herself invisible. Difficult, given she seemed to be the only woman.

She pushed around what was left of her breakfast, realizing she wasn't the only one who'd noticed that fact. She peeked from behind her lashes to catch them watching her, only to look away when she'd meet their gazes.

It was a familiar feeling. When she'd been forced here against her will by Guy all those months ago, she'd experienced the same thing. Only this time, no one had attacked her. Yet. Calay gripped her spoon, shivered. Guy was dead. For good, this time. She'd watched Tess execute him at point blank range. She could still picture the Rorschach shapes of his blood on the cavern floor. Still, something about him lived on in her mind, pooled like oil. The way his rank breath clung to her skin, the feel of his rough fingers against her belly.

She dropped her spoon and clasped her hands beneath the table, as if she could clamp her memory shut. Seal it forever. It could have been worse, she reminded herself; he could have raped her. She was grateful that hadn't been the case. Still, the threat was there.

Here.

Everywhere.

Since the Change.

Before it.

It'd been a while since Calay had felt this way. She'd forgotten how afraid she'd been, and for how long. How safe she'd felt in Jacob's company. His presence insulated her from it. Not that she needed him to protect her, but he'd been a safe place to land.

Until he wasn't.

Finding out he'd lied to her, betrayed her, manipulated her. They might have had a special connection, but Calay would never really know how much of that was real and how much was fabricated.

It didn't matter. The truth was all that mattered now. That, and the mission.

Calay pried her hands apart. Her heart ached. She traced her thumb across the thin dark outline of a heart she'd carved into her right wrist after they'd uncuffed her. She'd slipped a pen off the table after she signed her life away to them. Or at least, her loyalty. Late that night, she'd taken the pen apart. Using the ink and a thin piece of barbed wire she'd found in the yard on one of her escorted outings, she'd given herself the tattoo. A memento to remind her of the promise she'd made to herself. To Tess. It wasn't the lockets she and Tess shared, which Calay had tossed off the side of the Loft before going with Jacob to Téras, but it was the next closest thing. Something to remember their love by. Something to remind her to keep fighting when the going got tough.

Like now.

It wasn't fair. None of it was. Calay was going to see to it that women, gays, and theys had a safe space here. Hybrids, too. But first, she had to get these men to listen. She wasn't sure how she was going to do that, but she needed to do it soon. Locked away, she'd heard the guards whispering about increased attacks by the Others. Evidently they'd abandoned the pods, taken up their true form. A vision of Ash, half-transformed in the starship, lurked at the back of Calay's mind.

The Resistance didn't know what forced the change. Calay did. It was her.

Jacob had warned her they'd come for her. That they could sense her heat signature, and now that she'd destroyed their ship and killed Elora, their leader, they'd hunt her down. Her heat signature might be invisible to humans, but it was like a honing beacon for the Others.

Calay knew she didn't have much time. If she really was going to lead the Resistance—and humanity—to victory, she was going to need her strength.

She picked up her spoon and shoveled greens into her mouth. She grimaced at their bitterness. Though she had to admit it wasn't the worst, and at least it, for once, wasn't green beans. She took another bite.

"This seat taken?"

Calay dragged her eyes up a pair of dark pants, grey T-shirt, and dark journeyman jacket. They settled on Adam's clean shaven, well-chiseled face. Before Calay could answer, he tossed a heavy book on the table and slipped his tall frame into the chair opposite her.

"Do I get a choice?" Calay tilted her head.

"Not really. Last I checked, you're still on probation." Adam raised his eyebrows, settling.

"So what's this then? A performance review?"

"Something like that."

"Hm." Calay nodded, poked at her food some more. She eyed the book. The cover showed a drawing of a wild plant with thick thorns and dark berries. She reached forward, ran her fingers along the cracked spine. She flipped through the pages. Inside were sketches of other flora, notes in the yellowed margins about seasonality and companion planting. "You like reading?"

"I like eating." Adam smiled, scooped a spoonful of paste into his mouth. "This is how we're going to do that."

"We're going to eat books?"

"Ha-ha. Did you just make a joke, Calay?"

"I have my moments."

"You'll have more of them soon if you behave yourself this time. I know it's only been a few hours, but how's it going so far?" Adam's wide green eyes grew soft as he trained them on her. "Settling in?"

"Oh, you know." She placed the book back on the table. "Aside from being bullied by ogres, and aliens trying to kill us, and the only woman in a sea of men who can't keep their eyes to themselves, it's all hunky-dory."

Adam blinked through a curtain of dark lashes. "You aren't the only woman."

"The only one I can see."

"Then you aren't looking hard enough. What about her?" Adam pointed his spork over Calay's shoulder.

She turned, scanned the bustling crowd. It parted and her eyes grew wide when her gaze settled on the group perched just two tables over.

Adam was right. There was another woman.

Warm caramel skin, short dark hair styled into a fauxhawk of ringlets, strong cheekbones. Calay watched as the woman's shoulders shifted beneath an old, faded grey T-shirt, her hips curved beneath fitted blue denim jeans. She moved with a confidence Calay had never felt, a grace she couldn't name. The woman's lips turned upward, her smile reaching her wide, charcoal eyes. Calay couldn't look away. She was striking.

"Earth to Calay?" Adam's voice broke through her thoughts. "Now who's staring?"

Calay's cheeks flushed. He was right a second time. She'd just been wishing she could disappear under the weight of others' gazes, and she'd just done the same to someone else.

"She's not the only one," Adam continued, dragging a wide hand through his dark, floppy hair. "There's more."

"Why are there so few of us though? So many men?" Calay cleared her throat and turned back to him. "It doesn't make any sense."

"I'll admit the…leadership…under Smith was, how do I say this?"

"Sexist and misogynistic as fuck?"

Adam cleared his throat. "Problematic."

Calay grunted.

"We had rules and most of the time, the rules worked."

"Most of the time isn't good enough."

"Which is why I'm working to change things."

"Right." Calay shook her head and dropped her eyes to her tray.

Once Calay recovered from being waterboarded, Adam had explained what happened to Smith. He'd suffered serious injuries from Max's attack after Calay escaped the compound all those months ago. He would have recovered from them too, had they not become infected. He'd later died and in his place, Adam stepped up to lead the Resistance. To bring about change. To fight the Others. Calay was lucky he did. If Smith was still around, she wasn't so sure he would have let her go free. Or even live. After some serious word gymnastics, Adam did. She'd never say it to his face, but Calay knew the only reason she was still alive was because he'd believed her when she told him she wanted to help them. Adam understood the value of working together. Or at least, the complexities of it. And that had been Calay's Hail Mary.

"I know you don't believe it, but I told you the first time you were here, this is a good place. It's safe. You're right about it not being safe enough, though. We're working to bring more women in. Make it more equal. Safety in numbers, right? So that's one problem solved. There's not much I can do about the aliens, but we can see about that ogre."

Calay seized her opportunity. "I appreciate that, Adam. I really do. I know we didn't end things on the best of terms last time, and I'm grateful for everything you've done for me."

"Stronger together." He nodded.

Calay angled herself across the table. "That's exactly my point. We need to collaborate to fight the Others."

"We are."

"We need to do more."

"We're working on it."

"Not fast enough."

Adam frowned, lowered his spork. "How many times do we have to go through this, Calay? There's a process. Not to mention trust. Show me you can do things the right way. You'll see they work."

Calay's brows matched his furrow. She pushed her tray aside, leaned closer. "There is no right way, Adam. That's what I've been saying. We do things your way and people—these people—die."

"Not to be dramatic or anything," Adam muttered as he scraped the last of the food off his tray.

"Call it whatever you want, but you know I'm right. That's why you let me out after I—"

"Shh," Adam hissed. He glanced around, tossed a glare at Calay. He took a deep breath. When he continued, she could barely hear his voice above the hum of the cafeteria. "As far as anyone in this place is concerned, that was a Council decision. No one will ask; it's standard procedure. But I swear to God, Calay, no one can find out I ushered you through the system."

"Why not?" Calay was practically climbing over the table. She lowered her voice. "I mean, they're going to find out eventually. The Council will, anyhow."

"They'll find out when I know what the hell I'm going to do with you. I don't mean to be rude, but in the meantime, keep your head down and your mouth shut. You're right, I know we have to do more. The Others' attacks are getting worse. But now is not the time. Not yet. Calay, please. I took a huge risk and already sacrificed my convictions for you once. Don't make me regret it."

An unsettling anger rose in Calay's stomach. She clenched her teeth. The chair groaned as she leaned back in the seat. "Or you'll what? Lock me back up? Torture me again? You talk about trust—how am I supposed to trust you after that?"

"You know I'd never give that order. It's not okay to treat people that way. I stopped it as soon as I found out what was going on. I'm sorry it happened to you." Adam huffed, pushed his tray away. It clanged against Calay's. Calay watched a smile dance behind his eyes. "Though would you blame me? You did smash a computer over my head."

"You were going to shoot me." Calay raised an eyebrow and grinned back.

Despite Adam's unyielding morals, she'd come to like the guy. He was friendly from the beginning, albeit cagey with the details. He'd protected her from Guy, offered her friendship when she had no one else to turn to. He'd done nothing but try to help her until she'd forced his hand. It seemed like a lifetime ago that she'd broke into the records room and uncovered the Resistance propaganda, not to mention the truth about who—or what—Jacob was. It was one of the things Adam was trying to fix. Calay understood change happened slowly. And that was okay. As long as it did, in fact, happen.

"Guess we'll have to work on learning how to trust each other, then." Adam shrugged. "No one's clean anymore."

He wasn't wrong. The idea of good and evil, right and wrong—they were just that now: ideas. The fact of the matter was everyone had done something to survive. To get here. And if they hadn't, they'd been lucky. Sooner or later that luck was going to run out and in a way, Calay was grateful hers ran empty when it did. Everything she'd gone through had made her into the woman—the fighter—she was today. It was because of that that Tess's legacy would live on.

"I guess no one gets to be the good guy." Calay reached for her tray. She prodded the congealing mash. "I'm sorry I tried to electrocute you with an iMac."

"That thing was heavy."

"Yeah, why were the monitors so old anyhow?"

"It's not like we could have just walked into our local Genius Bar and picked out a top-of-the-line model. We needed something that was reliable, sturdy." Adam winked.

"I'm just saying there had to be better options around than that brick."

Adam crossed his arms over his chest. "Beggars can't be choosers."

Calay smirked and abandoned the spork upright in the leftovers. "You're just chock full of wisdoms today, aren't you?"

"Not just today." Adam's gaze fluttered to the far end of the room. Some freckled-faced kid was waving him over, his eyes wide like a deer in headlights. Adam rose, snapped up both their trays. "Finished?"

"Yeah, thanks." She watched as he made his way across the room and dumped them in a bin before following the young man around the corner and out of sight. Not quite ready to brave the walk past the endless rows of tables still overflowing with male bodies, she turned her attention back to her own and noticed Adam had left his book behind. She picked it up, flipped through the pages.

The smell of the musty paper reminded her of Jacob. He'd shoved his nose inside a book every night at the Loft, waiting for her to return from her self-imposed exile.

How many lifetimes ago had that been? It felt like a billion.

She knew nothing would bring him back from the inferno she'd left him to die in. Though someone had made it. She couldn't help but hope, despite everything he'd done to her, that it'd been him. Not that she ever wanted to see him again, she just didn't want him to burn to a crisp in the vast emptiness of deep space. He deserved better than that.

And yet, she'd left him behind.

Calay sighed, tucked the book underneath her arm, and pushed her chair in as she forced herself to stand. She figured she could sit there and lament the dreams she'd lost, letting the disappointment thrum in her heart, or she could make herself useful and learn how to forage for wild dandelion until Adam finally came around to her way of thinking.

She turned to quietly make her exit, but the curly fauxhawk woman's gaze locked Calay in place. And she wasn't alone. The two men she was sitting with just about tore Calay in half with the force of their stares.

The smaller one with the olive skin and black-rimmed glasses squinted at her, pressed his pouty, upturned lips into a thin line. The bigger one was more worrying, and not just because of his classic Hollywood good looks. Calay braved eye contact and the dark grey sweatshirt he wore bulged across his biceps. His nostrils flared. She watched his jaw twitch beneath a long, heavy beard as the smaller one whispered something in his ear.

Calay held her arms close and balled her fists, hoping they couldn't see the shake she felt. She didn't know what the hell their problem was, and she didn't want to find out. She may have been done with running from her fears, but that didn't make her stupid.

This wasn't a fight she could win.

She shuffled forward, averted her gaze, and hoped it would be enough to skirt by without incident. To her dismay, she practically felt the air ripple when the big one pressed himself up and away from the table. From the corner of her eye, Calay could see he'd begun making his way toward her, moving slowly between errant chairs and flowing bodies.

She tried to slow her breathing when something glinted in his hand against the overhead lighting.

Then, the lights went out.

The chatter in the room, too.

Calay halted. She forced her one free hand into a fist, raised the book in the other. It wasn't exactly her weapon of choice, but if push came to stab, she figured its ample page count could do some damage.

Despite it being mid-day, even the light outside seemed to fade to black.

She peered through the shadows, strained to hear the tell-tale shuffle of someone sneaking up from behind. Or rushing from the side.

The only sound was that of her heart against her chest.

She couldn't see more than a foot in front of her. There was nothing but darkness. The outline of bodies. But which one was his? She scanned the shadows for movement. It was as if the entire room and everyone in it froze, but how could that be? A vision of a million Eloras stacked one behind the other fluttered through her mind. This wasn't the starship. She wasn't trapped in that basement. Hell, she wasn't trapped here either. She could move any time. Still, the vast emptiness of the dark held her in place.

Calay could feel the scream rising in her throat, but before it could pass her lips, an alarm blared and the whole room went red.

Don't stop now. Keep reading with your copy of THE STARS INSIDE US.

And sign up for the latest news, giveaways, and more from Kristy Gardner here.

Don't miss book three of *The Broken Stars* series, THE STARS INSIDE US, available now, and find more from Kristy Gardner at kristygardner.com

She'll burn it to the ground...

The ashes have settled since Calay's harrowing escape back to Earth, but the threat from the Others–and humanity itself–hasn't. After surviving devastating losses and impossible choices, Calay drags herself to the doorstep of the one place she never wanted to return: The Resistance.

Forced to trust hidden motives and questionable loyalties, Calay intimately knows the only way they survive, is together. But as she dives deeper into alien territory, her new reality is even more alarming than she could have anticipated. A perma-winter has settled over the planet. A strange new league of mutations has emerged amongst the Others. And despite her best efforts, past decisions come back to haunt Calay–taunt her.

It doesn't take long for her plans to go horribly wrong. Her terror is compounded when she realizes she's not only trapped with the enemy–a group that would gladly kill her if they knew her secrets–but that she's actually started to care for them; especially Briar, the tea-loving, open-hearted woman who makes Calay feel like home.

In these final dying days, stars collide and the darkness within ignites. The world's future is in Calay's hands and she must decide what's more important: saving herself, or saving what makes us human.

Please sign up for the City Owl Press newsletter for chances to win special subscriber-only contests and giveaways as well as receiving information on upcoming releases and special excerpts.

All reviews are **welcome** and **appreciated**. Please consider leaving one on your favorite social media and book buying sites.

For books in the world of romance and speculative fiction that embody Innovation, Creativity, and Affordability, check out City Owl Press at www.cityowlpress.com.

ACKNOWLEDGMENTS

The Darkest Stars would not exist without those who shall be named, or the hell I went through to get here. It was eight years between the time I started writing The Stars In Their Eyes and this book. Together, they are a tribute to the pain I clawed through during that time, and the love that grew from it. It's unnerving to see how Calay's path so closely mirrors my own, but I believe there's power (and magic) in vulnerability. I hope you found this book dark, horrifying, beautiful, and healing. I sure did.

So, without further verbosity, let's name some people…

My eternal thanks to Julie Gwinn for shepherding this book into the world.

Huge thanks to my brilliant editor, Danielle DeVor, and her uncanny ability to peel open the story I'm trying to tell and help me shape it into something readable. To Lisa Carlisle for her endless patience and keen copy-editing skills. To Tina Moss, Yelena Casale, and the teams at City Owl Press and MiblArt for making this book whole. It wouldn't be here without you.

Immense gratitude to Shanna Pranaitis for always making space and time in your brilliant mind (and schedule) to be the first to read my stories before they become the books they're meant to be. It is an honor and a gift.

To my husband. You've brought me back from the dark place on more than one occasion with your humor, enthusiasm, and endless patience for my bookish obsessions–including this one. I love you.

To my friends, family, beta readers, and fellow authors who so generously offer their unending support, advice, love, and a safe space to lose my shit when everything gets to be too much–you know who you are, and I am beyond grateful.

To anyone who recommends this book, posts it on social media, stocks it in their bookstore or library, or leaves a rating and review on Goodreads and/or retail sites. You have my eternal gratitude.

To you: books are messages trapped in time; people are not. We flail in all directions, just trying to find something–someone–to hold onto, even if that is just ourselves. I'm grateful for you and this book that binds us together. As always, if the stars should align and we're fortunate enough to find ourselves in the same room, please say hello.

ABOUT THE AUTHOR

KRISTY GARDNER is a queer sci-fi, fantasy, and horror writer. She is the author of the *The Broken Stars* series and the award-winning cookbook, *Cooking with Cocktails*. Furnished with degrees in Gender Studies & Sociology, she crafts complex characters who adventure through space, time, and emotional maelstroms questioning what identity – and home – really mean.

When she's not jet-setting words on her laptop, she's chasing stars, mountain adventures, belly laughs, curating playlists for her books, and packing her carry-on for another escape to SE Asia. She resides in Vancouver B.C. with her partner.

kristygardner.com

instagram.com/kristy_gardner
tiktok.com/@kristy_gardner
goodreads.com/kristy_gardner
threads.net/@kristy_gardner

ABOUT THE PUBLISHER

City Owl Press is a cutting edge indie publishing company, bringing the world of romance and speculative fiction to discerning readers.

Escape Your World. Get Lost in Ours!

www.cityowlpress.com

facebook.com/YourCityOwlPress
x.com/cityowlpress
instagram.com/cityowlbooks
pinterest.com/cityowlpress

www.ingramcontent.com/pod-product-compliance
Lightning Source LLC
Chambersburg PA
CBHW060608030726
47498CB00005B/1591